Big British Bluff
Lesser-Known Feats of Netaji Subhas

Written by
Subir

Ukiyoto Publishing

All global publishing rights are held by

Ukiyoto Publishing

Published in 2024

Content Copyright © Subir

ISBN 9789364947046

All rights reserved.

No part of this publication may be reproduced, transmitted, or stored in a retrieval system, in any form by any means, electronic, mechanical, photocopying, recording or otherwise, without the prior permission of the publisher.

The moral rights of the author have been asserted.

This book is sold subject to the condition that it shall not by way of trade or otherwise, be lent, resold, hired out or otherwise circulated, without the publisher's prior consent, in any form of binding or cover other than that in which it is published.

www.ukiyoto.com

Acknowledgements

I extend my deepest gratitude to my family members, whose unwavering support and encouragement have been instrumental in bringing this story to life.

Sanchali (Spouse)

Sudipta (Daughter)

Sujata (Daughter)

Debopriya (Son-in-law)

Daivyik (Grandson)

Your belief in me and the various ways in which you contributed to this journey has made all the difference.

"History is not there for you to like or dislike.
It is there for you to learn from it.
And if it offends you, even better.
Because then you are less likely to repeat it.
It's not yours to erase. It belongs to all of us!"

U.S. Congressman Lt. Col. Allen West.

CONTENTS

Chapter 1 - Busting the Myth   1
Chapter 2 - Oatenization   28
Chapter 3 - The Vanishing Act!-How Bose Broke Away From His House Arrest?   65
Chapter 4 - Across the Globe by Submarine-German Reich to the Land of the Rising Sun   109
Chapter 5 - The Born Revolutionary: Rash Behari   131
Chapter 6 - Serious Setback   169
Chapter 7 - Finally, the Victory!   208
References/Sources   227

About the Author   *242*

Chapter 1

Busting the Myth

Today, many Indians, including those from the northeastern region, remain largely unaware that World War II once disrupted the peace and tranquillity of this remote part of the subcontinent. The twin battles of Imphal in Manipur and Kohima in Nagaland were fought fiercely in their backyard in 1944, dangerously disturbing the serene environment of their secluded homeland. These encounters were so intense that in 2013, a poll conducted by the British National Army Museum in London recognized the Imphal/Kohima battles as 'Britain's Greatest Battle.'

Renowned authors such as Martin Dougherty and Jonathan Ritter likened the twin battles of Imphal/Kohima to the "Stalingrad of the East" for the viciousness and aggressiveness with which the battles were then fought. The fighting was brutal, and at one point, these descended into primitive, cruel hand-to-hand combats, with only a tennis court separating the two rival sides dug in on a hilltop. Yet, the reminiscences of these harrowing days of India have all but vanished now from the annals of our historical memory.

While global narratives often frame these 1944 Second World War events as mere episodes of a Japanese invasion of India, the truth is far more radical and stirring. These battles orchestrated by the Azad Hind Fauj (Indian National Army or INA) under the leadership of Netaji Subhas Chandra Bose were crucial chapters in India's struggle for liberation from 200 years of British colonial (mis)rule. With the support of the Japanese army, Netaji's daring act was aimed at forcefully overthrowing the British Raj from the Indian subcontinent through armed struggle.

British Prime Minister Winston Churchill was well aware of Netaji Subhas's audacious attack. However, fearing a nationwide uprising in support of Bose's Liberation Army, Churchill organised a disinformation campaign, misrepresenting the attack as a mere Japanese invasion rather than acknowledging its true nationalist origins. The Wartime Allied propaganda machine executed this deception so skillfully that Indian soldiers fighting under the British flag during the Second World War's Imphal campaign remained oblivious that they were engaged in battling their fellow countrymen—the Azad Hind Fauj—who came to liberate India from alien British rule.

Thus, the story of Ruzazho village in the Naga Hills, once part of Assam, became a hidden gem in India's struggle for liberation. Despite being the first Indian village to be freed from the grip of British colonial rule, its unique tale has faded into obscurity, notwithstanding the fact that the Azad Hind Fauj, under the indomitable leadership of Netaji Subhas Chandra Bose, liberated Ruzazho from the clutches of British control as early as March 1944. Located just 33 kilometres from Kohima, the present-day capital of Nagaland, Ruzazho stands as an authoritative testament to India's struggle for liberation in the northeastern region. Recognizing these vital moments in India's history and honouring the exceptional efforts of the Azad Hind Fauj is not just essential but a tribute to the undying spirit of all freedom fighters.

The Azad Hind Fauj, commonly known as the INA (Indian National Army), was successful in liberating Ruzazho after crossing northern Burma's Chindwin River while advancing towards Kohima during the Second World War. As already mentioned, the INA was backed by the Japanese. Netaji Subhas Chandra Bose, along with his armies, reached Ruzazho village at dawn and called for a general public meeting at a place called 'Metho Chope'. Bose enquired if some among the villagers had studied or were studying in school. The villagers responded by mentioning Poswuyi Swuro's name as he was the only person who passed Class III. Netaji then called Poswuyi in the front and asked him if he would be DB (i.e. Dobashi or Interpreter) for the surrounding area. On agreeing to the proposal, Bose wrote Poswuyi Swuro's name in his diary. As per Poswuyi's description, Bose was very handsome and had a promising character and persona, which impressed the villagers to a large extent.

After that, Bose gave an opportunity to the villagers by asking who would be willing to be the Gaon Bura (Village Heads). When ten villagers responded by raising their hands, Netaji Bose wrote their names in the diary as well. Just then, some of the Assam Regiment soldiers, who were captured and came along with Bose, spotted Vesuyi Swuro (elder brother of Poswuyi who was on medical leave and staying in the village) and reported to Bose saying he was also from the same battalion. Netaji called Vesuyi to the front and questioned if the claim was true. He replied in the affirmative with great fear. However, to his surprise, Bose gently spoke to him in Hindi and asked him to be the interpreter. Vesuyi Swuro agreed.

The villagers were given their assignments, such as collecting rations, firewood, water, grass for their horses, etc. They were to report through their representatives, whom Bose had just appointed. Netaji and his team stayed at Ruzazho village for nine days. The villagers reported that during their stay in the village, the team ran out of their food grains, vegetables and most of their domesticated animals. Still, the villagers did not feel much pain in sharing these essential items with their guests, hoping that one day, they would see their village developed as promised by Bose.

Poswuyi Swuro DB was sent to neighbouring villages like Phugi and Suthozu for rations. He and his brother Vesuyi were also given a mission to lead their INA allied Forces to Sathakha via Dzulha, Kilomi, which involved a night's stay at Sathakha. The next day, on learning about the presence of the British forces at Zunheboto, Poswuyi Swuro and his brother Vesuyi decided to retreat to their base at Ruzazho village.

However, on that fateful day, while crossing Dzulha village, the British troops ambushed them, and one [1] Sema guy was shot just in front of them, succumbing to his injuries and dying on the spot. Luckily, Poswuyi and his brother escaped the attack and returned to their village.

It is worth mentioning that all the villagers, including womenfolk, were involved in helping Netaji and the INA soldiers in one way or another. The villagers were engaged in carrying their rations to different locations and camps and also carried their weapons. Some were involved in building their base camps, and others helped them as guides to various places and so on.

The Nagas, by and large, depended on Oral tradition (passing stories from one generation to the other) and gave no importance to recording them in written forms. They considered oral stories to be the most legitimate proof of any events or disputes that might have arisen between different parties, villages, or individuals in the past. Things have changed recently. Now, the educated Nagas are in pursuit of documenting all those oral stories in writings and recordings (both audio and videos). One such history about the presence of Netaji and INA with the Japanese at Ruazaho village during April and May 1944, as narrated above, has reportedly been duly recorded.

---

[1] Sema, also known as Sumi, are among the 15 officially recognized Naga tribes in Nagaland.

As per the research so far, there is no record of Netaji administering any village prior to this village, and hence Ruazaho stood as the first village administered by the INA under the leadership of Subhas Chandra Bose, where he gave powers to the villagers as DB (Dobashi, or interpreter) and GBs (Gaon Burah or Village Head) for administration. Many renowned scholars are on the same page on this, as reported by a Bangalore-based online magazine, 'My India My Glory'. [1]

THE MORUNG EXPRESS, the first print newspaper in English language published from Dimapur in Nagaland, with an online edition, reported on 18th January 2023,

The Assam Rifles (AR), a central paramilitary force responsible for border security, counter-insurgency, and maintaining law and order in Northeast India, held a function on 18th January 2023 at Nagaland's Ruzazho village in Phek district in celebration of the Iconic Week to commemorate the 126th birth anniversary of Netaji Subhas Chandra Bose to "remember the nine-day stay of Netaji in this village during the advance of the Indian National Army (INA) towards Kohima in March 1944 after crossing the Chindwin River."

A press release from the PRO, HQ IGAR (N), stated that Ruzhazho was also the first Indian village liberated from British control by Azad Hind Fauj. Subsequently, the village was administered by the Azad Hind Government under Netaji. The village has been identified due to Evangelist Poswuyi Swurov, a 104-year-old veteran freedom fighter and Cekrolhu Swuro, who served under Netaji and are living witness to narrate the heroic acts of INA. The PRO stated that Netaji had appointed Evangelist Poswuyi Swuro as the village's DB Area Administrator. [2]

News of Ruzazho Village also appeared in national and regional newspapers and news channels. For instance, The Times of India, dated 24th January 2019, under the caption "News channel adopts Ruzazho Village under CSR", reported that on the 122nd birth anniversary of Netaji Subhas Chandra Bose, a Delhi-based news channel adopted Ruzazho Village, which is claimed as the first Azad Hind government-administered village in 1944.

Making the formal announcement about the adoption of this village under Corporate Sector Responsibility (CSR), [2]Sudarshan News Channel Chief Managing Director and Editor-in-Chief, Suresh Chavhanke, said that with the

---

[2] Sudarshan News is an Indian right-wing news channel

adoption, Sudarshan Rastra Nirman Trust would endeavour to bring about all-round development of this remote village. He said that the Trust would pursue with the Central government for bringing about funds for the development of roads, converting the area into a Heritage village, developing the house where Bose stayed at Ruzazho into a national museum and also bringing Eklavya school into the village. He announced that the Trust would work towards transforming and equipping the village with modern facilities and connecting it with the mainland through social media and information technology. He said it would also move for granting pensions to those who helped Bose during his stay in this village. [3]

While news reports highlighted Netaji Subhas Chandra Bose's presence in the Naga Hills not very long ago, Krishna Bose, a three-term Member of the Indian Parliament, documented Subhas Chandra Bose's visit to Manipur as early as 1972. She recorded that Netaji was in Manipur around July 1944. Before this revelation, it was not widely known that Subhas Bose had entered India during the Second World War, despite persistent rumours.

Krishna Bose travelled the Indian sub-continent and the world to uncover Netaji's life from childhood to his mortal end in 1945. In one such tour to Manipur along with her husband, Dr Sisir Kumar Bose, the son of Netaji's elder brother and lifelong confidant Sarat Chandra Bose, they were surprised to be told that Netaji came to Churachandpur, some distance south of Moirang where the flag of the Indian National Army was first unfurled on 14th April 1944. There in Churachandpur, the Bose couple were told that the Raja of Saikot, who was still alive, had met Netaji during World War II. (It is customary among the tribes in Manipur to refer to the village chief by the title Raja.) So, they went to Saikot and met the Raja, named Kolbel, a very friendly seventy-five-year-old man. Raja Kolbel gave them a clear and detailed account of Netaji's visit to his village twenty-eight years earlier, on 2nd July 1944. According to Kolbel's account,

There was a large INA camp on the hill above the village. Netaji came to inspect that camp and met the soldiers. He then came down to the village and met the locals. Raja Kolbel greeted him. Netaji was in military uniform. He had a hip-holstered revolver and a short sword hung from the other hip. At 7 p.m., Netaji sat down under the large tree in Kolbel's garden. The villagers have preserved the tree with great care.

It was a brightly moonlit night. The garden slopes down to a river. The INA soldiers came down from their camp and gathered on the slope. They all sat down on the slope. They numbered in the hundreds, but the villagers prepared and served steaming-hot tea to all of them. Netaji gave a short speech to the assembled soldiers. Kolbel offered Netaji milk in a tumbler. Netaji asked why he was being given milk rather than tea like everyone else. Kolbel explained that it is their custom to offer milk to distinguished visitors. Netaji said that in that case, he would have the milk, but generally, he ate and drank only what his soldiers did.

Netaji told Kolbel that he knew the local villagers had been supplying essential foodstuffs to the INA soldiers for quite some time since their arrival. He was deeply appreciative of the help and told Kolbel that he would not forget their generosity once India was free. Before leaving, Netaji wrote a note of thanks on a piece of paper and gave it to Kolbel to keep but cautioned him that he would face adverse consequences if the note fell into the hands of the British. After INA retreated, Kolbel put the note along with some other items in a box, which he buried under the earth nearby. Water seeped into the box, and the handwritten note was spoiled.

During their discussion with Raja Kolbel, the Bose couple wondered why Netaji came to the Churachandpur area rather than to other areas of the Manipur front and then requested Kolbel to venture a guess. To this, the Raja said maybe because of rather easier access from Burma into India through the Churachandpur routes and comparatively shorter and somewhat less harsh terrain, they preferred this track, given that there were severe shortages of petrol on both sides of the border that made lengthy journeys by motor vehicles difficult. [4]

The initial success of the joint INA-Japanese forces' assault on the British Allied troops was spectacular. The following paragraphs quoted from the book, "A Beacon Across Asia: A Biography of Subhas Chandra Bose" by British writer, journalist, and war correspondent Alexander Werth provide a glimpse of the epoch-making happenings:

"When Imperial Headquarters issued a communique on 8th April saying that "Japanese troops fighting side by side with the Indian National Army captured Kohima early on 6th April", many Japanese began to expect Imphal to fall before the Emperor's birthday on 29th April." (Japanese Prime Minister) Tojo, who was a scowling and sulking man for many months, was smiling again and felt happy. He issued a statement and made it clear that "whatever area the Indian National Army liberated should be placed under the administrative control of the Provisional Government of Free India. It is the aim of Japan to crush the enemy and help to place India under the complete control of the Indian people."

Rash Behari Bose (Ref: Chapter 5, "Born Revolutionary: Rash Behari"), who was critically ill with tuberculosis, rose from his sickbed against medical advice and went to Radio Tokyo to record his speech expressing jubilation to be broadcast "when Imphal fell". He was carried back after he had recorded his speech at the studio. That speech, of course, failed to go on the air.

Nelaji issued a statement announcing that the INA, fighting under the command of the Provisional Government of Free India, had embarked on its sacred mission with the cooperation of the Japanese Imperial Army. At that historic moment, when the Indo-Japanese troops had crossed the border and started marching deep into India, the Provisional Government drew the attention of the world to the epochal event. He declared that the Provisional Government of Free India would continue to fight side by side with the Japanese Army until India was completely liberated. On behalf of the Provisional Government of Free India, he further urged upon the Indian people to give it full support, block the US-British war efforts by resorting to sabotage and cooperate in bringing about the success of the struggle for freedom as early as possible. Netaji urged Indian soldiers serving with the British Army to refuse to fight for the rulers and come over to the INA, and upon Indian officials working for the British Government to cooperate with the Provisional Government in fighting the holy war. He assured the Indian people that there was nothing to fear as long as they did not work as agents of the British and that the seat of the Provisional Government would, in due course, be shifted to Indian soil, liberated from British rule. He advised Indians to stay away from the US-British oil fields, ammunition factories and other military installations to avoid being hurt as a result of Indo-Japanese attacks. He concluded by saying that at this crucial moment in history, India expected all Indians to do their duty." [5]

The local leaders of Manipur had prior information about the movement of the INA towards India from the letters Netaji had written to prominent leftist leaders asking them to help the INA when it entered the Indian territory to fight for India's independence, according to Professor J. B. Bhattacharjee, the renowned historian and the founder General Secretary of the North-East India History Association (NEIHA). Professor Bhattacharjee added that in Naga Hills, Z. A. Phizo, who later headed the underground Naga movement, and his followers joined the Azad Hind. Many people from Cachar, Manipur, and Naga Hills moved to the liberated areas to work for the Azad Hind despite the strict vigil maintained by the British on borders.

The Congress had asked the party leaders in Assam to resist the Japanese advance. Still, some prominent Congress leaders of Assam, like Lakshmi Prasad Goswami and Debakanta Barua, publicly announced their resolve to welcome the advancing liberation forces. At the same time, the Forward Block, Revolutionary Communist Party and the Congress Socialist in Assam started preparation to welcome the INA. A section of the radical youths in Assam was excited by the rumour that INA had already crossed Kohima on its way to Brahmaputra valley. They prepared to receive the INA men at Lumding (in Hojai District of Assam state) and formed a local unit of the Forward Block. These INA supporters in the Northeastern corner of the country were inspired by the desire to see India free, and their confidence in the sincerity of the Azad Hind Government to achieve it was unshakable.

The British knew it well. A historian of Manipur wrote:

Churchill must have had all this information. If Azad Hind Fauj had succeeded in entering any populous area of India, a countrywide volcanic eruption against the government would have started. But in its stead, the presence of a Japanese force on Indian soil would have produced quite a different reaction. The Congress leaders would have fought the Japanese to the last. Pandit Nehru clearly announced his resolve both to the British and the Japanese and said that he would not hesitate to take up arms to resist the invasion of India by the Japanese forces.

But out of extreme nervousness, the British government arrested the Congress leaders, although it knew that it was definitely not the Japanese but the Azad Hind Fauj who were making time in Burma to liberate India. Hence, Churchill rightly apprehended a countrywide revolt. But he had not dared to disclose the reality.

On the other hand, the activities of the Azad Hind Fauj were given wide publicity by the government as a Japanese invasion. If the Indians had any sympathy for the Japanese, the government would not have done so. It showed that the government also believed that the Indians would have resisted the Japanese if they had really invaded India.

The historians, therefore, cannot rely on the British sources alone. The intelligence reports, and the records maintained by the British officers in Assam, Naga Hills and Manipur would be more reliable. The evidence and oral records available at the local levels provide a better comprehension of the nature of the relationship between the INA and the Japanese. The battle narratives collected from different sources clearly indicate that both INA personnel and the Japanese army actively participated in the warfare, overturning the British depiction of INA as a puppet army. The evidence is clear enough to disprove the hypothesis of a Japanese invasion. In fact, the Japanese Invasion of India was a myth consciously created by the British to alienate the INA from the Indian masses. In doing so, the British succeeded like their many other successes achieved through disinformation.

Notwithstanding, according to Prof J.B. Bhattacharjee:

When they entered India, the INA received massive support from the local tribal groups of Naga and Mizo extractions. The tribal villages like Taungian, Ukhrul, Tiddi, Sanghak, Molan, Morse, Tamu, Kabaw, and Hangdam voluntarily submitted to the INA. The Tri-Colour Flag of the Azad Hind flew over these villages for several months. The Bahadur Group of INA led the operations in Manipur. After encounters with the allied British-American forces, this group occupied Manipur's Mairang and Bishenpur areas. The Azad Hind Fauj remained in possession of about 1,500 square miles of territory in Manipur for about six months. Major General A. C. Chatterjee, appointed by the Azad Hind Government as Governor of the occupied territory, took charge of the civil administration. The Nikhil Manipuri Mahasabha joined Azad Hind en bloc under the leadership of M. Koireng Singh, H. Nilmani Singh et al. [6]

Besides, Seikhohao Kipgen, Assistant Professor in the Department of History, Manipur College (India), in Part V, Chapter 11, Trial and Tribulation, under the caption "KEEPING THEM UNDER CONTROL: Impact of the Anglo-Kuki War" among other things, wrote:

The outbreak of the Second World War heralded a new hope for the Kukis. When Mahatma Gandhi launched the 'Quit India Movement' in 1942, the Kukis' urge for freedom got a new lease of life. This hope soon became reality when the Japanese and Indian National Army (INA) under Subhas Chandra Bose appeared at the eastern gate to fight against the British and the Allied forces. To many Kukis who felt disheartened under the colonial regime, the coming of the Japanese and INA was seen as a 'God-sent messiah', as some writers would put it. They took every possible measure to reach out to the invading forces and joined the rank of the military establishment as fighters, informers, spies, campaigners, guides, and coolies.

Many Kukis had joined the Japanese and INA establishment before the war began. Once the war started, the entire Kuki population did whatever they could to help the advancing forces by supplying food, nursing the sick and wounded, providing information and guiding them in the rugged, roadless mountains. Thousands of Kukis also died in the ensuing war.

Significantly, according to 'Bande Mataram'– Freedom Fighters of Manipur who's who published by Freedom Fighters Cell/Department of Manipur Pradesh Congress Committee MPCC (I), 1985, among the 120 INA Pensioners (with their photographs), 75 of them were Kukis. [7]

Notably, Prof J.B. Bhattacharjee claimed that the INA and the Japanese had a prior agreement well before entering any Indian Territory that provided, inter alia:

- The two armies would work in a company.

- Officers and men of the Azad Hind Fauj would be under their own military law (The INA Act) and not under the Japanese law and police.

- The Japanese force would hand over the liberated territories to the Azad Hind Fauj.

- The only flag to fly over Indian soil would be India's National Tri-colour.

- Besides, Netaji maintained clear terms with the Japanese on all matters. An excellent example of this is the understanding of currency circulation in the liberated areas.

- Japanese civilians and institutions moving into the liberated regions, including Japanese banks and firms, would come under the control of the Governor-Designate and would use only the currency notes of the Azad Hind Government.

- The National Bank of the Azad Hind would be the only authorised bank of the Provisional Government, and the Japanese banks and firms would operate under the control and direction of the National Bank. [8]

History bears the testimony that the Japanese fully honoured their promises. The INA Memorial Complex at Moirang in Manipur (India) has a collection of letters, photographs, badges of ranks, and other war memorabilia, including INA currency notes inscribed with Netaji's portrait adorning the tiny museum that buttresses this fact. This author, Subir, had a blessed opportunity to pay his tribute to Netaji and the INA soldiers at Manipur's INA Memorial Complex sometime in 2005. The currency note inscribed with Netaji's portrait, in particular, kept alongside various war memorabilia displayed inside the museum, is a unique attraction for all those visitors who are aware of the history of the INA. For Subir, that item in the exhibit was a thrilling and unforgettable spectacle.

It must be emphasised here that Netaji believed Japan and India had a common goal of driving the British out of India. However, he clarified that this was not a favour from the Japanese to Indians but a mutually beneficial arrangement. He emphasised that he trusted neither the British nor the Japanese and asserted that the only way to safeguard against betrayal was to build up India's own strength. He warned his soldiers to be prepared to fight not only the British but also the Japanese if they attempted to replace the British in India. Despite working in cooperation with the Japanese Army, the INA maintained its independence, operating entirely on its own in certain sectors of the front. Netaji dismissed criticisms labelling the INA as a "puppet" force, arguing that if the British could accept American strategy in France, they had no grounds to criticise the INA's cooperation with the Japanese. [9]

In the daring joint campaign of the Azad Hind Fauj and the Japanese Army penetrating India's northeastern frontier, the Battle of Kohima was regarded as one of the most crucial battles in the Second World War. The entire operation in northeast India was fought with the intention of hurting the British Empire, where it would hurt them the most. The plan was to capture Kohima and Imphal, which were strategically important towns along the land route to Burma (now Myanmar) and China, in particular, blocking their supply line. For the INA, the success of this crusade would give a boost to their morale and encourage the Indian nationalists in their struggle to drive the British colonial rulers out of their motherland and win freedom for India.

The battle of Kohima was fought between 4th April and 22nd June 1944, which is regarded as one of the most significant events in the military campaigns during the Second World War. It was part of the larger Burma Campaign, where British and Indian forces, along with Allied troops, fought for the town of Kohima in India's Naga Hills against the joint Azad Hind Fauj and the Japanese troops. This battle marked a turning point in the Burma Campaign and had significant strategic importance in the Asian theatre of World War II. Lieutenant-General Renya Mutaguchi, a great veteran who was in charge of three Japanese divisions and one Indian National Army division, planned the attack meticulously. Lieutenant-General Kotoku Sato, Commander of the 31st Division, was deputed to attack Kohima. The plan was that as soon as Japan's 33rd Division would cut off the British Indian Army's 17th Indian Division in the southern part of Imphal, the 15th Division of the Japanese Army would stage the attack from the north-east side to cut off the link road to Kohima in Nagaland. Simultaneously, Sato's 31st Division was to encircle Kohima so as not to allow any relief from Dimapur to reach the British Indian Army. As per the plan, on 29th March 1944, the Japanese Army took steps to cut the Imphal-Kohima road and also surrounded the 17th Division of the British Army. Later, by mid-April, the Japanese 15th Army planned to disrupt the supply to British forces so as to deprive them of receiving any support for invading Burma. They had also planned to set up a base after their victory in Imphal to carry out further attacks from the sky and to disrupt air supplies to China as well. [10]

The battle, not skirmish, generally called the Battle of Kohima, was so fierce and formidable that in the final analysis, it was adjusted as Britain's greatest battle, fought over a vast jungle and mountain, and was distinguished by vicious hand-to-hand fighting. Cut off by the joint INA-Japanese armies, the Allied forces depended solely on supplies by air, and very few believed they could withstand the relentless onslaught. The Japanese troops attacked ceaselessly, coming in 'wave after wave, night after night'. The fighting was brutal, and the British-Indian troops were eventually confined to Garrison Hill, which overlooked Kohima. At one point, the battle descended into hand-to-hand combat, with only a tennis court separating the two sides dug in on the hill. Among others, Sosangtemba Ao from Naga Hills was also engaged by the British Army for two months for one rupee per day to cut the Burma road. He had a lot of admiration for the fighting ability of the Japanese soldiers. According to him:

"The Japanese army was highly motivated. Their soldiers did not fear death. For them, fighting for the emperor was divine. When they were asked to surrender, they would become suicide attackers." [11]

Similarly, the Battle of Red Hill, also known as the Battle of Maibam Lokpaching, took place in Manipur from 21st to 29th May 1944, where the intensity of the battles was so harsh that it involved some hand-to-hand combats. The joint INA-Japanese forces attacked this hill and occupied parts of it and the village of Maibam on 21st May. Intense fighting followed over the next nine days between the warring forces.

It's the rarest of the rare instances in the history of World War II where the Indian soldiers were up against India's Liberation Army men to kill each other as the arch-enemy. It was the deceitful, mischievous, incessant propaganda campaign launched by Churchill & Company, which continued uninterrupted throughout the Second World War and even after that, which made possible this extraordinary armed confrontation as well as hand-to-hand combat happening from the two opposing warring camps like never before.

Thus, the people of northeast India witnessed the heroic campaign of the INA men and their sufferings and sacrifices. The restoration of essential public services, law and order and reconciliation of the local population in the liberated areas by the Azad Hind had won their heart. The RCPI, CSP, the local units of the Forward Block, and a section of the Congress leaders had also enlisted the support of the people for the INA. It was heartening that the INA soldiers ruled out the retreat from the liberated areas at all stages, and the Naga chiefs offered to manage food for them despite the acute food shortage for themselves. Yet, eventually, the INA had to retreat under compelling circumstances, but it did so, casting a lasting spell on the people of northeast India. The role of Subhas Chandra Bose and the INA was appreciated by the press and public everywhere in Assam, even after the end of World War II in 1945.

The INA-Japanese campaign brought northeast India into prominence. It demonstrated the great importance that should be attached to this frontier of the country from the military point of view. Despite the mounting confusion from the beginning of the last century, the British government had not shown any genuine interest in guarding even the Sino-Indian border in the eastern sector.

Notwithstanding, shrewd British colonial rulers of India of those days knew that if the truth about Bose's extraordinary escapades spread to the Indian masses, there would be an uprising across the country in support of their beloved Netaji. Subhas Bose had already earned great respect and admiration among the rank and file in the British-Indian force since his magnificent escape from home incarceration in Calcutta, throwing dust into the British eyes. These British-Indian forces were the backbone of the British military service, enabling a comparatively limited number of British colonial officers to rule India for nearly 200 years. Their revolt in support of Subhash Chandra Bose had the potential to overthrow the British in no time. To avert such disastrous fallout, the clever colonial rulers deviously masked this daring success story of INA, India's Liberation Army led by Netaji Subhas Chandra Bose, as a Japanese invasion of India.

The British considered Netaji to be a dangerous revolutionary who possessed abundant talent for leadership. The reaction of the British administrators in India to his clarion call '"Dilli chalo" (On to Delhi) was mixed. They were certainly perturbed by developments in East Asia but, at the same time, had doubts about the prospects for the movement Netaji dreamt of. A British report on Netaji Subhas Chandra Bose ridiculed him, suggesting that during his tour of southern regions under Japanese occupation, he had announced his intention of flinging his purportedly well-equipped Indian National Army across the India-Burma frontier before the end of 1943 'no less than five times'. To deflate the movement, the British presented Subhas as a traitor and spoke of the INA with disdain.

Nevertheless, the Commander-in-Chief of the British forces, in a secret dispatch to the Secretary of State for India, was constrained to report that Bose should not be dismissed as 'a mere loquacious tool of the Japanese' for his influence on Indian soldiers both in India and abroad – if not actually on the Indians – was a factor to be reckoned with. An official analysis of Subhas' position at this time further stated forcefully that:

Bose has now finally burned his boats with us by virtue of his association with Germany and Japan, his political future being entirely dependent upon the continued military success of the Japanese and the paralysis of British rule in India by internal revolt.

British officials, however, were convinced that internal revolt was not possible since public morale and internal security were fairly steady. They believed that 'his chances of whipping up a major revolt would appear to be small. Had he arrived in East Asia last August or even during Gandhi's fast, his prospects would have been much better.' As the Director of Military Intelligence pointed out, one specific factor which stood in Bose's path was the uncooperative attitude of the Congress and its leaders, and since Bose had little chance of being recognised by Gandhi and the Congress high command, 'it seems unlikely that he would be able to win over the Congress to his plans for national revolution'. As such, his chances of stirring up a major revolt appeared to be small. Subsequent events, however, proved that the assessment was inaccurate.

The Anglo-American block had spread the word that the INA was a puppet army raised and equipped by the Japanese to serve their own ends. The British war machine had kept the Indian public in the dark about the INA and its activities. Throughout the war, they had been depicting the Japanese as a barbaric and inhuman race whose advances had to be resisted at any cost. The characterisation of INA as a puppet army and Bose as a stooge of the brutal Japanese Army by the British as a counter-measure proved very successful. It was quite common for the British to ridicule Bose's claim to be the leader of the INA. They depicted the Azad Hind Fauj as full of spies and those who would not hesitate to desert to the British at the first opportunity.

At the same time, to create mistrust of the Japanese within the INA, it was propagated that the Japanese considered the INA unreliable and, hence, were using them merely as spies and stretcher-bearers. The combatant roles played by the INA in the warfare in the Kohima and Imphal regions were, therefore, erased from the records. Anti-Japanese and anti-Bose propaganda were produced in Bengali, Punjabi, Hindustani, Tamil, Gujarati and English. The British depicted Bose as a dreamer who had degraded Indian self-respect by calling on Japan to secure the freedom of India.

Inside the country, British propaganda heavily influenced the perception of the Indian political leaders about Japan. Many prominent leaders began to view Japan as a hustling aggressor to be resisted no matter what. The success of the British propaganda nearly sandbagged the possible drive of the Azad Hind movement into India and prevented the Indian people from understanding the nature of the movement, which Bose had started to oust the British from India. [12]

While the British propaganda against Netaji Subash Chandra Bose and the INA, in tandem with the defamation of the Japanese brandished the world over, including the Indian Expats, back home in India, there was a total blackout of news about what actually was happening on the Indo-Burma frontier as well as in the Imphal-Kohima theatre. The censorship of the war-related news and the anti-Japanese/anti-Bose propaganda of the British was so comprehensive that the Indian soldiers fighting within the country under the British command were oblivious that they were at work fighting to kill their fellow citizens, who came to liberate India and the Indians from nearly 200 years of the brutish misrule of the alien forces when they penetrated the

North-East frontier of India in the garb of the INA troops with the backings of the Japanese.

The extent to which they manipulated the historical records could be gauged from the fact that Sir Winston Leonard Spencer Churchill was awarded in 1953 the Nobel Prize in Literature "for his mastery of historical and biographical description as well as for brilliant oratory in defending exalted human values" [13], whereas, according to Shashi Tharoor,

"Churchill has as much blood on his hands as Hitler does. The (1943) Bengal Famine – millions died because of the decisions he took or endorsed. Not only did the British follow its own policy of not helping the victims of this Famine, Churchill persisted in exporting grain to Europe, not to feed actual 'Sturdy Tommies' as he described them, but to add to the buffer stocks that were being piled up in the event of a future invasion of Greece and Yugoslavia."

UKAsia quoted Tharoor (India's Member of Parliament, former diplomat, bureaucrat, politician, and a noted writer and historian) as saying so in an interview while speaking to media during the launch of his book 'Inglorious Empire' in London. The Indian Express newspaper, updated on 22nd March 2017, reported it. [14] (Emphasis by Subir)

Interestingly, British Prime Minister Churchill, who guided his nation through World War II, wrote a comprehensive history of the War. The book series, titled "The Second World War", was published between 1948 and 1953. It covers the period from the end of the First World War to July 1945 in six volumes. Churchill wrote the history with the assistance of a team, using his own notes and privileged access to official documents that provided valuable insights into the War from his point of view. The book was a major source of information on World War II, especially in Britain and the United States.

The following two paragraphs quoted from Volume IV of the series titled "The Hinge of Fate", give a sense of how brazenly Churchill propagated disinformation across the board on India and the Indian National Army leader Netaji Subhas Chandra Bose through his book:

"NO great portion of the world population was **so effectively protected from the horrors and perils of the World War as were the peoples of Hindustan** (undivided India). They were carried through the struggle on die shoulders of our small Island. British Government officials in India were wont to consider it a point of honour to champion the **particular interests of India against those of Great Britain** whenever a divergence occurred. Arrangements made when the war was expected to be fought out in Europe were invoked to charge us for goods and services needed **entirely for the defence of India**, Contracts were fixed in India at extravagant rates, and debts incurred in Mated rupees were converted into so-called "sterling balances" at the pre-war rate of exchange. Thus enormous so-called "sterling balances"—in other words, British debts to India—were piled up. Without sufficient scrutiny or account we were being charged nearly a million pounds a day **for defending India from the miseries of invasion** which so many other lands endured. We finished the war, from all the worst severities of which they were spared, owing them a debt almost as large as that on which we defaulted to the United States after the previous struggle. I declared that these questions must remain open for revision, and that we reserved the right to set off against this so-called debt a counter-claim for the defence of India, and I so informed the Viceroy." [15] (Emphasis by Subir)

In this context, History Professor J. B. Bhattacharjee from North-East India commented:

"**Dragging India into the war** by a Viceroyal Ordinance within a few hours of Britain's declaration of war against Germany on 3rd September 1939 and the parallel enactment of the Government of India Amendment Act, which was rushed through the British Parliament in a matter of minutes **in total disregard of Indian public opinion** was in effect Britain's assertion of her right to decide the fate of India in the way she wanted and manifestation of how powerful were the administrative, legal and financial mechanisms created for the perpetuation of imperial interests in this classic colony. It was easy for British writers, like [1]Reginald Coupland, to argue in favour of the legitimacy of policy and action of their government in involving India in the war, the guarantee of provincial autonomy by the Government of India Act 1935 notwithstanding. On the other hand, [2]Maulana Azad's observation that the 'Viceroy's action proved afresh, if further proof was necessary, that the British Government looked on India as a creature of her will and was not willing to recognise India's right to decide her course for herself reflected the Indian sentiment." [16]

Note: [1]Reginald Coupland, a professor of the History of the British Empire, was deeply involved in Indian affairs as a member of some important commissions on constitutional reforms.

²Maulana Azad was an eminent Indian leader and the president of the Indian National Congress (1940–1946) during the crucial years of the war period.

Thus, it is clear that the Second World War was not our war. India's significant involvement in the conflict was merely as a part of the British Empire. As a British colony during this period, India's participation in the War was not by choice but rather as a result of British policy. The colonial rulers engaged over two and a half million Indians to fight for the British under their command against the Axis powers. They did not even consult Indian leaders before dragging India into the War. The reality was that the people of India were absolutely in no need of any so-called 'protection' from the Axis forces, especially the Japanese armies, as Churchill narrated in the book. He knew it better than any other person of his time.

Undeniably, Churchill was not only untruthful in his book, THE SECOND WORLD WAR VOLUME IV, THE HINGE OF FATE", but he was also trying to spread misleading information and downplay Subash Bose's resolve. Accordingly, what he wrote in the following paragraph of the same book about Netaji Subhas Chandra Bose needs to be taken with a pinch of salt:

"The atmosphere in India deteriorated in a disturbing manner with the westward advance of Japan into Asia. The news of Pearl Harbour was a staggering blow. Our prestige suffered with the loss of Hong Kong. The security of the Indian sub-continent was now directly endangered. The Japanese Navy was, it seemed, free to enter, almost unchallenged, the Bay of Bengal. India was threatened for the first time under British rule with a large-scale foreign invasion by an Asiatic Power. The stresses latent in Indian politics grew. Although **only a small extremist section in Bengal, led by men such as Subhas Bose**, were directly subversive and hoped for an Axis victory, the powerful body of articulate opinion which supported Gandhi ardently believed that India should remain passive and neutral in the world conflict. As the Japanese advanced, this defeatism spread. If India, it was suggested, could somehow throw off British connections, perhaps there would be no motive for a Japanese invasion. The peril to India might only consist of her link with the British Empire. If this link were snapped, surely India would adopt the position of Eire. So, not without force, the argument ran. [17 (Emphasis by Subir).

At the same time, the British did not leave any stone unturned to wipe out from the face of the earth the name of the INA and the dexterity of its leader, Netaji Subhas Chandra Bose. They even tried to assassinate Bose to achieve this end. Reality can be seen as the story progresses.

Towards the end of June 1944, on Southeast Asia's combat zone in Naga Hills, the Head of Southeast Asia Command, Nicholas Louis Francis Mountbatten, visited the battlefield of Kohima after the fighting had ended in 1944. Considering the ground developments and the course of the battle, he commented, "The Battle of Kohima will probably go down as one of the greatest battles in history." Field Marshal Sir William J. Slim agreed, writing in 1956 that "sieges have been longer, but few have been more intense, and in none have the defenders deserved greater honour than the garrison of Kohima." Later, in a message for issue 'to all ranks on the Manipur road', Mountbatten wrote that 'only those who have seen the horrific nature of the country under these conditions will be able to appreciate your achievements'. It sums up a great truth about the battle of Kohima. It also emphasises the magnitude of the victory brought at great cost by the combined British and Indian force of the 2nd British Division, the 161st Indian Brigade (which included the 4th Royal West Kents), and the 33rd Indian Brigade. [18]

Thus, one can easily make out how fiercely the opposite side, the joint INA-Japanese forces, fought in the battle for Kohima in India's Naga Hills. Yet, strikingly, the story of their fearless fight against all odds is missing in most history books, even today. On the other hand, the fact that the INA had suffered a setback in their war of liberation against the British colonial rule in North-East India's battlefields started trickling in gradually with sketchy details. Still, the attempt to liberate India through armed struggle cannot be termed a failure. Instead, it was a successful venture ultimately as far as its eventual outcome is concerned. That would also be evident as the story progresses.

As mentioned earlier, in a contest organised by the British National Army Museum in 2013, the Battle of Imphal/Kohima of World War II, fought between 8th March and 18th July 1944, was chosen as Britain's greatest battle. While Kohima was picked over the more celebrated battles of D-Day and Waterloo, Rorke's Drift in the 1879 Zulu War and the Battle of Aliwal in the Anglo-Sikh War in Punjab in 1846 brought up the rear. The contest's criteria included:

- A battle's political and historical impact.

- The challenges the troops faced.

- The strategy and tactics employed.

"Great things were at stake in a war with the toughest enemy any British army has had to fight," historian Robert Lyman said, making the case for Kohima in a debate at the museum. Lyman added that: If Lieutenant General William Slim's army of British, Indian, Gurkha and African troops had lost, the consequences for the allied cause would have been catastrophic. [19]

Unfortunately, INA forces that accompanied the Japanese in the liberation war of India did not have wireless transmitters/operators or any other means to regularly share information with the INA Headquarters about the details of their clashes against the Allied forces on Indian soil. Therefore, their side of the stories of the Battle of Imphal and, for that matter, the Battle of Kohima could not be adequately disseminated, even among their fellow soldiers and higher-ups.

Also, it has not been possible to lay hands on the Japanese accounts, if there are any, of the battles. It is understood that because of the censorship of the Japanese History Textbooks during the Allied Occupation of Japan (1945–1952) just after World War 2, the chronicled records of the campaign have been 'controlled' and rendered non-existent.

Over and above, whatever reports on these crucial battles were compiled at the INA Headquarters, almost all were destroyed by them at the time of surrender (as per standard military practice before a retreat). There are, therefore, little authentic written records of the INA per se. For all that, the readily available accounts are primarily based on the Anglo-American versions of the conflicts, which clearly and wittingly ignored and played down the triumphant roles of the joint INA-Japanese soldiers in general and the INA fighters, in particular.

The fact that the joint INA-Japanese Imphal campaign during World War II in 1944 to liberate India from British colonial rule ended in tragic failure is now well-known. The onset of the monsoon before the usual time, the shortage of air support, and, consequently, the disruption of the supply line were the primary reasons for the disaster. Different experts have attributed various causes to the fiasco from diverse perspectives. It's easy to find faults in hindsight when discussing military operations. However, when recounting history, it's crucial to consider the limitations and the compulsions of the time, and the events should be evaluated from a long-term perspective and their ultimate outcome.

From the Indian point of view, the INA's aim of liberating the sub-continent from British rule eventually succeeded, and the sacrifices of the Azad Hind Fauj personnel in the Imphal campaign did not go in vain, as will be seen later on. There is considerable concurrence on the argument that though the INA lost the battles of Imphal-Kohima, they won the War of India's Independence in the larger picture.

It is evident from contemporary government records that "Operation U" was successful at its initial stage. From 28th March, when the Kohima operation was inaugurated, up to 31st March, the entire road between Dimapur and Imphal was controlled by the Japanese army and the I.N.A. The then Deputy Commissioner Charles Pawsey has mentioned in the official records that seize of Kohima was unsuccessful no doubt, but for a slightest chance Kohima city proper, market and villages were under their control except the bungalow of the Deputy Commissioner as it was a top. (Reports of Charles Pawsey, 1946).

The feedback centre of the army was totally detached. If they had defeated the battalion, Dimapur would have been under their direct occupation. From there, they would have straight forward entered the plains of Assam because, by that time, sufficient soldiers were not there at Dimapur. (The same report by Pawsey) and Subhas wanted exactly this.

On 8th April, from the general Imperial headquarters of Japan about the dual attack, the following declarations were made:

(i) Our crack troop fighting side by side with I.N.A. captured Kohima early on 6th April.

(ii) Our attack on the enemy's airborne troops in the Kata area is moving along smoothly.

During those dark days of the British people, a handful of the Gorkha regiment, a few hundred of British soldiers and some exceptional patriots like Pawsey getting help from the local staff and Naga Labour Crops totally reversed the situation. (After the war, all of them were heavily rewarded by the British government.) Thus, the ill-fated campaign from lofty dreams doomed to failure. Netaji's planned march to the plains of Assam and undivided Bengal might not have changed the course of Indian history overnight. Yet, all said and done, it is such rare feats- the likes of Tipu Sultan to Subhas Bose – that make history and are remembered by the gen-next with awe and reverence. [20]

Anyway, as the spring of 1945 unfurled, the Axis powers found themselves on the brink of defeat. The relentless march of the Soviet forces from the East and the Western Allies from the West had Berlin in a vice-like grip. In a desperate bid to evade capture, Adolf Hitler and his companion Eva Braun chose death over dishonour, ending their lives in suicide.

Only three days after the end of the Second World War, Netaji Subhas Chandra Bose disappeared from the scene. On 18th August 1945, Netaji reportedly boarded a Japanese bomber plane at Taipei, Taiwan (which was at that time Japanese-ruled Formosa) to escape to Manchuria to seek a future in the Soviet Union, which he believed to have turned anti-British. But it seems his flight never reached its destination. There were reports that the plane crashed just after take-off. Bose suffered third-degree burns and died in a hospital in Taiwan.

The circumstances of his death remain a topic of controversy. Many Indians at that time refused to believe his death. Several commissions were established by the Indian government to investigate and find the truth about Bose's death or disappearance, but even today, a section of people refute claims of his death or its circumstances.

One theory suggests that the plane crash was a ruse set up by Netaji himself to evade Allied forces and continue his struggle from a safe location. Another theory posits that Bose survived the crash and lived in hiding in North India. Yet another belief insists that he was betrayed by Nehru and Gandhi and imprisoned in a Soviet gulag, which is a prison camp where the prisoners are forced to work very hard in extremely harsh conditions. These theories gained traction when the Indian government established the Netaji Inquiry Committee in 1956. While the committee concluded that Bose died in the plane crash, Netaji's brother refused to sign the report, alleging a cover-up and implicating several political leaders, including Jawaharlal Nehru. Despite several investigations reaching contested conclusions about Bose's death, the mystery persists due not only to popular longing for a different story but also the controversies surrounding some 'Netaji Files' officially classified by the Government of India initially supposedly for a variety of reasons, primarily due to the so-called sensitive nature of the information they contained.

Then, on 18th September 2015, the Government of West Bengal declassified 64 files related to Netaji Subhas Chandra Bose, followed by the Government of India announcing its decision to declassify all those files on 14th October 2014. Accordingly, the files have since become available for public scrutiny.

One of the most shocking revelations from the declassified papers was that the government of Prime Minister Jawaharlal Nehru spied on the family of Subhas Chandra Bose for nearly two decades. Intelligence Bureau (IB) officials intercepted, read, and recorded letters of the Bose family. They also discreetly followed family members as they travelled around India and abroad, recording in detail who they met and what they discussed.

The British CID had the two Bose family homes in Kolkata-1, Woodburn Park and the 38/2, Elgin Road-placed under surveillance since the 1930s when the two Bose brothers, Sarat Chandra and his younger brother, Subhas Chandra, emerged at the forefront of the freedom movement in Bengal was another significant disclosure. As the declassified intercepts show, independent India's government was just as keen to spy on the Bose family.

"If you were in India today," Sisir Bose (the son of Netaji's elder brother Sarat Chandra Bose) wrote to Netaji's wife in 1955, "you would get the feeling that in India's struggle two men mattered- (Mahatma) Gandhi and (Jawaharlal) Nehru. The rest were just extras." [21]

One of history's greatest infamies is the depiction of Azad Hind Fauj's valiant efforts to liberate India from nearly 200 years of British colonial rule as the Japanese invasion. The fact that Netaji allied with the Japanese forces penetrated India's northeastern frontier, aiming to engineer a country-wide mass uprising that would eventually drive out the British, was distorted beyond recognition of its true character. The sequel of British propaganda, coupled with the persistent rumours about Bose being alive and flights of fantasy in regard to his whereabouts, came in the way of the development of a sensible historical appraisal of the joint INA-Japanese extended Burma campaign that culminated in what the historian popularised as the Battle of Kohima and the Battle of Imphal.

Besides, the unceasing hype generated every now and then surrounding the disappearance story of Netaji Subhas Chandra Bose hindered the proliferation of the fantastic feats Netaji Bose accomplished in his endeavours to fulfil the lifelong aspiration of freeing India from the shackles of alien colonial rule got insufficient prominence than required. Furthermore, suitable efforts to counter the extravagant and intensive propaganda against Netaji by his adversaries were few and far between, if not totally absent. Those who slandered or downplayed the successes of Subhas Bose remained largely unchallenged. The unabated disinformation which surfaced during the Second World War was used in many cases as the so-called authentic source of information for many textbooks, academic papers, and articles, all with their domino effects.

Notwithstanding, the knotty questions on Netaji's disappearance after 18th August 1945 dominated the literary world, which saw the appearance of many books in the public domain in India, but, in contrast, only a very few of them deliberated on the twin battles of Kohima and Imphal that were one of the highest points in Netaji's life-long mission to see India liberated from the British colonial rule.

As mentioned earlier, while many authors all over the world have written numerous books about the battles of Kohima and Imphal, referenced primarily from British and American sources, only a handful have contradicted or doubted the prevalent narratives of Japanese invasions of India, trying to build the histories of India's Liberation War the Azad Hind Fauj fought under Netaji Subhas Chandra Bose. But these scarce and a limited number of them propagating the true story were not enough to kill the already well-established British propaganda that overshadowed or understated the heroic efforts of the INA and its leader, who fought valiantly to free India from the foreign yoke. Even today, most Indians, including those in Assam, Meghalaya, Tripura, as well as the people of Nagaland and Manipur, are more or less ignorant of the fact that Kohima and Imphal were not just battlefields of World War II but sites of India's deadliest struggle for independence. In other words, British propaganda triumphed over the true stories a few Indian authors tried to disseminate. On this sensitive aspect involving our national pride and dignity, we, the people of India, failed to properly propagate India's Liberation War that the INA had fought under the command of Netaji Subhas Chandra Bose.

The Indiatimes report on the 'Forgotten Battle' of Imphal-Kohima in 1944, published in its NE (North-East) Section as recently as on 22nd August 2023, authored by Srishti B Dutta, is a glaring example of how the British propaganda could wipe out the role of the INA and Netaji Subhas Chandra Bose in India's Liberation War from the memory of the people at large. The said report of 22nd August 2023 completely forgets to mention the involvement and contribution of the Azad Hind Fauj, led by Netaji, who fought alongside the Japanese to free India from British rule. Besides, what the report mentioned at the outset, as selectively quoted below, is in stark contrast with the factual story:

"Few in India know that the Japanese had a plan to invade India and, in fact, had come as close as Kohima, the capital of Nagaland, and Imphal, the capital of Manipur, in their effort to do.

So, India had come pretty close to become a Japanese colony. One wonders what trajectory history would have taken had they won the Battle of Kohima-Imphal. [22]

Many of our Army veterans and senior newspaper correspondents of the national press are also apparently in the dark about the reality, as appears from the Times of India newspaper report dated 28th March 2022. The report, titled "Veterans Commemorate the Battle that stall Japanese Invasion in Northeast", mentioned, among other things, that:

A group of veterans of the Indian Army commemorated the 78th anniversary of the battle of 'Sansak', which was fought by one Indian Light Infantry **under the British against the Japanese force during World War II in March 1944 in the North East region,** by laying a wreath at the war memorial in a locality situated in the eastern suburbs of Pune city on Saturday.

The bravery of the Indian Light Infantry soldiers on the battlefield enabled them to **successfully resist and thwart the fierce attacks** of the Japanese force in the treacherous hilly and forest terrains.

The battle was one of the highest points of the Burma campaign. The battalion, as part of a Parachute Brigade, sustained the brunt of 31 Japanese division's attacks attempting to breach the defence of Imphal and **yet turned the tide against the enemy force**.

The Indian soldiers displayed unprecedented courage and steadfastness in the battle and changed the equation of the battle. Because of them, the concentration of 4 Corps gained precious 10 days to rope in its resources in the defence of Imphal and Kohima then. **It had stopped the invasion of the Japanese force successfully**." states the records of the battalion.

Serving and retired soldiers of the battalion commemorate the day every year on 26th March to pay tribute to those who have laid down their lives in the battle.

The Lt Gen (retd), who commanded the battalion and, under his tenure as Director General Assam Rifle (DGAR), constructed a memorial at Sangsak in Manipur in 2002, told TOI, "It was the only battalion deployed in the most difficult terrain to stop the invasion of the Japanese force. The 'Ganpats' (soldiers fondly called) could fight without food and water for 10 days. It had fought against all adversities but did not give up. Even today, after visiting the place, one can understand how it could have been difficult for them to stand against the strong Japanese force then. It is a proud day for the battalion."

About 100 soldiers, including serving and retired officers from Pune and neighbouring districts, gathered at the Memorial to pay their respects and tributes to the battalion's fallen soldiers.

The battalion, which is presently deployed in Northern border areas, too commemorated the day by **organising 'Bara Khana'** for soldiers and veterans of the area." (Emphasis by Subir). [23]

Alas, little did they seemingly know that the Light Infantry, as part of the 50 Parachute Brigade, in reality, turned the tide against the valiant efforts of the Indian National Army (INA) when they came, allied with the Japanese, to liberate India from the British colonial rule. The soldiers of the Light Infantry unwittingly changed the course of our independence movement in favour of India's enemy forces - the British Allied forces of World War II. The Indian soldiers fighting under the British flag unknowingly risked their lives and displayed unprecedented enthusiasm and dogged determination in the battle of 'Sansak'. Unaware, they altered the equation of India's Liberation War and the course of Indian history all for the British by fiercely fighting against the Japanese and the Azad Hind Fauj. Such was the power of the British propaganda machinery that, nearly 80 years down the line, many Indians are still unaware of the truth behind the so-called Japanese Invasion.

Against that backdrop, it is crucial to recall what ELIZABETH ESTON, the Co-author of "Rash Behari Bose the Fahter of the Indian National Army", wrote in this context:

"We are living in a generation in which, ever since the triumph of British and American imperialism over Japan, a distorted version of history continues to be fabricated and propagated and is even now growing ever more complex. If one is distressed by the current state of the world even in the slightest, one must not simply stand by idly and accept Britain and America's interpretation of history as the truth. There is a vital need for the Indian independence movement and Japan's cessation of war to be revised and understood from the Asian point of view rather than continuing the present trend of automatically defaulting to the Western concoction of history."

Therefore, re-evaluating our historical narratives, particularly those surrounding our armed liberation movements and Japan's wartime actions, by adopting an Asian perspective is crucial to gaining a factual understanding of how India won its freedom from British colonial rule.

As we conclude this introductory chapter, let's reflect upon the fact that our history is not merely a chronicle of events. It is also a tribute to the unyielding spirit of the commendable people. The saga of the Indian National Army and its charismatic leader, Subhas Chandra Bose, extends beyond their attempt to expel the British to liberate India from colonial rule. Despite initial setbacks, including defeat in the Imphal campaign, the endeavour of the Indian National Army led by Netaji Subhas ultimately emerged victorious, as can be seen in the final analysis.

It is, in essence, a narrative of India's rewarding Liberation War, a heroic struggle against colonial subjugation. We bear the responsibility to ensure that the gallant efforts of the Azad Hind Fauj, Netaji Subhas, Rash Behari Bose and others are never forgotten. These must be documented in the correct perspectives. Their story intertwines with ours, echoing a tale of their sacrifice, determination and bravery that reverberates through the corridors of history. We must commit to keeping their memory alive, for their spirit and determination must motivate our resolve to be vigilant in guarding and defending our country from being subjugated by any alien force once more.

With this view in mind, let us delve into the vital aspects of Subhas Chandra Bose's life and briefly touch upon the biography of the born-revolutionary Rash Behari Bose. Together, we will explore the events leading up to the "Battle of Kohima" and the "Battle of Imphal," tracing the INA's journey through trials and triumphs. This journey unequivocally disproves the fabricated Anglo-American narratives of the Second World War against India's Liberation War in general and Subhas Bose in particular. So, let us begin at the beginning when the indomitable spirit of Netaji Subhas Chandra Bose first began to manifest.

* * * * * * *

Chapter 2

Oatenization

'Oatenization' is a noun in Indian English that has its origin in an episode, which took place in 1916 at India's Presidency College, Calcutta (now Presidency University, Kolkata), embroiling its Professor Edward Farley Oaten, who taught History and English. That was a unique dramatic incident because it involved a British Professor on one side and Indian students led by Subhas Chandra Bose on the other side. Subhas was expelled and rusticated from the Presidency College and Calcutta University allegedly for beating up the Professor on 15th February 1916. The Oaten incident, in a sense, was the beginning of the future of Netaji's political career, and Oaten has often been demonised in its Indian telling.

From the late 1960s, assaults on academics – and occasionally even murder – became common happenings in colleges and universities in Calcutta and West Bengal. But, in 1916, it was a unique dramatic incident that retrospectively acquired historic importance because it marked a turning point in the life of a future leader of India. The expulsion made Subhas Chandra Bose a hero at once. The exceptional happening at India's Presidency College soon gave rise to a new English verb – to 'oatenize' someone - and thence the noun 'Oatenization'.

The incident also immortalised the name Edward Farley Oaten. Though he had a distinguished career, his encounter with Subhas has made him memorable in the history of India's British empire. There are different versions of what truly happened on that day when Bose's Professor was Oatenized. [1]

Be that as it may, Subhas Chandra Bose was very perceptive from his early days and would notice things that others would miss. Thus, he developed a keen eye for detail - an important trait that often manifests in an upright leader. At the age of five, Subhas was admitted to a Protestant European school, which predominantly catered to Europeans and Anglo-Indians. The school, under the leadership of Mr Young, showed little regard for local culture and language, focusing instead on imposing Christian and European values on its students. Vernacular subjects were ignored, and Indian culture and history were omitted from the curriculum. Young Subhas found solace in the sympathetic Miss Lawrence. Otherwise, he found himself surrounded by an environment that emphasized European culture, history, and norms while discriminating against Indian students, even denying them access to scholarship examinations. Although, at that time, he harboured no hostile feelings toward the school authorities, he felt uncomfortable.

In 1909, Subhas Chandra Bose decided to leave this school and enrolled in Ravenshaw Collegiate School in Cuttack. Here, his life took a different turn. His headmaster, Benimadhab Das, was an ardent Nationalist, and the teachings of Swami Vivekananda profoundly influenced him. Subhas noticed a notable shift in the new school, where his family background began to earn him respect among his fellow students, a contrast to his prior European school experience. He initially faced humiliation due to his lack of knowledge in Sanskrit but rapidly excelled, becoming the top student in Sanskrit and Bengali. His primary academic rival and good friend was Charu Chandra.

While studying under a diverse set of Bengali and Oriya teachers, Subhas was particularly influenced by Benimadhab Das, who epitomized moral purity in his personal life. Benimadhab imparted to Subhas a love for the country, its culture, and its people, emphasizing the importance of moral principles in life. The idea that the individual must sacrifice for the nation's greater good became deeply ingrained in Subhas. He realized that he needed to dedicate his life to the service of India, striving for freedom and glory. This realization shaped Subhas Chandra Bose's actions and remained a guiding principle throughout his life. [2]

A couple of years before the infamous 'Oaten incident' in the Presidency College upset his student life, during the summer vacation of 1914, Subhas came to his hometown, Cuttack. About that time, his political awareness started growing, triggered by the following happenings. One day, he quietly left home with a friend in search of a guru - a spiritual preceptor, without telling his parents about the trip. His search for a guru landed him in all the major pilgrimage sites of northern India, including Lachman-Jhola, Hrishikesh, Hardwar, Mathura, Brindaban, Benaras and Gaya. A third friend joined the duo at Hardwar in the search party for a guru. In a couple of months' expedition, Subhas had a few meetings with some truly holy men, but overall, the mission ended in disillusionment and disenchantment. He personally witnessed the deeply ingrained caste prejudices in northern India and the petty sectarian rivalries of the men of religion. Brought face to face with the glaring shortcomings of Hindu society, he returned to Calcutta, becoming a wiser man, shedding much of his admiration for ascetics and anchorites. Within a few days of his return, he came down with typhoid. That was the price Subhas had to pay for his pilgrimage and guru-hunting. As he lay ill in bed, he received news of the outbreak of the First World War.

Subhas did not tell his parents clearly about the trip, leading them to think he had run away. His absence caused emotional distress to his parents, causing both parents to break down upon his return. Heated words were exchanged between him and his father, Janakinath Bose. It took the return of Subhas's favourite brother, Sarat Chandra Bose, from law studies in England for the tempers to subside. Subhas returned to the presidency and busied himself with studies, debating and student journalism.

It was at this time Subhas's political consciousness was truly aroused. The racism that India suffered at the hands of the British in the city of Calcutta was constant and ubiquitous. Subhas encountered this haughty superiority on his daily tram-car journeys from home to his college. He often had to engage in verbal duels with arrogant Englishmen. At the same time, the shock of the eruption of global war affected him greatly. Lying in bed and reading newspapers, he began to question whether it was possible to divide a nation's life too into two compartments and hand over one of them to the foreigner, reserving the other to ourselves. He doubted the efficacy of separating the home from the world, the inner spiritual life from the outer material domain. Yet, the year 1915 passed without any major crisis. Subhas busied himself with studies. His extracurricular activities were numerous; he was the class representative on the students' consultative committee, the secretary of the debating society and a famine relief committee for East Bengal, and a member of the board of the newly launched college magazine. That was the time when Subhas came close to his fellow student, Dilip Kumar Roy and forged what was to become a life-long friendship. Dilip later reminisced that from their earliest meetings, he noticed that Subhas had a native power to lead, and he knew it.

Nevertheless, a dramatic incident shattered the normal life at the Presidency College in early 1916. As every day, Subhas was studying in the college library on 10th January 1916 when he was told that Professor Edward Farley Oaten had manhandled some students who were Subhas's classmates. As the class representative, Subhas took up the matter with the principal, Henry R. James, and demanded that Oaten should apologise to the students. The Professor claimed that, being disturbed by the chatter of these students outside his classroom, he had merely taken them by the arm, a gesture that could not be interpreted as an insult. He was a member of the government's educational service, and the principal did not have the power to extract an apology from him. The disaffected students then called a general strike for the next day. The news of the successful strike in a college meant to be a bastion of loyalism caused much excitement in the city. It encouraged young students at other institutions to follow the rebellious example. Toward the end of the second day of the strike, Oaten met the student representatives and settled the dispute. The principal, however, refused to withdraw the fine of five rupees that he had imposed on the striking students. The next day, Oaten ordered ten students out of the twelve in his history course – those who had taken part in the strike – to leave the class.

On 15th February, the students learned that Oaten had manhandled another student belonging to the first-year chemistry class for being noisy in the corridor. On this occasion, a group of students decided to take the law into their own hands. Oaten was given a solid thrashing at the bottom of the Presidency College's imposing main staircase. The incident lasted forty seconds, according to the official inquiry. Oaten later recalled that he suffered no injury except a few bruises.

Subhas Chandra Bose was allegedly connected with the affair, although Oaten never had any proof of it. He had seen ten or fifteen students milling around as he came down the stairs but could not be sure who had hit him as he was putting up a notice about a cricket match. An orderly identified Subhas and another student, Ananga Dam, as being among those he had seen leaving the scene. [3]

Among other documents preserved in the archives of London's India Office, this 1916 incident has been documented in the 'Oaten File' where it is noted that in January 1916, there was an altercation between Professor Oaten and some students. The students complained to the principal that one of them had been manhandled by the young professor. There was a students' strike at Presidency College for two days. A successful strike at Presidency College, a premier government institution, was big news. Principal James called the students and asked them to make up with the professor; quietly, he advised Oaten to do the same. There was an apparent reconciliation – everyone shook hands and agreed to forgive and forget. However, the students were again upset when they were compelled to pay a fine by the college authorities for participating in the strike. Only those who pleaded poverty were exempted.

Soon after, on 15th February 1916, another incident took place. A professor was absent, and his class was taken by a substitute teacher, who let the class off a few minutes ahead of time. The boys came out in the corridor and were noisy. Oaten was taking his class in a nearby room and got annoyed. He came out and scolded the students. The students dispersed, and Oaten was about to return to his classroom when one of the boys called out loudly to another student. Possibly, this was not deliberate, but Oaten thought it was.

What happened after that is a matter of controversy. The boy said he was grabbed by the neck by Oaten and called a rascal. Oaten said he only took the boy by the arm. The students became agitated, and although they lodged a complaint with Principal James, they reportedly felt there was no hope of justice from a British principal.

Principal James asked the students to come to his room at 3 p.m. the same day to discuss the matter. But it was precisely at that time some students took the matter into their own hands and assaulted Oaten. A common story is that he was pushed down the steep staircase of Presidency College.

The official story is different. The professor had come down the stairs and was standing near the notice board on the ground floor when he was suddenly surrounded by a small group of students and beaten up. Another professor, Gilchrist, who was coming down the stairs at that time, saw the incident, but the boys ran away before he could identify any of them. The assault lasted barely a minute, but the consequences were far-reaching.

The governing body of the college started an enquiry immediately. But the Bengal government announced another high-powered enquiry committee, which eventually submitted its report signed by the following members – Ashutosh Mookerjee, W. W. Hornell (Director of Public Instruction), C. W. Peake, J. Mitchell, and Haramba Chandra Maitra of the City College.

Principal James, meanwhile, fell out with Mr Lyon, the member of the government in charge of education and, as a result, was suspended and later made to retire. But before his suspension, Principal James called Subhas Bose, who had admitted that he was 'an eyewitness' to the Oatern incident, to meet him. This is how Netaji Subhas describes the meeting in his autobiography:

> 'To me he said – or rather snarled – in unforgettable words: "Bose, you are the most troublesome man in the college. I suspend you." I said, "Thank you" and went home'.

The Oaten incident, in a sense, was the beginning of the future of Netaji's political career, and Oaten has often been demonized in its Indian telling. [4]

Another version went like this: Oaten was highly disrespectful towards Indian culture and its people. One day, he had maltreated a few students on flimsy grounds. As the students' leader, Subhas went to the Principal, James, and asked for an apology from Oaten. But the Principal said he couldn't force Oaten to apologise for his behaviour. Subhas and the students then decided to call for a strike. All the students stayed away from the class. None of them budged, even when they were fined for being absent. The students' strike at Presidency College became a sensational news item nationwide. On the second day of the strike, the authorities asked Oaten to settle the matter. Oaten agreed, discussed, and settled it with a few student representatives. After some time, Oaten again started misbehaving with the students, and it was reported that he had beaten a first-year student. The students got mad as the authorities were unable to take any action. So they decided to take the matter into their own hands. Oaten was pushed down the steep staircase of Presidency College, creating a hue and cry.

Subhas was reportedly not directly involved, but he was made a scapegoat, being the student leader. The Government decided to close down Presidency College and formed an investigative committee. The Principal was enraged by the Government's unilateral decision and misbehaved with the education ministry. The Principal was suspended, but he wielded his rod of chastisement before his suspension was effective. He called Subhas and suspended him from Presidency College. The investigative committee supported his decision. Even Calcutta University expelled Subhas, and all avenues for his higher education were closed. The president of that committee was Sir Ashutosh Mukherjee. The committee had asked Subhas if it was proper to have beaten Oaten. Subhas said it was improper conduct, but he supported the students on the grounds that they had been enraged by the deliberate insults and abuses hurled at them over a period

Travelling back home to Cuttack after the Oaten affair, his future apparently in ruins – expelled and rusticated - Bose oddly felt supreme satisfaction and joy that he had done the right things, standing up for a noble cause of defending their honour and self-respect. With this strange feeling after expulsion from the Presidency College, Subhas went back to his hometown, Cuttack.

For two years, he remained there, unable to continue his studies because of his rustication. He asked his parents to send him abroad, but his father refused. In a kind of limbo, not knowing when or where he might resume his studies, the young Bose searched for an outlet for his energy and idealism. Soon, he took to social service with a passionate zeal.

Finally, in 1917, the Vice-Chancellor of Calcutta University, Sir Ashutosh Mukherjee, helped him get admission into Scottish Church College for the final two years of study for his B.A. During his first year at this college, he enlisted in a university unit of the Territorial Army that was being formed and devoted most of the year to his newly discovered enthusiasm for soldiering, in which he found a positive pleasure. It was only in his last year that he commenced serious study for his B. A. examination. In the examination, he received first-class honours in Philosophy but fell below his expectations in that he ranked second in order of merit.

Interestingly, in 1929, while in his early thirties and already well into a spectacular political career, Subhas Chandra Bose recalled his expulsion in an address to a student conference:

> My Principal expelled me, but he had made my future career. I established a precedent for myself from which I could not easily depart in future. I had stood up with courage and composure in a crisis and fulfilled my duty. I had developed self-confidence as well as initiative, which was to stand me in good stead in future. I had a foretaste of leadership – though in a very restricted sphere – and of the martyrdom that it involves. In short, I acquired character and could face the future with equanimity.

This was the day when I realised what heavenly bliss awaited all of us to compensate for persecution for serving a noble cause! ....Having passed the most difficult test successfully, I found that the course of my life and its future programme had been decided once and for all.

This Oaten incident, as it is commonly known, gave a foretaste of leadership to Subhas Chandra Bose that eventually turned him into the renowned Netaji, bestowed the young Professor of Presidency College, Edward Farley Oaten, in 1916 a unique notoriety but immortalised Oaten in the history of India's British empire, and a new English emerged in India - to 'otanize' someone - and its use in the academic campuses, especially in Bengal, became very much in vogue, and thence its noun 'otenization' came into being. [5]

"**Nearly a century after he was expelled, Netaji finds pride of place at Presidency**", under this caption The Indian Express newspaper on 10th April 2010, among other things, reported that ninety-four years after he was expelled from the college, Subhas Chandra Bose returned to Presidency College on Friday (9th April 2010) as a statue.

Academicians, historians and the entire staff and students of Presidency College came together to welcome one of its greatest alumni, as the statue next to the Derozio hall was unveiled today. On 16th February 1916, two students, Ananda Mohan Dam and Subhas Chandra Bose, were expelled from the college on charges of assaulting a teacher, E F Oaten.

Head of the Political Science department of the college, Professor Nandalal Chakraborty, said: When the principal told Subhas Chandra Bose that he had been expelled, his reply was, Thank you very much. And he left the college. Professor Amal Kumar Mukhopadh, a former principal of the college who has done extensive research on Netaji's stay at the college (July 1913-February 1916), claimed there had been a number of attempts to give Netaji the recognition that he deserved, but the college failed to do so in the past. [6]

In the Proceedings of the International Netaji Seminar 1973, "NETAJI AND INDIA'S FREEDOM", EDITED BY SISIR K. BOSE, Executive Directory, Netaji Research Bureau, Netaji Bhawan Calcutta, Amiya Nath Bose, the son of Netaji's elder brother Sarat Chandra Bose, among other things, said:

> "One evening, Netaji expressed his annoyance at the way my father, the late Mr. Sarat Chandra Bose, generously tolerated and gave importance to a certain gentleman in public life. Netaji told me that he could never forgive that gentleman because of certain things that he had known about him during his student days. To satisfy my curiosity, Netaji related the following about the second Oaten incident:
>
>> Mr. Oaten used to condemn everything Indian in his lectures, and he was contemptuous of Indian culture and history. A feeling of animosity thus grew up between him and his Indian students. Students held many meetings amongst themselves to decide what was to be done about it. Protests registered in the classes were not of any avail. The direct reason for the second incident was this: In one of Mr. Oaten's classes, one of the students may have talked. Mr. Oaten felt very annoyed, walked up the student and boxed his ears. The gentleman who had his ears boxed is alive and available. After this incident, a number of students, including Subhas Chandra Bose, met and decided that Mr Oaten should be thrashed for his violence against the students. And the assault was neither accidental nor sudden.
>>
>> I asked Netaji many many times whether he had himself physically assaulted Mr Oaten. He never answered the question. He only smiled." [7]

As Subhas Chandra Bose completed his graduation with a B.A. in Philosophy in 1918 from the Scottish Church College, affiliated with the University of Calcutta and prepared to take up studies leading toward an M. A. degree, his father had proposed that he go to Britain to study for the entrance examination for the prestigious and exclusive Civil Service (ICS). There was probably no more nearly universal and intensely held aspiration of Western-educated, upper-middle-class Indian parents than that a son gains a coveted appointment to the ICS.

At that time, the examination was held only in Britain, and most successful candidates were British graduates of Oxford or Cambridge. The young Bose decided to go, although there seemed little prospect of his success in the examination since he would have only eight months in Britain to prepare for it. Anyway, he went on to study at Cambridge. After briefly studying there, Bose sat for the rigorous examination. Again, he had revealed his remarkable studiousness and intellectual ability. Bose passed the Civil Service open competitive test brilliantly in 1920, attaining fourth place, a considerable achievement for one who had been in England barely eight months.

But the direction of Indian nationalism was now changing. Subhas thought of dedicating his life to the freedom struggle of India and thought of going back and sacrificing the ICS job under the British.

He debated the matter with his family, particularly with his brother Sarat, who urged him not to resign. But to Subhas, they seemed to miss the point. He said to himself: I must chuck this rotten service and dedicate myself wholeheartedly to the country's cause, or I must bid farewell to all my ideals and aspirations.

"As he stood on the verge of taking the plunge by resigning from the Indian Civil Service, he wrote to his elder brother Sarat on 6th April 1921:

> 'I know what this sacrifice means. It means poverty, suffering, hard work and possibly other hardships to which I need not expressly refer but which you can very well understand. But the sacrifice has got to be made— consciously and deliberately. Father says that most of the so-called leaders are not really unselfish. But is that any reason why he should prevent me from being unselfish?'

An overpowering sense of mission impelled the young Subhas Chandra Bose to set an early example of leadership as he dedicated himself to a life of selfless service", wrote Sisir K. Bose and Sugata Bose in the EDITORS' INTRODUCTION of the book "An Indian Pilgrim – An Unfinished Autography: Subhas Chandra Bose". [8]

No Indian had yet resigned from the Indian Civil Service. If he failed here, he would never respect himself again. His mind was made up in January 1921: he would offer himself for work at the Congress in Calcutta. He resigned from the Indian Civil Service in April. His father was grieved, but the son had faced the father's distress and would not be diverted. When the Under-Secretary of State for India had sent for Subhas and asked him why he was resigning, Subhas said that one could not be loyal to the British Raj and yet serve India honestly, heart and soul. Finally, in April 1921, Bose withdrew from taking up this post with the ICS and returned to India in the summer of 1921.

This gesture of defiance and self-sacrifice added to Bose's aura of dedication and martyrdom, spreading his fame far and wide. Before he departed from Britain, Bose wrote to Deshbandhu Chittaranjan Das, a prominent nationalist leader from Bengal, expressing his wish to devote himself to the cause of national independence.

After landing in Bombay from London on 16 July 1921, Subhas Chandra Bose first met Mahatma Gandhi at Mani Bhavan and had long discussions with him about his future plan of action in the service of the Congress. But, somehow, Bose was not impressed by Gandhi, who himself suggested to Bose that he should meet C. R. Das in Calcutta for his guidance.

Returning back to Calcutta, Bose met the Bengali leader Chittaranjan Das, popularly called Deshbandh. During his very first meeting, Subhas Bose accepted him as his leader. The first assignment of Bose in the Congress was the office of the Principal of the National College, and along with it, he was also made the Chief of the Publicity Board of the Bengal Provincial Congress Committee and the Head of the National Volunteer Corps. Das also gave him the responsibility of keeping contact with the revolutionaries, some of whom were underground. From the very beginning, Bose proved his leadership ability, and within the next four months, he became famous as an important leader not only in Bengal but throughout the country. In the Hartal in Calcutta, on 17 November 1921, organised by the Congress in protest against the visit of the Prince of Wales, he proved his organising capacity, and in the Civil Disobedience movement started at that time, C. R. Das nominated him as one of his successors for the leadership of the movement. This was the first taste of movement for Bose, and he came out with flying colours and justified by his leadership the confidence and faith reposed on him. He was arrested on 20 December 1921 and was awarded six months' imprisonment. [9] That was the first time, the British administration in India arrested Subhas Chandra Bose.

Here is a digression. Over the years, the British Raj started regarding him as the most dreaded Indian revolutionary due to his uncompromising militant struggle for India's freedom. His activities unnerved the British administrators, and they marked him out as their 'arch enemy'. To restrict his movements, the British Government put him to prison - seven times in the course of his twenty years' struggle at home (1921-1941) – 'on trumped up charge of his active complicity with the terrorists.' [10] The last time Subhas Bose detained was on 3rd July 1940 .in connection with the Howell Monument movement. Bose then engineered a daring escape on the night of 16-17 January 1941 from his house arrest to Germany surreptitiously. We shall come to that narrative as the story progresses.

Now, returning to where we deviated, the next few years were just like a hurricane for Bose, to put it mildly. He addressed a number of conferences of students and youth, both within and outside Bengal. He did a very excellent work for flood relief in North Bengal. He campaigned successfully for the elections held under the Montague-Chelmsford Act but could not contest himself because his name did not appear in the voters' list. He became the General Secretary of the Bengal Pradesh Congress Committee (BPCC) in 1923. He was elected to the Corporation of Calcutta in 1924 from Ward No. 22 in Bhowanipore. In the same year, the Mayor of the Corporation, C. R. Das, appointed him as its Chief Executive Officer (CEO). He was arrested in October 1924, when he was the CEO of Calcutta Corporation, for his alleged involvement with the 'terrorists'. Bose was ultimately put to Mandalay Jail in Burma and was kept detained there for years. Though he was in prison in far-away Mandalay, in 1926, he was elected to the Bengal Legislative Council from North Calcutta Constituency, defeating the then-famous moderate leader Jatindra Nath Bose. Subhas Bose was one of the main organisers of the Calcutta Session of the Congress in 1928, held under the presidency of Motilal Nehru. He became famous for organising the Volunteers' Corps in military uniform and with almost full military discipline. Subhas Chandra Bose became the General Officer Commanding (GOC) for this volunteer force.

Afterwards, it appeared to be the embryonic beginning of the INA in Southeast Asia during the Second World War. Subhas became the leader of the trade unions, particularly with the Tata Workers' Union at Jamshedpur, and was elected as the President of the All India Trade Union Congress. He presided over its all-India conference in Calcutta in July 1931. Subhas Chandra Bose was closely associated with all Congress programmes from July 1921, when he first met C. R. Das in Calcutta, till January 1941, when he left his Elgin Road house incognito. During his stay in Europe and Southeast Asia in the forties, Bose watched the activities of Congress very closely and always considered himself to be one who belonged to it. He participated in all the movements started by the Congress and attended the Congress sessions as one of the prominent leaders of the Congress. Even when Subhas was in Europe in the thirties, in exile, Bose did not idle away. He devoted his time, in spite of his ill health at that time, to propagating the ideas of Congress in different countries of Europe. [11] [12] [13] [14] [15]

Earlier, in 1915, Mahatma Gandhi joined the Indian National Congress after returning from South Africa at the invitation of Gopal Krishna Gokhale. Gandhi's ideologies, markedly different from the combative policies of the extremists within the party, slowly gained wider acceptance. His coming to power in the nationalist movement signalled a shift of power centres in the party. For decades, the nationalist movement had been concentrated in the three coastal

Presidencies, but now the man from Gujarat came to the fore, with support in the Hindi heartland of North India and South India. This shift meant a loss of predominance with the movement for Maharashtra and Bengal mainly. Leaders from these two areas did not quietly step aside to pave the way for Gandhi. From 1918 to the end of 1920, the moderates – or the newly rechristened Liberals – left the Congress to Gandhi and Das.

From the beginning of what Jawaharlal Nehru called Gandhi's 'super presidency' of the Congress, Gandhi insisted that the working committee should be a homogeneous body with unanimity of view. The AICC (All India Congress Committee) and the annual sessions were envisioned as forums for diverse opinions, but the executive was to act as one. Gandhi could listen to others, but accompanying his strong desire to persuade others of his views was an authoritarian streak. From 1920 to 1925, there were always men more devoted to Gandhi and his ideas who wanted control of the provincial Committees, but Das was generally recognised by Gandhi as well as the Government of Bengal as the Congress leader in Bengal. At the same time, he achieved national stature within Congress. Mahatma Gandhi was chosen as Congress president in 1924.

'I have observed that Subhas is not at all dependable. However, there was nobody but he who could be the President' Gandhi had written in a note to Sardar Patel on 1st November 1937 prior to Subhas Chandra Bose being selected in the Congress session at Haripura, in Gujarat, President of Congress Party in 1938. Exactly who was consulted and when their consensus was communicated to Subhas Bose is not clear. Netaji found it very hard to work as he would have liked to because of behind-the-scenes manoeuvring by certain groups in Congress. He could realise that even though he was a Congressman, he was still an outsider to the Gandhi group which controlled the party. Gandhi remained 'willfully blind' on the issues. There was a strong feeling among many people in Bengal as well as the rest of the Country that 'it was that part of the Mahatma's contribution to the eventual partition' of Bengal/India. For instance, the correspondence between Gandhi and Subhas when he became Congress president clearly proves that Gandhi did not let Subhas act according to his own wisdom even after his due consultation with the Mahatma and others. Bengal had to pay dearly for Gandhi's unreasonable interference with the workings of Netaji as the President of the Congress Party, as could be seen subsequently.

After the election of 1937, no single party could secure enough votes to form the government in Bengal Province without forming a coalition. "Left to himself, Subhas would have liked to join Fazlul Huq's KPP; he tried even afterwards to upturn the KPP-League coalition but found himself powerless to defy Gandhi. As late as 1938, Gandhi wrote to Bose, then Congress president:

> "A long discussion with Maulana Abul Kalam Azad, Nalini Ranjan Sarkar and Ghanasyamadas Birla has convinced me that the present ministry in Bengal (a coalition of the Muslim League and the KPP) should not be changed. The change will be of no avail. Rather, if the Congress forms a coalition ministry in Bengal with the Krishak Praja Party, it may be injurious to the province. Nalini Sarkar has told me that if the present coalition ministry takes any measure which is against the Country's interest, he will not hesitate to resign from it."

Subhas Bose's reply to Gandhi (21st December 1938) was:

> Your letter came as a profound shock to me. I have had many discussions with you over the formation of ministry in Bengal. The matter was also discussed with you some days back in Wardha. My elder brother Sarat Chandra Bose, too, has talked with you over the matter. Both of us clearly recall that you have supported the idea of a coalition ministry of Congress and Krishak Praja Parties in Bengal. I cannot understand how you changed your views so soon after the discussion at Wardha. It is quite clear that your talks with Azad, Nalini, and Birla are responsible for the changing your views. The position, therefore, appears to be you prefer to give more importance to the views of the above three persons than those of persons who are responsible for running the Congress in Bengal.

There had been a hint that Gandhi was unduly influenced by G. D. Birla, representing Indian business interests. Birla, as the leader of the Marwari business interests, strongly felt that political unity between the Muslims and Hindus in Bengal would threaten Marwari dominance of the business landscape in Kolkata. The existing arrangement in which the Muslim League, a party of vested interests, played a dominant role with strong links with up-country business interests through non-Bengali industrialists like Ishpani would suit both Marwari and British industrialists.

In retrospect, there can be no doubt that the Congress's mistake in turning down Fazlul Huq's request (to have a Congress-KPP coalition ministry) in Bengal, together with its blunder in the United Provinces, did pave the way for the partition of the subcontinent ten years later. The Muslim League took full advantage of its governmental authority in Bengal to extend its base over the Muslim masses."

Before the end of 1938, another conflict began over the presidency of the Indian National Congress for the following year. The controversy changed the position of the Boses (Subhas and Sarat Chandra Bose) in Indian politics and had significant consequences for the history of the left and Hindu-Muslim relations. Subhas Chandra Bose contested the election of the President, defying the 'wish' of Gandhi and against the likings of Sardar Patel and many other senior Congress leaders of its working committee, who put forth Sitaramayya as their candidate. They even asked Subhas Bose to step aside and allow the election to be a unanimous one. Bose declined.

The victory of Subhas Bose, with 1,580 votes against his opponent's 1,375 votes, in the Congress presidential race came as a surprise to Mahatma Gandhi and his closest colleagues. It awakened Gandhi from his somnolence, and he issued a hostile and self-accusatory statement two days later. In part, the Mahatma said:

> Shri Subhas Bose had achieved a decisive victory ..... I must confess that from the very beginning, I was decidedly against his re-election ..... I do not subscribe to his facts or the arguments in his manifestos. I think that his references to his

colleagues were unjustified and unworthy. Nevertheless, I am glad of his victory....... After all, Subhas Babu is not an enemy of his Country. He has suffered for it. In his opinion, his is the most forward and boldest policy and program...... The minority may not obstruct on any account. **They must abstain when they cannot cooperate**. (Emphasis by Subir)

Here, Gandhi gave hints of what was yet to come. Gandhi and his men, angry with Bose's description in his book "The Indian Struggle" as 'tired old reactionaries', were preparing to teach Bose a lesson. On 22nd February 1939, all the Working Committee members – except the Bose brothers, Subhas Chandra Bose and his elder brother Sarat Chandra Bose – including Jawaharlal Nehru, resigned, leaving the Congress with a president marked for the helm but without a crew to run the ship.

To cut a long story short, Netaji was not allowed to work in discharging his duties as a Congress President despite having won the election with convincing majority support of the Congressmen, and amidst allegations and counter-allegations, Subhas Bose tendered his resignation on 29th April 1939. Within a week, he announced in Calcutta on 3rd May 1939 the formation of a new grouping WITHIN the Congress to be called "Forward Block".

Even after the resignation of Bose from the Indian National Congress Presidency on 29th April 1939, as desired by Gandhi due to their ideological and tactical discordance with him, Gandhi was not entirely satisfied with it. Gandhi and Nehru could not stand Bose as he had been working intensively from the platform of his new-born Congress wing, the All India Forward Bloc. Gandhi felt that the Forward Bloc made Bose more popular with a bigger following than when he was the Congress President. On 19th August 1939, Gandhi got a resolution passed disqualifying Bose as the President of the Bengal Provincial Congress Committee for three years on the imposed ground of 'deliberate and flagrant breach of discipline'. (It is noteworthy that Gandhi formally resigned from his membership in Congress in 1934 and often said that he was not even a 4-anna member of the party. But it showed the extent of extra-constitutional influence he still used to exercise!) Nevertheless, it made no difference to Bose as his popularity and mass following all over the Country was due to his sincere and dedicated work and impressive speeches. But it created a rift between the two. On 18th June 1940, at the second All India Conference of Forward Bloc, Bose proclaimed, 'It is for the Indian people to make an immediate demand for the transference of power to them through a provisional National Government... When things settle down inside India and abroad, the provisional National Government will convene a Constitutional Assembly to frame a full-fledged Constitution for the Country.'

In his writings and speeches during this period, Bose portrayed himself as a courageous rebel and a challenger to the status quo in the Country and Congress. He contrasted his 'fighting mentality' with the 'constitutional mentality' of the Gandhians. He also continued, though he was in his early 40s, to identify with the young, calling upon them to join him in his 'manly' fight against all the reactionary forces of imperialism and within the nationalist camp. Some left voices in the Congress were quite critical of his course, and Nehru went so far as to call the Forward block an 'evil'. These dissent voices did not slow Bose down, for he firmly believed that he was right and the other Congress leaders were wrong on the issue of putting maximum pressure on the Raj.

On 3rd September 1939, Subhas Chandra Bose was addressing a rally of 200,000 people by the oceanfront in the city now known as Chennai. The ambitious Congress leader had acquired an impressive national following. He could draw crowds of similar sizes throughout the country, luring them with his charismatic style and his uncompromising demands for Indian freedom. During the speech, a member of the audience thrust an evening paper into his hand. Bose paused to glimpse the headline on the front page. War had broken out in Europe. It was the event that he, an inveterate opponent of the British, had eagerly anticipated. The moment he would go on to write in his memoir offered Indians 'a unique opportunity for winning freedom'.

In India, Bose was a distinguished leftist with pronounced views on equality. He regarded Mohandas Gandhi's wing of the party as too weak and too right-wing for his taste. Earlier that year, he formed his own faction within the party, the Forward Bloc, to break Gandhi's grip on Congress and steer it in a more progressive direction. When it came to the wider world, however, Bose was an ultranationalist. For years, he had been busy ingratiating himself with Europe's foremost fascists. He met Benito Mussolini multiple times in Italy, a fact he advertised with pride, provoking cringes from Jawaharlal Nehru, who suspected Bose fancied himself a local variant of the Duce.

Nehru had travelled to Spain during the Country's civil war to express solidarity with the republican cause. In London, he spoke at anti-fascist rallies alongside leading British socialists. Bose, who by this time had developed a weakness for military uniforms, was unbothered by the character of the Italian and German regimes. Getting the British out was all that mattered to him. A fascist victory in Europe, he hoped, would break up the British Empire to finally deliver the dream of Indian independence. Over the next ten months, Bose addressed hundreds of rallies like the one in Madras. He openly agitated for a British defeat. Much to Bose's dismay, other Indian leaders didn't share his enthusiasm.

After some wavering, Gandhi came out on the side of the British. He had earlier urged the British people to resist Hitler only through 'spiritual force', while counselling the German leader, in an undelivered letter addressed to 'my friend', to discover the virtues of peace.

Nehru was resolute in his hostility to fascism. But he wanted to ensure that any Indian support for the Allied forces would be contingent on a promise of Indian freedom. Lord Linlithgow, the British viceroy of the time, had already declared India a participant in Britain's war with Germany without consulting a single Indian. He saw no need to do otherwise. After all, Indian troops had long served the British Empire. They had loyally tamed rebellions both at home and in other colonies abroad. Over a million Indians had fought in the First World War under the British flag. None of this had even slightly weakened the Raj. Since 1857, Indian soldiers had been the upholders of its order.

Nehru had scant faith that Linlithgow would yield a promise of full independence. The Congress leader had memorably described the viceroy as 'heavy of body and slow of mind'. Linlithgow, who was too carapaced to let the slight wound him, tried to turn it to his advantage. He mockingly pleaded with Nehru to slacken the pace of his insistent demands, arguing that his 'slow Anglo-Saxon mind cannot keep pace with your quick intellect'. As far as the addlepated viceroy was concerned, Indian independence was satisfyingly remote, even though a new generation of Foreign Office understrappers had begun to appreciate its inevitability. Linlithgow made some placatory noises about India being granted 'dominion status'. To complicate the issue, he suggested this might not be possible until Muslim grievances were addressed. This infuriated Nehru but must have elicited a rare smile from his habitually stone-faced rival Muhammad Ali Jinnah, the leader of the Muslim League."

Through the series of controversies in which Subhas Bose had been involved from late 1938 through late 1939, one prominent figure, the giant of India's cultural life, Rabindranath Tagore, supported him stoutly. Tagore had had his doubts about Subhas, but now, with Subhas besieged, the poet spoke eloquently for him and to him in an essay entitled "Deshanayak" (The Leader of the Country). He wrote, in part:

> As Bengal's poet, I today acknowledge you as the honoured leader of the people of Bengal. …… Suffering from the deadening effect of the prolonged punishment inflicted upon her young generation and disintegrated by internal faction, Bengal is passing through a period of dark despair. …… At such a juncture of nationwide crisis, we require the service of a forceful personality and the invincible faith of a natural leader who can defy the adverse fate that threatens our progress. …… Today, you are revealed in the pure light of the midday sun, which does not admit of apprehensions … Your strength has been sorely taxed by imprisonment, banishment and disease, but rather than impairing, these have helped to broaden your sympathies… You did not regard apparent defeat as final; therefore, you have turned your trials into your allies. More

than anything else, Bengal needs today to emulate the powerful force of your determination and self-reliant courage... Long ago ..... I sent out a call for the leader of Bengal, who had yet to come. After a lapse of many years, I am addressing ..... one who has come into the full light of recognition.

Privately as well, Tagore had made every effort to help Bose, asking Gandhi and Nehru in late 1938 to accept Bose as Congress president again without a squabble. In December 1939, Tagore asked Gandhi to have the ban on Subhas lifted and his cooperation cordially invited in the "supreme interest of national unity". They declined his advice throughout.

Jawaharlal Nehru had been taking from 1939 an ever more negative view of Bose's actions. Writing in early 1940, Nehru said:

> Subhas Bose is going to pieces and has definitely ranged himself against Congress....... The pity of it is that Bengal is badly affected by all this development.... I have no doubt that the Working Committee has acted on occasion very wrongly in regard to Bengal, but I also have no doubt that Subhas Bose has made it exceedingly difficult for the Working Committee to act otherwise...... Subhas Bose does not seem to have an idea in his head, and except for going on talking about leftists and rightists, he says little that is intelligible. [16]

The British government was alarmed by the activities of Bose. Gandhi was perceived as naïve and harmless, but Bose, in contrast, was seen as dangerous and a threat to them, and they were looking for any opportunity to control him and his activities. The fact that the British CID had the two Bose family homes under surveillance at least since the 1930s, when the two Bose brothers, Sarat Chandra and his younger brother Subhas Chandra, emerged at the forefront of the freedom movement in Bengal, bears its testimony. [17]

The following paragraphs quoted from the book "SUBHAS AND SARAT: An Intimate Memoir of the Bose Brothers" written by Sisir Kumar Bose, Netaji's nephew and son of Netaji's elder brother Sarat

Chandra Bose, buttresses the assertion of how seriously the British took Netaji Bose's latent threat potential and shows the extent to which were they prepared to go to combat the underlying threat:

> The British government played a trick on Uncle Subhas when they allowed him to proceed to Europe for medical treatment in 1933. I discovered this while studying old papers in the India Office Library in London in 1971. On the one hand, they alerted British diplomatic representatives in a number of countries in Europe to the visit of this very dangerous person and impressed upon them the necessity of keeping a close watch on him. At the same time, the India Office in London, responsible for the government's India policy in those days, informed them that only two counties, Italy and Austria, were mentioned in his passport as his destinations. It might appear from such entries in the passport that he did not have an entry permit to other countries, including England.
>
> The paper admitted confidentially that, in reality, any subject of British India holding a British Empire passport could not be prevented under the law from visiting England. The government added in secret despatches that Subhas Bose was under the wrong impression that he could not lawfully enter England. This impression, they said, should not be dispelled on any account. This is because, the papers say, Bose should be kept away from two places – London and Berlin. At both these places, there were a large number of Indian students. The government apprehended that Subhas Bose's influence on them could be dangerous. [18]

Subhas Chandra Bose was indeed the most dangerous person to the British in India during their colonial rule of the sub-continent, and it needs to be realised why the British perceived him to be so. Clearly, Netaji's ideals, principles, actions, attributes and all were against the interests of the British in the country to the highest degree. Among these, Subhas Chandra Bose posed the greatest threat to their primary principle of 'divide and rule' based on which they framed most of their colonial rules and regulations of the Indian administrations. Netaji aimed to replace the loyalty of Indian soldiers working under the British to the causes of India's freedom movement. That was most threatening, no doubt.

When Subhas Chandra Bose had gone to Europe in early 1941, the war situation had not fully evolved. Germany was then fighting Britain on the Western Front. The Soviet Union was neutral. The United States and Japan were not yet part of the conflict. With Italy's support, Germany planned to attack British interests and outposts in the Mediterranean. Against that backdrop, Subhas Bose made certain proposals to the German government. In the interest of the freedom struggle in India, he wanted to bring the war closer to the northwestern frontier of India. Bose told the Germans that three or four routes could be used to approach the India-Afghanistan border from Europe. The task would be easier with some support, direct or indirect, from the Soviet or armed force he had organized in Europe, from POWS captured by the Germans, to enter India with the support of armed tribal militants of the northwest frontier. Large numbers of Pathan and Punjabi revolutionaries would then join the invasion. However, that blueprint became defunct once Germany attacked the Soviet Union in June 1941. [19]

So, Subhas had to think and plan afresh. He succeeded remarkably during World War II and in its aftermath, even when he was no longer there. That way, Netaji Subhas was a master strategist. He was aware of his constraints and limitations. At the same time, Netaji Subhas knew when and where to counter the British with his limited resources that would hurt them the most, and Subhas Bose aimed at that point – their 'divide & rule policy'- in India. He also saw an opportunity in World War II and tried to take full advantage of the developing situation that very few Indian leaders could think of at that time.

Interestingly, after the Indian Rebellion, or the Sepoy Mutiny, of 1857, the British colonial rulers could gauge the strength of the Indian masses when they worked together on any issue. The British knew that if they were to govern the country, they could not let the Indians unite. So, they created artificial fissures among them, which were based primarily on religion and then on other bases like their caste, mother tongue and all. However, the way Subhas Bose generally acted, behaved, and conducted himself was against the principle of the British-sponsored 'divide and rule'.

Thus, Netaji Subhas Chandra Bose was seen to be the most successful among the contemporary leaders of the Indian nationalist movement in uniting Hindus, Muslims, Sikhs, and Christians based on equal rights and respect for all. He had the unwavering trust of the minorities and was found to be totally against any type of discrimination. In his numerous speeches and writings, he voiced that Indians felt conquered only with the advent of British rule in India, stressing that even when there were Muslim rulers, whether in Bengal during the Sultanate period and the Nawabi or in India during the Mughal Empire, the administration was run jointly by Hindus and Muslims. His final goal was to reach the Red Fort of Old Delhi. He was less concerned about New Delhi because he saw the Red Fort as a symbol of sovereignty, dominance and control.

He visited the grave of the last Mughal emperor, Bahadur Shah Zafar, in September 1943. There was a parade of the Indian National Army in front of that tomb, and that's where Netaji gave his clarion call, "Jai Hind" and "Chalo Delhi". He respected the Mughals and felt that Akbar, in particular, had brought together all the different religious communities of India during his rule.

It's important to recall that there were many Muslims in the Azad Hind Movement that Subhas Bose led. Netaji's closest associates were Muslims. During his escape from India, the man who received him in Peshawar was Mian Akbar Shah, a Muslim freedom fighter from North-West Frontier Province (NWFP). The only Indian companion on his submarine voyage in early 1943 was Abid Hasan, a Muslim from Hyderabad, who was perhaps his closest aid both in Europe and Asia. The commander of the first division of the INA was Mohammed Zaman Kiani. An INA officer named Shaukat Malik, a Muslim, unfurled the Indian tricolour in Moirang near Imphal in 1944. The last journey he undertook was a tragic one, and the only companion he had on the trip was Habibur Rahman. As luck would have it, in the Red Fort Trial, the British made an unexpected blunder by putting on trial a Hindu, a Muslim and a Sikh – Prem Sahgal, Shah Nawaz Khan and Gurbaksh Singh Dhillon – that boomeranged on them.

Netaji, for one, never accepted the charapterisation of Indian history by the British as Hindu, Muslim and then finally, British Period. In his book 'An Indian Pilgrim - An Unfinished Autobiography of Netaji Subhas Chandra Bose, he mentioned, "It is a misnomer to talk of the Mughal period as Muslim rule." He went out of his way to show that the commandant chiefs, the generals and many influential cabinet ministers were Hindu. In other words, that was a joint rule. It wasn't slavery. It wasn't Muslim rule.

When Netaji revamped the INA, he chose Tipu Sultan's springing tiger as its insignia, which was worn on every epaulette. Once he came to Southeast Asia, he decided to adopt the flag, the tricolour with the charkha in the middle. That was because he wanted to make common cause with Mahatma Gandhi. But on all the shoulder pieces of the INA uniforms, there was the insignia of Tipu Sultan's tiger. The army's motto was three simple Urdu words, "Etihaad (Unity), Etmad (Faith) and Kurbani (Sacrifice)."

He also had very fine Anglo-Indian Christian officers in the INA. For example, Cyril John Stracy built the model of the INA Memorial in Singapore. Netaji wanted to inaugurate the memorial expeditiously before the British landed in Singapore. Stracy completed the task against all odds.

All along, Netaji made deliberate and conscious attempts to forge unity and develop religious harmony in his Indian National Army. He chose Hindustani – a mixture of Hindi and Urdu with lots of Urdu words in it – as the link language of his movement. He used the Roman script so that the many Tamils and people from South India who joined the movement could easily read some of the orders of the day that he issued.

> "For him there were no religious or provincial differences He refused to' recognise these. He looked at everyone— Hindu, Muslim and Sikh— without distinction and his spirit animated

his men. In the I N A there was no "communal" feeling of any sort in spite of the fact that every men had full liberty to practise his religion in any way he liked He made his soldiers realize that they were the sons of the same motherland, and, as such, there could be no differences between them We were all completely united and it was realized by us that the communal differences in our country were the creation of an alien power The success of this can be gauged from the fact that the most ardent supporters and admirers of Netaji were to be found among Muslims. Netaji respected every man for what he was worth and not for his religion or the province he came from," – according to Shahnawaz Khan, who served as an officer in the Indian National Army during World War II. He wrote it in his book "INA And Its Netaji 1946". [20]

In a speech Netaji gave as Congress president on 14th June 1938, he specifically addressed the problem of communalism. He said, "We hear voices of Hindu Raj, these are useless thoughts. Do the communal organisations solve any of the problems confronted by the working class? Do any such organisations have any answer to unemployment and poverty?"

In 1943, Netaji Subhas Chandra Bose visited Singapore and was invited by the Tamil business community to see the Sri Tendayuthapani Temple, also known as the Tank Road Temple or the Chettiar Temple. Aware of the temple's discriminatory practices against subordinated castes and other religious faiths, Netaji initially declined the invitation. However, he agreed to attend after the temple authorities allowed admission of all castes and communities. Flanked by Abid Hasan and Mohammad Zaman Kiyani, Netaji participated in the ceremony. The temple was filled with INA uniforms and black caps of South Indian Muslims. A tilak was put on them in the Garba Griha, creating a memory of unity and common purpose among all Indians. This event left a lasting imprint on public memory.

The following narrative has been reproduced from Shahnawaz Khan's "INA And Its Netaji 1946". It depicts a heart-rending scene portraying multi-dimensional aspects of the Indian freedom movement launched by Netaji Subhas Chandra Bose in a foreign country:

> By organising the Indian Independence League all over East Asia, Netaji was able to instil a spirit of patriotism in the heart of every Indian, rich and poor alike, from whom voluntary contributions flowed freely. A large number of Indians, among whom were included members of almost every community, gave their all to the Azad Hind Fauj and became 'Fakirs' (one who lives solely on charity) for the sake of their country. Whole families joined the I. N. A., father the I N A Fauj, mother Rani of Jhansi Regiment and little children Balsena. "Karo sab nichawar, Bano sab Fakir " was the slogan that Netaji gave them, and men like Habib Betai, Khanna and numerous others willingly gave all their fortunes amounting to several lakhs to 'the Azad Hind Govt.' and became fakirs. A total sum of 20 crores was collected and deposited in the Azad Hind Bank Rangoon.
>
> Rich and moneyed people were not the only ones that contributed. In fact, a greater proportion of our funds was donated by comparatively poor people. It was always the poor labourers, Gwalas (milkmen), and others like them who made the greatest sacrifices. I should never forget a scene I witnessed at one of the meetings addressed by Netaji in Singapore.
>
> After Netaji had finished his speech, he made an appeal for funds. Thousands of people came forward to donate. They formed a queue in front of Netaji, each one coming up on his turn, handed over this donation to Netaji and left. Most of the people who formed the queue were donating large amounts. All of a sudden, I saw a very poor labourer woman go up to the stage to hand in her donation. She was in tatters and had even no cloth to cover her head. With bated breath, all of us watched her. She took out three rupees notes and offered them to Netaji. He hesitated. She said to Netaji, "Please accept these This is all I possess." Netaji still hesitated. Then, great big tears

rolled down his cheeks. He extended his hand and accepted the money from her.

After the meeting was over, I asked Netaji why he had hesitated to accept the money from that poor woman and why he had cried. Netaji replied, "It was a very hard decision for me. When I looked at the condition of that poor woman, I knew that those three rupees were all the wealth that she possessed. If I took it, she would probably suffer terribly. Still, on the other hand, when I thought of her sentiment, her desire to give her all for Indian freedom, I felt that if I refused, she would feel hurt and probably think that I accepted only large sums from the rich. In the end, in order not to hurt her feelings, I accepted the money. To me, those three rupees have a greater value than lakhs contributed by rich man out of their millions." [21]

Overall, the narrative is a powerful depiction of the depth of human emotions generated by Netaji during the struggle for India's independence. It not only displays a range of profound human emotions and sentiments but also shows Netaji's compassion, humility, and charisma in instilling a deep sense of patriotism in every Indian, regardless of their socio-economic status. Besides, the real-life story of Netaji in Singapore also highlights the spirit of sacrifice among the expat Indians.

No wonder, therefore, Indians from all walks of life, irrespective of their caste, creed, religion, race and region where they came from, were avid followers of Netaji, and that was what the British colonial rulers were scared of in their beloved Indian leader, Subhas Chandra Bose. His simple, benevolent nature, complete honesty, and friendliness towards fellow Indians were danger signs to the colonial rulers. It made Subhas Bose the enemy number one of the British administration in India. [22] [23]

In the 1920s, 1930s and 1940s, Subhas Chandra Bose was in and out of jail on various occasions for his drastic political actions and often radical protests against the British. He was imprisoned eleven times in various jails due to his stand for India's complete independence. The last of the eleven times the British detained Subhas Chandra Bose took place against the backdrop of a significant historical event. Since its context is essential to comprehend the significance of his actions fully, it is briefly narrated here. By examining this event, we can gain insights into not only Bose's deeply held beliefs but also his remarkable ability to identify and champion causes that had profound implications for India's fight for independence. His strategic foresight and commitment to his country's freedom struggle are noteworthy.

Earlier, the British had set up a port and trading base at Calcutta and built Fort William for its protection. However, their efforts to strengthen the fort's defences against the French displeased the new Nawab of Bengal, Siraj ud-Daulah. Ignoring his orders to halt fortification work, the British provoked Siraj ud-Daulah to march on Calcutta with a large army.

On 20th June, Siraj's forces attacked Fort William. The governor and many of his staff and the British residents ran for safety to the ships in the harbour, leaving women and children behind and a garrison of only 170 English soldiers to defend the fort under the command of John Zephaniah Holwell, who was the Company's zemindar, responsible for tax collection and keeping law and order. He had no military experience, and the situation was hopeless in any case. By the afternoon, he was forced to surrender in return for what he thought was a guarantee of the quarter. That night, according to Holwell's statement, 146 British prisoners were crammed into the fort's 'black hole', a small lock-up. The intense heat and overcrowded conditions led to the death of most prisoners. Only twenty-three survived.

Holwell's account of the event stirred patriotic fervour and anger towards India in Britain. However, it's believed that Holwell exaggerated the numbers. Research suggests that around sixty-four prisoners were confined in the black hole, with twenty-one surviving. Evidence also indicates that Siraj-ud-daula was unaware of the incident.

News of the fall of Calcutta and the Black Hole incident stirred the East India Company (EIC) into action. Retribution followed swiftly. Robert Clive, East India Company's clerk-turned-colonel, laid siege to Fort William, and the Battle of Plassey ensued. Clive's small army defeated Siraj's much larger force through the betrayal of Siraj ud-Daula's trusted generals, with whom Clive made some underhand dealings. Siraj fled but was killed by his own people, whom he trusted with his life.

The 23rd of June 1757 marked a turning point in the annals of British colonisation in the Indian subcontinent. Robert Clive spearheaded a military expedition replete with disaffiliation and deception of his own supporters to reclaim Calcutta. He ingeniously orchestrated the defection of Mir Jafar, one of Siraj ud-Daula's trusted generals. This act of betrayal, engineered by Robert Clive, proved instrumental in decimating Siraj's army and securing a definite victory for the British. The East India Company used Holwell's exaggerated story as a justification for taking over Calcutta completely. This ruse heralded the dawn of British colonial rule in Bengal and laid the groundwork for their eventual nearly 200 years of British colonial exploitation over the vast expanse of the Indian sub-continent.

Despite the incident's grip on the popular imagination, there were long rumours that the entire episode was an invention by the British to justify further military conquest. A notable study by J. H. Little in 1916, published in Bengal Past and Present, cast severe doubts on Holwell's reliability and the accepted version of the Black Hole story. It may also be true that focusing on the Black Hole incident was a convenient way to draw attention away from the EIC's shambolic defence of Fort William, where the officers had disgracefully abandoned their men before the capture of the fort. The incident also drew public attention away from the EIC's general policy change in this period from a mere trading company to a full colonial power. The story of the Black Hole of Calcutta continued to stir emotions, and the incident became one of many dubious justifications for what the British considered their 'civilizing' presence in India and (to them) a measure of just how awful the previous rulers had been.

As one of the survivors of the Black Hole incident, John Zephaniah Holwell took the initiative to erect a tablet on the site of the cell to commemorate the victims of the 'Black Hole Tragedy'. However, this plaque somehow disappeared from the area before 1822. More than a century later, when Lord Curzon came to Calcutta as the Viceroy in 1899, he noticed nothing to mark the spot of the Black Hole. In 1901, Curzon commissioned a new monument, often referred to as the Holwell Monument, which was erected at the south-west corner of Dalhousie Square (now B. B. D. Bagh) in the heart of central Calcutta, the site said to be the location of the 'Black Hole'.

The Holwell monument represented the alleged savagery of the last Nawab of Bengal, Siraj ud-Daula, and the so-called bravery of the British soldiers who sacrificed their lives. It was argued that the monument must go because it was not merely an unwarranted stain on the memory of the Nawab but had stood in the heart of Calcutta for over 150 years as a symbol of slavery and humiliation. So, Subhas Chandra Bose launched a campaign to remove it and restore the honour of Siraj ud-Daulah and the nation.

Subhas Bose organised agitation and, in a meeting, resolutions were adopted that paid homage to Siraj ud-Daulah, condemned the falsity of foreign historians and urged deletion from school textbooks of matters derogatory to Siraj ud-Daulah. It was agreed that if there were no ministerial decisions on the Holwell Monument by 15th July, satyagraha (nonviolent resistance) by the council of action would start on 16th July. In Calcutta, Hindus, anti-government Muslims, and the Muslim League Student Organization attended the meeting. Netaji announced that he would personally lead the first batch of satyagraha in a march on the Howell Monument on 3rd July 1940, but on that day, Subhas Bose was arrested as a preventive measure. [24] [25].

From July to December 1940, Bose was imprisoned at the Presidency Jail, Calcutta. The members of his family met him several times in the jail. He was pretty cheerful and cracked jokes with the jail officials. There was no inkling at first that he was about to take the most difficult decision of his life. As Subhas and other inmates did in Mandalay prison in Burma in 1926, Netaji and other prisoners decided to perform Durga Puja (Bengal's biggest annual Hindu festival) inside the jail. All necessary arrangements for the Puja were, of course, made outside, and an idol of the deity was sent in. On the immersion day, Vijaya Dashmi, his friends and relatives were at the jail gate in strength. The idol was brought out on a truck. Subhas Chandra Bose and other prisoners were seen standing in a body behind the iron bars. A band of young men took charge of the immersions.

Ever since his arrest, Subhas Bose had been contesting the grounds of his detention without trial. During this time, he was elected to the Central Legislative Assembly in Delhi from a constituency in Dacca (Dhaka). After the Pujas, he wrote long letters to the Government about the illegality of his detention. Finally, he told the Government that if he were not released, he would, as a last resort, go on a fast unto death. After writing his last letter to the Government, he asked that his letters be preserved in government archives. He called one of the letters his 'Political Testament'.

Some documents show that since the early 1940s, Subhas Bose has been exploring the possibility of leaving the country. In the Punjab, there was a political outfit called the Kirti Kisan Party, a breakaway Communist group that wanted to develop relations with the Soviet Union. Across north-west India, Subhas had a large number of adherents. He tried to get some of these people to help him develop his plans. But, these early efforts did not yield results, and his efforts to establish contacts with Russia were unsuccessful.

Nevertheless, when he was arrested as a preventive measure on 3rd July 1940 as he planned to lead the first batch of satyagraha demanding the removal of the Howell Monument, he was not prepared to waste his time in prison while the British Empire faced an unprecedented crisis of the World War II. He was convinced that his duty was to do something decisive for the country's freedom by exploiting the British predicament. The Government arrested him under the Defence of India Rules and also filed two court cases against him, one on account of a 'seditious' speech and the other for an 'objectionable' editorial in his weekly paper, Forward Bloc.

During his detention, the authorities used to bring him out of jail and produce him at Alipore Court for hearings under heavy police escort. At the end of one hearing, the magistrate granted him bail on sound legal grounds but added that he was doubtful if Subhas would be allowed to avail of it. Because the Government was holding him in jail without trial under different draconian laws, Subhas started challenging the two-faced government policy. He also demanded his release as an elected member of the Central Legislative Assembly. But the Government would not budge. They made it clear that they intended to be very tough with him.

Yet, in the latter half of November 1940, Subhas Chandra Bose resolved to go on a hunger strike. His family members became very worried. Friends close to the Government had pressed his elder brother Sarat Chandra Bose to persuade Subhas to desist from the extreme step of a fast unto death. Sarat Bose was told that the government's attitude was highly rigid and that Subhas would not be released under any circumstances. On the other hand, Sarat Bose knew his younger brother well. Subhas's resolve was unalterable. Until his demand was conceded, no power on earth could make him relent. In defiance of advice from his well-wishers to desist from taking the extreme step of a fast unto death, Subhas made up his mind. After telling the Government: 'Release me or I will refuse to live.' Anxiety gripped everybody as he began his fast unto death in the prison.

What went on in official circles during the period when Subhas was on fast was interesting. After a week of his determined fasting, the jail superintendent gave a rather grim report on his health, which indicated that death from fasting was a distinct possibility. Consequently, the Bengal Government developed cold feet. After detailed consideration of its pros and cons, it decided to set him free. However, the India Government was still not keen to release him. As the issue of letting Subhas Bose off was taken up with the Indian Government, they wrote to the Bengal Government disapprovingly. However, the Bengal Governor, John Herbert, replied to the Viceroy of India, Lord Linlithgow, saying that they were just playing 'cat and mouse' with Subhas Bose and would put him back in jail as soon as his health improved. Lo and behold, it was not a mouse but a lion the cat thought of playing with - as it soon turned out!

The jail superintendent was a sympathetic person. He came again and again to Subhas in his cell to plead with him to give up the fast. He would say: 'Why don't you understand, even a living donkey is better than a dead lion.' Anyway, when the order of release arrived, Subhas broke his fast with a glass of fruit juice offered by this jail superintendent.

As soon as the news of his amnesty became public, the relatives rushed to see him at the Elgin Road house. An ambulance was still parked in the portico. Subhas could be seen in his room, lying in bed, looking pale and weak. But his eyes were bright and shining. He had started growing a moustache in jail, which had since developed further. He now also had a shaggy beard noticed. As the close relatives were standing at the door and watching while things were rearranged in the room, Uncle Subhas gestured for his beloved young nephew Sisir to come to him. When Sisir went to his bedside, Subhas Bose looked up at him and grasped his hand in a long, warm handshake. [26]

The following paragraphs reproduced from Shanawaz Khan's book "I.N.A. And Its NETAJI" provide some idea of what prompted Netaji Subhas Chandra Bose to begin his fast unto death inside prison, what Gandhi would think about his flight and all:

> "The choice before me," he said, "was that of being imprisoned for the duration of the war or of escaping from India, joining hands with the enemies of England, and through their help raising an army to fight for India's liberation." He explained that it was not easy to choose between the two alternatives and that before he finally made up his mind, he discussed the world situation with Mahatma Gandhi and the part to be played in it by India. He pointed out to Mahatma Gandhi that it would serve no useful purpose if Indian leaders were shut up inside jails for the duration of the war and that the only way in which India's liberation could be achieved was for some Indian leaders to escape, raise an army outside India

and then invade India as an army of liberation. Netaji explained that in saying so, he had before him the examples of Garibaldi and Gen Franco.

Mahatmaji replied that he personally did not believe that it was possible to secure India's liberation by these methods. If, however, Netaji succeeded in freeing India by these means, he (Mahatmaji) would be the first one to congratulate him. Thus, Netaji felt that he had secured Mahatmaji's blessings for an enterprise that Netaji thought would prove successful in freeing India.

As was expected at the outbreak of World War II, Netaji found himself behind prison bars. The first problem for him then was how to get out of the prison. Netaji said that he thought over it for several days and finally decided that he would go on hunger strike as a protest against his illegal detention. He knew that having once started the fast, there would be no going back for him, and if the British persisted in detaining him, he would have to starve himself to death like Jatin Das. Knowing the British as he did, he felt that there was an even chance that he may have to starve to death. "Anyhow," he said, "I took the plunge and went on hunger strike". For the first few days, the British authorities were adamant, and it looked as if they would never give in. The jail Superintendent approached him and pointed out to him the futility of such a move. But Netaji would pay no heed to him, and after a fast lasting 12 days, his condition became very grave, which alarmed the British Jail, who finally released him, and Netaji returned to his ancestral home. Once back home, Netaji began to prepare for his next move —that of escaping from India to one of the Axis countries.

The house in which he was residing was under the closest watch of the C.I.D. and local police. It is unofficially learned that there were as many as 62 men from various police departments who were detailed to keep watch over him. He shut himself up in his bedroom for several days and allowed no one except a young niece to enter it occasionally to serve his meals. It is learnt that he even divided his bedroom into two parts. One was curtained off as his prayer room, and the other portion was used as his bed and dining room. He rarely came out of his prayer room. Finally, how unnoticed he escaped from his house by completely deceiving the guards and reached Afghanistan must, for the time being, remain a mystery. [27]

What was a mystery during those days is no longer so at present. How Subhas Chandra Bose performed the vanishing act and deceived the wide-ranging surveillance network of the British colonial rulers has been revealed by the very person who was hand in glove with Bose from its preliminary plan to its actual execution, as can be envisioned from the narratives in the next chapter, "The Vanishing Act"!

* * * * * * *

Chapter 3

The Vanishing Act!

How Bose Broke Away From His House Arrest?

'Can you do something for me?'

("আমার একটা কাজ করতে পারবে?" Amar ekta kaj korte parbe?)

Subhas Bose, fondly called Rangakakababu (meaning the radiant uncle), asked his nephew -the silent boy.

He nodded slightly and made an indistinct noise- perhaps meaning 'Yes'.

'How well can you drive?''

Rangakakababu asked the second question.

"I can drive more or less well,' came the reply.

এই একরকম ভালই পারি (Ei ekrokom bhaloi pari)

'Have you ever done long-distance driving?' Rangakakababu asked the third question.

'No,' was the reply.

'Look, you will have to take me by car to a certain destination without a soul knowing about it. Can you do it?' Subhas Bose continued asking - opening up a little.

Initially, 'the silent boy' did not react; he just fixed his gaze on his Rangakakababu. Only after some time, there might be some visible reaction, if at all. Then Rangakakababu added:

"In this house, Ila (the favourite cousin of 'the silent boy') will know. I have tested her. She can be trusted. We must work out a 'foolproof' plan of escape that should remain absolutely secret."

With this simple, innocuous conversation began the most intricate and downright dangerous journey Subhas Chandra Bose had ever undertaken, which eventually changed the history of India's struggle for independence from the British colonial rule of the sub-continent.

A beacon of the Indian independence movement, one of India's pioneering and finest Paediatricians, a former Member of the West Bengal Legislative Assembly, and an author, Sisir Kumar Bose (1920–2000), in his book titled "SUBHAS AND SARAT: An Intimate Memoir of the Bose Brothers" admitted:

> Till then, I felt diffident and nervous whenever I came face to face with Father or Uncle Subhas; I hesitated to have a proper conversation with either of them. That is why Uncle Subhas gave me my moniker - 'the silent boy.'

At that time, Sisir might have been merely a cog in the daring escape planning of Subhas Chandra Bose, which was a prelude to Subhas Bose's war against the mighty British. But by assigning a vital role to Sisir in his escape from India, Subhas Bose gave a revolutionary twist to the boy's life that was beyond the imagination of Sisir Kumar Bose. Sisir never thought he would get deeply involved in inaugurating a new chapter in India's history.

On that winter afternoon, the silent boy's life was transformed when the stormy petrel of India's independence movement, Subhas Chandra Bose, lying in bed in his room of their 38/2, Elgin Road, Calcutta, asked his quiet, shy nephew, Sisir Kumar Bose, a deceptively simple question in Bengali: "আমার একটা কাজ করতে পারবে?" (Amar ekta kaj korte parbe?) 'Can you do something for me?' [1]

Sisir Kumar Bose (1920-2000) was the son of Netaji's elder brother, Sarat Chandra Bose and Bivabati Bose (née Dey). He wrote the book "SUBHAS AND SARAT: An Intimate Memoir of the Bose Brothers", which included a blow-by-blow account of the planning and execution of the escape. The beginning of this chapter, "How Bose Broke Away?" has been mostly taken from it.

During the Quit India Movement launched by Mahatma Gandhi in 1942, Sisir Bose was severely injured in a police attack on a student protest and imprisoned in Presidency Jail in Calcutta and later interned at home in 1943. For assisting his uncle and his continued involvement with the Indian independence movement, Sisir Bose was arrested again by the British colonial government and imprisoned in the Red Fort in Delhi, the Lahore Fort and Lyallpur Jail, including long periods in solitary confinement until the end of the war.

Anyway, after the unforgettable casual discussions Sisir Bose had with his Rangakakababu Subhas Chandra Bose on that winter afternoon and his uncle mentioning the need for drawing out a 'foolproof' plan of escape, Sisir went back to his room at 1 Woodland Park, Calcutta, his head reeling as he analysed the facts of the meeting. It was not very clear to him what his Uncle Subhas was up to at that time. He could feel it would not be an ordinary political game of hide-and-seek. Subhas asked him to think about the matter in depth, chalk out a plan of escape and go to him at 38/2 Elgin Road, Calcutta, again the following evening.

Thus, they started their long and detailed conversations every evening, sometimes late into the night. But that first meeting on a winter afternoon in wartime Calcutta changed Sisir forever. It dispelled his inborn shyness and diffidence and gave him a sense of self-confidence, which was entirely new to him. Sisir realised that his Uncle Subhas similarly instilled a sense of purpose and direction in so many ordinary persons like him and gave them the courage to undertake big tasks.

Sisir Kumar Bose was amazed at how freely he talked with his Uncle Subhas every time after that. Along with the transformation of their relationship with his Uncle, he also became very free and open with his father and began to discuss various subjects and exchange views with him without a trace of nervousness. The work on their hand in the winter of 1940-1941 could not have been carried out without this fundamental change in their relationship.

Apart from working out a practical escape plan from the Elgin Road house, other thoughts also came into Sisir's mind. He wondered: Why did Uncle Subhas call on him? There were others in the family who were also good drivers and, in fact, knew more about cars than he did. Sisir also pondered whether it might have been better, in the interest of secrecy and safety, to select a young man from outside the family to do the job, particularly when Uncle Subhas wanted to keep the rest of the family in the dark. Then, he mused if he would have to do the job without his parents' knowledge. Sisir Kumar Bose brooded over these questions till the early morning hours.

Eventually, he told himself not to bother about these issues and to leave it to his Uncle to decide. Sisir concentrated on how to disappear from the house with Uncle Subhas without anyone knowing about it. From then on, his studies at the Calcutta Medical College - studying anatomy and physiology, dissecting human cadavers and identifying blood cells and germs - took a back seat to the plan of Subhas Chandra Bose's great break away from India.

In the initial stages of planning the escape, the first consideration was to find a safe and sure exit to avoid being noticed at the time of leaving. Disguise might work in general, but with relatives, it won't be of much use, it seemed. It was known that if any family member became suspicious, the plan would fail. Most people cannot restrain themselves when curiosity or suspicion is aroused. They talk to others. If such an eventuality arose, Subhas Bose thought it might become necessary to change the plan altogether or to take one or two additional persons into confidence to stop them from whispering. There was another way, as well, to send the suspicious person away from the scene on some pretext. Sisir discussed these delicate issues in detail with his Uncle Subhas.

The house at 38/2 Elgin Road was a long, narrow structure from north to south, much like a barrack. There were a series of rooms with corridors on both sides along the entire length of the building. One could go from one end of the house to the other along the open corridors without entering any room or hall. There were altogether four staircases. In the middle of the house was an old-style wooden staircase from the ground to the second floor, which visitors used to take. The second staircase was on the east side of the rear two-storeyed annexe. The annexe, which had the toilets, was also provided with a wrought-iron spiral staircase used by cleaning personnel to access the toilets from outside and the ground floor directly. At the southern end of the main building and annexe, there was a small two-storeyed structure called 'the school-house', facing the end of the driveway. This structure, which also had stairs, does not exist anymore.

One could walk down the corridor from the main entrance in the north, on Elgin Road, and reach any stairwells without disturbing anyone in any of the rooms opening off the corridor. The house had three exits. One was the main gate on Elgin Road, providing access to the driveway. A smaller entrance was on the west side, which was also accessed from Elgin Road. There was a third possible exit. Right at the rear of the building, there was an open yard where a third paternal uncle, Suresh, ran a machine tools workshop. A rear exit from the yard could also be made.

Due to the possibility of slipping out by the small side entrance or sneaking out from the rear, who would think of the large main gate at the front of the building as the exit? Sisir did not. He toyed with an exit plan that involved Subhas going down the length of the building from his bedroom on the first floor by the corridor on the east, down the open staircase of the annexe, then taking the western corridor of the ground floor to return to the front of the building and exiting to the street through the small side entrance. Alternatively, Subhas could use the south-facing stairs of the 'school house' to the backyard and leave by an improvised exit on the south boundary wall to the narrow alley called Elgin Lane, which runs alongside the building. It was presumed that his disguise would make his short walk up the alley to Elgin Road safe late in the evening. Sisir would wait on the road with the car near the Elgin Road post office, a couple of minutes walk to the west, or at the spot where Elgin Lane opens onto Elgin Road.

As Sisir met his Uncle the following day and narrated his ideas, Subhas listened to Sisir quietly and patiently. When he paused occasionally, Subhas looked at Sisir or the wall pensively, with the tip of his left index finger raised to his lips, as was his habit. Then he said to Sisir: 'Think more, think hard. We are in a hurry. We may have to set out around Christmas". Subhas said he was expecting a signal from the other end (wherever that was). As soon as it arrived, he would tell Sisir.

In December 1940, Subhas Chandra Bose awaited a signal from Mian Akbar Shah, his loyal follower in the North-West Frontier Province. As Akbar Shah revealed to Sisir in 1983, it was settled that Subhas Bose would arrive at Peshawar on 19th January 1941. He would, therefore, have to leave Calcutta by 16th January. It was clear that Subhas did not find it necessary to tell Sisir about the exact departure date in advance. Instead, he wanted his nephew to be in full readiness for the journey at all times. It was an example of his modus operandi. He found no need to tell individuals about every specific.

Sisir's frequent visits and closed-door conversations with his Uncle Subhas naturally made some people in the Elgin Road house curious and even suspicious. Ila reported on this new development. Subhas used to listen to the radio, particularly to foreign broadcasts, every evening to keep himself informed of the war's progress. Throughout 1940, the Germans were getting the better of Britain and her allies. Subhas felt happy about this, and so did Sisir. Even in prison, Subhas Bose had compelled the government to give him a radio in his cell. Sisir had also developed a craze for listening to the radio. People in the Elgin Road house who were curious or suspicious about Sisir's visits were told he was very good at tuning into foreign radio stations. Hence, he frequently visited Subhas's room.

However, some people were incorrigibly inquisitive. One such person was Palan. He grew up with the Bose family and spent his early life in Cuttack and later life at 38/2 at Elgin Road or 1, Woodburn Park. He would often gently push open the door of Subhas's bedroom and peep in when Subhas and Sisir were planning. As soon as Subhas learned about it, he persuaded Palan, who was unemployed, to get a job and gave him a letter of introduction to the boss of Tata Steel in Jamshedpur. Thus, Palan was safely away in Jamshedpur when the escape took place in January 1941. Later, taking advantage of his simple nature, the police tried to use Palan. He once approached Ila and told her that the police had offered him money if he could get them some information about Subhas Bose's escape.

A large number of people lived in the Elgin Road house - a typical Indian joint-family establishment- and a large number of visitors came there daily. Different people had different routines, hours, and lifestyles in this sprawling residence. Moreover, there were quite a few domestic servants all over the place. To make matters even more complicated, one 'doctor uncle' or 'Uncle Sunil" residing with the Bose family had a ferocious Alsatian dog called 'Sunny Boy'. It would pounce upon visitors whenever it got a chance, especially at night.

While Sisir was exploring ways of making a safe exit from the house at night, Subhas suddenly changed his line of thinking. He said: "It will be difficult to do this (escape secretly) from this large, complex establishment. Why not leave this house openly? It is well known my health is in bad shape. I may as well move somewhere easier to escape from, citing health grounds, and then disappear from there." The discussions then took an entirely new turn.

Moving out of the Elgin Road house and organising the escape wase possible through two methods, Subhas thought. The first was to move to 1 Woodburn Park, his brother Sarat Bose's house on the street, running perpendicular to Elgin Road. The second was to move to Sarat Bose's farmhouse (Bagan Bari) at Rishra, about sixteen miles up the Hooghly River from Calcutta.

Subhas mentioned it was widely known that he had been released after a hunger strike and that his health was far from satisfactory. A medical bulletin issued by Dr. M.N. De, professor of medicine at Calcutta Medical College, could be published in the newspapers. It could be announced that for his recovery, he badly needed fresh air, sunshine, and more space to move around than was available in the large but crowded Elgin Road residence. It could be followed by his moving across the road to the Woodburn Park house, where he would have a nice room and the terrace all to himself on the second floor. From the 'health' point of view, the Rishra house was even better. The house was on the river and had a garden. Both possibilities were attractive for a case made on medical grounds. But did they have their own share of problems?

Subhas felt it would be easier for Sisir to make the necessary arrangements at Woodburn Park. As for the Rishra house, only one caretaker lived there, and he would have to be taken care of somehow. Sisir thought over both proposals carefully and critically and felt that after talking with Uncle Subhas so freely for a while, his opinions mattered , and it was welcome to Subhas. He concluded that it would be very unwise to move out of the Elgin Road house openly and then carry out the escape from either of the two places. He told his Uncle bluntly:

> 'You are known to be ill, confined to one room, and you have not been seen to move out of your room even once. Plainclothes police agents stationed around the house have that impression. Watching them daily, I think that they have become complacent and lazy as a result. In these circumstances, if you move to another place, everybody concerned will sit up and take notice. There would immediately be new and special police arrangements in the other place, to our disadvantage. Besides, order and discipline at 1. Woodburn Park is strict. Those who live on the ground floor, namely the gatekeeper, the office attendants and the two drivers, are all old, reliable, and alert employees. They would raise a ruckus at anything unusual. We indeed have to deal with only one person in Rishra. But once you move outside the city, special police arrangements would also be made by the authorities there."

Subhas immediately concurred and said: "You are right. That is not the way to do it. Regardless of all the problems, we have to plan on the basis that the escape will take place from 38/2, Elgin Road.'

Sarat Bose, Sisir's father, was not keeping well throughout 1940. Soon after Subhas's release in early December, he left for Kalimpong in the Darjeeling hills for health reasons. A few days after he departed from Calcutta, Sisir's mother and the rest of the family went to Bararee, near Dhanbad, to spend the winter vacation. As a result, when Sisir started preparation for his Uncle Subha's escape from Elgin Road, he was entirely alone at 1 Woodburn Park.

When, eventually, it was agreed that the escape would be from the Elgin Road house after all, Subhas started thinking and planning afresh. But he did not indicate how he planned to depart unnoticed from the house. Meanwhile, there were other arrangements to be made, and they got busy with them.

First, Subhas needed a disguise. He wanted to look at his warm clothing and arranged to have his available warm clothing brought from 1 Woodburn Park across to the Elgin Road house. He returned some of the clothing and asked Sisir to keep some for the journey. After his escape, there were whispers about the 'operation clothing' conducted between the two houses.

A very important episode in connection with the escape plan took place in December. Subhas called a party executive meeting to which members from all parts of the country were invited. Apart from his desire to meet close comrades once before leaving the country, it was essentially a cover. The real business was with Mian Akbar Shah, Forward Bloc leader of the North-West Frontier Province. One evening, on Sisir's arrival in his Uncle's room, he found a handsome Pathan gentleman talking to Subhas, who introduced Sisir to Mian Akbar Shah, telling him that Akbar Shah was leaving Calcutta by the night train from Howrah. Subhas requested Sisir to take Mian Sahib to the station in his car. On the way, Mian Sahib would pick up his baggage from his hotel on Mirzapur Street and visit a department store on Dharmatala Street to make some purchases. Sisir noticed that a measuring tape was lying on the bed.

Mian Akbar Shah and Sisir sat in the rear seat of the Wanderer driven by the chauffeur on their way to shopping. After a while, speaking in

English, Mian Sahib said that Subhas Bose had told him that Sisir would assist him with the escape at this end while Mian Akbar was taking charge of arrangements at the other. He said it was good that they had a chance to meet. They first drove to the hotel on Mirzapur Street in central Calcutta, where Mian Sahib picked up his bags and then made the necessary purchases from Dhamatala Street. On the way, they agreed that Mian Akbar would 'forget' the shopping packet in the car when Sisir dropped him at Howrah station. Subhas had advised Sisir not to alight at the station.

Accordingly, after Mian Sahib's shopping, he returned to the car with Sisir holding the packet and duly placing it on the seat. At Howrah station, Sisir quickly passed Mian Sahib's baggage to a porter, bade goodbye to him and asked the chauffeur to drive home. But as fate would have it, the chauffeur noticed the packet lying on the rear seat even before they had left the station premises. He offered to run back and give the package to Mian Sahib. Sisir pretended to be irritated and said: 'I cannot be responsible if people are so forgetful. We shall send him his things by parcel post. I am in a hurry; please drive home fast. Back at Woodburn Park, Sisir threw the packet into his wardrobe.

After the encounter with Mian Akbar Shah, what his Uncle Subhas Bose was planning became clearer to Sisir. Soon after that, Subhas asked Sisir to buy some items for his daily use. Accordingly, Sisir got them from the Stuart Hogg Market (New Market') in central Calcutta, a pair of flannel shirts as well as a comb, toothbrush and paste and soap, all British make. Then, he bought a pair of the 'Kabuli' chappals from a Chinese shop on Bentinck Street, a suitcase of medium size, an attache case and a bedroll from a shop on Harrison Road, and finally a pillows, a quilt and sheets from Dharmatala street. In between, Sisir got the letters 'M.Z.' inscribed on the suitcase and the attache case. Returning home, Sisir silently carried the items to his room and kept them in the wardrobe, except for the suitcase under his bed.

Sisir then had to print a fake visiting card for Subhas Bose, who gave the text written in block letters on a small piece of paper. He told Sisir to go to an obscure shop, dress, and behave as if he were ordering the cards for himself. Accordingly, one evening, as he was about to leave home, dressed formally in Western style, he ran into his cousin Rabindra Kumar Ghosh (Dantida). He was surprised to see him dressed like that and said: 'Oh, you have a dinner invitation?' Sisir fumbled momentarily and said awkwardly: 'Yes, yes, a dinner invitation, of course!' He took a taxi to Radhabazar behind the Writers' Buildings. There, he went into a shop and placed an order for the visiting card in a very serious manner and in a superior tone. The visiting card read:

MOHD. ZIAUDDIN B.A., LL.B.

Travelling Inspector

The Empire of India Life Insurance Co. Ltd.

Permanent address:

Civil Lines

Jubbulpore.

After a couple of days, Sisir handed the printed card to Subhas Bose. He seemed to like it.

In the Bose family, there were two cars. One was a Studebaker President, a convertible limousine Sarat Chandra Bose used. The other was the Wanderer, which Sisir's mother and others in the family used; Sisir drove it mostly. The Studebaker was a powerful car, ran well, and was comfortable riding in. The Wanderer was also a robust and reliable car. They wondered which car would be more suitable for the long drive.

Subhas Bose initially seemed to be in favour of the Studebaker. But when they discussed the matter, it was felt that the big car was much too well-known. If it passed through Calcutta's streets, people would remark: "There goes Sarat Bose's car! There goes Sarat Bose!' So they decided to go for the Wanderer for the journey.

One day, Subhas took Sisir's endurance test, requesting him to drive the Wanderer non-stop to Burdwan, a little over seventy miles from

Calcutta, up the Grand Trunk Road, have lunch at the railway station there and immediately drive back to Calcutta. Sisir was told to report to him about the car's performance and how tired he felt after the drive. Sisir took this test drive on Christmas Day. It went well. Sisir did not feel too tired.

Subhas then wanted Sisir to drive to his Father's Rishra farmhouse just outside Calcutta and spend a night there one evening. He wanted the caretaker-cum-gardener at Rishra to be prepared to receive Sisir without notice and also for people at Woodburn Park to get used to seeing Sisir spending nights away from home. Accordingly, Sisir drove out to Rishra late one evening. On arrival, he told the gardener that he had been delayed on the way and would stay there overnight instead of returning to Calcutta. Sisir asked him to get some food and prepare a bed. Subhas had said that he might need to spend a night at Rishra after being taken to a railway station (at the time of escape) much further from Calcutta. That would also give him a pretext to say he had been taking a snap getaway at the Rishra farmhouse.

As December 1940 drew to a close, Subhas seemed increasingly restless. He had once mentioned that he might set out around Christmas. Sisir then thought his Uncle Subhas was getting restive because of a delay in receiving the 'signal' from Mian Akbar Shah. But later on, he knew there was no question of receiving any signal. The departure date had already been fixed between them.

In the early stage of their discussions in December, Subhas had expressed deep anxiety about Sarat Bose's health. He thought his elder brother Sarat Bose was in a delicate, nervous condition. Subhas mentioned that he had received advice and support from his elder brother at all the critical moments of his life. His apprehension was that if Sarat Bose advised him to desist from the dangerous undertaking, given his own weak health, Subhas would be in a real dilemma. However, when Sisir met his Uncle Subhas the next day (8 January 1941), he did not get the impression that Sarat Bose had raised any objection to his going ahead with the daring plans. On the contrary, Sisir got the impression that the brothers discussed and analysed the plan in great detail. In fact, Sarat Bose had suggested some significant changes.

For instance, he believed it would be unwise to leave the entire responsibility of keeping the secret and maintaining the bluff after Subhas's departure on a young woman like Ila. In that case, Ila would be fully exposed to police harassment. Subhas then asked Sisir, who, among the other young men in the house, could be taken into confidence and assist in carrying on with the deception for a few days. Sisir suggested the name of his cousin Dwijendranath, the younger son of Uncle Satish. Subhas accepted his suggestion and co-opted Dwijen to join the plan.

In the next few days, Subhas revealed his deception plan to Sisir, who was amazed, expressed his reservations and doubted the plan would work. Subhas decided to announce to the family that he would go into complete seclusion for a few days and not stir out of his bedroom, meet anybody or talk on the telephone during this time. There would not be any public or press announcement, however. Visitors or telephone callers would be told Subhas Bose was in seclusion and could not meet or talk to anybody. The news should be allowed to percolate slowly. The cook, Sarbeshwar, would serve him food from behind a curtain. Subhas wanted people to believe he was self-isolated in his room and engaged in religious and spiritual exercises. He would assign Ila and Dwijen the task of eating the food and switching the lights on and off at appropriate times. Besides, Subhas wrote out a number of messages in his own hand on small pieces of paper to be given to visitors. The notes read: 'Please see Ashrafuddin Sahib in Congress office about this', 'Please ask one of our councillors in the Corporation to deal with this', and so on. He also wrote several post-dated letters, mainly to comrades in prison, to be mailed after his departure on different dates. Letters passing through police censors would convince the interceptors that Subhas Bose was safely in his house in Calcutta.

It was now the second week of January, and Sisir had a feeling that the big day was fast approaching. His Uncle Subhas asked him repeatedly during that previous week if he was ready and all arrangements were in place. Now, Sisir paid particular attention to the car. He spoke to his father, Sarat Bose, and arranged a new spare tyre and battery. He contacted International Tyres and Motors, their regular car-servicing firm, for a service appointment. But the problem was how to get rid of the chauffeur of the Wanderer car for a few days. As luck would have it, a telegram arrived that the chauffeur's mother was ill and he must go home at once. His leave was granted. Sisir reported to Uncle Subhas that there was some good news, looked at him in surprise, and asked what it was. Sisir told him that the chauffeur's mother had been taken ill. At first, he looked at Sisir gravely, then broke into laughter.

A few days before departure, Subhas asked Sisir to take Ila in his car to the famous Kali temple at Dakshineswar, north of Calcutta. It was understood that paying reverence at the Dakshineswar Kali temple was a part of Subhas Chandra Bose's mental preparation for the journey he was about to undertake. So, one beautiful moonlit evening, Sisir drove Ila in his Wanderer car to Dakshineswar. He waited on the steps as she entered the temple with a small copper bowl. She returned with some flowers and holy water in the bowl after a while.

Although there were speculations about Subhas's religious beliefs, there was no doubt among his family members that Subhas believed in God and was deeply religious. He proved through his life that true faith brings limitless strength to a human being, makes him selfless and prepares him for sacrifice. This kind of faith, according to Subhas Bose, has nothing to do with superstition and meaningless rituals. In family and social matters, Subhas was always very liberal and progressive. He was free of blind superstition, pseudo-devotion and excessive attachment to showy rituals, which were prevalent in many of his family members. He was never seen participating in rituals on particular social or family occasions. He used to say that whatever one's beliefs might be, one should never unnecessarily wound others regarding their faiths.

In this context, two other events may be recollected. Subhas Bose had launched his fast unto death in Calcutta's Presidency Jail on the day of Kali Puja in November 1940. And, in December 1943, in a secret message, Subhas had sent to Sisir written in his own hand in Bengali, at the top of the letterhead it was written: 'Sri Sri Kali Puja, 29 October 1943'. There must have been a deep spiritual significance to invoking total devotion to one's God-Divine Mother, in this case, before embarking on noble missions in the service of the country and humanity.

Be that as it may, it became necessary to take precautions and pre-emptive steps to avoid any difficulties during the actual exit from the house. Studying the habits of all the residents and domestic servants was essential. Most elders retired early to their respective bedrooms on the second (top) floor. The servants, fortunately, were all deep sleepers. Subhas's personal servant, Karuna, used to close the front door before going to bed. Subhas had decided that he would walk down the length of the house, windows overlooking Elgin Road, to the southern end and then come along the internal corridor from his north-facing first-floor room down to the ground level by the open staircase of the two-storeyed annexe at the rear of the building. There was no door at the ground floor end of that staircase, and Sisir would park the car at the rear end of the house's driveway, just where he would exit from that staircase. At the front end of the longish driveway, the house's main gate, opening out on Elgin Road, was permanently closed at night but, crucially, never locked. It only had to be pulled open when they would be ready to drive out of the house.

The Alsatian dog, Sunny Boy, was a problem. As mentioned earlier, it had the habit of pouncing on people moving about in the building at night. A difficult situation arose when, one night, he jumped on Subhas's close associate Satya Ranjan Bakshi, a small and frail man, when he was leaving the house late after meeting Subhas. Ila was asked to speak to their Uncle Sunil about restraining his Sunny Boy at night, to which he had agreed.

One evening, Sisir found Subhas in a particularly cheerful mood. Surprisingly, it turned out that the reason was that he (Subhas) had tried on his Mohd. Ziauddin, the travelling insurance salesman, disguise the previous night. He thought it was jolly good and that nobody would recognise him. But, Sisir was not so sure and said: 'It is challenging to disguise your appearance, however much you may try. He did not appreciate Sisir's comment.

Towards the end, Sisir was making more than one visit daily to the Elgin Road house just in case there was some news. On 14th January 1941, Subhas told him that the 'signal' had come, and they would have to leave on the evening of 16th January. Sisir rushed for an early appointment for servicing the car. Unfortunately, no booking was available before the 16th, but the garage assured Sisir that the serviced car would be returned by early evening. Subhas asked for the bedroll Sisir had bought to be sent to the Elgin Road house so he could do some last-minute packing.

Getting the bedroll from Woodburn Park to Elgin Road was difficult, but Sisir managed it somehow through Karuna on the pretext of sorting Subhas's clothing. On the evening of 15th January, it suddenly struck Sisir that the height of Subhas's suitcase might be too much for the boot of the Wanderer car to hold it. After ascertaining its dimension with a measurement tape, it was indeed found to be big! Sisir had to replace the suitcase with one belonging to his father, scratch off 'S.C.B.' written on his father's one and inscribe the initial 'M.Z. for the fictitious Mohd. Ziauddin in Chinese ink in its place in bold capitals. He also had to work on the suitcase he had bought for Subhas. He removed the 'M.Z.' from it with some difficulty, clumsily inscribed 'S.C.B.' on it, and put it back with the other suitcases in the hall.

Then Sisir repacked the things he had purchased for his Uncle in the replacement suitcase. Next, two copies of the Quran were put in the attache case. After that, the items were appropriately arranged inside the two bags. The night Sisir spent in some anxiety as all sorts of problematic scenarios regarding the escape plan filled his mind.

The next day, 16th January, was a Thursday. Thinking that it would be a good idea to be seen in college, Sisir spent some time in the anatomy dissection room and also attended a lecture with the feeling as if he was about to leave that ordinary world for a long time and enter into an unknown, dangerous zone. He sat through the lecture without listening, mind wholly distracted. At the dissection table, his partner was Prabhat Kumar Bose, a fellow student known for his simple nature was there. He just told Prabhat casually that there were a few things to attend at home, so he might be unable to participate in the college for the next couple of days.

In the late afternoon, Sisir peeped into his Uncle's room. As too many people were around, he could not have any conversation with Subhas. They just looked at each other, locked their eyes briefly, and perhaps silently conveyed to each other that everything was all right and they were ready to go. The previous night, Subhas had told Sisir to arrive by car at around 9 p.m., as he would like to leave as early as possible.

In the Calcutta winter, dusk fell early. Sisir got anxious as the car had not returned from the service centre. He had sent his father's chauffeur, Shamsuddin, who drove the Studebaker, to fetch it. Sisir kept looking out of the street-side window again and again. What if the servicing mechanics failed to finish their work the same day, as they had promised, and wanted to keep the car overnight? At the droning noise of the Wanderer's engine, Sisir heaved a sigh of relief and saw Shamsuddin driving it into the driveway of 1 Woodburn Park. By then, Subhas's baggage was ready.

Sisir was going down to the first floor occasionally and looking this way and that. He saw his father, Sarat Bose, resting on the divan in the south verandah after he returned from the High Court. Sisir wanted to talk to him, but there were other people around. As he was thinking what to do, he heard his father coming up the stairs at a slow pace. He asked Sisir to switch on the light of the terrace and took him out there. Sisir had never before in his life had a conversation with him in such a sombre and charged situation. Sarat Babu looked really worried, but he smiled gently to put his son at ease and asked: 'Well, will you be able to do it? (Ki, thik parbe to?)' Then he asked if he anticipated any problems with driving a long distance and if there was much risk of mechanical trouble. Sisir told him quite confidently: 'I shall have no difficulty driving a long distance, and the Wanderer is a very reliable car.' It appeared that his father was surveying the entire journey mentally and told his son that he was not as confident as Subhas about his prospects. It was wartime, and they had to pass through areas with rigorous police or military watch. He particularly apprehended that they might be challenged while driving through Chandernagore, a French enclave in British India. They knew that the French police there stopped passing vehicles frequently to combat smuggling. Sarat Babu told Sisir that a private car driving through Chandernagore in the dead of night was bound to arouse suspicion and advised his son to be extra careful while passing through there.

He also told Sisir that he had discussed with Subhas a reasonable alibi for them to account for the sudden trip to Bararee. If necessary, we would tell people that his father had sent him there upon receiving news of the sudden illness of their sister-in-law. The plan was that he would send a telegram to his father after their arrival there to say that the sister-in-law was better and there was no cause for anxiety. As he talked, while strolling on the open terrace that winter evening, Sarat Babu also said that secret conversations should always be held in public view -in his words, 'conspiracy under the lamppost' was the best way to avoid suspicion! Then he looked at Sisir for a while with a philosophical gaze, gave him an affectionate smile, said 'All right', and slowly went down the stairs. The son could sense his father's great anxiety.

Sisir's mother told Sisir later that his father stayed awake until 2 a.m. that night and anxiously waited for the sound of the Wanderer passing in front of the house. He repeatedly came out of his bedroom and looked out from the small streetside verandah. He had evidently thought that they would go north along Woodburn Road, which they did not.

The clock was ticking, and the questions coming to his mind were how to load Subhas's luggage into the car without being seen; if someone caught him in the act, what would he say? First, Sisir went down as if to check how the car had been serviced. Shamsuddin had put the Wanderer in the garage. Sisir took it out and parked it close to the side door of the small kitchen on the ground floor. He avoided going out by the front door as servants were sitting there. Then, he took the luggage down in three stages.

First, he quickly took the cases from his second-floor room to the first floor and put them in the darkened drawing room by the hallway. Apart from the servants on that floor, he had to dodge younger sister Gita, who usually kept a close watch on whatever was happening in the house. They were close in age, and she monitored him quite a lot. Then Sisir went down to the ground floor to see if anybody was around. When he found the coast clear, he quickly took the cases down to the dining room. Fortunately, there was nobody there, and the room was dark. Finally, Sisir went out by the side door of the kitchen on tiptoe and opened the left rear door of the car. Then, after taking a quick look in all directions, he swiftly took the two cases out of the dining room and put them inside the boot. Nobody saw the operation. But he had an eerie feeling, then and later, that their tall grandfather clock standing in the ground-floor hallway with its gleaming face had seen it all!

Sisir wanted an early dinner. Their cook, Satyabadi Panda, had been with the family for a long time and had worked with his grandmother in the past. Satyabadi was very affectionate but could be pretty domineering as well. The younger children of the house had not yet been served their dinner. So, the cook might turn Sisir away. In Mother's presence, Sisir told him he was tired and wanted to retire early after a quick dinner. As he ate, his mother sat quietly and pensively by his side.

Chauffeur Shamsuddin was also an impressive and intelligent person. He lived on the premises but had his meals elsewhere. As mentioned earlier, the driver of the Wanderer had left for his home to see his ailing mother. But Sisir had to get rid of Shamsuddin. So he told his mother to send Shamsuddin off to have his dinner.

After dinner, Sisir went into his parents' room and asked his mother for cash for expenses on the road. She opened her wardrobe for the money and said: 'God knows what you all are up to!'

Earlier, Subhas had asked Sisir not to change his usual dress. After all, many people in both houses would see him that evening. So he wore a shirt, dhoti, a warm jacket and Kabuli chappals. Uncle Subhas had given him a Kashmiri cap while sorting his things. He asked Sisir to wear it while driving during the day to change his appearance and project a non-Bengali look. Subhas Bose used that cap quite often in Europe, and there are many pictures of him wearing it.

It was now past 8 p.m. Sisir went downstairs in a leisurely fashion. His father's office attendant Dhonu was sitting in the portico. Sisir told him that he was going towards Rishra and would spend the night at their farmhouse if he got delayed for any reason. So, he should close the front door if Sisir was not back by 11 p.m.

Sisir rolled out of the driveway and turned right, got onto the Lower Circular Road and then turned left, driving west until he reached the petrol station at the junction of Lower Circular Road and Lee Road. There, Sisir filled the tank and took an extra two gallons in a can for emergencies. He entered Elgin Road from the Chowringhee side on the west and drove into the driveway of 38/2, then turned the car around and parked it by the open staircase of the annexe at the rear of the house. It was now nearly 9 p.m.

In this room, Subhas sat on the floor for a specially prepared vegetarian dinner before starting his purported meditation exercise in seclusion. His mother, two of Sisir's aunts and three or four youngsters were seated around him. It was the drama being enacted to fool people before the escape. Sisir sat on his grandfather's large bed, watching and impassively checking the proceedings.

After the special dinner, senior members of the family retired to their rooms one by one. Sisir's grandmother, Prabhabati, went to her room next to Subhas's and closed the door. This door between the two rooms remained closed until 26th January. Sisir moved to the next room, where Ila lived, and started a hilarious conversation about movie stars with his older cousin Ganesh, whom they called 'Mejda'. Subhas's radio had been removed to this room. They listened to the radio and chatted. Mejda was a jovial person, and they all liked him.

After the elders had left, the re-arrangement of Subhas's room began. Ila, Dwijen and Aurobindo, another cousin, helped in the process.

Apparently, Aurobindo had been taken into confidence about Subhas's departure at the last moment. Large bedsheets were used as curtains to divide the room into three compartments. The northern half, looking onto Elgin Road, was kept separate, ostensibly for Subhas's seclusion. The southern half was divided into two parts. The larger portion included the grandfather's large bed, and then a small area was created near the door. It was announced that nobody should venture beyond this area. Grandmother Prabhabati's cook, Sarbeshwar, was instructed to gently pass the food under the curtain and leave it on a small teapoy. He would also remove the plates in reverse order. Ila and Aurobindo then removed Subhas's pillowcases, bedsheets, and undergarments. The linen was then packed into the bedroll. The cook Sarbeshwar played a crucial role in the deception without his knowledge. Ten days later, in the morning, he was the person who discovered when he went to collect the plates that Subhas's dinner was untouched. Naturally, he raised the alarm but that story came later.

Subhas wanted to set out as quickly as possible to reach Dhanbad before dawn. But as it turned out, they had to wait another four hours before the coast cleared for them to leave! Subhas was getting restless during that time. Ganesh used to go to bed early. After listening to the radio for a while and chatting with Sisir, he started yawning. Sisir, too, started yawning. He said he should go to bed. Sisir said he was also feeling sleepy and wanted to go home. Meanwhile, Dwijen came once to tell Sisir that his Uncle Subhas wanted him to turn to the right twice after getting out of the house, first onto Elgin Road and then take the first right turn onto Allenby Road.

Mejda left for his room, yawning. But the trouble was with another cousin, Ranjit (also known as Kartik), the eldest son of Uncle Suresh. Sisir was sure that Ranjit suspected something fishy was afoot. He even asked Sisir why he was staying so late and why he had the car with him! Ranjit paced up and down the long corridor in front of Subhas's first-floor room for quite a while.

After some time, Sisir saw him moving away towards the central staircase of the house. Encouraged, Sisir said loudly, 'I must go home now!' and went downstairs, stamping his feet on the wooden stairs.

After a few minutes, Sisir sneaked back upstairs on tiptoe. To his horror, he saw Ranjit descending the stairs from the second floor. Sisir mumbled that he had left something behind in Ila's room and moved away. Karuna, Subhas's servant, had already been told to shut the ground-level door of the central staircase and retire. Ila ensured the rest of the servants had all gone to bed. But Ranjit stuck around. When it was past 1 a.m., Subhas asked Dwijen to take Ranjit with him upstairs to their second-floor bedroom and somehow keep him there. Dwijen was also asked to clear his throat loudly after his cousin was brought under control and after he checked the road in front of the house was clear of any loiterers. After getting the signal, they would move.

The night was quiet and still. The old wall clock in Subhas's room chimed half-past-one. Sisir could hear his own heartbeat. The tension of the last fifteen or twenty minutes was hard to describe. Then they heard Dwijen's throat-clearing signal. Subhas came out of his enclosure into the area just in front of the door to his room. Sisir was struck by his Uncle's impressive disguise. He observed with amazement Subhas Chandra Bose's transformation into Mohd. Ziauddin, a north Indian Muslim! It was the same with Ila and Aurobindo.

Subhas kissed Ila tenderly on the forehead, whispered 'God bless you' to her in English and moved out of the room, gesturing to Sisir to proceed down the long corridor leading to the staircase at the rear of the building. Aurobindo carried the bedroll and walked in front, followed by Subhas. Sisir brought up the back.

The late moon was shining by then. Subhas had already instructed them to keep close to the wall so that there were no shadows. They all walked on tiptoe. Sisir had already noticed that his Uncle was wearing the tough laced shoes he had brought from Europe, not the Kabuli chappals he had bought for Subhas, who had told Sisir that he might have to walk a lot. So, the Kabuli footwear won't be suitable. The spectacles Subhas usually wore were left behind. Instead, Subhas wore the gold-rimmed oval glasses he had used as a student and in the 1920s. Subhas mentioned that he would wear them only whilst walking and when absolutely essential. Otherwise, he would go without spectacles.

The three of them went down the entire length of the long corridor to the south, passed through the dark passage of the annexe and reached the top of the open staircase. There was not a sound to be heard. They came down the stairs. Aurobindo quietly put the bedroll on the front seat by the driver. He then opened the left rear door for Subhas and moved swiftly along the driveway towards the main gate to open it. Subhas got in, took the back seat on the left and held on to the door without closing it.

Sisir went around as usual, climbed into the driver's seat and slammed the door with a bang. Then he switched on the ignition, drove down the driveway out of the house by the open and turned right. Again, he turned right immediately, a second time, and entered Allenby Road, as Subhas had instructed. Then, from Allenby Road, Sisir turned left on Justice Chandra Madhab Road to reach Lansdowne Road. Going in a southerly direction at first, rather than on their northbound route, was to throw any watchers off-track. In case any plainclothes police agents saw the car leaving the house, they would report that the car went south, perhaps to drop a late-night visitor home.

Until they turned, Subhas firmly held on to the door and shut it only after they had gone some distance along Allenby Road. The reason was that if someone were awake in the Elgin Road house and heard the noise of a car leaving, he or she would recall one car door being slammed shut, not two. It was 1.35 a.m. on the night of 16-17 January 1941.

It was already decided that Subhas would sit in the back, not in the front, besides Sisir. That way, Subhas Bose could conceal himself better. Also, the arrangement was that if they were challenged on the road, Sisir would pose as the master and remain in the driving seat. Subhas would pretend to be his chauffeur. If necessary, he would smartly come out of the car, do 'salaam' and start a conversation in Hindustani.

After looking at both, Sisir dared to ask how anyone could believe Sisir was the master and Subhas the chauffeur! Subhas told Sisir not to worry but to remain behind the wheel with a dignified posture without uttering a word. Subhas would do the talking. Thus, the most incredible escape in the history of modern India was underway. Subhas Chandra Bose's journey from Subhas Babu to Netaji Subhas Bose began!

For a while on Lansdowne Road, Sisir saw a car's lights behind them, so he kept looking back through the rear window for some time. Then, that car turned into a side road, and Sisir felt relieved.

During the nocturnal drive, Subhas's first words were about the unforeseen delay in their departure. They had been delayed by at least three hours beyond the intended time of leaving. Sisir was startled when Subhas said he had contemplated giving up the plan for that night. He also noted that in such a hazardous undertaking, one sometimes had to take relatives or friends into confidence, but only if that became unavoidable, to keep things secret. But generally, the fewer people involved, the better. He said it was not a question of trust or lack of it. Subhas admitted that at the last moment, he had thought it wise to take Aurobindo into confidence and ask him to assist in escaping the house when he learned that Aurobindo had been voicing his suspicions openly and loudly. Despite the seriousness of his Uncle Subhas's words, Sisisr still felt optimistic about the journey ahead.

A week or so before the escape, Subhas had told Sisir that the fact that he had driven the escape vehicle would not remain secret for long. The Elgin Road house had so many residents and visitors that a leak was more than a possibility. He also told Sisir in a matter-of-fact tone about the risk he was running and that the worst that could happen to him was an extended spell of imprisonment. After all, he added, so many revolutionaries in India had suffered lengthy jail terms and continued to do so. About himself, he was confident. He said that if his departure could be kept under wraps for about four days, it would give him sufficient time to make good his escape from British India.

From Lansdowne Road, Sisir took the Lower Circular Road toward the Sealdah railway station (Calcutta's second railway station after Howrah). He came across some phaetons and hackney carriages near the station, so he slowed down a bit. There were hardly any pedestrians on the street, though. Two questions bothered him: whether they were being followed and if there was too long a delay for a safe arrival at the other end. The light on the car's dashboard clock was not working. So, Sisir used a hand torch to check the time on the clock repeatedly. Subhas asked him to avoid doing it because the light from the torch was reflecting right on his face as he sat in the back.

When they entered Harrison Road and drove towards Burrabazar, Sisir was struck by the emptiness of Calcutta's streets in the dead of night. As they passed a couple of taxis at the entrance to Howrah Bridge, Sisir felt his car made far too much noise on the cobbled street and the bridge's wooden planks. The steamers and country boats on the Hooghly River were all in deep slumber. He suddenly remembered that as Congress president, Uncle Subhas had been taken in a massive procession down this bridge on his return from the Haripura Congress in 1938, but what a change this present journey was! The city of Howrah was utterly silent as they passed through at high speed. There was bright moonlight by this time, and Sisir was enjoying the drive. As he got on the Grand Trunk Road, he felt a surge of freedom and speeded up further.

Subhas now revealed his plans for the next stage of the journey. He said it would not be a good idea for Sisir to send a telegram home from Bararee as they had planned. There is no need for Sisir to unnecessarily leave a record of his trip with the postal service. Before departure, Subhas told him about his decision to spend the day of 17th January at their house in Bararee rather than in a dak bungalow in disguise. Rather than running the risk of being recognized by strangers, Subhas felt that it would be preferable to be with members of the family who could then be asked to keep their mouths shut. He was confident that the plan of a halt at Bararee would work out well.

As they passed by Rishra, Sisir indicated to his Uncle Subhas the way that led to their farmhouse. They passed the industrial complexes off the Grand Trunk Road at fairly high speed and saw armed police stationed at several points. The police looked at them curiously, but nobody attempted to stop them.

To keep track of the distance covered and the speed at which they were driving, Sisir used his torchlight on the passing milestones from time to time. He did not want to take any risks of driving too fast by maintaining a moderate speed. About halfway to Burdwan, the car had to be stopped at a closed railway-level crossing. Ila had given a flask of hot coffee, and Sisir thought of taking a sip as they waited. Subhas intervened and suggested (in Bengali): 'I should pour you coffee from time to time as you drive.' It was as if Sisir was on an important mission, and his Uncle Subhas was there to assist and support him. He spoke with such affection and humility that Sisir felt embarrassed. But Subhas kept on pouring coffee for him from then on.

Sisir, in turn, tried to return the courtesy and asked: 'Why don't you take a nap?' Subhas said: "The only passenger in a car must not sleep. It makes the driver lonely and, consequently, drowsy. Subhas added that he had been on so many long tours by car across the country that made him used to remain awake during long drives, including at night. Then, he described a few such trips to Sisir.

The train passed the level-crossing, but the guard at the gate seemed to have dozed off. Sisir sounded the horn, but there was no response. He switched off the engine, got out and called out loudly. The man came out of his little kiosk and opened the gate. But then the car would not start! There was an overflow of petrol into the carburettor. Subhas became anxious. Sisir assured him that there was nothing seriously wrong. Sure enough, after a few tries, the self-starter worked, and the Wanderer sped forward.

They reached Burdwan around 4.30 a.m. when most people were sound asleep, so there were no problems. Sisir took the road to Asansol. From Howrah to Burdwan, the road zigzagged a lot. It was straight on long stretches between Burdwan and Asansol, but there were gradients along the way.

They passed Durgapur, a town which became an important industrial centre in post-independence India, which was completely different at that time. Sisir drove along a road of red soil winding through thick forests. It was known that dacoits sometimes pounced on travellers on this road. Sisir now got a real sense of adventure as we drove along.

There was no sign of dacoits, but they encountered another hazard. Suddenly, the headlights illuminated a pack of buffaloes as they appeared on the road, followed by two lathi-wielding men. Sisir hit the brakes as quickly as he could, and the car screeched to a halt just short of the animals. The buffaloes swarmed around the car and bumped against it from all sides before being herded onwards by their owners. Sisir had a bit of a fright then.

As they approached Asansol, dawn was breaking. They had wanted to avoid driving in daylight, but nothing could be done given their delayed departure from Calcutta. Sisir thought of re-filling the tank, but Subhas did not like the idea. 'Can't you do without it?' he asked. 'I don't want to take any chances,' Sisir replied.

He pulled up at a petrol station just before Asansol town. He parked the car as far ahead as possible so that the attendant could not see the passenger in the back seat easily and got out with the Kashmiri cap on. He paid the man at some distance behind the car. As the man returned to his shed, Sisisr started the engine and drove off quickly.

Between Asansol and Dhanbad, they passed several cars coming from the other direction. He accelerated a bit whenever Sisir saw a car or people on the roadside. As they approached the checkpost at Gobindapur, he saw the bamboo barrier slowly come down across the road. He slowed down. A man came out from the shed and noted the number of the car (BLA 7169). But the barrier went up again before he had brought the vehicle to a complete stop. He drove on. A little later, he turned left in the direction of Dhanbad. Uncle Subhas asked twice: 'Are you sure he took down the number?' Sisir briefly replied 'Yes' each time.

As the car passed by Dhanbad town, there was clear morning light. Sisir felt insecure and drove as fast as possible. But perhaps of the bright daylight, he had no difficulty locating the road of Bararee and felt immediately relieved when he spotted his elder brother's bungalow from a distance. The tall chimneys of the Bararee Coal Works provided a good landmark.

It was now nearly 8.30 a.m. on 17th January 1941. Subhas had thoroughly coached Sisir about the bizarre drama they would enact at Bararee. Sisir would drop Subhas a short distance from the bungalow and proceed there alone to tell his brother, Asoke, that he had brought in his car their Uncle Subhas in disguise, who would arrive on foot after some time. Subhas would ask for Asoke on arrival. Upon being informed by his servant of the visitor, Asoke would come out. Uncle Subhas would then ask for a discussion on behalf of the insurance company he represented as Mohd. Ziauddin. Asoke would reply that he was in a hurry to go to the factory and did not have time for a meeting. Subhas would then say that he had come a long way and there was no train before evening. Therefore, he would appreciate being kindly allowed to stay for the day in the guest room so he could have a talk in the evening and then leave. All conversation would be in English and within earshot of his brother's servants.

Asoke would then instruct the servants to arrange the visitor's stay in the guest room. Subhas would be brought into the living room and introduced to Sisir in English in the presence of the servants. After being served tea, the visitor would be taken to his room. After his brother returned from work, they would discuss plans for the evening and the onward journey.

When Sisir pulled in in front of Asoker's house, Sisir found two persons outside. One was the driver cleaning his car. They saw him arrive alone. Sisir felt happy and walked into the house with his little bag and the empty coffee flask without wasting time. Sisir asked the driver to put his car in the garage. Subhas's luggage was inside the boot. Later in the day, the driver asked Sisis if he should bring the things inside. Sisir was a little worried that he had noticed but managed to brush off the query.

On entering the living room, Sisir found his brother's bedroom door closed. He banged on the door and became impatient as there was a delay in his opening the door. Sisir did not want Subhas to arrive before the situation could be explained to Asoke. As soon as he opened the door, Sisir blurted out the instructions he had to convey to him. Asoke turned pale.

After a few minutes, the bearer came in to say that a Muslim gentleman wanted to see Asoke, who then went out into the verandah and talked to him (Subhas in disguise) in English as scripted. Sisir could hear the conversation from the living room. Asoke asked the visitor to come in for a cup of tea after he had asked for shelter for the day. He asked the bearer to serve tea and introduced him (Subhas in disguise) to Sisir. It was amusing, but Sisir managed to control his laughter. After a while, Sisir retired to the back of the house and started chatting with his sister-in-law, Mira.

The bearer was asked to serve breakfast to the guest in his room. Sisir had no direct contact with his Uncle Subhas for the rest of the morning. The bearer reported to Mira that the visitor appeared to be a Khandaani (aristocratic) Muslim gentleman from the United Provinces. Asoke came home for lunch. After lunch, he talked to Subhas in the front verandah, and plans for the evening were drawn up.

Subhas thought it would not be wise to catch the train for his onward journey from Asansol or Dhanbad. These were big stations and always crowded. He picked Gomoh, the next station after Dhanbad. It was a smaller station and would not be crowded, especially late at night.

There were two routes to Gomoh from Bararee. One option was to go along the Grand Trunk Road and then take a connecting road to Gomoh town and its railway station. The other route went through coal-mining areas, rice fields and forests along poorly lit kuccha roads. Subhas preferred the latter because he wanted to avoid the Grand Trunk Road. The problem was that Sisir was not too familiar with the second route. He suggested that Asoke come along as a guide. That led to another problem; Asoke said that he could not, in those parts, leave Mira alone in the house late at night. So Subhas decided that Mira should also come with them. Accordingly, Asoke tutored Mira.

While Asoke, Mira and Sisir had their lunch together, their Uncle Subhas, disguised as a visitor, stayed in the guest room and was served food there. Sisir kept well away from him so nobody would suspect that he had anything to do with Subhas. After lunch, Subhas slept soundly for quite some time. They could hear his heavy breathing as he slept. In the afternoon, Sisir went out with the car to a petrol pump in a nearby Jharia town, filled the tank, and checked the tyres. Then, he also took some rest.

It was winter and already dark when Asoke returned from work. Uncle Subhas had a final talk with him in the verandah. The servants were told that Asoke and Mira would go out after an early dinner to visit friends, with Sisir driving them. The guest was served dinner in the guestroom. After dinner, Uncle Subhas - or rather Mohd. Ziauddin - came out onto the verandah. He bade goodbye to Asoke and Sisir in English in a rather demonstrative manner in the presence of the servants and walked off into the evening.

Soon afterwards, Sisir drove out in the Wanderer with Asoke and Mira. Subhas was waiting for them by the road. Sisir picked him up, and all three sat in the rear seat. Sisir had the bedroll by his side in front and drove with Asoke, giving him directions. They had plenty of time to reach their destination. The Delhi-Kalka Mail from Howrah was due at Gomoh station after 1 a.m. The distance they had to cover was around thirty miles. They drove through forests and rice fields after getting out of the colliery area, the headlights of the Wanderer illuminating the pitch-dark route.

Subhas repeatedly told them in the car that everyone must keep their mouths shut. He specifically asked Sisir to remind Ila, Dwijen and Aurobindo, who knew about his departure, of the need for absolute secrecy on his return to Calcutta.

They made two stops on the drive to Gomoh, once in a forest lined with tall trees and once among rice fields bathed in moonlight. During the stop in the forest, a long line of bullock carts with twinkling lights and bells jingling around the necks of the animals passed them. It was a fantastic and romantic scene otherwise. During the second stop, the rice fields on either side gleaming in the moonlight made for an equally enchanting atmosphere. Sisir felt strangely moved and wondered whether this tranquillity in the heart of nature was the prelude to a storm in the country. Was it the eye of the hurricane?

When they reached the station at Gomoh, there was still some time before the train's arrival. They parked the car outside the station and took Subhas's luggage out of the vehicle. The station was very quiet. Asoke and Sisir could find a sleepy porter after some difficulty. He picked up the luggage. Uncle Subhas looked at them in silence for a few moments. They all looked at each other. Then their Rangakakababu said: 'I am leaving; you go back (Ami chollam, tomra phire jao)'. Then, he walked calmly with deliberate steps towards the overbridge leading to the train platform.

Sisir, Asoke and Mira watched as their Uncle Subhas crossed the overbridge with his usual purposeful stride behind the porter carrying his luggage. Then he disappeared into the darkness. The 'Silent boy' suddenly remembered, too late, that he had forgotten to touch his Radiant Uncle's feet as per the traditions of the Bose family.

They waited for a while outside the station for the train to arrive. The train pulled in. They still waited. Then they heard the puff-puff sound of the steam engine and the rattle of the carriages as the train pulled out of Gomoh station. The Delhi-Kalka Mail moved out, and they saw a chain of lights moving further and further away from them, dancing to the rhythm of the clattering wheels until it was swallowed up by the night.

That was the last time they saw Uncle Subhas at a lonely railway station in Bihar at about 1 a.m. on 18 January 1941. Sisir's tryst of destiny with him was far from over. It would not only dominate the next few years of his life. It defined the rest of his life. But, that's a different story. [2]

The escape was kept a closely guarded secret for ten days, and during this time, the bluff of his home in seclusion was carried on by Subhas Bose's niece Ila and two nephews living on the premises. On 25th January, Sarat Bose gave instructions to all concerned on the manner of the disclosure of the disappearance and left for the weekend for his garden house outside the city. Bose's departure was ostensibly revealed by the discovery on the morning of 26th January that his food plate was left untouched. On receipt of the 'news', Sarat Bose rushed back to the city, driving in the same historical car by Sisit. Among the many diversionary tactics, Bose had left several post-dated messages to be despatched in the days following his departure as a cover for his safe journey.

The escape news was deliberately broadcast to the world on 26th January because his case was coming up for hearing the following day to prevent the initiative from passing into the hands of the British police. His own people raised a hue and cry, and a frantic hunt was on even before enemy Intelligence could gather its wits and start operations. Wild rumours spread throughout Calcutta about the disappearance, one of them being that he had been secretly done away with by government agents. Another reaction was that Bose had left for the Himalayas in a mood of disgust and frustration. This impression was sought to be supported by members of the Bose family. Sarat Bose sent messengers searching for him to various pilgrimage centres. Replying to an enquiry by Mahatma Gandhi, for instance, Sarat Chandra wired him, "We as much in the dark as the public about Subhas's whereabouts and intentions and even the exact time of leaving No news in spite of best efforts for the last three days. Circumstances indicate renunciation."

It was widely suspected that Bose had left India to ally himself with foreign powers in his quest for freedom. Japan was not at war then, and it was surmised that he might have boarded a Japanese steamer which had left the Calcutta docks about that time. The mystery over Bose's disappearance was maintained for over a year until he began his broadcasts over the Azad Hind Radio, though even then, his exact whereabouts were not disclosed. To add further piquancy to the situation, Reuters reported on 28th March 1942 that Bose had been killed in an air crash near the coast of Japan. The news agency soon contradicted the news, and speculations over his whereabouts became rife again. Like the elusive Sealet Pimpernel, Bose was reported to be here, there and everywhere for nearly sixteen months. [3]

Late in the evening of 19th January, the Frontier Mail from Delhi turned into Peshawar cantonment station. Mian Akbar Shah, hovering next to the exit gate, spotted a distinguished-looking Muslim gentleman coming through it. Confident that this was Bose in disguise (and it was), he walked alongside and asked him to get into a waiting tonga. Akbar Shah instructed the tongawallah to take the gentleman to Dean's Hotel and got into another carriage to follow. Akbar's tongawallah asked Mian Sahib why he was taking such an obviously devout Muslim, who looked like an alim (a leaned Islamic scholar), to a hotel for infidels; he suggested going to the Taj Mahal Hotel, where the guest would be provided with a prayer mat and water for ablutions. It struck Akbar that the Taj Mahal might be the safer place since Dean's Hotel was likely to be crawling with police agents - and so the two tongas changed course.

The manager of the Taj Mahal was as impressed with Muhammad Ziauddin as the tongawallah and found the visitor a nice room with a working fireplace and a jai namaz (prayer rug). The following day, Akbar had intended to shift Bose to the home of a well-to-do friend. But on the way back from the Taj Mahal Hotel, he encountered Abad Khan, a close political associate from a humble background, who insisted on playing host to Subhas Chandra Bose. Before dawn, Muhammad Ziauddin was shifted to Abad Khan's home, where, in the next few days, he transformed from a north Indian Muslim gentleman to a deaf-mute Pathan. It was necessary since Bose did not speak the local language, Pushto.

Prior to his leader's arrival, Akbar had already identified two possible escorts- Muhammad Shah and Bhagat Ram Talwar- for the next stage of Bose's journey across the border of British India. Both were, at that time, active members of the Kirti Kisan Party and also to the NWFP Forward Bloc. Akbar yielded to Bhagat's eagerness and entrusted him with the task of accompanying Bose to Kabul. Bhagat Ram, under the assumed name "Rahmat Khan, would be taking his deaf-mute elder relative Ziauddin to the shrine at Adda Sharif in an attempt to cure him of his affliction. Abad Khan taught Ziauddin how to drink water from a kandoli and partake of food from a common plate with his fellow Pathans. With a new set of clothes, complete with the local headgear,

Subhas Chandra Bose fully looked the part but had to be careful not to utter a word.

Bose was held up in Peshawar for seven days of acute anxiety and suspense as it was decided just before his arrival to change his route to Afghanistan. The new road was the shortest but stiffest, and a reliable guide was necessary. At last, on the early morning of 26th January, the very day the news of his disappearance was disclosed in Calcutta, he left Pasluwar in a car accompanied by Bhagat Ram, Ahad Khan, and the guide. Bhagat Ram passed as Rahmat Khan and Bose as Ziuddin, his sick uncle whom the former was taking to the shrine at Adda Sharif in Afghanistan. The first halt for the customary police check was made at the Jammad Hamiler, after which the party drove to Khajani Maidan Military Camp. Beyond this point lay the tribal area as a buffer between British India and Afghanistan. Bose, Bhagat Ram, and the guide got off at a point where a track goes towards the mountains, which was a furlong away from the actual tribal border. Abad Khan was asked to return to Peshawar after an interval.

The party trudged on for nearly two hours, during which they could cover only one and a half miles of steep ascent. Bose was visibly tired and lay down for rest. But he quickly recovered when told they had crossed the border and were now safe in the tribal area. With frequent stops for rest, as Bose was not accustomed to mountain climbing, they reached the top of the pass at about 8 pm and reached the village of Pishkan Maina at the foot of the other side of the mountain at midnight. Resting there that night, they resumed the trek the following day and reached the next village at about noon.

Bose was now visibly tired and asked Bhagat Ram to get a mule for him. It was done, and they managed to reach the first village in Afghan territory at about 1 am on 28th January. The guide was sent back from this point. During this 12-hour ride, they had to cross another pass covered with snow, and Bose suffered a fall. Resuming the journey after a night's rest, they reached the village of Gardi, situated on the Peshawar Kabul highway. It had taken them two days of cross-country walking to cover a distance, which could usually be done in a few hours by bus. The rustic Pathans they had encountered in these two days and were to meet subsequently were naturally suspicious of those two strange travellers, but somehow they managed to bluff their way.

Nevertheless, one of them insisted on feeling Bose's tongue to satisfy himself that he was really dumb. They were now on the highway, and as they walked along, they tried to hitchhike on passing trucks. Eventually, they caught one truck loaded with tea chests and reached Jalalabad at about 10 pm on 28th January. In the bitter cold of January, they made themselves as comfortable as they could on the top of piled tea chests.

To lend credence to their pretence, they spent 29th January at the shining of Adda Sharl and performed the customary rituals. However, Bhagat Ram's real purpose was to contact one Ilaji Mohammad Amin, a political worker who was once Bhagat Ram's fellow prisoner in Peshawar Jail. He gave them several valuable tips for their journey ahead and asked them to be cautious when they reached The Bud Khak chock-post, 13 miles east of Kabul. Everybody visiting the Afghan capital had to disclose his identity and other particulars. Fortunately, there were no formal passports between India and Afghanistan in those days.

The next morning, 30th January, they set out in a tonga on the road to Kalal. They changed the tonga on the way and ultimately reached Mimla in the late afternoon. The truck reached Bud Khak the next morning, 31st January, at 5 am. It was still dark, and there was plenty of snow. After a short rest, they hired a tonga for the last time and reached Kabui at 11 am. Both Bose and Bhagat Ram were utter strangers to the Afghan capital. They had neither friends nor reliable contacts there. Though Bhagat Ram could speak fluent Persian, he was not quite at home with the local language. They searched for a shelter and were guided to one near the Lahm! Gate, which was scarcely fit for human habitation. But they hardly had any alternative, and in their plight, any kind of shelter was welcome to rest their weary limbs and protect themselves from the biting cold winds that raged that day. All they had for food was bread dipped in cloying sweet tea.

Bose had reached Kabul, the first safe haven on his adventurous journey. However, he soon discovered that his ordeal had only begun rather than ended. In fact, it started the very next morning, 1st February 1941, when Bose and Bhagat Ram began to seek contacts with foreign embassies in Kabul for his journey to Europe. They first sought to contact the Russians because the Soviet Union lay next to Bose's route to Europe. Taking advantage of the Soviet-German Non-Aggression Pact was his primary political tactic in his fight against Britain. There is no reason to doubt that Bose's destination was Germany, the major opponent of his enemy. But a rapport with the Soviets would naturally be welcome to a political realist like Bose.

Clearly, the intermediaries, through whom Bose had sought to establish contact and come to definite or tentative arrangements with the Russians before he embarked on his journey, had failed to achieve anything. Why they failed is yet a closed book.

The result was that when Bose actually arrived in Kabul, nothing was ready for him, and everything was left to luck and improvisation. The delays and dangers inherent in such a situation began to bother Bose. It was crucial for Bose to leave Kabul as quickly as possible. If, by any chance, the Afghan government could come to know of his presence there, it would unceremoniously hand him over to the British.

As the frequent efforts of Bose and Bhagat Ram to establish contact with the Soviet Embassy proved futile, Bhagat Ram, in desperation, even tried to accost the Russian Ambassador once when his car had halted at a road crossing, with Bose standing about seven yards away. But the Ambassador refused to oblige.

While Bose's unsuccessful attempts for contact with foreign embassies dragged on, his stay there was becoming more and more risky. Soon, Bose and Bhagat Ram came under the suspicion of an Afghan plain clothes policeman who began to harass and question them - or rather Bhagat Ram, since Bose's deaf and dumb show was still on. Bhagat Ram tried to fob him off with the offer of a bit of money, but the policeman's eyes were also firmly fixed on the gold watch on Bhagat Ram's wrist. The wristwatch actually belonged to Bose. Eventually, one day, when the policeman insisted on taking Bose and Ram for questioning at the Kotwali (police station), he had to be placated with the gold watch.

Further, staying at the same place was becoming dangerous, so Bose was shifted to the house of Uttam Chand on the afternoon of 13th February. Uttam Chand was a former acquaintance of Bhagat Ram, whom the latter had located after some efforts. Uttam, who had a radio and crockery shop in Kabul, was taken aback when he learned about Subhas Bose's Identity and the purpose of his presence in Kabul. Uttam Chand readily agreed to shelter Bose and help him in whatever other way he could.

Meanwhile, a drama was enacted in Calcutta on 26th January. Sisir had returned to Calcutta on the evening of 18th January and had accompanied his father to the wedding of the granddaughter of Subhas's political guru, Deshbandhu Chitta Ranjan Das. There, he had dutifully answered questions about the poor state of his uncle's health. On the homefront, the niece and nephews in the know continued to consume their uncle's food daily to keep up the pretence that he was still confined to his room. Subhas had told Sisir that he would have enough time to get away if they could only hold for four or five days.

Since a court hearing was scheduled for 27th January concerning one of the sedition cases, the conspirators in Calcutta decided to report that they could not find Bose rather than cede the initiative to the police. After leaving clear instructions on how Subhas's disappearance should disclosed, Sarat and Sisir left for their garden house in Rishra, outside Calcutta. Subhas's food, consumed by his niece and nephews during the previous few days, was now left uneaten, and the cook, upon discovering this, naturally raised a hue and cry. Two anxious nephews hurried to Rishra to inform Sarat that Subhas had disappeared. Sisir drove his father back to the Elgin Road home in Calcutta to hear family members and domestic staff give their version of events and to take stock of the situation. Subhas's mother, Prabhabati, was distraught. Seeing her in distress, Sarat tried to reassure her and moved the headquarters of his cover-up operations to Woodburn Park. Sisir was sent with the Wanderer to search the areas around the Keoratala burning ghat and the temple at Kalighat. A holy man who believed Subhas had renounced the world promised to wake the goddess at night to seek further information.

The news of Subhas's disappearance was published in two friendly papers, the Ananda Bazaar Patrika and the Hindusthan Standard, on the morning of 27th January. Reuters then picked it up and transmitted it to the world, leaving British intelligence officers embarrassed and questioning everyone. Sisir observed them as they looked at all the wrong points of a possible exit from the house. One agent reported that Subhas Chandra Bose had left his home on 25th January for Pondicherry to join his old friend Dilip Kumar Roy in religious seclusion. Sarat and Sisir made subtle efforts to propagate the renunciation theory.

An anxious telegram from Mahatma Gandhi elicited a three-word reply from Sarat: "Circumstances indicate renunciation". But he would not deliberately mislead Rabindranath Tagore, who had stood by Subhas during his political battles with Gandhi in 1939. "May Subhas receive your blessings wherever he may be," the poet received the cable from Sarat Bose in response to his query.

The police could see that Prabhabati was genuinely inconsolable. While most of the police officers and intelligence agents floundered and blamed one another, the most astute among them, J. V. B. Janvrin, Deputy Commissioner of Police of the Special Branch in Calcutta, believed there were "grave reasons to doubt that sudden religious fervour was the "true explanation" for Subhas's disappearance. On 27th January, Janvrin forwarded to Delhi an intercepted letter dated 23rd January from Sri Aurobindo to a colleague, saying the reason he could not accept an invitation to travel outside Bengal would become evident on 27th January. But this error brought the police no closer to fathoming what had really taken place. One report from Punjab claimed to know of a plot to fly Subhas toward Russia. Another conjectured that Subhas's friend Nathalal Parikh, who had visited from Bombay in December, may have got him a false passport to travel to Japan. There was serious speculation that Bose may have left Calcutta on 17th January on a ship called the Thaisung, which had sailed for Penang, Singapore, and Hong Kong.

All this bungling made Viceroy Linlithgow furious with Governor Herbert, who had ventured to suggest that if their inveterate opponent had indeed left India, this might not be such a bad thing. Linlithgow believed that Bose's escape reflected very poorly on those responsible for keeping him under surveillance. If he had left so easily, he might just as easily return to torment them.

Richard Tottenham of the Home Department in Delhi was categorical that the government had wanted to prevent Bose from harming from within India or abroad, but he had hoodwinked the police. On 13th February, he wrote, "How Bose arranged to escape and where he now is still a mystery." He told Linlithgow that Herbert was by no means proud of the performance. Deputy Commissioner of Police Janvrin, in Calcutta, may have been out-manoeuvred, but his assessment of Subhas Chandra Bose was on the mark. Even if Bose had left home to become a sannyasi (an ascetic), his police detective was sure it was not for religious reasons but to plot a mass revolution. The other alternative was that Bose had gone abroad to seek foreign help for his country's freedom. Eventually, Janvrin concluded that Subhas Bose would strive his utmost to achieve his life's aim- the complete independence of India. [4]

It was sometime during this period the British Government decided to get rid of Subhas Chandra Bose by hook or crook. In fact, the Special Operations Executive (SOE) - an irregular war-time sabotage agency set up at the instance of British Prime Minister Winston Churchill -had been ordered soon after Bose disappeared from Calcutta to "eliminate" him, including by assassination. The SOE's branch office in Istanbul had been conveyed this direction because British intelligence expected Bose to move into Europe through Turkey. In the event, Subhas Bose travelled to Berlin via Soviet Russia, foiling the British attempt.

According to the BBC News, dated 15th August 2005:

The British told their agents to assassinate India's independence war leader, Subhash Chandra Bose, in 1941, an Irish historian has claimed. Eunan O'Halpin, who has written several books on British intelligence, says the order came after Bose sought support from the Axis powers in World War II. British agents were told to intercept and kill Bose before he reached Germany via the Middle East. Once they found Bose was planning to oust the British with the active support of the Axis powers, British intelligence was given "clear orders" to assassinate him in 1941.

In a lecture in Calcutta, Mr O'Halpin cited a recently declassified intelligence document referring to a top-secret instruction to the Special Operations Executive (SOE) of British intelligence to murder Bose. He says the British were initially puzzled about the whereabouts of Bose after he escaped from Calcutta in January 1941.

"They thought he had gone to the Far East, but they soon intercepted Italian diplomatic communication and came to know Bose was in Kabul, planning to reach Germany through the Middle East. Two SOE operatives in Turkey were instructed by their headquarters in London to intercept Bose and kill him before he reached Germany," said Mr O'Halpin and added that the SOE operatives in Turkey failed because Bose reached Germany through Central Asia and the Soviet Union. "Every time [the operatives] checked back, headquarters told them the orders were intact, and Bose must be killed if found." Describing the decision as "extraordinary, unusual and rare", Mr O'Halpin said the British took Bose "much more seriously than many thought" and added: "Historians working on the subject tell me the plan to liquidate Bose has few parallels. It appears to be a last desperate measure against someone who had thrown the Empire in complete panic."

Other historians who have worked on Bose say this will add to the mystique of India's British agents to kill Bose, (the) most charismatic independence war figure.

"Bose would have reasons to compliment himself if he knew the British were desperate enough to plan his assassination. That's a measure of how seriously they took him," says Calcutta historian Lipi Ghosh. In retrospect, she says, the British had correctly assessed the potential of Bose.

Sugata Bose, Gardiner professor of history at Harvard University and a grand-nephew of Bose, said: "Since he ultimately managed to swing the loyalty of the Indian soldiers to the national cause from the King-Emperor, they had all the reasons to contemplate the worst." [5]

Interestingly, on the issue of Subhas Chandra Bose's assassination attempt by the British Government, what Professor Sugata Bose, who is Netaji's brother Sarat Chandra Bose's grandson, wrote in his book, "HIS MAJESTY'S OPPONENT: Subhas Chandra Bose and India's Struggle against Empire" illustrated that not only the British colonial rulers activated their Special Operations operatives on 7th March 1941 to liquidate Subhas Chandra Bose, they also reconfirmed that their decision of murdering him was still valid. The relevant part of the narrative is depicted below:

> In June 1941, long after Bose had safely reached Europe, the Special Operations Executive (SOE) in Istanbul sought confirmation of the continuing validity of the March order from London to assassinate him. In late May, Delhi had informed London that they had thought Bose "would be used for Radio Propaganda from Russia, Italy or Germany, but nothing of the sort has eventuated." Therefore, they believed Bose might still be in Afghanistan and wondered "whether demand should be presented to Afghan Government to deal with him under rules of practice." It was on June 13 that SOE in Istanbul inquired whether the assassination order was still in effect. Sir Frank Nelson, the chief of SOE, was reported to be

"in a minority of one at that morning's meeting in insisting that it should be referred to the Foreign Office. He said he was sure the Secretary of State for India. [L. S. Amery], who was also interested in this question, would not take kindly to Sir Hughe Knatchbull-Hugessen [the British ambassador to Turkey] objecting to Bose being liquidated on Turkish territory." Reconfirmation of the assassination decision having been obtained, London cabled SOE in Istanbul telling their operative Gardyne de Chastelain that "the Foreign Office agreed to the liquidation of Chandra Bose being carried out on Turkish territory," but that Gardyne de Chastelain should tell no one about this. [6]

Nevertheless, in Kabul, Bose had already managed to establish contact with the German Legation. On 6th February, he had practically gate-crashed into the Legation alone. He succeeded in meeting Minister Hen Pilger, who became extra-cautious, thinking that Bose might be an agent provocateur. Bose was asked to keep in touch with them through Herr Thomas, a representative of Steinens in Kabul. The Minister had promised to get in touch with Berlin immediately for instructions. Bose had to return reluctantly to the caravanserai at the time. Till 15th February, when Bose had already shifted to Uttam Chand's house, there was nothing encouraging from the German side. While Uttam Chand and Bhagat Ram were busy with their rounds of foreign embassies and legations, Bose mainly shut himself up within the four walls of Uttam Chand's house. He could not expose himself to the risk of recognition. Any Indian might be a British agent, any Afghan a police informer. The suspicious behaviour of a neighbour of Uttam Chand's had compelled him to shift himself to a new location again for a few days. But as he fell ill there, he had to return to the friendly shelter of Uttam Chand's house. He could no longer make personal approaches to any foreigner, for he had nothing more than his word to establish his identity or bona fides. The Russians remained unapproachable, and the Germans lukewarm.

Bose was getting disgusted with his unending stay in Kabul. So, about the middle of February, they thought of crossing into the Soviet Union on their own. They went to the extent of examining the possibilities of crossing into the Soviet Union with the help of a man from Peshawar who had absconded to Kabul years ago on account of a murder charge. The Peshawar man, in turn, would have enlisted the support of his dacoit brother-in-law living on the frontier for this purpose. However, on 23rd February, they got word from Herr Thomas to contact the Italian Minister Alberto Quaroni for further arrangements. Bhagat Ram met Quaroni first and then arranged a meeting between the Italian Minister and Subhas Bose. Their first interview lasted a whole night. Bose was already quite clear about the technique of his future struggle. He told Quaroni of his intention to go to Europe to create a Free India Government and to form out of Indian prisoners of war in Germany and Italy an Indian Liberation Army. He also told Quaroni that he wanted a wireless station at his disposal to carry on propaganda for Indian independence.

Quaroni was sceptical about how Bose's revolutionary programme would be received in Berlin or Rome. Still, as he felt that Bose had already burnt his boats behind him, he did not wish to discourage him. Arrangements were made that Mrs Quaroni would visit Uttam Chand's shop regularly to pass messages to and from Bose. During this time, the German and Italian governments jointly took up the question of Boss's transit through Russia with the Soviet government. Bose utilised the time to arrange reliable contacts for future work in Afghanistan and the tribal territories. He also wrote his well-known thesis "Forward Bloc-Its Justification" at that time. Contact with Italians was maintained in two ways - Mrs Quaroni visiting Ullam Chand's shop and Bhagat Ram visiting Signor Crescini of the Italian Lagation at his private residence.

The Soviet answer came after nearly four weeks. The agreed formula among the two governments was that Bose would travel across Russia on an Italian diplomatic passport, impersonating a clerk at the Italian Legation in Kabul, Orlando Mazzolta. The Afghan government was asked to issue a courier visa. About a week before Bose departed from Kabul, Mrs. Quaroni brought the vital message to Uttam's shop. Arrangements were made to take Bose's photograph, which was to replace Mazzottia's on the original passport and to get his clothing ready. The Italians collected Boso's suitcase on 16th March, and Bose himself shifted to Crescini's residence the next day. He handed over to Bhagat Ram several documents to carry back to India with the necessary instructions. It was arranged with the Italians that Bhagat Ram would be the link between India and Kabul and that they would provide the means of communication between Bose and Kabul.

On 18th March, early morning, Bose left in a car for the Soviet frontier, accompanied by a German engineer of the Todt organisation and two others. He spent two nights on the way in German houses. They travelled through the Hindu Kush's high passes and the Afghan steppes' dead expanse and crossed the Oxus at the Afghan frontier post at Pala Kisar until they reached the fabled city of Samarkand. On 20th March, they left Samarkand for Moscow, from where they flew to Berlin, arriving at the beginning of April 1941.

On the evening of 31st March 1941, a visitor from the frontier arrived at the Calcutta residence of Sarat Chandra Bose at 1 Woodburn Park and asked to see Sisir. The latter immediately fetched his father, who received from Bhagat Rum three documents- a personal letter from his brother in Bengali, the thesis 'Forward Bloc-Its Justification' and a 'Message to My Countrymen' from 'Somewhere in Europe dated 22nd March 1941. The next morning, Bhagat Ram joined Sarat Bose for his morning walk at the Victoria Memorial Gardens. He told him about Bose's journey from Peshawar to the Russian frontier. Sarat Chandra put Bhagat Ram in touch with Satya Ranjan Baksi, a trusted lieutenant of Bose and leader of the underground Bengal Volunteer Group. It is now known that the Bose brothers maintained contact with each other until November 1941, using wireless messages exchanged via Tokyo with the secret assistance of the Japanese Consulate General in Calcutta. After two months and eleven days of adventure, suspense and anxiety since leaving home, Bose arrived safely in Berlin in his new Avatar as 'Signor Orlando Mazzotta'.

Bose's journey from Calcutta to Berlin through a dragnet of British policemen, spies and informers ranks among the most sensational escapes in history. [7] But that was not all. Subhas Bose's journey from Berlin to the 'Land of the Rising Sun', Japan, was even more breathtaking and incredible. It's narrated in the next chapter.

Chapter 4

Across the Globe by Submarine

German Reich to the Land of the Rising Sun

On the morning of 3rd April 1941, 'Signor Orlando Mazzotta', posing as an Italian diplomat, walked up the steps of the German Foreign Office in Berlin. The Under-Secretary of State, Dr Ernst Woermann, immediately received him and carefully listened as he spoke of establishing a government-in-exile and launching a military offensive. The government he had in mind was Indian, and the target of his offensive was British India. 'Orlando Mazzotta' was, in fact, Subhas Chandra Bose, who eventually became the only Indian to lead a military assault against the British Empire in the twentieth century.

That was not the first time Subhas Chandra Bose visited Berlin. His earlier visit here in 1933 was also under some extraordinary circumstances. At that time, British Colonial rulers in India imprisoned more than a hundred thousand activists, including top leaders like him, and declared the Congress organisation unlawful. The new Governor-General and Viceroy of India, Lord Willingdon, was unwilling to make concessions to the nationalists. Consequently, at Gandhiji's call, there was a countrywide resumption of civil disobedience in January 1932.

Subhas Chandra Bose was sent to a rather remote jail in a place called Seoni in the Central Provinces. There, he began to experience severe abdominal pain in February 1932 and by mid-May, he had lost twenty pounds. He was then transferred to Jabalpur Central Jail and subsequently shifted to the Madras Penitentiary, the Bhowali Sanatorium and Lucknow Jail in quick succession. Thus, he was kept far from Bengal. Stringent bureaucratic instructions were issued by the government to the Superintendents of the Bhowali Sanatorium, the

Balaram Hospital in Lucknow and the Madras Penitentiary regarding the treatment of 'state prisoner' Subhas Chandra Bose. Eventually, the government agreed to allow him to travel to Europe for treatment at his own expense. Accordingly, on 13th February 1933, Subhas Bose was carried in an ambulance to the port of Bombay and released from detention only after he was put on board the Italian ship S. S. Gange, sailing for Europe.

In March 1933, Subhas Chandra Bose came to Vienna as a political exile seeking a cure from the illness that had beset him in colonial prison and hoping to promote his country's freedom struggle in Europe. On 11th March, Subhas Bose was admitted to Furth Sanatorium and underwent an X-ray and clinical examination. He had suffered a series of bronchial pneumonia in Mandalay Jail in Burma in 1925 (that was described by him as a 'kingdom of dust' for its adverse climate). Doctors suspected that he might even have contracted tuberculosis from a fellow prisoner. More recently, severe abdominal pain had indicated the possibility of stones in the gallbladder. The medical facilities in Vienna were outstanding. Even though the chest and stomach ailment were not immediately remedied, Bose soon felt rejuvenated after the relief he got from the stresses and strains of being shunted from one jail to another during the previous year.

Despite restrictions imposed on him, Bose soon found ways and means to travel around the European continent as the spoke person for India's freedom. He travelled tirelessly for the next three years, inspiring Indian students studying abroad, establishing associations to promote friendship between India and various European countries and meeting opinion makers and leaders of governments wherever possible to win over their support for Indian independence. His visits to Czechoslovakia and Poland were particularly encouraging, but at the same time, his first visit to Germany was, in contrast, disappointing. On 17th July 1933, he travelled by train from Warsaw to Berlin.

Berlin was a critical diasporic space where Indian revolutionaries had gathered since World War I to strengthen the international dimension of the anti-colonial movement. Bose followed his predecessors' trail and decided to travel to this German metropolis. Now, it had become the capital of the Third Reich, led by Adolf Hitler, who would "rather see India under English rule than under any other". Hitler viewed the British as a superior race. His deep-seated racial prejudices severely influenced his dim view of Indians. Besides, Bose felt there was a distinct possibility of an imperialist collaboration between Germany and Britain for global mastery in the future, which made him very unhappy and disillusioned. [1]

Why did Subhas Chandra Bose come to Berlin in 1941, given that his first visit here in 1933 was disappointing? In 1933, the Italian government offered him hospitality under very favourable conditions and showed readiness to help him carry on his political activities in Europe. During Subhas Bose's stay in Europe, Mussolini received him on several occasions, but Hitler refused to have any conversations with him. Yet, in 1941, Bose preferred to come to Berlin because he was a pragmatist who looked at problems realistically. It appeared vital to him to seek asylum in a country of greater military importance among the Axis Powers. He could have lived more comfortably and had an easy life in Italy. But, from the beginning, he wanted to go to a place where he could find the best possible working opportunities for Indian independence. Perhaps Bose would have gone even to Moscow if the world situation had been different and the Soviet authorities had shown some eagerness to help him with his work when he contacted them in Kabul. [2]

While in Kabul, Bose also discussed his plan for an Indian revolution with Italian ambassador Pietro Quaroni. On 2nd April 1941, the day Bose arrived in Berlin, Quaroni sent a favourable report to Rome on Bose's proposal about India. As a first step, Bose wanted to constitute a Government of Free India in Europe, something along the lines of various free governments that have been constituted in London. Quaroni had asked Bose about the possibilities in the field of terrorism. According to Quaroni's report, Bose had replied that 'the terroristic organisation of Bengal and other similar ones in different parts of India still exist', but he was 'not much convinced of the usefulness of terrorism.' He was, however, prepared to consider sending instructions about 'large-scale sabotage' to impede Britain's war effort. The encounter with Bose had convinced Quaroni about the value of using the 'revolution weapon' with regard to India, the 'cornerstone of the British Empire.'

Just a week later, on 9th April, Bose submitted a detailed memorandum with an explanatory note to the German government setting out the work to be done in Europe, Afghanistan, the Tribal Territory and India. He pointed out that the overthrow of British power in India could, in its last stages, be materially assisted by Japanese policy in the Far East. He wrote with precognition: "A defeat of the British Navy in the Far East, including the smashing up of the Singapore base, will automatically weaken British military strength and prestige in India." Yet he felt that a prior agreement between the Soviet Union and Japan for a settlement with China would pave the way for a settlement with China and free Japan to move confidently against the British in Southeast Asia.

In April 1941, Subhas Chandra Bose met with German foreign minister Joachim von Ribbentrop to discuss his plan for an Indian fighting force against the British. However, Ribbentrop felt it was premature and refused to support Indian independence publicly. Despite initial disappointment, Bose submitted a supplementary memorandum on 3rd May, urging the Axis powers to declare their policy regarding the freedom of India and the Arab countries. He also proposed four possible communication routes between Germany and India, favouring the one through Russia and Afghanistan.

Before implementing any of his plans, Bose demanded that the tripartite powers make an unambiguous and unequivocal declaration recognising Indian independence. In the latter half of May, he wrote up a draft of such a declaration and tried his best to get the German and Italian governments to issue it publicly. The Germans and Italians gave various excuses for delaying it. One reason for this prevarication was that the tripartite powers had tacitly agreed that India was within the Russian sphere of influence, and they could not publicly repudiate that position at this stage.

Bose was on a visit to Rome when he received news that on 22nd June 1941, Germany had invaded the Soviet Union. He was utterly dismayed. The international scenario "looked gloomy." Bose's strategy had been critically dependent on the continuance of the German-Soviet pact. He even indulged in wishful thinking that a rapprochement between Japan and China could be facilitated through Soviet mediation. Hitler's Operation Barbarossa, secretly in works even as Bose passed through Moscow, upset all his plans. [3]

Nonetheless, he gathered a group of dedicated Indians around him in the Free India Centre in Berlin, which began operating in October 1941. He provided leadership to the Indian Legion, a force of several thousand men recruited mostly from POWS captured by the Germans in North Africa. He made his first broadcast to India over Azad Hind Radio, based in Berlin, on 19th February 1942, days after the fall of the British citadel, Singapore, to the Japanese.

Ever since his arrival in Germany, Bose ceaselessly tried to persuade the German, Italian and Japanese Governments to make an official declaration on the question of Indian independence. In this, he always received the support of his German friends. The Special India Division often tried in a big way to make the Government in Berlin agree with Bose's suggestion. Until May 1942, the progress he was able to make in this matter was minimal. In fact, though Mussolini had declared his readiness to issue such a declaration and although the Japanese Prime Minister Tojo had let it be known that Japan would be ready to support a German-Italian declaration to this effect, yet Hiller did not agree to make such a declaration, probably because he did not want the end of British domination in India on racial grounds. As long as Bose was in Germany, the Italian and the Japanese Governments could not act otherwise, for that would have been an act of discourtesy towards the German government. [3]

By the time Subhas Bose could meet Hitler on [3]29th May 1942, the Japanese had swept through Southeast Asia and were poised on the

---

[3] In the original record of Hitler's official interpreter Paul Schmidt, filed with the office of the Foreign Minister, the date of the meeting is given as 27 May, 1942. From other sources via, records of the Supreme Command of the Wehrmacht, 'The Fuehrer's Diary' and the report of German News Bureau (DNB), it is clear that the conference took place on 29 May, 1942.

Burma-India frontier. The Indian National Army (INA) had been formed in Singapore in February 1942, and tens of thousands of Indian POWs taken by the Japanese in Malaya and Singapore had joined. It was clear that Bose's role now lay in East and Southeast Asia and that he must reach there as soon as possible.

The official transcript of the Hitler-Bose meeting in Berlin was initially not made public, according to Paul Schmidt, the interpreter present at the meeting. Mr Schmidt later said in Munich in 1959 that he was very impressed by the dignified manner in which Bose conducted himself during the meeting with Hitler. Subsequently, the transcript of the Hitler-Bose meeting was found in the archives of the Foreign Office of the Federal Republic of Germany (West Germany) and published in the original German in 1970. The Netaji Research Bureau (Kolkata) quickly obtained a microfilm of the transcript, and it was published as an appendix (page 310-315) in English translation in "Netaji and India's Freedom (Sisir K Bose, Ed., 1975), the proceedings of the First International Conference held at Calcutta's Netaji Bhawan in January 1973.

Bose tried to deal as tactfully as possible with Hitler, thanking him for the hospitality he had received since his arrival in Germany almost fourteen months earlier and addressing him as 'an old and experienced revolutionary' from whom he sought 'advice'. There were three substantive points of discussion, and Hitler did most of the speaking.

The first matter was the public declaration of support for India's independence by the Axis Powers, which Netaji had been trying to secure for over a year. He had a few supporters in the German foreign office's special bureau for India, notably Adam von Trott and his deputy, Alexander Werth. There were several drafts of the declaration, the first in May 1941, and an updated version was prepared on 22nd February 1942. As mentioned earlier, in May 1942, the Japanese, as well as Mussolini, were in favour of issuing a joint declaration supporting Indian independence, and Ribbentrop tried hard to

---

As to the place of the meeting, the original record mentions the 'Fuehrer's headquarters' which is also not correct. The meeting took place in the Reich Chancellory in Berlin.

persuade Hitler. But Hitler refused to budge. He told Netaji during their meeting that India was geographically very remote from Germany, and he was not in favour of making 'proclamations' for rhetorical effect, which could not be followed up through military action.

In the meeting, Subhas Bose also brought up the matter concerning the adverse remarks Hitler had made about India and Indians in [4]Mein Kampf and on other occasions, which, Bose said, 'had been greatly distorted by British propaganda and was being used for propaganda against Germany'. Bose 'requested the Fuehrer to say something clarifying Germany's attitude towards India at a suitable opportunity', as 'this would clear things up as far as the Indian nation was concerned'. Hitler was in no mood to oblige and gave a convoluted and evasive response. But it showed something of the grit of Subhas Chandra Bose that he was prepared to raise the matter with the arch-racist.

The other topic was the urgent necessity of Bose's travel to East Asia. Here, Hitler agreed that Subhas Bose should go there as soon as possible and take the help of the Japanese. However, the Fuehrer advised Subhas Bose against an air journey as too dangerous. Instead, he suggested Bose make the journey by submarine and offered to place a German submarine at his disposal. He even showed Subhas the journey route on a map and estimated it would take six weeks (it actually took three months).

However, the departure by submarine took another eight months to materialise, and Netaji finally left the port of Kiel in northern Germany on a U-boat only on 9th February 1943. So when a mass uprising broke out in India in August 1942 in response to the Congress's 'Quit India'

---

[4] "Mein Kampf" (German for "My Struggle") is an autobiographical manifesto written by the leader of the Nazi Party, Adolf Hitler. The book, published in two volumes in 1925 and 1927, outlines Hitler's political ideology and future plans for Germany. It became the bible of National Socialism (Nazism) in Germany's Third Reich. The work is known for its anti-Semitic content and remains controversial today.

call, Netaji was still stuck in Germany, and the INA and the Azad Hind movement in Southeast Asia were somewhat leaderless. Netaji became so impatient with the delay that he wanted to risk going by air, but a planned departure by air from Rome in October 1942 had to be cancelled when it leaked out from the Italian government. [4]

Eventually, when on the morning of 9th February 1943, Subhas Chandra Bose's voyage from Berlin to Tokyo with his aide-de-camp started from the North of Hamburg's Baltic Sea Port Kiel, it was a top-secret project. Notwithstanding the delay and the clandestineness, the mission succeeded beautifully, thanks to the superb teamwork of the German and Japanese navies. In the jet age of the 1970s, a flight from Berlin to Tokyo took hardly twenty hours. For Netaji and his adjutant, the voyage from Germany to Japan was perilous and took more than ninety days. Navy experts from many nations have termed their success as a near miracle. As a matter of fact, it was not repeated for anyone else throughout World War II.

German and Japanese authorities secretly and most carefully studied various transportation possibilities for several months after Japan agreed to receive Subhas Chandra Bose in August 1942. The overland formula was ruled out first. Germany was fighting the Soviet Union on one side and Britain and its allies on the other. Serious consideration was given to the air-lift idea since an Italian plane successfully flew from Turkey to Paotou, Innes Mongolia, about 650 KM west of Peking on 2nd July 1942. After drafting many plans, German authorities ultimately discarded the idea of a transcontinental fight as too risky, given the intensified patrolling activity of Allied fighters over the vast areas which had to be flown over. The only remaining possibility was in the seas - not by surface ships but by submarines.

After long and complicated discussions with the respective Military Attaches at the Italian and Japanese Embassies in Berlin and Rome, the following was agreed upon: Netaji, accompanied by only one friend, should be taken by a German submarine by way of the English Channel, Bay of Biscay, then down the Atlantic Ocean along West Africa to the Indian Ocean below South Afries and finally to the south of Madagascar where he should be transferred to a Japanese submarine. The latter would take him to the nearest Japanese base in East Asia. This plan was successfully carried out, thanks to the joint efforts of Netaji and the Special India Division, the initiative of Conoral Oshima, the Japanese Ambassador in Balin, his Military Attache Mr Yamamoto and other members of Japanese Embassies in Berlin and Rome and the co-operation of competent German military authorities. An interesting anecdote related to this historic journey may be mentioned here: Shortly before Boss's departure, the Japanese Naval Command raised objections because of an internal Japanese regulation not permitting civilians to travel on a warship in wartime. When Adam von Trott received this message by cable from the German Ambassador in Tokyo, he sent the following reply: "Subhas Chancha Bose is by no means a private person but Commander-in-Chief of the Indian Liberation Army." Thus, the bureaucratic interference was overcome.

Transhipment of passengers midway was the final compromise formula agreed upon by the two navies. But, many problems had to be solved before the plan could be implemented. Sabmarine-to-submarine transhipment is an extremely difficult performance at any time, anywhere. Especially in wartime, it is very dangerous since submarines which have surfaced are helpless once spotted and attacked by enemy planes or warships. Both nations classified the whole project as top-secret. Once any information about the plan leaked, all aboard the submarines were doomed. The German Navy deserved to be particularly commended for successfully guarding the secret. The embarkation point was Kiel in northern Germany.

The ciphered go-ahead message from Tokyo reached the embassy in Berlin early in February 1943. The message outlined the dangerous transhipment formula and concluded with none-too-encouraging remarks: "The Ambassador is requested to tell the passengers that they will be travelling at their own risk and unconditionally." Told of the contents, Netaji smiled quietly and said: "That's perfectly all right with me and my aide-de-camp. I am grateful to the two Governments for their extraordinary efforts."

At the beginning of February, Subhas Chandra Bose and one adjutant disappeared from Berlin after telling a few close friends that they would make a one-month trip to Vienna. The two secretly headed to the U-boat base at Kiel. Thus began Netaji's long, perilous voyage aboard a [5]U-boat, probably of Type IX, which could make 18 knots on the surface and 7.3 to 7.7 knots when submerged. Such speeds were almost academic when U-boats operated on high seas, eluding enemy patrol ships and aeroplanes day and night. On 20th April 1943, Japanese submarine I-29, a sister boat identical to I-30, slipped out of Penang, Malaya, on a purportedly routine mission of hunting enemy vessels in the Indian Ocean. Cermin Indian port workers were, however, intrigued to see Captain Masao Teraoka, submarine flotilla commander, going aboard the boat. A Japanese submarine I-29, a sister boat identical to I-30, slipped out of Penang, Malaya, on a purportedly routine mission of hunting enemy vessels in the Indian Ocean. Certain Indian port workers were intrigued to see Captain Masao Teraoka, submarine flotilla commander, going aboard the boat. A Japanese submarine on a lone wolf mission seldom carried a flotilla commander. Soon afterwards, words spread fast among Penang's large Indian community that the boat's cooks had bought a lot of supplies for making Indian meals. The next day, Indian residents were mumming to one another: "Netaji is coming here!" If any capable British spy had heard the rumours and alerted the British navy, it could easily have bagged two birds.

I-29 sped towards the rendezvous point in the Mozambique Channel, a comparatively safe zone near the neutral Portuguese territory. The Japanese submarine reached the position about 400 nautical miles south-south-west of Madagascar on 26th April, more than 10 hours ahead of schedule. Crew members were then told for the first time of the real mission of the sortie. All of them braced themselves up for the forthcoming ordeal. I-20, skippered by Commander Juichi Izu, roamed

---

[5] U-boat is a translation of the German U-boot, which is short for Unterseeboot, or "undersea boat." In other words, a U-boat is a World War I and World War II German submarines.

around the area for several hours until, at last, Izu and his man spotted a small submarine emerging out of the gathering darkness. From the silhouette, they could tell that it was unmistakably a German U-boat. But the dangerous transhipment could not be handled in darkness. All aboard the Japanese boat sweated it out for many hours until the sun rose again. Then they looked around, and their hearts sank. The sea was quite rough. It was out of the question for the two boats to get near and still less tranship passengers. There was no way to discuss matters because the enemy could intercept radio conversation at once. The crew of either boat at wit's end, I-29 began sailing to the northeast while the German U-boat joined the movement alongside. They could not switch off their engines to save fuel because surfaced submarines must be prepared to dive at any moment once spotted by the enemy.

The bizarre twin-formation manoeuvre of two surfaced submarines went on for several hours. "It was like an eternity for all aboard the two boats", said Captain Teraoka, who survived the war. It was a miracle that no enemy planes came swooping down to the easy targets for so many horns. "Or perhaps they saw us but refused to take us to be enemy boats, Teraoka added, "because our manoeuvre was so fantastically naive and audacious."

The sun was setting again. Japanese officers on the surfaced deck spluttered, "Oh, No!" when they saw two men jumping overboard from the German U-boat and swimming energetically toward the Japanese. When they got near, Japanese sailors threw ropes and hauled up the two dare-devil swimmers. They were Germans — one officer and one signalman. The officer told the Japanese that the U-boat with low fuel could not continue the voyage in that fashion. Teraoka replied that he was waiting for the rough waves to subside. The German officer heaved a sigh of relief, and the signalman began sending messages with his hands.

The two submarines continued the north-easterly voyage for another 12 hours or so, and the 28th of April dawned on the horizon. Waves were still high, but neither the Japanese nor the Germans were inclined to hold on to the dangerous surfaced operation any longer. The decision was made. The two Germans rode a rubber raft, dragging a strong Manila Hemp Rope back to their boat. Then Netaji and his adjutant rode the raft and clung to the rope, inching their way amid kicking waves and lurking sharks. Both drenched to the skin, Netaji and his aide climbed onto the Japanese submarine at last. Captain Teraoka and Commander Izu personally and very warmly welcomed them aboard. The indomitable Indian leader stammered thanks as he was ushered into the narrow vessel. The German U-boat turned round and went away while Japanese officers and men waved them "auf wiedersehen (goodbye)."

Throughout the entire annals of World War II, this was the only known submarine-to-submarine transfer of passengers in an area dominated by enemy air and naval strength. One other rare transhipment success was scored by the Japanese submarine 1-8 to the south of the Azores in the Atlantic from a German U-boat. In this case, however, a radar and not passengers were transhipped. Incidentally, 1-8, which left Penang on 6th July 1943, became the lone submarine that safely returned to Japan in late December 1943. From the German side, one U-boat, IXC, reached Japan as a gift to the Japanese government that year, but no German U-boat made a return trip of the 30,000-nautical mile voyage.

A day after the transfer, on 29 April 1943, the crew of I-29 held a double-count celebration party- welcoming the Indian guests aboard and observing the Japanese Emperor's birthday. At the party, some sake (rice wine) was even served. The boat's cooks did their utmost to prepare Indian meals with materials acquired at Penang. The Indian guests showed no fatigue after their long, gruelling, and often hair-raising 'voyage from Europe and, at the special dinner, chatted cheerfully with the Japanese hosts.

On 30 April, the ship embarked on a monotonous return trip with four meals a day, the wartime standard of the Japanese Navy. The flotilla commander's cabin was vacated for Netaji. The Indian leader tried to take exercise by moving around the narrow interior of the submarine, but that was not enough to build up an appetite. From the third day, he quipped with a shy grin when the chow arrived, "Do we have to eat again, Captain Teraoka?"

After the submarine had left the British patrolling radius, it picked up a radio message from Ponang for the first time. It instructed the ship to divest and land the passengers at Sabang, an isolated offshore islet north of Sumatra, because of the widespread rumours that accurately told of Netaji's arrival. I-29 reached Sabang on 6 May 1943. Shortly before disembarkation, a photograph of the passengers with the crew on the surfaced deck was taken. To a print Netaji autographed, he added this note in his own hand:

> It was a great pleasure to sail aboard this submarine. I am deeply grateful to the Japanese Imperial Government for having made it possible. The Captain has always treated me and my aide-de-camp so nicely that we felt quite at home during the voyage. I hereby express my sincere thanks for the kindness shown us by all the crew members from Captain Downwards. The voyage aboard this ship will evoke pleasant memories for the rest of my life. This will mark a milestone in our fight for victory and peace.

As I-20 readied itself for its final leg of the voyage back to its base at Penang, Netaji shook hands with Teraoka, Izu and practically all 100 crew members, wishing them continued victories in the fight. Netaji did not know that he was looking at many of them, including Commander Izu, for the [6]last time. [5]

The aide-de-camp or the officer acting as a confidential assistant to Netaji Subhas Chandra Bose in his voyage from Berlin to Tokyo in the top-secret project was Abid Hasan (1911-1984) - one of Netaji's closest associates from 1941 to 1945. He joined Netaji's struggle in May 1941, a month after Netaji had arrived in Berlin following his historic escape

---

[6] Commander Izu was soon transferred as skipper of I-11, which was reported missing in the Central Pacific in January 1944. I-29 with a new skipper, left Penang again in November 1943, reached Brest, France, and returned to Penang. But it was sunk by an American submarine near the Philippines on 26th July 1944 on its way to Japan. Only Teraoka and a few others survived the war.

from India. Hasan was one of the first civilians to enlist in the Indian Legion, a military force drawn mainly from Indian prisoners of war taken by the Germans in North Africa. During Netaji's epic submarine voyage over three months from Europe to East Asia between February and May of 1943, Abid Hasan was his sole Indian companion. He was with his leader in Tokyo, Singapore, Rangoon, Nanking and Shanghai in Asia, almost like a shadow. In 1944, Abid Hasan fought with distinction on the Imphal front as an officer of the Indian National Army. On 17th August 1945, a handful of senior INA officers and ministers of the Provisional Government of Free India saw Netaji off at Saigon airport on his last journey. Abid Hasan was one of them. Thus, Abid Hasan was a unique source of information on Netaji's struggle to liberate India from 1941 to 1945. The following paragraphs on Abid Hasan's submarine voyage from Berlin to Tokyo as Bose's aide-de-camp are a synoptic outline taken from the tape-recorded interview author Krishna Bose conducted with him in Calcutta in 1976 that has been noted in her book "Netaji Subhas Chandra Bose's Life, Politics, & Struggle." It provides a little bit of an idea of the inside scenes, challenges, and hardship of the 90-day constricted submarine journey the two guests had to negotiate and how best they put to use their free time on the long trip.

As mentioned earlier, Subhas Chandra Bose's voyage from Berlin to Tokyo was such a top-secret project that until the last moment, even his aide-de-camp on the trip, Abid Hasan, was unaware that he was to accompany his leader for 90 days in a submarine. So, when on the morning of 9th February 1943, in the North of Hamburg's Baltic Sea Port Kiel, he entered the cramped and claustrophobic submarine, his heart sank. The submarine was one of the legendary German U-boats of World War II. Netaji's craft, numbered U-180, was commissioned into the German Navy in May 1942. Its commander during Netaji's journey was Werner Musenberg. U-180 was sunk in August 1944 while operating under a different commander in the Bay of Biscay in the Atlantic, and all its fifty-six crewmen perished. Of course, Subhas Bose had told Hasan beforehand that the task he was chosen for did not involve fighting as such but would be extremely dangerous and asked Abid if he was ready to take it on, to which Abid Hasan had consented.

The fearful, constricted submarine had a long, narrow passage with sleeping bunks against the walls. The bunk allotted to Netaji was in a small alcove, but all the other bunks were in the corridor, with no privacy at all. There was hardly any space to move around, and Hasan realised he would have to either lie on his bunk or stand in the passage during the journey. There was only one sitting small table where six could sit if they sat very close together. Meals were usually taken at the table, but sometimes they also ate sitting on their bunks. As soon as Abid Hasan entered the submarine, the stench of diesel hit his nostrils and made him nauseous. The whole craft, even the blanket on Hasan's bunk, reeked with the smell. The pungent smell was everywhere, even in the food they ate. Abid Hasan's excitement evaporated as he realized that he would have to spend three months in these surroundings and conditions.

On the very first day, Abid Hasan noticed at the 'dining' table that Netaji was eating hardly anything. He could tell why. There was plenty of food, but the military rations for frontline combatants consisted of thick bread, tough meat, and tinned vegetables, which looked and tasted like gum. Abid became concerned. How would Netaji survive on this diet for three months? He also felt annoyed that Netaji had kept the round-the-world submarine voyage secret until the departure from Berlin. Had he known even a little in advance, he could easily have acquired provisions for the journey, both foodstuffs and spices with which to cook. But now it was too late, so he would have to improvise.

Abid Hasan raided the U-boat's larder. There, he found a packet of rice and a packet of lentils, which he promptly appropriated. There was also a large tin of egg powder. Abid considered taking this, too, but then thought it might look selfish. Nonetheless, the egg powder provided omelettes for breakfast for the next few weeks. For the other meals, Abid relied on the precious packets of rice and lentils. He cooked khichuri (the rice-lentil mix popular in Bengal) for Subhas Bose. Netaji was pleased to see khichuri on the table. He immediately called the German officers and offered them a share of the Indian dish. Abid Hasan was aghast. He was determined to preserve the rice and lentils for Netaji's consumption, and if other people started eating khichuri, the supply would run out in days. But he could not bring himself to tell Netaji this. So he discreetly spoke to the officers instead. It turned out that the Germans did not particularly like the rice-lentil concoction anyway but had thought it impolite to decline Netaji's offer. From then on, Abid Hasan sparingly used rice and lentils for Netaji's meals – sometimes Khichuri and sometimes the traditional Bengali daal-bhaat (rice with lentil gravy). Abid Hasan's limited cooking abilities came in very useful as the U-180 traversed seas and oceans for the next three months.

When the U-180 left Kiel, it was part of a small convoy of U-boats. The lead submarine was a minesweeper whose task was to detect and detonate mines scattered on the surface of the sea by the enemy. For some distance beyond Kiel, the Germans had full dominance of the sea, and the U-boat convoy was able to travel above water some of the time. They travelled along the Danish coastline. Sweden was next, and it was a neutral country so caution had to be exercised in Swedish waters. The Norwegian coastline came next. Close to Kristiansand, on Norway's south coast, the convoy broke up and the U-boats went off in different directions; the minesweeper too departed. From that point, the U-180, with Subhas Chandra Bose and Abid Hasan on board, commenced its solitary journey.

The submarine moved into the deep waters of the North Sea. This was a dangerous area, lying between Scotland and Iceland. The British air force bombed this area almost constantly, using depth charges. Indeed, incessant 'boom- boom sounds were clearly audible as the U-boat glided underwater through the North Sea towards the Atlantic Ocean.

Abid Hasan soon got used to the submarine's day-night routine. During the day, the submarine travelled underwater. At night, it would surface. Modern submarines can remain submerged underwater for days on end. But their World War II submarine ran on diesel and used battery power for its equipment. So, every night, it needed to surface to charge the batteries. Just before dawn broke on the eastern sky, it would disappear under the water.

When the submarine surfaced at night, its captain, Werner Musenberg, would often ask Netaji and Abid Hasan to come and sit on the bridge (roof). It was a relief from being cooped up inside during the day and a chance to stretch out a bit. On hitting the Atlantic, the submarine went northward, in the direction of Greenland. For a while, it seemed to Hasan that they were on an expedition to the North Pole! The detour was necessary to reduce the risk of being spotted and attacked from the air. But the circuitous route brought magnificent vistas with it. When they surfaced, they could see striking ice formations on the sea. A wonderful sight, Abid Hasan recalls.

Then the submarine gradually turned south and approached the coastline of France. Near the Cherbourg peninsula, which juts out of the Normandy coastline, a 'U-tanker', also known as a]'mothership' among sailors, approached their submarine. The U-tanker was a submarine used for refuelling U-boats at sea. The U-tanker supplied Netaji's vessel with the diesel required for the long trans-oceanic journey that lay ahead.

Netaji gave the crew of the U-tanker some important documents for delivery to the Free India Centre in Berlin. There were some letters, but the most important was the revised manuscript of his book, The Indian Struggle. Netaji had been working on the revisions on the submarine and had completed them by the time of the rendezvous near Cherbourg.

On the second day of the submarine journey, Abid Hsan was ruing to himself that he had not brought along some books to read, to pass the time and relieve the tedium of the long voyage that lay ahead. Had he known what he was getting into even a little in advance, he would have made sure to do so. Suddenly, Netaji said to him: 'Hasan, tum to typewriter le liya, na? (Hasan, you have brought the typewriter, haven't you?)

Indeed, Hasan had brought his typewriter. That was the beginning of almost incessant work until they arrived in Sumatra three months later. The work kept both men occupied and enabled them to cope with life on the submarine. Otherwise, the claustrophobic environment would have been unbearable. There was no space to walk around or even exercise properly. And, of course, there was no daylight - it felt like one continuous night on the submarine, with the lights on all the time.

First, The Indian Struggle was revised. Then, Netaji started meticulously planning his activities on arrival in East Asia. He began to dictate the speeches he would give. Netaji's habit was to write out his speeches in advance. But - except on very formal occasions and for radio broadcasts – he would always speak without any text or notes. People did not realise that the extemporaneous speeches had, in fact, been prepared in advance in 'homework' style, with all the major points written out. Before the event, Netaji would study that carefully and then tear up the sheets and throw them away. Abid Hasan said, 'my heart used to bleed' when Netaji threw away the sheets he had typed out.

Apart from the speeches, there were other preparations. Netaji started planning how he would interact and negotiate with the Japanese government and its officials. He even asked Abid Hasan to play the role of Hideki Tojo, Japan's Prime Minister. He asked Abid to assume Tojo's role and ask him pointed questions about his plans and intentions.

The breaks from work came when the submarine surfaced at night. When they sat on the bridge amid the vast, dark oceans, Netaji would be in an informal, talkative mood, and they would chat. During these chats, Abid Hasan would sometimes ask Netaji questions. On one occasion, he asked Netaji what he found most difficult about public life. Netaji replied: 'Chhote chhote logoko khoshamad karna (having to flatter the vanity of small people).' Another time, he asked Netaji what his most painful experience in life had been. Netaji replied without a moment's hesitation: To be in exile,' away from India. Sitting on the submarine's bridge that night, Abid Hasan felt this remark had a particular poignancy.

There were two remarkable moments Abid Hasan recalled from the journey in the German submarine. On one occasion, their U-boat spotted and torpedoed a British oil tanker. It was quite a sight - it was as if the sea was ablaze as the flames engulfed the ship. They could see that there were some crew aboard the burning ship who looked Indian and possibly Malaysian. These brown-skins were left to their fate, while a large lifeboat that was launched was packed with white men.

The other incident was even more memorable. Commander Musenberg spotted a British warship through his periscope and ordered his crew to torpedo it. As the torpedoes were being readied, a sailor made a mistake with some equipment, and the U-boat rose up and surfaced! The British ship came charging towards the U-boat. Musenberg frantically called out, 'Dive! Dive!' and the U-boat barely managed to disappear underwater and get away, but not before the ship rammed the railing on its bridge (the roof/ deck), and it keeled over partially.

Abid Hasan was frozen with fear when he suddenly heard Netaji's calm voice, in a tone of mild reprimand: Hasan, I just repeated the same point twice.' Netaji had been dictating the draft of the speech he planned to deliver to the soldiers of the Rani of Jhansi Regiment, the INA Women's regiment he intended to form upon arriving in Singapore. With shaking hands, Abid Hasan resumed taking notes. Once the danger was past, Musenberg gathered the crew and told them that their distinguished Indian guest and his companion had set an example of how to remain calm in dire danger. Abid Hasan knew that was in fact true only of Netaji, while he himself had been terrified.

Netaji's submarine skirted the long western coastline of Africa. On the day they crossed the equator, there was a small party on the submarine. This 'baptism' celebration was a longstanding tradition of seafarers. Netaji and Abid took part in the ritual, which involved dousing each other with water.

In the last week of April, the U-180 approached the island of Madagascar in the Indian Ocean. The seas around Madagascar were relatively unaffected by the maritime hostilities of the war, so the area had been chosen for the U-180 to rendezvous with a Japanese submarine which would carry Netaji to East Asia. Netaji would be transferred from the German U-boat to the Japanese submarine. That mid-ocean transfer was, in Abid Hasan's words, 'a very fascinating experience'.

On 26 April 1943, the two submarines approached each other. First, the German submarine raised its periscope above the water, and then the Japanese submarine did the same. Then, the two submarines surfaced at the same time. But the seas were extremely choppy, which made the transfer very difficult. Buffeted by the waves, the two submarines could not come close enough to each other for Netaji to cross from the deck of the one to the other on a plank, as planned. It was decided to wait for the sea to calm down, but on 27th April, it was just as turbulent. The transfer could not be delayed any longer. Finally, just before daybreak on 28th April, a rubber dinghy was lowered from the German submarine into the Indian Ocean's waters. Netaji said his thanks and goodbyes to the crew of the U-boat and got into the rubber dinghy, and sat down, followed by Abid Hasan. The dinghy swayed crazily in the choppy sea, and the waves cascaded on it, completely drenching Netaji. They could see the crew of both submarines assembled on the roofs of their respective craft, watching with anxious faces. After some effort, the dinghy was pulled towards the Japanese submarine. A minute later, Subhas Chandra Bose and Abid Hasan stepped on the roof of the Japanese submarine.

After the rather hair-raising transfer, Netaji and Abid Hasan quickly settled in as passengers on the Japanese submarine, designated as I-29 in Japan's navy. Abid Hasan discovered, to his delight that, unlike the German U-180, the I-29 was a spacious craft. It was not cramped, and the claustrophobic feel was absent. There was even a good-sized lounge, just about enough to accommodate two dozen or so people. The day after they boarded, the Japanese Emperor's birthday was celebrated on the submarine.

Although he had spent several years in Germany, Abid Hasan felt more at home in the company of the Japanese submariners compared to the Germans. The crew of U-180 had been nothing but cordial, but somehow, the atmosphere on the Japanese submarine was different, and Abid Hasan sensed a touch of human warmth. He thinks that the tradition of Asian hospitality, which he knew so well, may have been a factor. To top it off, the food served on the Japanese submarine was excellent!

Netaji and Abid had experienced two encounters with enemy ships on the German U-boat. That was because the U-boat's commander and crew were under orders to attack enemy vessels they came across during the journey. By contrast, the [7]I-29's commander and crew were under strict orders not to get involved in any hostilities- their task was simply to transport Subhas Chandra Bose speedily and safely to East Asia. The journey passed without incident. The only difficulty, Hasan recalls, was the language barrier. Both Netaji and he were proficient in German, but they had no clue about the Japanese language, and there was no translator on board. But they coped with this minor problem.

On 6th May 1943, the I-29 arrived at the north-westernmost point of Indonesia, Sabang, an island just off the northern coast of Sumatra. As they stepped off the submarine, Subhas Chandra Bose and his aide-de-camp, Abid Hasan, were greeted by a familiar face - Colonel Yamamoto, who had been the military attache in Japan's Berlin embassy and had now been assigned to head Hikari Kikan, the Japanese intelligence and liaison organization responsible for coordination and relations with the Azad Hind movement and the INA. Yamamoto was accompanied by another official, Mr M. Senda, as well as by a translator, 'Sasaki.' Mr Sasaki came to Calcutta a few years ago, accompanying General Fujiwara Iwaichi, who, as a Major in the Japanese army and its military intelligence wing, had been principally responsible for launching the Indian National Army in Singapore in February 1942.

Stepping out of the submarine, Abid Hasan felt as if he was released from jail after finishing his term of confinement, with a short-lived

---

[7] The I-29's name was Matsu', the Japanese word for a pine tree. It was commissioned in the Japanese Navy in February 1942. The mission to collect Netaji southeast of Madagascar and bring him to East Asia was personally commanded by Masao Teraoka, the commander of Japan's submarine fleet. The I-29 was sunk off the Philippines in July 1944 in a combined attack by three American submarines. All but one of its 101 crewmen perished.

feeling of exhaustion after the round-the-world voyage by submarine. Netaji, however, showed no sign of fatigue and immediately started to discuss his plans with Yamamoto and Senda. [6]

Nevertheless, Bose and Hasan were taken to quarters arranged by the Navy and advised complete rest before departing for Tokyo again. "No, sir, I am not tired at all", Netaji mildly protested. "I am ready to leave any moment." His hosts smiled and bowed without saying anything more. Japan had to withdraw from Guadalcanal in the Central Pacific in February of that year, losing one bastion after another in the southern region. Making even one aeroplane available for important guests was demanding.

Five days later, a plane came to Sabang to pick them up. It was a short-range combat plane that landed at numerous places for refuelling. It had a one-night stop-over each at Penang, Saigon, Manila, Tapel, and Hamamatsu before reaching Tokyo on 16th May 1943. The guests were taken immediately to the Imperial Hotel near the Imperial Palace and the Prime Minister's office. All through the trip, the identities of Netaji and his adjutant were kept secret for security reasons. Bose was supposed to be a Japanese VIP named Matsuda. [7]

* * * * * * *

Chapter 5

The Born Revolutionary

Rash Behari

Nearly 28 years before Subhas Chandra Bose reached the capital of Japan on 16th May 1943, undergoing a 90-day perilous submarine journey from Germany, another radical revolutionary from Bengal, Rash Behari Bose, had set foot on the shores of Japan on 5th June 1915. He remained an uncompromising challenger of British alien rule in India until he died in Japan in 1945 – the same year Netaji Subhas disappeared. The mighty British could never arrest Rash Behari despite their unrelenting pursuit. All the resources of the British bureaucracy were pressed into service to put him behind bars, including a reward offered for his arrest, and his photographs circulated widely. Still, all these attempts came to nought in the long run.

More than sharing their last name, Bose, the two firebrand patriots, Rash Behari and Subhas, were obsessed with dreams of freeing their beloved Motherland, India, from the clutches of the alien British rule. Both recorded legendary escapes from British India, successfully deceiving their elaborate intelligence network by using fake identities to reach Japan. Rash Behari as Preo Nath Tagore, a distant relative and emissary of poet Rabindra Nath Tagore and Subhas Chandra Bose as a Japanese VIP named Matsuda. Their audacity extended beyond these aliases, exhibiting several other remarkable similarities in their deeds.

Rash Behari Bose and Subhas Chandra Bose had identical visions of freedom and a remarkable idea of achieving the independence of India, snatching it from the mighty British. Both realised that the backbone of British rule in India was their military might, the significant parts of which consisted of Indian soldiers that facilitated a numerically negligible number of British officers in India to dominate zillions of Indian people of the sub-continent for over a hundred years. It occurred to both Rash Behari and Subhas severally that if a mass revolt by the Indian soldiers against British rule could somehow be engineered, ousting the British from the country and gaining India's independence from the exploitative alien rule would not be as difficult a task as it seemed otherwise. In fact, the two of them, in their own way, actually worked in that direction at various levels and at different times. Their tireless efforts converged in their friendship with Japan, and they played pivotal roles in shaping the Indian National Army (INA), the Azad Hind Fauz, that was floated to free India from British colonial rule.

Interestingly, in the early days, too, Rash Behari Bose was a student with a radical mindset, and so was Subhas Chandra Bose. Similar to the Oaten incident, Rash Behari had a share of confrontation with his British teacher Howard Rothman at [8]Chandernagore Dupleix College as a student of the Second Class (Class 9) in 1902 that steered the course of his life away from school altogether.

On the fateful day, after the school hours were over, students from all the classrooms were preparing to leave as they were hurrying down the staircase. Three British teachers employed at Dupleix College at that time were standing near the corridor and overheard the boys' conversation. Among these three, Howard Rothman was reportedly the most notorious. Rothman intercepted Rash Behari and his friend Shrish and said sternly, 'I believe that you two gentlemen have a serious grudge against the British teachers. Alright, then speak up.'

Rash Behari came forward and said calmly, 'Sir, we don't have a grudge against the British. We simply don't support your colonial rule that is forcibly imposed on this country and on her people. Moreover, this is

---

[8] Chandannagar (Bengali: চন্দননগর Candannagar, French: Chandernagor), formerly Chandernagore.

my personal conviction. None of my companions have any opinion on this.'

While the other students gathered around them, Rothman came closer to Rash Behari and shouted, "This country was always destined to be ruled and will remain so in future as well. That is why Bakhtiyar Khilji was able to conquer Bengal with just seventeen cavalrymen. You must feel blessed that the British have chosen to rule you. That is the reason why you fools are getting a good education.'

Rash Behari could not control himself further. He shouted back, "That is a wrong statement, Mr Rothman. The vile Bakhtiyar Khilji had many more men behind him... your knowledge of history is incomplete. Mother India and her children are not cowards. One day, we will prove that to the entire world and overthrow the colonial rule.' Rash Behari then stormed out of the premises of the school,

The next day began within the closed chamber of the Principal of Dupleix College. In front of a small assemblage of teachers, Rothman pointed at Rash Behari and screamed, "This boy has the audacity of confronting the teachers with contempt. He dared to insult me in front of the entire school. His mindset dwells upon radical nationalism. He does not have the right to study at Dupleix College. He must be expelled from here before he corrupts the minds of other students.'

The teachers gathered in that room nodded in agreement. None of them dared to oppose Rothman's opinion. He was British, and speaking against him was considered taboo. Thus, silence prevailed. The Principal of Dupleix College was like a puppet who dared not say a word against Rothman even though this school was in French Chandannagar, beyond the administrative control of British India.

Rash Behari replied in a furious tone, 'I reject the allegations. It is Mr Rothman who inflicts heinous abuse upon Indians. I had simply put forth my objection. Yes, I did because I am proud of my birth and ethnicity as a son of Mother India. Moreover, I won't allow you an opportunity of expelling me. Before that, I am leaving on my own,' and the angry young man strode out.'

As the door of the Principal's room was flung open, Rash Behari walked out with a conqueror's stride. Students of the entire Dupleix College witnessed the final departure of Rash Behari Bose from the school. Standing by the corridor, his buddy, Shrish Ghosh, silently wiped away his own tears and whispered to himself, 'One day, his strides will jolt the entire colonial Raj.' That was the last day for Rash Behari at Dupleix College. The school etiquette had been breached, and Rash Behari's name was permanently removed from the school's rolls.

At home, Rash Behari's father, Binod Behari Bose, was furious. The news struck him like a thunderbolt, and he sat speechless for some time. Then, he said in a grim voice, 'Rasu, my boy, your desperate views and your growing inclination towards revolutionary activities is making me feel scared and worried. I was never so afraid in my entire life. I feel apprehensive about your future.'

Rash Behari sat down beside his father. There were tears in both their eyes. He understood that his rebellious behaviour was causing pain to his father. He touched his father's hands lightly and said softly, 'Baba, I cannot restrain myself when someone abuses my motherland. The behaviour of these British teachers at Dupleix College had crossed the threshold of my tolerance. Please forgive me for whatever happened. It was beyond my patience. However, I promise you that I will obey whatever you tell me to do.'

Binod Behari hugged his son lovingly and said, 'Rasu, on Saturday, I will take you to Kolkata. From now onwards you will stay in Kolkata, at my cousin's house. I will use my influence and get you enrolled in the Morton School. You must complete your studies from there.'

The decision was a painful one for Rash Behari Bose. The life of a revolutionary is never painted in the hues of stability. A revolutionary is like a vagabond who roams around the world to create his vision of freedom, and he remains a nomad. Rash Behari did not know that his life as a nomad had already been written in his stars.

Although revolutionary stories from his grandfather and teacher kindled nationalistic passion in him in the early days, interestingly, it was the same Dupleix College where Rash Behari Bose earlier got immense inspiration and limpid vision on revolution from none other than the College Principal Charu Chandra Roy, who said, "Revolution is not defined by just opposing something with sheer repulsion. It is not about stubbornly resisting. Neither is it about doing outrageous acts without a proper focus. The life of a revolutionary is extraordinary, and it needs astonishing skills." On that occasion, Rash Behari looked at Charu Chandra with utmost attentiveness while the guru spoke,

> 'A revolutionary must take tremendous strides but must protect himself from being crumbled by the opponent. He must be a master of disguise, a commander of mass conviction and a person who can accomplish a mammoth rebellion. Yes, he must do that. However, the rebellion must rise like a wildfire and consume the entire woodland. Even though a wildfire often mellows and is contained by mankind, the human mind grapples with the impact it leaves behind. The aftermath of a revolution must be like that of a wildfire. Even though the revolution might not be able to accomplish its target, its jolt must unnerve the opponent with its sheer strength.'

Charu Chandra's words were like arrows piercing his heart. The rush of adrenaline brought with it visions of great adventure and excitement.

Renowned Bengali novelist Bankim Chandra Chattopadhyay's "Ananda Math" and the fiery speeches of Rashtraguru Sir Surendranath Banerjee and Swami Vivekananda acted as a further catalyst to his radical patriotic thought. Charu Chandra Roy introduced him to the revolutionary wing of the [9]Anushilan Samiti, of which Jugantar was the wing that was active in Calcutta.

---

[9] Anushilan Samiti means "Self-Culture Association". Inspired by the thoughts, speeches and writing of **Swami Vivekananda** and influenced by **Bankim Chandra Chatterjee's** *'Anandmath'*, the concept was formulated with its roots in **Sashakta Hinduism**. Their main aim was to create an urge amongst the Hindus to become vigorous spiritually,

After Rash Behari's name was permanently removed from Dupleix College over the Rothman incident, his father, Binod Behari, arranged for his enrolment at the Morton School in Calcutta. But no sooner had Rash Behari restarted his routine student life in the high school than he found himself increasingly engrossed in the work of the Anushilian Samiti and its fledgling wing, Jugantar. Rash Behari tried to focus on the school curriculum, but his young mind was bubbling with zeal, and he felt that whatever was being fed to him as a student was irrelevant to him or unrelated to the need of the hour. Eventually, he left school and went back to Chandannagar.

Rash Behari then made unsuccessful attempts to join the Indian Army. Later on, according to his father's wish, he joined the Government Press in Shimla for a brief period, was appointed as a copyholder, and then attended the Pasteur Institute in Kasauli. At last, upon the advice of a close acquaintance, Rash Behari Bose went to Dehradun in 1906 and began work as a guardian tutor in the house of Prafulla Nath Tagore. At the same time, he managed to get employed as a clerk under Sardar Puran Singh, in charge of the Chemistry Department at the Forest Research Institute, where he soon mastered the careful art of mixing chemicals under the Sardar. Over the years, Rash Behari, with utmost dexterity, immersed himself in the lethal art of making explosives. Grasping the dangerous ingredients and mixing them in the right quantities, Rash Behari Bose became an expert in the art of making country bombs, an essential part of a militant freedom fighter's arsenal. By then, he also became a master of disguise, which played a crucial role in his revolutionary activities against the British Empire. His ability to disguise himself helped him escape the authorities multiple times. While at Dehradun, he secretly got involved with the revolutionaries of Bengal through Amarendra Chatterjee of the

---

physically and intellectually. As a result, unnumbered youth clubs denominated as Anushilan Samiti were formed. By 1902, it turned into a conglomeration of local youth groups and gyms (akhara) in Bengal that was actually used as an underground society for anti-British revolutionaries. In the first quarter of the 20th century, it supported revolutionary violence as the means for ending British rule in India. It challenged British rule in India by engaging in militant nationalism, including bombings, assassinations, and politically motivated violence. It had two branches: the Jugantar Group in Calcutta and the Dhaka Anushilan Samiti in Dhaka.

Jugantar. Subsequently, he also came across revolutionaries of the Arya Samaj in the United Provinces (currently Uttar Pradesh) and the Punjab. [1]

On 23rd December 1912, a significant event unfolded in Delhi, the new capital of India. Lord Hardinge, the British Viceroy of India, was making his grand entry on the back of an elephant during the transfer ceremony of the capital of British India from Calcutta to New Delhi when a homemade bomb was thrown into the Viceroy's howdah as the ceremonial procession was moving through the Chandni Chowk suburb of Delhi. The bomb, intended to assassinate Hardinge, instead resulted in him being injured by shrapnel and led to the unfortunate death of his attendant.

Although the attack did not succeed in its primary objective of killing the British Viceroy of India, it served different purposes. It dented the British pride and sent a powerful message to the world that there were Indians who were ready to resort to force to drive out the British colonisers. It marked a pivotal moment in the fight against colonial rule and the beginning of the daring revolutionary activities of one of the greatest Indian patriots, Rash Behari Bose, the mascot of the armed struggle to free India from British colonial rule.

Hardinge's assassination attempt was condemned by media outlets around the world, even attracting criticism in the Christmas greeting of Pope Pius X. Investigation into the attack became the top priority of British intelligence services in India, who, in the absence of reliable information, were willing to consider increasingly farfetched tactics for uncovering information on Hardinge's attackers such as offering a free pardon to co-conspirators in the bomb plot and importing detectives from Scotland Yard to assist in the investigation. Despite the offer of a reward of a hundred thousand rupees, the identity of the attacker remained a mystery until much later information surfaced in connection with a separate conspiracy case, revealing that the man who had thrown the bomb was a Bengali revolutionary named Rash Behari Bose.

Rash Behari Bose's assassination attempt against Hardinge was not an isolated incident. It was against the backdrop of a broader Indian revolutionary movement that played a significant role in shaping anticolonial politics during the early twentieth century. Primarily, it was the British plan to partition Bengal in 1905 that gave broader impetus to the development of networks and organisations that adopted assassination and intimidation as explicit tactics of anti-colonialism. While British officials claimed that the partition of the Bengal province was simply an administrative necessity, coming on the heels of carving out of the Assam Division and three districts, Sylhet, Cachar and Goalpapra, from the Bengal Presidency and creating a new Bengali majority Province with the name Assam in 1874, was widely seen as an attempt to fragmentise Bengal and divide the Bengali community along racial and religious lines to undermine the authority of the Bengali political class centred in British India's capital, Calcutta. The decision to partition Bengal for the second time in 1905, after the 1874 break-up for the first time, sparked a storm of protest throughout Bengal, manifested in both the nonviolent Swadeshi movement, which sought to undermine British rule through economic boycott and mass agitation, and organisations that sought to disrupt colonial authority through the targeted murders of British officials and members of the colonial information order.

Although these revolutionary organisations first developed in Bengal, they quickly spread to other parts of India and soon became transnational in their ambitions and areas of operations. The most significant of these organisations was Ghadar, a network of Indian anticolonial radicals based out of California, which reached a global membership of eight thousand at its height. Founded in 1913 by Har Dayal, a radical political thinker and anti-imperialist, the Ghadar party expanded during the First World War into a global network that sought to destabilise the British Empire through the transnational circulation of arms, ideas, and revolutionaries. Ghadar's global reach stirred imperial anxieties during the war, stimulating the rapid growth of Britain's imperial intelligence services as officials desperately sought to keep up with revolutionary activities. It is within this context that Rash Behari Bose became one of the leading figures in a plot that had as its goal nothing less than an all-India uprising, in the line of the Indian

Rebellion of 1857, which the British administration tried to play down by naming it as the [10]Sepoy Mutiny. [2]

After the assassination attempt on British Viceroy Lord Hardinge, the next highly notable overt act was the Lahore Bomb outrage on 17th May 1913, believed to have taken place under the inspiration of Rash Behari Bose. The target of the bomb was the Assistant Commissioner of Punjab, Mr Gordon, under whose orders the police raid on the Ashram of Swami Dayananda was conducted in 1912, killing Mahendra Nath De, the ex-head Master of the Habiganj National School, while Gordon was the Sub-Divisional Officer of Sylhet District in Bengal. Unfortunately, instead of killing the target, Gordon, the explosion eventually caused the death of an innocent chaprasi (Peon). This attempted act of revenge was part of a larger series of revolutionary activities against British rule, and it was often clubbed together with the assassination attempt against Hardinge and conjointly referred to as the Delhi-Lahore Conspiracy, for which a Special Tribunal held the trial constituted under the Defence of India Act 1915. The two narrowly missed attempts severely dented the prestige of the British Raj in India, and there was a deep sense of outrage in the colonial government. Eventually, out of a total of 291 convicted conspirators in the Delhi-Lahore Conspiracy, 42 were executed, 114 got life sentences, and 93 got varying terms of imprisonment. Forty-two defendants in the trial were acquitted. [4]

Meanwhile, the mastermind behind the two attacks, Rash Behari Bose, continued his peaceful life in Dehradun and did everything possible to safeguard his alibi and remain in the good books of the intelligence services. He took great precautions to keep a low profile and not draw the slightest attention from the intelligence services while, all around,

---

[10] The word mutiny implicitly implies that the British monarchy had the right to rule over India and that there was just one small group of Indians who objected to this and launched a rebellion. This was by no means the case. The uprising was a heroic battle in which vast numbers of Indians in various places throughout India shed their own blood in their struggle to expel the British East India Company from their land. [3]

his revolutionary friends were being arrested, prosecuted and punished. Later, finding an opportune moment, Rash Behari again started commuting between his hometown Chandannagore and work station Dehradun, often taking a detour here and there to keep in touch with his comrades in arms.

By the beginning of 1914, the police had gathered some incriminating evidence against Rash Behari Bose. Anticipating arrests, Rash Behari quietly bid farewell to Dehradun and arrived at Chandannagore to remain underground within the inner quarter of his house. Very soon, he was marked 'Wanted for the Delhi-Lahore Conspiracy', and the colonial government tried its best to find him. Secretly, Rash Behari continued to strengthen the links between the revolutionaries of Bengal, Benares, United Provinces and Punjab. He knew the day would come soon when he could use these connections to fulfil his objective of a free India. On 8th March, when the police raided Rash Behari's home in Chandannagore, he managed to escape arrest by hiding behind the mango trees in his garden not far away from his dwelling house. After hours of desperate search, the police officers were left abashed as their suspect had again managed to outwit them. As the cops left the place red-faced, Rash Behari Bose quickly went back to his home, knowing that nobody would suspect him to be there because it had just been raided.

As the days passed, Rash Behari was again forced into an unspecified period of hiding and became restless before long. He decided to leave Bengal and selected Benares as a new base of operations. The constant turnover of pilgrims, sadhus, and merchants ensured that a stranger could stay in the holy city of Benares without arousing curiosity about an unfamiliar person like Rash Behari Bose and his private affairs. Benares became especially important for Bose and his allies as the place was in the middle of Punjab and Calcutta, as well as a shield and a refuge for revolutionaries like Rash Behari Bose. In Benares, Bose quickly adopted a leadership position within the existing revolutionary organisations, taking over from a young man of Bengali descent named Sachindranath Sanyal. Eventually, he took control of the revolutionary efforts across the United Provinces, Bengal and Punjab.

On 28th July 1914, a significant event occurred. Austria-Hungary declared war on Serbia in response to the assassination of Archduke Franz Ferdinand, the heir presumptive to the Austrian-Hungarian throne. It marked the beginning of World War I. This global conflict stirred up various anti-imperial rebellions worldwide. Among these was the Ghadar movement, which originated in the USA and Canada.

It may be recalled that during the late nineteenth century, many Indians immigrated to foreign lands in search of employment and livelihood to alleviate their financial difficulties and overcome India's economic downturn. Many of them settled in Canada and North America. Most of that demography comprised people from the then-Punjab region in undivided India.

These people had been loyal legions behind the British Raj since the 1860s. They expected equal rights and warmth for their communities across the British and Commonwealth countries. However, when Canada promulgated strict laws against the emigrants, the Punjabi communities faced the harsh reality of racism and discrimination for the first time. Some members migrated from Canada to the United States, but the same humiliation followed them there. The enraged Punjabis felt cheated and tricked. Hungry for justice, they swore retribution, setting up a party in 1913 in the USA. It was initially named the 'Pacific Coast Hindustan Association'.

The organisation quickly gained popularity among Indian expats, particularly in the United States, Canada, East Africa and Asia. The key members of the Hindustan Association were Indian immigrant students, mainly from the Punjab. Many of them were students at the University of California at Berkeley. Some influential individuals were Vishnu Ganesh Pingley Pingley, Har Dayal Singh, Kartar Singh, Tarak Nath Das, et al. The sense of betrayal metamorphosed within them into a profound sentiment of patriotism. The intense loyalty towards their motherland exhibited itself in their weekly paper, Ghadar, which the party circulated. Using the Arabic word Ghadar, meaning revolt, the group eventually became known as the Ghadar Party – an enemy of British rule. Far away from home, these young and brave men felt the call of nationalism and the urge to uphold the honour of their motherland. Eventually, they decided to return to India in large numbers to participate in the ongoing revolutionary activities which were taking place in the country against the British Raj.

The efforts of the Congress-led mainstream movements for dominion status for India were considered a soft approach, and the Ghadar members were in favour of winning freedom through armed rebellion. Against this background, thousands of the party members returned to India with their audacious intentions, joined their families and plunged into action with the fuming Punjabi and other North-Indian brotherhoods.

Several failed attempts at isolated mutinies opened the eyes of the Ghadar Party's primary members to the flaw in their plan. These were poorly designed, and the attempts were disparate and without finesse. The failures made them introspect. With deep concern, when the members assembled to discuss the way ahead, they eventually concluded that they needed a suitable leader under whom the sense of collective patriotism could be consolidated and properly channelled. [5]

As World War I broke out intensely and Britain now engaged in a total war that seemed to threaten its very survival, the continuation of the Indians' loyalty to the British armed forces was considered more vital than it had been ever before. In an internal memo, one colonial official noted, 'As long as the Native Army is sound, the civil population will not give us much trouble.'

Interestingly, this perspective on the Indian soldiers in the British army was also echoed in the publications of the revolutionaries, but for the opposite reasons. The revolutionaries targeted the army barracks and cantonments in which Indian troops resided to seduce the soldiers to act against the British colonial rulers' interests. The 'seduction of troops' was the primary objective of the revolutionary strategies of Rash Behari Bose, who believed that a mass revolt by Indian soldiers in the style of the Great Indian Rebellion of 1857 (Sepoy Mutiny in British parlance) would spark a widespread popular revolt that could expel the British from the subcontinent.

That was the backdrop against which an active worker of the Ghadar Party, Vishnu Ganesh Pingley, called on Rash Behari Bose in Benares in late 1914 as part of a wider goal of developing closer relations between the Punjabi and Bengali wings of the revolutionary movement. Pingley met Rash Behari Bose on the recommendation of Bengal's Anushilan leader Jatindranath Mukherjee.

During their meeting, Pingley apprised Rash Behari of all the earlier failed attempts of their isolated insurrection and their eventual assessment that the absence of suitable leadership guidance in the Ghadar party had so far doomed their prospect of success. He added that 4,000 men had already returned from North America with the intention of overthrowing British rule, with another 20,000 ready to mobilise once the rebellion began. Bose gave a patient hearing to the Ghadar activist and then instructed his trusted lieutenant Sachindranath Sanyal to accompany Pingley to Punjab to connect with the Ghadar revolutionaries, who had manpower but little expertise in bomb-making. Sanyal did not speak Punjabi but found Pingley helpful in connecting him with Sikh farmers and labourers prepared to take up arms against the British.

Early in 1915, Sanyal and Pingley returned to Benares and informed Bose that the Punjab was simmering with discontent. Around this time, Bose had moved house again to a property near Harish Chandra Ghat. He had been changing his residence frequently since his arrival at Benares to remain incognito. Upon the return of Sanyal and Pingley, Rash Behari called a meeting of the Benares revolutionaries and announced that the time had come for a widespread rebellion against the British. Not wanting to risk transporting too many bombs at once on the crowded trains, Bose split up instructions for ferrying small numbers of bombs from Bengal to the Punjab via Benares. Accompanied by Sanyal and Pingley, Bose took the train to Amritsar and rented a house with the help of local revolutionaries. With Bose's headquarters secured, Sanyal returned to Benares to resume command of local operations in this crucial hub.

At this point, the party was so low on funds that Bose had suggested that Sanyal turn him to the police and use the reward money to finance the revolution, although it is unclear if this was said in jest.

To raise money, Bose and his associates in and around Amritsar planned a series of robberies in nearby locations. As the robberies attracted increasing scrutiny from local police, Bose and some of his close associates shifted their operations to nearby Lahore, the provincial capital. The revolutionaries found five houses to rent, and a female revolutionary named Yamuna Das moved in with Bose to pose as his wife and thus allay the suspicions that could attach to a lone bachelor moving in from out of town. At this point, the police still had no idea Bose was anywhere near Punjab, and even many of his associates only knew him under one of his various aliases. The move to Lahore proved wise, as police soon arrested Bose's top lieutenant, Mula Singh in Amritsar, in connection with one of the robberies.

On 12th February, Bose and his associates decided that the revolution would begin on 21st February, with Lahore as the epicentre of a full-fledged rebellion comprising a series of connected uprisings in Ferozepore, Rawalpindi, Ambala, Meerut, Benares, Agra, and elsewhere. For this purpose, Bose sent emissaries to cantonments across northern India to convert as many soldiers as possible to the revolutionary cause and to muster groups of armed villagers to join the uprising. Bombs were arranged; arms were collected; flags were made ready; a declaration of war was drawn up; arrangements were made for destroying railroads and telegraph wires. Rash Behari Bose thus became one of the leading figures in the daring plot.

Everything hinged on a successful strike in Lahore. There, the rebels of the 23rd Cavalry would first disarm the soldiers who remained loyal to the British before massacring the Europeans living in the nearby cantonments. While 50 or 60 men presumably agreed to the plan, it was anticipated that the whole regiment would join the revolution once the fighting began. With the Lahore assault underway, a separate group of rebels would initiate a second attack in Ferozepore, a short distance to the southeast. The plan was to gather at the Ferozepore cantonments, where sympathetic soldiers would arm the rebels and then join them in a midnight attack to seize the armoury.

The preparations of the revolutionaries, however, had not escaped the attention of the police. Realising that the string of local robberies carried out by Mula Singh and his accomplices was linked to the wider Ghadar movement, Deputy Superintendent Liakat Hyat Khan hired a spy named Kirpal Singh to infiltrate the organisation. Kirpal was known to one of the rebels from having previously met in Shanghai and was the cousin of Balwant Singh, the revolutionary who had joined the 23rd Cavalry in December with the express purpose of sparking mutiny within its ranks. These relationships helped Kirpal secure the trust of high-ranking rebels and enter the inner circles of the movement quite easily. [6]

When the revolutionaries, in their secret meeting, decided on the date of the uprising, Kirpal Singh eavesdropped this vital information and rushed to his Commanding Officer Liakat Khan. But Khan was out of the station. Therefore, Kripal Singh had to pass on the information to a British Agent for onward transmission to Liakat Khan. However, by a stroke of luck, a faithful member of Rash Behair's team saw Kripal Singh speaking to a British official and knew what had transpired between the two. He reported the matter back to their team.

Showing strong emotion at the news of Kripal Singh's betrayal, one of Rash Behari's trusted associates, Sachindra Nath, asserted that the plan must be called off and they should pass on the information to the native troops across the country immediately. He was apprehensive about a strong retaliation from the British. However, Rash Behari thought differently. He said in a sad tone that there was no looking back at this juncture, and they must not behave like cowards by abandoning their well-thought-out scheme for the revolt. Everyone's morale would take a hit nationwide if they dropped the plan at this stage.

Rash Behari then surprised everyone by saying that they would advance the date of the uprising by two days. Kirpal Singh must not know that they discovered his act of betrayal. He should be allowed to play his tricks, and the punitive actions against him must wait until they achieve their goals.

So, finally, they decided that 'The Uprising' would definitely happen, but not on 21st February. It would start on 19th February, two days before the scheduled date. The British must not get a hint of this changed timetable. Rash Behari then advised Sachindra Nath to send emissaries to inform everyone that the Day of the first uprising would now be on 19th February to stay one step ahead of the authorities. [7]

However, Kirpal Singh was not the only mole. There were others, too, through whom Kripal Singh found out the date had been changed. He immediately managed to sneak out and inform the police while the others were having lunch. When he returned, Rash Behari and the others seized him and placed him under guard in one of the rented houses near Mochi Gate. Bose had to leave to deal with other matters, but he provided clear direction to the men who remained: execute Kirpal Singh.

Kirpal originally planned to wait until all the leaders were assembled before signalling to the police, but when he realised that Bose had left instructions to kill him, the spy had to act quickly. Telling his guards that he needed to use the toilet, Kirpal managed to gain some privacy on the roof long enough to give a pre-arranged signal to the constable stationed outside the house at around 4:30 p.m. Police stormed the building while coordinating simultaneous raids on the other houses throughout Lahore. [8]

Inside the house, Rash Behari quickly assessed the seriousness of the situation and instructed Pingley, Sachindra Nath and others to flee from the scene instantly. Then he silently went inside and took out his prized briefcase cum makeup box. However, a commotion started outside, and Rash Behari heard the voice of a British Officer, 'Don't let anyone escape.' The police stormed the house and began a thorough combing operation. They ransacked everything and arrested the revolutionaries still present in the house.

However, even as the grand dream of revolution crumbled, the police failed to notice a nondescript man timidly carrying night soil on his head and leaving the house. The man nervously walked past the officers, who shooed away every passing spectator. This timid man was actually Rash Behari Bose in disguise. So skilful was his disguise that he was able to escape from the location and quickly reached a secluded lane. Then, he took out another set of disguises and like a chameleon, within a flash of a moment, he changed into a fierce Pathan.

At the Lahore Railway station, the Pathan met with an accomplice and boarded a train to Benares. As the train started moving out of the station, the Pathan looked at his companion and whispered, 'Pingley, you must get off at Meerut. You need to gauge the pulse....'

With tearful eyes, Pingley said, 'My heart is paining beyond all imagination. I cannot believe that a traitor has trampled our dreams to dust. I feel so much despair. This cannot happen. We cannot let this happen.'

Rash Behari looked at Pingley and said, 'We must not shed tears. Perhaps today is not the day of glory. Maybe that is what destiny has ordained for us. However, we are fighters. We must never give up. I shall never surrender as long as I live. And the British will never be able to capture me. I promise you, we shall fight, strive and finally bring Freedom to our motherland.'

At the Meerut station, Pingley got off the train and vanished in the crowd. Within the relatively empty compartment, Rash Behari, dressed as a Pathan, folded his arms and dug his head into their hollow. Tears didn't come from his eyes. However, his heart wept tears of blood as he knew that his biggest plot so far, his master plan, had failed to make landfall. The Ghadar Movement had just been totally crushed. The British colonial rulers were elated by the massive success of suppressing the meticulously planned revolt. They realised that if they had failed to prevent the uprising, the damage to the British rule in India would have been colossal, jolting the very foundation of the British Raj.

Returning to Benares, Rash Behari remained holed up in a top-secret hideout and maintained a low profile. While introspecting on the failure of the February revolt, Rash Behari felt it would be difficult to bring about a total revolution with the help of the Indian soldiers alone. There was a need to first honey-comb the people with 'small arms' all over the country for a full-fledged revolution to succeed. Moreover, raising money through political banditries and robberies or receiving money through gifts from a few rich men was unrealistic and insufficient given the vast needs. Further, robbing Indians to meet the finances undermined public support for the revolutionary causes. He started considering securing international assistance to pursue his dream of an India free from foreign rule.

However, after some days, Pingley came from Meerut, acquainted Rash Behari with the pulse of the troops there and proposed to plan another revolt by the soldiers at Meerut, where Pingley had worked during early February among the 128th Pioneers and the 12th Cavalry. Interestingly, the British intelligence services were still in the dark about the identity of the mastermind of the attempted Lahore rebellion.

Still, Rash Behari did not favour inciting the army at Meerut for a revolt then, as Pingley proposed. However, on Pingley's repeated pleas, Rash Behari gave a green signal to the proposal against his will. Unfortunately, however, before Pingley could start the mutiny, one of his accomplices betrayed him. He was put under arrest at once and subsequently hanged on a charge of treason. Ultimately, the intelligence officers discovered Rash Behari Bose's roles in the Ghadhar movement and the Delhi-Lahore conspiracies.

Amidst this scenario, Rash Behari Bose finally decided to leave for Japan, even though he had earlier rejected the suggestion from his associates to leave India to evade capture by the British on several occasions. He planned to travel in the name of P. N. Tagore, posing as a relative of the Nobel Laureate Poet Rabindra Nath Tagore, whose journey to Japan was scheduled for the near future, to create a general impression in the interested circle that P. N. Tagore was preceding the Poet to oversee the Nobel Laureate's smooth reception. On the eve of his travel to Japan, Rash Behari, dressed as P. N. Tagore, even went to the Police Commissioner at Calcutta to receive his identity card. [9]

At first glance, Japan may seem an odd choice for an exiled Indian revolutionary, Rash Behari Bose, given that in 1915, Japan and Britain were still in alliance for stalling Russian expansion in Asia and safeguarding their own interests in China and Korea. However, despite that, Japan was also an emerging centre of Asianist thought, and the country's rapid industrialisation and victory against Russia in 1905 cemented its reputation as a leader among Asian nations with the potential to challenge the hegemony of the West. In due course of time, he was proven correct. [10]

Authors Elizabeth Eston and Lexi Kawabe, in their book "RASH BEHARI BOSE THE FATHER OF THE INDIAN NATIONAL ARMY (Volume 1)", however, noted that:

> "At that time, Asia was suffering under the evil hand of colonisation by England and by the various countries of Europe and America. In the midst of this, when Japan defeated the powerful country of Russia in the Russo-Japanese War of 1904 to 1905, Asia came to hold a small glimmer of hope that it might be possible to escape the colonialism of the West. When the Russo-Japanese War ended, able-bodied young men from various countries throughout Asia fled to Japan on a mission to learn how they might rescue their own homelands. In a manner of speaking, Rash Behari Bose was also one such youth." [11]

It was into this milieu of expectation that, on 5th June 1915, with a fake identity, a great deal of hesitation and almost no acquaintances, Rash Behari Bose set foot in Kobe, the port city of Japan, whose demography, social etiquette, food habits, weather and many other factors were new to him. There was still a price on his head, put there by the world's most powerful empire, and his fight for Indian independence was far from over. Yet, in the land of the rising sun, the born revolutionary, Rash Behari Bose, was ready to take the second innings of his unfamiliar journey in stride. At that time, Bose was able to speak just four Japanese words.

When he got off the ship, Rash Behari was in for a surprise. A customs officer rushed to him, shook his hands and told him that there were many letters for him he had brought along. On glancing through them, Bose realised that they were all addressed to Nobel Laureate Poet Rabindranath Tagore. Rash Behari explained to the customs officer that he was P. N. Tagore, a relative and not Rabindra Nath. When the officer heard this, he exempted Bose from screening and even had him dropped in a car to his hotel.

When he reached Tokyo's Shimbashi Railway Station on 8th June, he was at a loss since he neither knew the language nor where to go. Luckily, a Policeman, conversant in English, came to his rescue. He not only arranged a hotel for him but also helped him from the following day to find a house to live in.

Still, the initial months were extremely difficult for Rash Behari. However, in due course of time, Bose was lucky to receive protection and patronage from an influential Japanese right-wing political figure and co-founder of the ultranationalist Genyosha Society, Mitsuru Toyama (1855-1944). Bose's life, survival, and activities in Japan spanning 30 years would not have been possible without the active financial and moral support from Toyama and other prominent Pan-Asianists, all of whom saw Bose's goal as part of their larger aspiration of an 'Asia for Asians'.

A few weeks later, he came in contact with a man of Indian origin, Bhagwan Singh Giani, a staunch supporter of the Ghadar Movement who had been deported from Canada and fled to Japan. Under the Anglo-Japanese Alliance, the Japanese government was closely monitoring Bhagwan Singh at the instance of the British government, and the police had been tailing him continuously since June 1915. Consequently, in the Japanese Ministry of Foreign Affairs records, the name of P. N. Thakur (fictitious name of Rash Behari) started appearing almost daily as and when Rash Behari and Bhagwan Singh met.

Perceptibly, Rash Behari was becoming conversant in the local language. Side by side, Bhagwan Singh helped Rash Behari make contact with the German Consulate. At that time, their activities were mainly procuring weapons and secretly sending them to their comrades in India to carry out a revolt on a national scale. First, Rash Behari tried to smuggle small arms into the revolutionaries in Calcutta, but unfortunately, the consignment fell into the hands of the British authorities in India. Later on, he even managed to send two shiploads of arms to India with the help of the Germans, but yet again, these two ships were intercepted by the British and the arms were confiscated even before they reached India.

Meanwhile, British administrative officials in Singapore discovered that Rash Behari, the most wanted man, was hiding in Japan under the false name of P. N. Tagore. The shocking revelation prompted the British Foreign Ministry to request their counterpart to arrest P. N. Tagore alias Rash Behari Bose. When the Japanese government refused to comply with the demand for the arrest, the British government on 16th October relented somewhat and demanded deportation, mentioning German and Indian agents were collectively exporting weapons from South East Asia to India and that Bhagwan Singh and Bose were involved in these activities.

It was a moment of crisis for Bose, even though he did not know that the British had discovered his real identity. He proactively began to establish contact with Japanese journalists to arouse public sentiment of the Japanese people through the press about the miserable situation in India and the sad plight of Indians in their own country under British colonial rule. Soon, a righteous indignation in the Japanese media against the British surfaced

Bose's unwavering commitment to the cause of India's fight against British rule then saw him moving energetically to arouse feelings of ASIA FOR ASIANS amongst the people of the Asian countries in general and Japan in particular. He was convinced that if the sense of oneness and unified spirits in the midst of Asian people could be suitably generated, India would get the much-needed allies and faithful friends in Asia who would support her necessities in the freedom movement. That was the moment when Rash Behari met Michiru Toyama and some other influential Japanese opinion makers.

Thus began Rash Behari's campaign to sensitise the Japanese in Tokyo and throughout Japan. The ordeals that India and her children had been suffering for decades under British colonial rule were vividly picturised. With the assistance of Bhagwan Singh and his contacts, Rash Behari continued to generate friendly sentiments amongst the Japanese as well as in the Indian society residing in Japan. Within six months of his arrival in a country where he was utterly unknown, Rash Behari developed good relations with some top-ranking Japanese politicians, newspaper editors, writers and public figures.

On 27th November 1915, Rash Behari Bose, another Indian revolutionary, Heramba Lal Gupta and Okawa, the editor of Michi (the mouthpiece of the Dokai Christian organisation), decided to hold a political gathering for Indo-Japanese exchange called 'Celebratory Meeting for the Coronation of the Emperor'. The gathering convened in [11]Lala Lajpat Rai's name was held in the Astar Hotel at Ueno Park, Tokyo. About one hundred people, primarily Japanese and Indians, as well as a few officials of the British embassy, attended it. Lala Lajpat Rai and three others delivered speeches on the occasion. All the speakers emphasised the need for Indo-Japanese friendship, except one. The speech by a Japanese (Oshikawa) was particularly anti-British, and it was considered 'radical' in nature as it called on Japan to support India's independence.

Although British embassy officials were present, the Union Jack was not hoisted. Even the British national anthem was not sung, and the mood was 'full of indignation' and anti-British sentiment. Obviously,

---

[11] Lala Lajpat Rai, (1865-1928) also known as the "Lion of Punjab," was a prominent leader of the Indian independence movement during the British Raj. He was a political activist, lawyer, and writer who fought for the rights of Indians and worked tirelessly to end British rule in India.

the British were infuriated and took strong exception to the happenings. [12]

At an urgently convened closed-door high-profile meeting, the British ambassador to Japan flexed his diplomatic muscles before the government of Japan, and its ultimate result was on the morning of 28th November, Bose awoke to news from the maid that the police had come by and requested Rash Behari to report to the police station. Accordingly, Bose arrived at the station around 10 a.m., where the police informed him that he had five days to leave the country. Bose checked in with Heramba Lal Gupta, who had received similar orders. They conferred with their various Japanese contacts and gave interviews in newspapers such as the Tokyo Asahi Shimbun to deliver scathing public critiques of the Japanese government's capitulation to British demands. Bose and Gupta cleverly leveraged the resentment of Japan's nationalist intelligentsia to kick up a storm of widespread anger against the deportation orders, which Bose called 'shameful'. For opposition figures within the increasingly powerful Imperial Diet, who were already critical of centrist Prime Minister Ōkuma Shigenobu for being too cosy with Britain, the incident was an embarrassing reminder of the lopsided nature of Anglo-Japanese relations.

Among the members of the Japanese public who read about the looming deportation of the two Indians in the press were a married couple, Aizō and Kokko Sōma. Aizō owned the famous Nakamuraya bakery in the busy Shinjuku area of Tokyo, and the couple had cultivated a loyal clientele that included influential Japanese nationalists. Upon reading of the deportation order, the couple became annoyed that the government was 'deporting guests who were here as political refugees, succumbing to British Imperialist Power'. On the eve of deportation, Rash Behari Bose went into hiding in a location that the police would not think to look at – he received shelter in the basement of Nakamuraya bakery! [13]

Thus, Rash Behari Bose changed from P. N. Tagore to become Bose of Nakamuraya. Some influential personalities like Mitsuru Toyama and a few members of Genyoisha and Kokuryukai played vital roles in this exceptional settlement that finally worked out. In time, Rash

Behari Bose and Heramba Lal Gupta lived in the studio behind the shop vacated by a reputed artist. They could not leave the studio and remained holed up the whole day inside in what looked like a hole dug in the ground. They could not slip out of the dark studio nor get a view of the world outside.

Fortunately, the studio had a kitchen, and Rash Behari could cook. He asked the maids to buy the foodstuff and spices and cooked Indian food for themselves. Watching the preparation of the typical Indian cuisine, the maids gradually learnt to cook Indian food, and in due course, Kokko also grasped the knowledge. It soon became a family favourite and ultimately a sensation in Japan as an authentic Indian curry. That was the origin of the 'Indian curry' introduced commercially by the Bose of Nikamuraya twelve years later in 1927. Teaming up with his father-in-law, Rash Behari launched the Nakamuraya Indi Karri, which 'retained the taste and flavours of Bengal', reminiscent of the simplicity of a *patla murgir jhol* (পাতলা মুরগীর ঝোল), in Bengali language, meaning the light-chicken-broth.

Nakamuraya's curry clicked instantly with the locals, quickly becoming more popular than the bakery's signature item, custard buns. The curious citizens of Tokyo began flocking to the restaurant to taste authentic Indian food, and soon, the restaurant grew into such a big venture that it became one of the first food companies to go public on the Japanese stock exchange. Thanks to newspapers that zealously wrote about his struggles against imperialism and his romance with Toshiko, 'Bose of Nakamuraya' became a household name in Tokyo, and his 'Indo-Karii' was famously christened the 'taste of love and revolution'. With over 6 billion helpings being served annually, the Nakamuraya Indo-Karii (still made according to Bose's original recipe) remains a Japanese favourite, supplying packaged ready-to-eat meals to supermarkets nationwide! The flagship restaurant still stands in its original location in Shinjuku (Japan) with a foyer adorned by vintage photographs of the Soma family and the Indian revolutionary they sheltered. [14] [15]

Meanwhile, further afield, in April 1914, the Komagata Maru incident occurred. A British naval ship had fired at the Japanese ship, Tenyamaru. Seven Indians on board were captured and taken to Singapore. The Japanese foreign ministry made a strong official protest to England and withdrew the deportation order against Bose and his companion. Bose was thus a free man. He left Nakamuraya for a house after nearly three and a half months in the confines of the studio. But the British authorities were still after him.

The British Embassy engaged a private detective agency to find out where Bose was hiding and take him into custody. Under these circumstances, he changed his residence as many as 17 times in a desperate game of hide-and-seek.

It became apparent that Bose was not yet out of danger. Mitsuru Toyama, by now firmly committed to maintaining Bose's security in Japan as a foil to British imperial interests in Asia, approached the Somas with a bold proposal: Rash Behari could marry their eldest daughter, Toshiko, and thus consolidate his presence in the country.

The Sōmas were initially taken aback. Although the couple had come to admire Bose and love him like a son, they also understood the enormous risk their daughter would be taking in marrying a committed revolutionary from a foreign country. Yet, Kokkō spoke to her daughter. After delaying for a few days, Toshiko eventually agreed to marry Bose.

Toyama was thrilled at the news and arranged for the two to wed in secret in a small ceremony that he presided over himself in July 1918, further rooting Rash Behari to the soil of Japan. The couple had two children in quick succession. Sadly, on 4th March 1925, Toshiko died from pneumonia. The end came as Rash Behari was chanting Sanskrit shlokas and Toshiko, repeating them faintly on her deathbed. [16] [17] [18]

The First Pan Asiatic Congress, held in August 1926, can be said to be the stage where Bose played a significant role in the 1920s. During this Congress, he worked out various compromises and conciliations, suppressed self-assertion, and made strenuous efforts as a mediator for the success of the Congress as a whole. This stance led to Japan's conciliation on the Twenty-One-Point Demand, and he played a major role in arriving at various specific resolutions. In the tug-of-war between Japan and China, Bose showed an understanding of both sides. Had he not been there, perhaps this Congress would not have been possible. In this respect, Bose's presence had an extremely weighty meaning.

After the Congress, Bose refrained from criticizing Japan in public as much as possible. He strengthened his relationships with influential people in Japan and tried to pursue India's independence movement while cooperating with them. This attitude led to compromises with the Japanese leaders on various aspects and enhanced his position and influence in Japan.

His active role in the First Pan Asiatic Congress became a major turning point for Bose. He found a practical path based on pragmatism and laid emphasis on securing specific progress and results. He was, after all, a revolutionary aiming at Indian independence and did not aspire to be a critic or an ideologue. He returned to the arena of the independence movement from which he had drifted since his years in India and recalled once again the principle of action as a revolutionary. Hereafter, Bose, as a pragmatist, pursued the attainment of India's independence and coordinated flexibly with Japanese imperialism. He gradually widened his scope of activities and acquired political influence.

By this time, Bose had attained tremendous command over the Japanese language and could speak it fluently. He even delivered long speeches in Japanese. However, he could never master writing Japanese using Chinese characters. Therefore, his books or papers were either based on oral statements or someone else rewrote the text written by him in the Roman script in Japanese. [19]

Soon after the commencement of hostilities in the Far East, Rash Behari Bose called on the Chief of the Imperial General Staff of the Japanese Army, Field Marshal Sugiyama, and requested him to help

Indians in East Asia to organise themselves to launch an armed offensive against the British from the East. Besides, in the Japanese-occupied countries, Indians should not be treated as enemy subjects. However, Sugiyama could not agree but contended that India was a part of the British Empire, which was at war with Japan, and as such, all Indians were to be treated as enemy subjects.

Rash Behari then met the Deputy War Minister and persuaded him to agree to his suggestion. Consequently, an Indian Independence League, with the objective of organising Indians in the Far East, was formed in Japan with Mr. Rash Behari Bose as its President.

Interestingly, before the outbreak of the Pacific War, there were about fifty-five thousand Indians, predominantly immigrants in Thailand. There were several Indian organisations, both religious and educational. The leading exponent of cultural activities among them was Prafulla Kumar Sen. In Thailand, he was famous as Swami Satyananda Puri. There were also some ardently nationalist Indians, mainly from the Sikh community, who were ready to take up anti-British activities to facilitate India's freedom from British rule. Most active among this group was headed by [12]Giani Pritam Singh, who, along with some nationalist Sikh revolutionaries, formed a secret organisation known as the Independent League of India (IIL). It was influenced by India's Ghadhar. After the occupation of Thailand by the Japanese forces, representatives of this League went with the Japanese troops as they advanced into Malaya and, with the help and under the leadership of local Indians, set up IIL branches in all the states of Malaya. Later, the IIL branches were formed all over East Asia, including the Philippines, Thailand, Dutch East Indies, French Indo-China, Shanghai, Burma, Korea and Manchuria. Eventually, all

---

[12] Giani Pritam Singh, son of Sardar Maya Singh and Mata Fateh Kaur, born on the 18th of November, 1910, in the village Nagoke Sarli, District Lyallpur, currently in Pakistan, was actively involved in the Indian Independence Movement and Gadher Party. He was instrumental in the failed 1915 mutiny that he stirred among a Bengal Lancers regiment. To avoid arrest, he fled via Burma to Bangkok in 1919, where a number of Indian revolutionaries from other parts of India were living. [21]

these League branches owed allegiance to India and were under the leadership of Rash Behari Bose. The tale of IIL will be further discussed as the story progresses. [20]

As the plans of the Greater East Asia War rapidly took final shape, Japan's Military headquarters, sometime in April-May 1941, sent out a senior officer, Major Iwaichi Fujiwara, to South Asian countries in disguise to keep them informed about the composition, location, etc. of the Indian troops. After a while, Fujiwara realised that the subversion of loyalty of Indian soldiers in the British Army would indeed facilitate Japan's impending military campaigns in Southeast Asia. He also helped a group of Indian revolutionaries contact the Indian nationalists in Bangkok.

On 18th September 1941, Fujiwara received an order from the Imperial General Headquarters (IGHQ) to form a small group with a few junior officers. The group later became known as Fujiwara Kikan. He was then ordered to go to Bangkok to help Military Attache Col. Tamura in liaison, particularly with the Indian Independent League and anti-British organisations in Malaysia and Chinese. In the event of the outbreak of the war, Fujiwara was to facilitate the Japanese campaign in Malaya and, from the point of view of the establishment of the Greater East Asia Co-Prosperity Sphere, he was tasked to pay close attention to the Indian affairs and somehow arrange to sow the seeds of subversion among Indian soldiers in the British Army.

On his arrival in Bangkok in October 1941, Fujiwara came to know about the two Indian groups headed by Pritam Singh and Swami Satyananda Puri. He chose to work with Pritam Singh, who had already been engaged in such activities in which Fujiwara was interested.

On 4th December 1941, Fujiwara and Pritam Singh reached an agreement of collaboration, which, among other things, mentioned that the Independent League of India would fight the British power for India's independence with overall support from Japan and Pritam Singh's organisation would work for propaganda against the British among the Indian soldiers in British Army and achieving harmony between these Indian soldiers and the Japanese. It was further agreed that, in the event of war, Pritam Singh's organisation, the Indian Independence League (IIL), would march with the Japanese army and carry out propaganda among the Indian soldiers of the British.

On 7th December 1941, two hours after the Japanese attack on American military installations at Pearl Harbor, Hawaii, Japan declared war on the United States and Great Britain, marking America's entry into World War II.

On 14th December 1941, while Fujiwara and Pritam Singh were on their job concerning one of their new missions at the city of Alorstar, a message from an officer of the British Indian Army, Major 13Mohan Singh, reached them. Earlier, on 11th December, Major Mohan Singh's 1/14 Punjab Regiment of the Allied Forces was utterly shattered by the Japanese Army in a surprise attack at Changlun. Consequently, the Commanding Officer, Lt. Col. L. V. Fitzpatrick and Major Singh and others were cut off from the Regiment. For twenty hours, Mohan Singh was stuck in a marsh along with two other Indian Non-Commissioned Officers (NCOs). Because of his earlier resentments on various issues against his own commanding officer or the European community in Malaysia as a whole, Mohan Singh was fed up and decided not to join the retreating British Army. At about noon the next morning, they reached a small village about six miles from Alor Star,

---

[13] Mohan Singh was born in a Sialkot village in 1909. The father died before the baby was born, and the mother died when Mohan Singh was a child of five. Her brothers brought up the orphan. After Matriculating, the lad joined the 2/14 Punjab Regiment as a sepoy. Later, he was selected for the Kitchener College and later joined the Indian Military Academy, from where he passed out in 1935 when he was posted in the 1/14 Punjab Regiment. Promoted Captain in 1940 and Major in 1941, he was sent to Malaya. As the senior-most Indian in his battalion and persistent in advocating the Indian point of view, he frequently came into conflict with his European officials. He protested against the anti-Indian attitude of his Commanding Officer in the selection for Emergency Commissions. Singh was not happy serving the British. He realised the difference between the soldiers of a free nation and soldiers of a subject nation. Mohan Singh even had a minor clash with his Commanding Officer, whom he did not like. Besides, Mohan Singh had a lot of grievances against the European community, especially the British. Several tactical mistakes by the British Army at the initial stage of the war in Malaya made him bitter and he was having a second thought of continuing with the British Army. [22]

where they met some more troop members. On the morning of 14th December, they reached and halted at a rubber plantation at Kuala Narang from where, with the help of an Indian civilian, Mohan Singh sent a message to the Japanese at Alostar, where it reached the duo of Fujiwara and Pritam Singh.

After receiving the message, Fujiwara went unescorted and unarmed to receive Mohan Singh and the party. On its arrival at Alorstar, the surrender took place without any formal ceremony. There were two immediate tasks for Mohan Singh's party. Since the fall of Alorstar, the lawlessness and disorder gripped the city. Fujiwara Kikan had no troops of its own to protect the city. Therefore, Mohan Singh was requested to help the Fujiwara Kikan in restoring peace and order in the city. The Indian troops welcomed the task as it would restore their prestige in the eyes of the civilians and prove their usefulness to the Japanese authority. The task was delicate. Yet, with his men's strenuous efforts, Mohan Singh restored order in the city. At the same time, Mohan Singh had to send some of his men to collect stragglers whom the retreating British forces had left behind.

On the same night of 15th December 1941, Mohan Singh, Fujiwara, Pritam Singh and another army officer, Capt Akram, were engaged in a lengthy discussion. Given the emergent situation, they did not want to lose any time to start the initial exchange of views. Fujiwara inspired Mohan Singh with the idea of liberating India with Japanese assistance. Mohan Singh pondered over the idea, found it worth consideration and sought some time to decide.

On 27th December, Mohon Singh informed them that he was ready to cooperate with the Japanese in raising an army from the Indian POWs if the Japanese would accept certain conditions. These were mainly:

(i) The Japanese Army should cooperate fully to raise a liberation army for India.

(ii) The Independent League of India and the Army would run independently.

(iii) The Japanese Army should allow the Indian POWs to be controlled by Mohan Singh.

(iv) These Indian POWs who would join the Army should be freed from concentration camps.

(v) Those who would not would also remain POWs under Mohan Singh.

(vi) The Japanese Army should give the liberation army the status of an allied army.

Under the above conditions, Mohan Singh agreed to organise the Indian army units being abandoned by the British into a well-knit armed force, which would work with the Indian Independence League of Sardar Pritam Singh and eventually fight alongside the Japanese when they invaded India.

By the end of December 1941 and the beginning of 1942, the attitude of Mohan Singh and the ordinary ranks of the Indian troops taken prisoner by the Japanese Army so far was one of conditional promise. At that stage, the name of the new Army to be raised was decided. Major Fujiwara wished the Army would be known as 'Volunteers for Indian Freedom'. Mohan Singh suggested that the Army would be national in character and that its name should be 'Indian National Army'. Fujiwara accepted Mohan Singh's suggestion, and that is how the Indian National Army (INA) came into being.

Interestingly, when the idea of raising an army comprising Indian Prisoners of War (POW) was mooted earlier, and the question of its leadership agitated the minds of the POWs, it was overwhelmingly resolved that the political leadership of Subhas Chandra Bose alone would be acceptable to them in the long run. So, when it was finally decided on the question of having INA, Fujiwara also promised to try to make Subhas Chandra Bose's leadership available in East Asia. So far as the conditions put forward by Mohan Singh were concerned, Fujiwara vowed to get the replies of the 25 Army Command but insisted that the Propaganda War among the British Indian troops should start at once. To this, Mohan Singh agreed.

With the declaration of War by Japan on 7th December 1941, Rash Behari Bose and his group in Tokyo lost no time in organising themselves to make use of the opportunity thrown up by the War to achieve India's independence. After the fall of Singapore to the Japanese Army on 15th February 1942, which saw the largest British surrender in its history, Rash Behari broadcast twenty-three messages addressed to the Indians and their political leaders, highlighting the extreme difficulties the British were in. According to Rash Behari Bose, it offered a golden opportunity to the revolutionaries. He pointed out that Japan and her allies, being England's enemies, were India's friends. By denying support to the English people and treating Japan as a supporter of India's independence, British rule in India could be ended easily. [23] [24]

At the same time, Rash Behari started contacting the Japanese high civilian and military authorities to enlist their support in organising movements in East and Southeast Asia for India's freedom. It became clear that a huge portion of the world was under the British colonial rule. The British Empire expanded by the use of military force, and it was India that supplied them with the necessary soldiers and financial strength to do so. England stole wealth from India and forcefully drove the Indian people to launch attacks and invasions throughout the world. In reality, the majority of the British soldiers were Indians who were being threatened and tricked into supporting the British agenda. If India were not freed from British rule, Indian soldiers would be used to destroy countries throughout the world and to force these countries into becoming British vassal states. Japan must understand this. Otherwise, it would also face the same fate. If India did not become independent, Indians would be used to attack Japan. Bose tried his best to spread this message. [25]

Side by side, General Sugiyama and others in the Japanese high command appointed Rash Behari Bose's companion, A.M. Nair, as Chief Liaison Officer for Indian Affairs, tasked with coordinating between the Tokyo command centre and a newly established regional office in Bangkok. Nair proposed that Bose be appointed leader of India's pro-Japan faction in the Far East, and the two men worked together to coordinate Indian freedom fighters throughout Thailand, Malaya, Burma, Hong Kong, Shanghai, and elsewhere.

In February 1942, radios and newspapers across Japan announced the establishment of the Indian Independence League (IIL), led by Rash Behari Bose and headquartered out of the Sanno Hotel in Tokyo, room 302. In their daily meetings, Bose and Nair concerned themselves with the well-being of the roughly two million Indians living in the swathes of territory recently conquered, or soon-to-be conquered, by the seemingly unstoppable Japanese war machine. It was, therefore, necessary to formulate a clear mandate for the IIL. They resolved that only Indian nationals would be eligible for membership in the IIL and that the IIL would retain autonomy in formulating its own policies.

Meanwhile, the collapse of Britain's imperial defences on the Malay Peninsula had left large numbers of Indian soldiers at the mercy of the victorious Japanese forces, with around 45,000 Indian prisoners of war (POWs) in Singapore alone. Mohan Singh was working with Major Fujiwara to arrange for the nucleus of a new fighting force, the INA.

According to A.M. Nair, the appointment of Mohan Singh as leader of the new INA caused immediate friction with senior officers, who were generally resentful of the relatively junior officer being given such an important role.

Wanting to ensure coordination among the various branches of the IIL and the Japanese high command in Tokyo, Bose and Nair arranged a conference in Tokyo on 28th March. Around this time, Bose also suggested that Nair be recognized as co-founder of the IIL and alternate president in the event of an emergency. During the planning of the conference, Bose and Nair learned of Mohan Singh's recruitment efforts among Indian POWs in Malaya and Singapore. The IIL co-founders were surprised that such an important initiative was being undertaken under Mohan Singh but did not want to undermine the efforts Singh had already taken to bring some officers on board and establish the bones of an INA. In the spirit of cooperation, Bose and Nair proposed that the INA faction of Indian expatriates send two representatives to the Tokyo conference, for which the Japanese proposed Mohan Singh and another officer, Colonel N.S. Gill. During the conference, Bose and Nair found Gill to be a promising man, while, in their opinion, Mohan Singh was invariably truculent and non-cooperative.

Although the twenty-five delegates assembled at the Sanno Hotel voted unanimously to elect Rash Behari as conference president, the event was marked by significant frustration for Bose and Nair, who struggled to bring about agreement among the guests. Gill had little confidence in Mohan Singh's leadership abilities, while Bose found the Malaya delegates unhelpful.

Many doubted Bose's fitness to lead an Indian league, given his adopted Japanese citizenship, a perspective Nair called grossly irresponsible, given Rash Behari's proven dedication to India's freedom struggle. Bose led the conference with great dignity and ability and managed to corral the various factions into a consensus resolution, reiterating their commitment to achieving India's immediate independence.

After three days of discussions, the delegates agreed to hold a second meeting in Bangkok, where further action could be decided by a Council of Action that would comprise Rash Behari Bose as president and four members, including Mohan Singh.

On 15th June, Rash Behari Bose inaugurated the Bangkok conference as IIL president and delivered his speech with characteristic dignity. He called upon the assembled participants to replace words with actions in fighting to achieve freedom for India once and for all. In Rash Behardi's words:

"Our brothers and sisters have, in hundreds of thousands, laid down their lives and have suffered and sacrificed for more than a century so that our country may be once again free. Let us rise to the occasion and carry their efforts to success so that the souls of the martyrs in heaven may find peace and be pleased. Let us stand shoulder to shoulder and march hand in hand to success. Remember, we have one indivisible nation – INDIA; One enemy – England; One goal - complete Independence.

Despite this stirring opening to the proceedings, the mood noticeably shifted when Mohan Singh took the floor to announce two controversial proposals. The first was that the INA should be a separate body entirely under his control, not subject to the authority of the IIL. The second was that all soldiers joining the INA take an oath of personal loyalty to Mohan Singh. A commotion broke out among the other delegates while another member of the Action Council stood up and denounced the suggestions as undemocratic and, therefore, undeserving of consideration.

Bose temporarily adjourned the meeting to allow tempers to cool down. At the same time, Nair reached out to his contact in the Japanese high command, who confirmed that the INA should be considered the military arm of the IIL and not a separate body. When the conference proceedings resumed after lunch, Bose announced the decision, framing it as an order not open for further discussion. The rest of the nine-day conference went much smoothly, and the assembled delegates unanimously agreed on a long list of resolutions.

Back in Singapore, Captain Mohan Singh persisted in treating the INA as his own personal army. He continued to demand personal oaths of loyalty from new members and allegedly resorted to extreme measures to secure recruits. Rumours began to reach Bose and Nair in Bangkok that Singh was placing Indian POWs who refused to join the INA on starvation diets as punishment. One report claimed that 'he placed the officers and men who hesitated to go with him in concentration camps surrounded by barbed wire fencing and ordered them to be beaten.' Trying to gain control of the situation, Rash Behari left Bangkok and took up lodgings in the Park View Hotel in Singapore, accompanied by two Indian assistants, one of whom doubled as a bodyguard due to his proficiency in judo.

Bose found the situation even worse than he had anticipated, learning that the Japanese commander Iwakuro found Mohan Singh 'absolutely impossible to deal with.' Singh refused to listen to Rash Behari or even meet with him. Finally, on 29th December 1942, Rash Behari arranged a meeting with the local Japanese commander, Colonel Iwakuro, in which Bose berated Singh and relieved him of his duties, ordering him to be placed under house arrest. Mohan Singh remained in a Japanese jail till the war ended. As a parting gift, Singh had left orders for the INA to disband in the event of his arrest. The removal of Singh thus triggered massive confusion and the disintegration of the INA, throwing Bose and Nair's plans into chaos. Nair shifted the ILL's headquarters from Bangkok to Singapore and began working with Bose to reconstitute the INA.

They soon found the army to be something of a paper tiger! In place of forty thousand soldiers reported by Mohan Singh, there were only about ten thousand army personnel. After much deliberation, Bose and Nair selected an army colonel named J.K. Bhonsle as the new head of the INA, a decision that garnered support from other respected officers. [26]

Rash Behari Bose lost no time in the work of salvaging the INA. On 6th February 1943, he put forward a scheme to the Iwakuro Kikan to reform the Indian National Army, which was approved on the same day. One notable feature of the scheme was that it took away the independence of the Army Command. It was decided that a military department would be established within the League that would deal with matters concerning the military administration and operations. The scheme reaffirmed that the INA would be under the direct control of the Indian Independence League. The Army would be organised on a voluntary basis and governed by the Indian National Army Act to be framed by the Council of Action. The Army should consist of (a) Headquarters, (b) Field Force Group, (c) Guerilla Regents, (d) Special Service Group, (e) Intelligence Group, and (f) Reinforcement Group. By early 1943, the INA had achieved a new life as a cohesive organization, thanks to the leadership of Bose, Nair, Bhonsle, and others.

From the beginning of February 1943, things started changing for the better. Prime Minister Tojo, in reply to an interpellation in the House of Representatives of Japan on 4th February 1943, reiterated that Japan had no territorial ambitions in India and, on the contrary, Japan would give all-out assistance to see India free. While a formal Japanese declaration on the issue was still to be made, the Indian Independence League and the Japanese press made the fullest use of Gen. Tojo's comment to allay the looming suspicion among the Indians and many others about Japan's intentions. The Indian Independence League published a statement on Gen. Tojo's remarks about India and observed that his reply 'has given the greatest inspiration of Indians who now realise all the more Japan's lofty spirit for the construction of Greater East Asia...' The Syonan Shimbun editorially wrote, 'Premier Tojo's reiteration of Nippon's policy vis-a-vis India should spur Indian Nationalists on the further efforts...'

Similarly, the events in India were used to stir up anti-British sentiments among the Indians in East Asia. It was expected to divert their attention from the recent troubles and forge a sense of unity among them. Indian Independence Day was observed on 26th January 1943 with great enthusiasm in all countries of Greater East Asia. Greetings were sent to the People of India from the Tokyo Broadcasting Station. [27]

Interestingly, to a gain better understanding of the Japanese people, Rash Behari Bose honed his language ability in just fourteen years to the level that he was able to write books in the Japanese language. One after another, he published books and delivered speeches wherever he was invited. He put his faith in the Japanese people, and the Japanese put their faith in him.

Rash Behari left behind many of his publications written in the Japanese language. At least forty of them are presently preserved in the National Diet Library in Tokyo. Among them are journal articles, book chapters, speeches, and translations written by Bose, in addition to eighteen other books. In particular, immediately following the outbreak of the Greater East Asian War in 1942, within a single year, he published six books and two articles."

Bose produced so many publications because he knew Japanese people needed to understand India to save it from British imperialism. He believed that only Japan, which had been victorious in the Russo-Japanese War, could save India and Asia at large. He fled to Japan in 1915, and for the next thirty years until his death in 1945, he dedicated his life to saving India. His greatest weapons were his pen, his network, and the mutual trust he shared with Japan.

On 21st January 1945, Rash Behari Bose breathed his last, calling out the names of his two children in the midst of the nine-month-long Tokyo air raids. A few days earlier, Japan had conferred the Order of the Rising Sun, Second Class, upon him. Until 1945, Japan greatly approved of and respected Rash Behari Bose, and the Japanese people extolled the extent of his greatness en masse from the bottom of their hearts.

On the other hand, the born revolutionary, who dedicated his whole life to the liberation of the Indian sub-continent from the shackles of colonial British rule, making tremendous sacrifices, was more or less unrecognised in India. Rash Behari Bose has long been forgotten pretty much by the people in his beloved motherland. There are now very few people who know of his extraordinary exploits. [28]

* * * * * * *

Chapter 6

Serious Setback

Subhas Chandra Bose's presence in Japan was shrouded in mystery for over a month, though from the port city of Sabang, he landed in the capital, Tokyo, on 16th May 1943. It was kept secret until 18th June when Tokyo Radio broke the news to the public for the first time that 'Chandra Bose' had reached Tokyo from Germany. Nonetheless, the news report did not mention his arrival date in Japan. The next day, when the Japanese press carried the news of arrival, it was a pleasant surprise to Japan's Indian community. Their enthusiasm rose to a feverish pitch.

Throughout East Asia, the first public announcement of the dramatic arrival of Netaji Subhas Chandra Bose in Tokyo on 18th June 1943 all the way from Berlin caused a wave of jubilation among Indians, and they enthusiastically celebrated his arrival. Overnight, the atmosphere was electrified. The INA and the Indian Independence movement suddenly assumed far greater vitality in the eyes of all. The Axis Press and Radio did not fail to stress the significance of Bose's arrival in East Asia. The Syonan Shimbun newspaper, published during the Japanese occupation of Singapore from 1942 to 1945, editorially commented that the arrival of Subhas Chandra Bose marked another milestone in India's progress in her fight for freedom... His presence in Tokyo would signal that the Indian Independence movement had reached its crucial stage. [1]

Previously, when Subhas Bose's arrival remained confidential, Netaji met the Japanese Army and Navy Chiefs of Staff, the Navy Minister and the Foreign Minister in rapid succession from 17th May onwards. But these meetings were not more than courtesy calls for none elected to talk shop. Netaji was politely turned down when he asked for a meeting with Prime Minister Tojo, who was concurrently War

Minister. "General Tojo regrets he cannot see anyone for the time being because of the pressure of work," was the reply he received from the protocol office.

As his proposed meeting with Prime Minister Tōjō in Tokyo was not materialising, Subhash Chandra Bose was quite uneasy. The long wait forced on Subhas Bose was, however, not without its merits. During the twenty days of waiting, Bose studied hard and familiarised himself with the delicate political situation in Japan. He also learned a lot about Tojo's background and personality.

Nonetheless, during that period, Subhas Bose's first-ever meeting with Rash Bihari Bose also took place on 1st June 1943. Despite his poor health, Rash Behari flew to Tokyo to meet Subhas in person at the Imperial Hotel. For the first time in their life, the two great Indian revolutionaries came face to face in room 217 of the hotel in Tokyo at 5 p.m. Subhash Chandra Bose was waiting for Rash Bihari Bose. The door opened, and the moment Rash Behari and his companion Yamamoto of the Hikari Kikan entered the room, two Boses looked at each other and embraced like long-lost brothers; no words were exchanged for some time before they could start a conversation. When they finally started talking, they spoke in Bengali- their mother tongue. The duo spoke for around an hour, during which time Rash Behari conveyed to Subhas his intention to hand over the leadership of the IILand the INA to the younger man. Subhas readily accepted. The Japanese admiral, Yamamoto, later remarked that Rash Behari's face after the meeting 'was brighter than he had ever seen.' The long-time resident of Japan, Rash Behari, also delivered an elaborate briefing about Tojo and the Japanese military that was very timely and quite useful to Subhas Bose. Two Boses also held several more meetings in Tokyo after that day. [2] [3]

Note: According to Yamamoto of the Hikari Kikan, who accompanied Rash Behari, the meeting was held on June 12th or 13th, 1943. However, in Rash Behari's diary for that year with his family, there was an entry scribbled under 1st June: 217 Teikoku Hotel: Hiradate: Matsuda: 5 p.m. Matsuda was the Japanese code name for Subhas Chandra Bose. The fact that Subhas Bose was in Japan was not yet public then. To maintain secrecy, he was given this code name and '217' must have been the room number at the Imperial Hotel where he was staying. These are mentioned in Takeshi Nakajima's book. [2] Accordingly, the date of the meeting has been taken as 1st June 1943. 5 p.m.

Subhas Chandra Bose had to wait twenty days before Tojo finally agreed to see him on 10th June 1943. The absence of any official communication from the Prime Minister's office explaining Tojo's delay in meeting the Indian leader who took enormous risks to visit Japan gave rise to wild speculations and mischievous rumours from the propagandists showing Subhas in poor light in the eyes of the Japanese filled the vacuum. The fact that the pressure of work delayed the meeting was not a mere excuse. Tojo was, in fact, a hauled man in those days during an aggravating and adverse war situation. The German and Italian collapse on the African front shocked him, just as the German withdrawal from Stalingrad had done six months earlier.

It was an excruciating exercise in self-criticism for Tojo, a German-educated officer, to discover whether he had overestimated the German strength when he decided upon Japan's entry into World War II. He was getting nervous about expressions of growing disappointment and dissatisfaction among the Japanese public. And as a matter of fact, Tojo did not know what exactly to talk to Netaji about.

Just eight days before Netaji arrived in Tokyo, the Independence Preparatory Committee for Burma was organised after many months of dispute between the local Army Command and Tokyo's local army officers in Burma. The latter wished to postpone the independence of Burma for tactical reasons. Tojo finally overruled their objections. He was unwilling to face repetitions of similar disputes with regard to the Indian Issue. Moreover, until then, the Indian National Army hardly appeared to be an asset. To the Tokyo high command, it seemed to be an ill-disciplined, overgrown outfit likely to cause trouble again. Tojo also understood that Netaji intended to lead the INA in an operation against India, and that was quite a question that Japan had to settle. Prodded repeatedly by the Army Chief of Staff and the Foreign Minister, Tojo finally decided to see Netaji with an open mind or a blank paper before him. The meeting opened with Tojo's distinct reservations.

When the meeting with Tojo eventually took place on 10th June 1943, Netaji conducted himself quite discreetly, watching his language and studying Tojo's reactions at every turn. Gradually, he became passionate and dynamic as he dwelled on his determination to liberate India. By that time, Tojo was already enchanted by the tall, dignified and sincere Indian visitor. Netaji won Tojo's heart or rather conquered him personally. The two leaders did not go into detailed discussions at the first meeting. But Tojo offered to meet Netaji again four days later.

At the second meeting, Tojo outlined the basic concept of the Greater East Asia Co-Prosperity Sphere and its policy of encouraging India to become independent. Netaji produced his trump card and asked straightforwardly, "Have you, sir, considered the question of sending the Japanese Army into India for the liberation campaign if it is deemed necessary?" Tojo clamped his mouth, gulped, turned around and watched the clouded faces of the Foreign Minister and the Chief of Staff, who were also present at the meeting held at his spacious office. After a long pause, the Prime Minister cleared his throat before speaking up softly, "My dear friend, I cannot answer that question offhand. You see, it involves a lot of tactical, logistic and political problems."

Netaji nodded, saying, "Very well. sir." He would not pursue the subject. But the second meeting was another great success for the Indian leader. After he left, Tojo turned to Foreign Minister Mamoru Shigemitsu, saying, "He is a great Indian, fully qualified to command the INA."

Shigemitsu quietly replied, "Yes, sir, I fully agree with your appraisal."

Two days later, on 18th June, Subhas Chandra Bose was invited to visit the Diet (Japanese Parliament), where an unexpected but great and pleasant surprise awaited him. At the plenary assembly of Japanese legislators, Tojo declared in the course of a long speech:

> We are indignant about the fact that India is still under the ruthless suppression of Britain and are in full sympathy with her desperate struggle for independence. We are determined to extend every possible assistance to the cause of India's independence. It is our belief that the day is not far off when

India will enjoy freedom and prosperity after winning independence.

Tojo's assurance of extending "every possible assistance" was his answer to Netaji's important question, which had been withheld at their second meeting. For the first time, Tojo indicated the possibility of extending Japanese military operations into India. Netaji's moral victory during his first visit to Japan was unparalleled.

After attending the Japanese parliament session, Netaji dropped his veil and held a news conference in his real name on 19th June for about 60 Japanese and foreign reporters. He said in part,

> For many long years, British jails in India and Burma had been my residence. But the fact that today I am standing before you in the heart of Nippon instead of sitting idly in a prison house in India is symbolic of the new movement that is now sweeping over my country. .. British Imperialism meant for India - moral degradation, cultural ruin, economic impoverishment and political enslavement. Is it any wonder, therefore, that the Indian people have at last solemnly resolved to end the British yoke?
>
> The Tripartite Powers have rendered the greatest help to India's struggle by waging war against our eternal foe. They have earned our lasting gratitude by offering us sympathy, active support, and assistance. Nevertheless, we must pay for our liberty with our own blood. We should, therefore, actively participate in the war against the common foe.
>
> The enemy that has drawn the sword must be fought with the sword. Civil disobedience must develop into armed struggle. And only when the Indian people receive the baptism of fire on a large scale will they qualify for the freedom." [4]

In that first press conference in Tokyo, when Subhas Bose was asked if any independent status for India should be given from outside, he said: "Independence must not be given by anybody, but should be obtained by Indians themselves through their own struggle and sacrifice."

On 2nd July 1943, during his first visit with Rash Behari to IIL Headquarters in Singapore, Subhas Bose was asked about the sincerity of the Japanese intentions. He replied, "Do you believe that I have brain enough not be fooled by them? Then trust in my word when I assure you that I am sure Japs cannot double-cross us." On another occasion, he concluded his argument in favour of trusting in Japan's sincerity by saying, "If anybody has still any doubt in his mind on this point, I shall ask him to place his trust in me. If any cunning British officer could neither cajole nor deceive me, no one else can do so."

The most important factor, which seemed to have enabled Subhas Bose to work out a plan of campaign for India's freedom without drawing wholly on the Japanese aid, was the existence of an Indian community in Southeast and East Asia - economically affluent and numerically strong. Moreover, an armed force of about twelve thousand strong was in existence when Subhas took over the leadership of the movement in East Asia. He based his plan on these two factors: the economic strength of the Indian community and the numerical strength of the army.

How would the liberation army fit into Bose's plan to achieve India's independence? Its role, Subhas Bose said, would be unique. In his speech on the occasion of reviewing the army in Singapore for the first time, Subhas Chandra Bose said:

"Throughout my public career, I have always felt that, though India is otherwise ripe for independence in every way, she has lacked one thing, namely, an army of liberation. George Washington of America could fight and win freedom because he had his army. Garibaldi could liberate Italy because he had his armed volunteers behind him. It is your privilege and honour to be the first to come forward and organize India's National Army. By doing so, you have removed the last obstacle in our path to freedom." [5]

Bose convinced the Indians in East Asia of the sincerity of Japan and boosted their morale by dispelling their doubts about the ultimate victory of Indian nationalist forces. He made them realise that Japanese military assistance to the INA against the British was as necessary for the Japanese to ensure the security of their co-prosperity sphere as it was for the achievement of India's independence. Bose further pointed out that the British were their common enemy and that they would like to fight together to end British domination of India. The Axis powers, Bose said, were doing no favours to India, as simple common sense should indicate that the most natural thing for an enemy of British imperialism would be to support India's demand for liberty.

On 21st October 1943, about 1,000 Indian representatives from all over the Ear East assembled in Singapore and unanimously adopted Subhas Chandra Bose's proposal for the establishment of the Provisional Government and elected him as the Chief Executive of the Government. Netaji issued a statement that, among other things, read:

> In setting up this Provisional Government, we are, on the one hand, meeting the exigencies of the Indian situation and, on the other, following in the footsteps of history. In recent times, the Irish people set up their Provisional Government in 1916. The Czechs did the same during the Last World War. After the last World War, the Turks, under the leadership of Mustafa Kemal Pasha, set up their Provisional Government in Anatolia.
>
> In our case, the Provisional Government of Azad Hind will not be like a normal peace-lime government. Its functions and composition will be unique. It will be a fighting organisation, the main object of which will be to launch and conduct the last war against the British and their allies in India. Consequently, only such departments will be run by the government as necessary for the launching and prosecution of the struggle for liberty. When the Provisional Government is transferred to Indian soil, it will assume the functions of a normal government operating in its own territory. Many new departments will then be started.

> With the formation of the Provisional Government of Azad Hind, the Indian Independence Movement has obtained all the preconditions of success. It remains now to start the final struggle for freedom. This will begin when the Indian National Army crosses the frontier of India and commences its historic march to Delhi. This march will end only when the Anglo-Americans are expelled from India, and the Indian National Flag is hoisted over the Viceroy's House in New Delhi.

The Japanese government's official recognition of Netaji's Provisional Government came two days later, on 23rd October. The following day, the Provisional Government of Free India declared war against Britain and the U.S.A. as its first sovereign act. The Supreme Command of Japanese in the South, headed by Taiauchi, since promoted to the rank of Field Marshal, issued a statement pledging to provide full support to the Indian Independence Movement and declaring that Japan had no territorial or economic designs on India. Two days later, Netaji, accompanied by Generals Chatterji and Bhonsle, left Singapore for Tokyo to attend the Greater East Asia Conference that was held in Tokyo on 5th and 6th November 1943. [6]

Before the INA could develop into an independent and strong force, however, it was necessary for Bose to settle the question of its relationship with the Japanese army. The Anglo-American block had spread the word that the INA was a puppet army raised and equipped by the Japanese to serve their own ends. This impression had to be obliterated from the minds of the INA soldiers before they could be expected to play their rightful role in the war for India's liberation. Besides British propaganda, even some Japanese army commanders thought that the INA was fit only for intelligence work and could not be relied on for actual fighting. For instance, Field Marshal Terauchi Hisaichi, Commander of the Southern Expeditionary Force, told Bose that in the event of a Japanese advance towards India, the Japanese army would bear the main burden of fighting, and the INA would be utilised for propaganda purposes. This role was not acceptable to Bose or other INA commanders. He told Terauchi frankly that the only role acceptable to the INA during their advance towards India was that of the vanguard; Indian freedom had to be won by Indians, for freedom secured through Japanese sacrifice would be worse than slavery. He declared that the first drop of blood shed on Indian soil should be that of a soldier of the INA." Though Terauchi's reaction was not very favourable, the Japanese Chief of the Army Staff, General Sugiyama, promised that in the ensuing Imphal campaign, the INA would rank as an allied army under Japanese command.

Bose attended the conference as an observer as, in his view, India had not yet come into the Greater East Asia Co-prosperity Sphere, and Japanese opinion concurred with his. Despite this limitation, he stood out as an outstanding politician among those attending the conference. The Times, on the other hand, described Bose as a quisling and head of the puppet government of free India when he arrived in Tokyo to attend the conference.

The conference ended with the enunciation of a joint declaration about mutual respect for each other's independence and cooperation. Bose regarded the declaration as the charter of freedom. On the other hand, the Anglo-American nations regarded it as mere propaganda and asserted that Japan had no intention whatsoever of carrying it into effect, even partially, including Tōjō's promise to hand over the Andaman and Nicobar Islands to the Provisional Government of Free India. Whether the conference was a major propaganda offensive or not, the fact remains that it marked the apogee of the goodwill effort of Japan's whole Southeast Asia programme. [7]

In the subsequent weeks of his stay in Tokyo, Netaji kept himself quite busy, as usual, conferring daily with Japanese leaders. When he met Dr. Shumei Okawa, an ultra-nationalist Japanese philosopher who had made certain studies of India, Netaji stupefied Okawa by suggesting that he would, if necessary, join hands with Russia or the 'devil himself' for the purpose of defeating the British. Okawa later said that he found Netaji to be a man devoted entirely to the cause of Indian independence and not at all a pro-Nazi politician, as some of his critics insinuated.

In a matter of less than five months, Netaji Subhas toured practically the whole of East Asia and met with its people and their leaders, in spite of all wartime handicaps and difficulties. He won the hearts of the three million Indians living in the region. On 29th December, Subhas Chandra Bose visited the Andaman Islands to officially take the area over as the sovereign territory of the Provisional Government of Free India from the Japanese possession. He appointed Lt. Col. A. D. Logfinndhan as Chief Commissioner of Andaman and Nicobar Islands.

It may be recalled here that the surprise attack by some 350 Japanese aircraft on the US naval base at Pearl Harbor on 7th December 1941 marked the US entry into the Second World. But it wasn't just Pearl Harbour that came under attack. Imperial Japanese forces launched a series of campaigns throughout the Asia Pacific region that day. Just two weeks later, Japan captured Hong Kong from the British Empire. By 8th February 1942, Singapore had fallen. In the early months of 1942, Japanese forces swiftly invaded Burma, capturing the capital city of Rangoon by 8th March. The British Empire's defences crumbled, and over the next two months, the Japanese drove Allied troops out of the rest of the country. British and Commonwealth forces stationed in Burma withdrew over 1,000 miles across the border to India. This remains the longest retreat in British military history. The situation in the Far East in 1942 and early 1943 was dire.

Incidentally, Burma played a crucial role in the broader context of the conflict during World War II. For the British, Burma was a useful barrier between their prized colony, India, and China under Japanese military occupation. The Americans viewed Burma as a vital lifeline. It was contemplating to help China break free from Japanese control and become a viable partner of their international community. Nevertheless, the fall of Burma marked a significant setback for the Allies in the Pacific theatre. The reoccupation of northern Burma especially became a priority for the Allied forces because the Burma Road, almost the sole supply route to Chiang Kai-Shek's Nationalist Chinese Army, passed through that region. Keeping this supply line open was essential for supporting China's resistance against Japanese aggression.

However, Japan's swift victories in the early stages of the war and their military efficiency surprised many at that time. The Pearl Harbour attack caught the United States off guard and demonstrated Japan's ability to strike decisively. While the United States was recovering from the Great Depression, Japan, by that time, had emerged from its own economic downturn by the mid-1930s. Japan had devoted much of its national income to building a powerful navy. Their Army was better prepared for war. While the British Empire was overstretched, and its resources were limited, Japan's early victories, economic strength, strategic positioning, and military preparedness, on the other hand, emanated a perception that the Japanese forces were invincible.

Interestingly, soon after the Japanese conquest of Burma in June 1942, they contemplated an attack on Imphal, the capital of India's Princely State of Manipur. The Japanese think tank considered that their army should strike against India without giving the defenders time to recover from their disastrous retreat. Imphal's capture at that time would rob them of the best base for launching a counter-offensive against Burma. However, it was argued that the jungles of Burma were impassable for large bodies of operational troops and that any attack on Indian Territory would provoke anti-Japanese feelings in India. Therefore, the plan was abandoned around December 1942.

But, with the arrival of Subhas Chandra Bose in Japan in 1943, the plan was revived. His passionate insistence on launching the Imphal campaign for the liberation of India at the earliest time, when the Allied forces were least expecting it, prompted the Japanese military strategist to reappraise an immediate assault on Imphal. Netaji hoped that such capture of Imphal and Chittagong would be strategically necessary to start an Indian revolution. He had, therefore, programmed that once Imphal was liberated, he could install an effective Provisional Government of Free India on Indian soil, which would offer an opportunity for more and more Indians to organize an anti-British revolt. The rationality secured the support of the Commander of the 18th Division, Lt-General Mutaguchi. He was convinced that the jungle was not impassable for well-trained troops, and the leaders of the Indian National Army had repeatedly declared that they and their Japanese allies would be welcomed as liberators of India. Given these two significant factors, Lt-General Mutaguchi pressed for an attack to destroy the threat to Burma rather than waiting for the Allied attack and fighting a defensive battle on the thinly held fronts. He had been appointed the Commander of the Japanese Fifteenth Army in March 1943. Hence, his views naturally carried greater weight. A reconnaissance of the Chindwin area also showed that the river was easily passable by rafts during the dry season.

At that time, the Imperial Headquarters in Tokyo was keen to produce a spectacular victory to offset the effects of the Japanese defeats in the Pacific on civilian morale. Moreover, Netaji Subhas Chandra Bose strongly favoured a joint attack by the Indian National Army and the Japanese Army to liberate India. He discussed the basis of cooperation between the Japanese and the INA forces. In his negotiation with General Kawabe, Commander-in-Chief of the Burma Area Army, he insisted that both would enjoy equal status in all respects. They also agreed that the territories liberated on Indian soil must be handed over to Major-General A. C. Chatterjee, Governor-designate of the liberated areas. If this plan succeeded, the Allied threat to Burma would be removed for many a long month, and another dazzling Japanese victory would stupefy the world.

Tokyo agreed to provide Burma with reinforcements for 14Operation U-go when it issued the directive for 'preparations' in August 1943. However, shipping shortages and other setbacks slowed down the implementation. Scepticism grew at Imperial Headquarters. In October, War Minister Tojo transferred Lt. Gen. Kitsuju. Ayabe, G1 or top operations officer at the General Staff, to Singapore as Teraucln's deputy chief of staff. Ayabe was instructed to 'realistically reappraise' the Imphal Operation formula but was also reminded by Tojo that Netaji's return to India could produce a significant political

---

[14] **Operation U-Go was a Japanese military campaign in 1944 during World War II** *aimed at capturing the* **Imphal and Kohima regions** *in northeastern India.*

impact. After two months of study and fact-finding, Ayabe concurred with Mutaguchi's formula.

In December, Ayabe, accompanied by two staff officers, went to Tokyo to ask for execution orders for the operation. They portrayed a favourable situation regarding the planned operation and obtained Tojo's sanction on New Year's Eve. Execution orders became official on 7th January 1944. The preparation for assault moved at a fast pace, and the INA HQ was moved from Singapore to Rangoon on 7th January 1944. It was decided inter alia that the only flag to fly over the Indian soil would be Indian National Tricolour. The decision coincided with the entry of Netaji's Provisional Government of Free India into Rangoon with a vanguard unit of the INA, the consent of the Burmese Government having been obtained after four months of negotiations. Soon, the Japanese-Indian-Burmese military group was established in Rangoon for coordination. Eventually, it was decided that the Burmese Army would not join the great operation, for it was just one division strong and too small.

In Tokyo, Prime Minister and War Minister General Tojo concurrently made himself the Army Chief of Staff based on the reasoning that the intensification of war required perfect coordination between the Administration and the High Command. Thus, Tojo became Japan's first and the last general to control politics and the military simultaneously, not without strong resentment of other generals who considered it unconstitutional. In other words, Tojo staked his political existence on Imphal. It was undeniable that Tojo was "keen to produce a spectacular victory to offset the effects on civilian morale of the Japanese defeats in the Pacific" and his own ebbing popularity. Mutaguchi was ready to act when the execution orders came in January. He wished to wind up the whole schedule before the dry season ended in Burma, that is, early May. But his men were not quite ready.

As a matter of fact, the Japanese strategists in Tokyo, on the whole, took too long to move. This delay, in particular, gave sufficient opportunity to the Allied forces to intensify their war preparations for their defence of Manipur. The official Japanese decision taken on 12th August 1943 was revealed to Netaji only on 26th August, and the concerned executive order to attack Imphal was issued from Tokyo on 10th January 1944. Mutaguchi was ready to spring into action when the execution orders came in January. As mentioned earlier, he wished to wind up the whole schedule before the dry season ended in Burma, that is, early May. But everything was not just ready, as the forthcoming proceedings demonstrated.

Of three Japanese divisions made available to him, only the 33rd Division had been in Burma for long and consisted of veterans of a series of actions. The 31st Division, which was reorganised around the nucleus of a regiment decimated in Guadalcanal in the Pacific, came from Bangkok in time. But the arrival of the 15th Division from Nanking, China, was long overdue. Shortage of shipping forced the 15th Division to come in a piecemeal fashion. Moreover, the Singapore command ordered the 15th Division to stay for a while in Thailand, ostensibly for the construction of a 300-kilometre military road from Chiang Mai in north Thailand to Toungoo, Burma. The undisclosed ulterior reason for the non-scheduled stay of the 15th Division was the necessity of ensuring the security of Thailand, which was becoming more and more unruly against Japan. The delay exasperated Mutaguchi, who sent a blistering protest message to Singapore on 11th February 1944. Some 20,000 men of the 15th Division marched on foot for 1,200 kilometres from Bangkok to Rangoon and looked groggy when Mutaguchi finally greeted them at the end of February. Mutaguchi consequently set 15th March as the D-day.

Thus, even though the Japanese High Command was keen on launching the proposed assault on Imphal well ahead of the monsoon, there were unescapable delays for unforeseen reasons. Such delay proved costly because they had to postpone the offensive for some time. Ultimately, by 10th February, General Kawabe issued the final assault orders to the 15th Army commanded by Lt. Gen. Mutaguchi Renya with a rider that the campaign be completed within a month because, thereafter, the monsoon was to commence.

Be that as it may, despite numerous bungling in the course of groundwork, the deployment of well over 120,000 troops along the Chindwin River, a front of some 200 kilometres, went on so smoothly and under such a cloak of secrecy that British spies planted in the area failed to detect anything unusual. Thus, the operation 'U-go' started moving with great optimism and undaunted spirit, as expected from the Japanese army, which had hitherto been undefeated by any power in the land battles in their military history so far.

The Japanese, by then, had built a fearsome reputation as jungle fighters. Far from looking at the jungle as an obstacle or hindrance, they were able to use it to their advantage and mastered the art of jungle warfare. They were able to move swiftly through the jungle, often undetected. Their ease of movement was helped by the fact that they travelled light, carrying with them only the bare minimum of arms and supplies required. They also used the sights and sounds of the jungle, initially unfamiliar to the British-Indian forces at the start of the Burma Campaign in 1942, to instil fear in them.

On the offence, a favourite Japanese tactic was to strike deep behind their opponents' bases/positions and cut their supply and communication lines. The forces thus cut off would be rendered acutely vulnerable, and that feeling of vulnerability, more often than not, induced panic. The besieged forces would conduct a disorganised and disoriented retreat, only to be attacked and cut off again by the Japanese farther behind. This pattern repeated itself on several occasions in 1942 when the Japanese chased and inflicted a humiliating defeat on the retreating Allied forces through Burma.

As defenders, especially in mountainous and jungle terrain, the Japanese Army was arguably the best in the world during the Second World War, barring none. Once in place and given sufficient time, the Japanese would dig in deep, creating a vast network of tunnels, bunkers and trenches. Defensive positions were often interlocking, making them almost impregnable. Dislodging Japanese defenders required the combined effort of the infantry, artillery and armour, almost always supported by air strikes. Even after a defensive position was captured, a watchful eye had to be kept for barely alive Japanese soldiers who would emerge hours or even days later from the rubble to try and attack their opponents.

What made the Japanese Army truly formidable at Imphal was the determination and dedication to the cause unfailing - indeed, fanatic of the individual soldier. A Japanese soldier sought to abide by bushido, the ancient samurai code. For him, giving himself up or surrendering was not an option; fighting to his death was the only honourable and acceptable way out. He believed that he was fighting to defend the honour of his emperor; his war cry, banzai, referred to his wish that the Japanese emperor live a thousand years. And so whether he was defending his own position or launching himself in a wave of attacks - attacking in waves being another preferred tactic - the Japanese soldier fought to the end. [8]

The Japanese Army had used its prowess in the jungle and its tactics to devastating effect against Allied forces in Burma in 1942. As a result, there was a certain arrogance or at least overconfidence about its own fighting abilities in 1944 and a related disdain for its previously vanquished foes. This was reflected in the time frame the Army set for itself to capture Imphal.

Initially, General Mutaguchi sought to have the job over and done within just three weeks; a subsequent deadline became the emperor's birthday on April 29. In any event, Fifteenth Army was to have been in Imphal before the rains began.

The tight deadlines meant that speed was of the essence to the Japanese units advancing towards Manipur's capital in 1944. It also meant adopting a risky strategy when it came to supplies. Keeping tens of thousands of soldiers supplied over the hills of the India-Burma border and across the Chindwin River was always going to be a challenge. The emphasis on speed required the men to carry the bare minimum of supplies, backed up by an unreliable and untested supply line. The assumption was that they would be able to help themselves to the bounty of the Fourteenth Army's supply depots and bases that were expected to fall into their hands in little to no time.

If Imphal had been taken by the Japanese Fifteenth Army according to its original timeline, the problem of supplies would have automatically been solved. Unfortunately for the Japanese, Imphal did not fall in a matter of weeks. In fact, Imphal did not fall at all. The fundamental reason for this was that the British-Indian forces they faced in 1944 were quite unlike those they had so roundly defeated only two years prior.

Anyway, when D-day finally came, Mutaguchi assembled war correspondents at his headquarters in Maymyo on Central Burma highlands and declared cheerfully:

I am firmly convinced that my three divisions will reduce Imphal in one month. In order that they can march fast, they' carry the lightest possible equipment and food enough for three weeks. Ah, they will get everything from British supplies and dumps. Boys, I see you again in Imphal at the celebration of the Emperor's Birthday on 29 April.

The Japanese army was in high spirits and prepared for the thrilling adventure of entering the Indian Territory across the mountainous Indo-Burmese border without the slightest doubt about their success. The plan was that the 55 Division was to attack the British Division in the Arakan, the coastal sector of Burma, on 4th February 1944 as a diversion to the main offensive. When the British had committed their reserve in the battle, the main attack to capture Imphal was to be launched. Then, the Japanese 33rd Division would cut off the Allied 17th Indian Division south of Imphal. Shortly afterwards, the Japanese 15th Division would attack from the northeast, severing the road to Kohima, some 80 miles (120km) away in Nagaland. Sato's 31st Japanese Division would simultaneously surround Kohima to prevent any relief from Dimapur, which was a further 40 miles (64km) to the north. Accordingly, by the first week of March, they planned a three-pronged attack using the following three principal formations:

> a) 15th Division (RETSU), commanded by Lt. General Yamauchi; consisting of five regiments (15th Infantry, 60th Infantry, 67th Infantry, 21st Field Artillery, & 15th Engineer);
>
> b) 31st Division (MATSURI), commanded by Lt. General Sato Kotuku, consisting of five regiments (58th Infantry, 124th

Infantry, 138th Infantry, 31st Divisional Mountain Artillery, Divisional Engineer,

c) 33rd Division (YUMI), commanded by Lt. General Yanagida: five regiments: (213th Infantry; 2 14th Infantry; 215th Infantry, 33rd Divisional Mountain Artillery; 33rd Divisional Engineer, 13

Notwithstanding certain initial reservations by the Japanese Generals about the battle-worthiness of the regular INA divisions, they finally agreed that some INA units and the Burma National Army were to accompany the above-mentioned Japanese Divisions. Netaji exerted his own pressure, pleading that the battles of Imphal and Kohima would represent basically the crucial battles for the liberation of India and, therefore that, not only the INA should spearhead the attack, but the first drop of bloodshed should be that of an INA soldier. Hence, two of the best INA Divisions were earmarked along with some special combat forces:

1) The 1st INA Division (Gandhi Brigade) commanded by Maj. General Md. Zaman Kiyani;

2) The 2nd INA Division (Subhas Brigade) commanded by Maj. General Shah Nawaz Khan;

3) Special Task Force (Intelligence Group) commanded by Colonel S. A. Malik joined the first offensive in the first week of March and

4) The Azad Brigade, commanded by Colonel Gulzara Singh, later joined and also fought together with Yamamoto's Force at the Tamu-Pallel sector,

Altogether, some 8,800 INA combatants participated in the campaign.

Tragically, unlike the IV Corps of the Allied forces then defending Imphal, the Japanese had no permanent allotment of air support. They had to depend on a few Japanese air squadrons temporarily attached to the armies or divisions for particular operations despite the fact that the Imphal Valley was of immense strategic importance at that time. A failure here would be disastrous, given that altogether, around 1,55,000 active combatants of the Allied forces were reportedly involved in the defence of Imphal. Besides, they were also supported by some 13 Groups/Wings and Squadrons of Air Force units operating in different parts of Imphal, Dimapur, Kumbhigram, Patharkandi, Pallel, and Sapam.

As planned, the Japanese 55th Division launched the Arakan diversion on 4th February, but the British Division holding that sector did not retreat, as Mutaguchi had expected. They stood firm and fought resolutely, receiving their supplies by airdrop. However, Allied General Slim had committed his reserve – the 5th Indian Division – and Mutaguchi was not totally disappointed. It, however, upset his tight schedule to some extent, causing a slight delay in their main planned attack.

In March 1944, three Japanese Army Divisions, along with the Subhas Brigade, entered the mainland Indian Territory after crossing big rivers, different hill ranges and thick forests for their attempted thrust and assault deep inside the Indian territories towards Delhi.

The 33rd Division was the first in the Japanese U Go offensive, launching its attack towards Tiddim on 7/8 March. It was a full week before the other Divisions - the 15th and 31st - began crossing the Chindwin River. The aim was to cut off and destroy the (British) 17th Indian Division and, by attacking early, draw in reinforcements from Imphal, leaving it more vulnerable to attacks by the other Japanese columns. The main infantry units of the 33rd Division involved in the fighting on and along the Tiddim Road in Manipur were the 214th Regiment, commanded by Colonel Sakuma Takanobu, and the 215th Regiment, commanded by Colonel Sasahara.

The 17th Indian Division of the Allied forces was supposed to withdraw to the Imphal Valley as the Japanese attack developed, but instructions from their Headquarters in Imphal came too late. By the time the Division started withdrawing from Tiddim, the Japanese had already got behind them and cut the road back to Imphal. From then until early April, the 17th Indian Division tried to make a fighting withdrawal to the Imphal Valley with the help of two brigades of the 23rd Indian Division sent down the Tiddim Road from Imphal to rescue it. Most key battles during this period -Tonzang, Singgel, Sakawng - took place in the hills on the Burmese part of the Tiddim Road. In early April, the Allied 17th Indian Division eventually managed to escape to the Imphal Valley.

Like the Imphal-Kohima Road, the Silchar Track was another route connecting Imphal to Assam and the rest of India. During the Second World War, the volume of traffic on this track was minuscule compared to that which came to Manipur via Kohima and the main railhead at Dimapur. Nevertheless, the Silchar Track was a target for the Japanese as they sought to encircle Imphal and cut off all land routes to the Imphal Valley. A raiding party from the Japanese 33rd Division, together with some INA men, blew up the 300-foot suspension bridge spanning the Leimatak River on the night of 14/15 April. This was where the track descended from the western hills into the Leimatak River valley. The Silchar Track was so cut, and the Japanese siege of Imphal truly began. On the Tiddim Road, the 214th Regiment, commanded by Colonel Sakuma, and the 215th Regiment, commanded by Colonel Sasahara, of the Japanese 33rd Division were active in this sector.

Previously, the 15th Japanese Division of Lt. General Yamauchi marched towards Tamu and Ukhrul in two columns. They captured Ukhrul before advancing towards the Imphal-Kohima road for their assault on Imphal from the northwest. At the same time, the 1st INA Division, under the command of Major-General M. Z. Kiyani, joined the Imphal campaign and fought with the Yamamoto force at the Pallel sector. Simultaneously, the 31st Japanese Division (MATSURI), commanded by Lt. General Sato, advanced to Kohima (now the capital city of Nagaland) through Homalin (North Burma) and Ukhrul and Major General Shah Nawaz Khan's 2nd INA Division could reach Ukhrul to help Sato. By 7th March, the daredevil (jungle warfare) Japanese crack force of Lt. General Yanagida's 33rd Division (YUMI) spearheaded the thrust from the south via Tiddim Road.

In the beginning, the Indo-Japanese columns advanced very fast with heavy guns and tanks, which the 17th Allied Division could not resist. As such, the Allied forces had to retreat, leaving completely behind the entire range of southern hills (now Churachandpur District) of Manipur up to Potshangbam into the hands of the advancing joint INA and Japanese columns. Jubilation ran high among the local people of Moirang at the progress of the war, and some leaders, including M. Koireng Singh, spent a sleepless night on 13th April, hiding under the Moirang Lamkhai Bridge and watching out eagerly for the British 17th Division retreating from Tronglaobi. The INA forces kept on occupying the vacated areas.

Finally, Colonel S. A. Malik's Bahadur Group (Special Task Force-Intelligence) of the INA was fighting with the 214th Japanese Regiment of the 33rd Division menacing in the Bishnupur sector by establishing its Headquarters at Moirang (14th April 1944). This was the supreme moment of ecstasy for the INA and its Supreme Commander Netaji Subhas Chandra Bose, because the National tricolour flag of INA was hoisted for the first time at the historic Kangla of Moirang, near where, incidentally, the INA Memorial complex is now lodged in lasting memory of the historic moment.

While the 33rd Japanese Division was fighting some of its fiercest battles in and around the Bishnupur-Moirang sector and the Silchar track (old Cachar road) against their enemy, the Imphal-Dimapur road remained closed due to the heavy fighting on the Kohima war front along the route. All the essential commodities for the Allied Forces had to be brought in by air. That proved to be a critical moment for the Allied forces since Imphal was then encircled by the Indo-Japanese combatants from all the three accessible approach roads and directions, and an imminent fall of Imphal was expected by Tokyo any time. [9] [10]

The Japanese-Indian offensive took the British by complete surprise. The Japanese and INA troops, mostly foot soldiers lacking vehicles and artillery or any air support, literally galloped through mountains and jungles, smothering or routing the enemy on the way. The advance of the 31st Japanese Division in the north to Kohima and the 15th

Japanese Division to Imphal was swift. Both crossed the Indo-Burmese borders by traversing some 200 kilometres of rugged terrain of the Arakan Mountains in two weeks on foot. However, the performance was marred by a grave mistake made by the 33rd, which was believed to be the crack force of the advancing Japanese. This Division drove rapidly initially and successfully entrapped the British 17th Division in a narrow valley tucked in by rugged mountains, some of which were as high as 2,324 metres. The destruction or wholesale surrender of the highly motorised 17th Division appeared only a matter of time. Blocked at its head by a powerful Japanese regiment and pressed hard from its tail, the 17th appeared doomed.

The official history of the British-Indian Armed Forces says:

Early the following day (26 Mach), however, a 2/5 Royal Gurkha Rifles patrol found that Japanese defenders had evacuated the south ridge. The battalion moved forward again, reaching the road and establishing contact with the Pany Foce before the morning was out. At 11 hours, on 26 March, the whole 48th Indian Infantry Brigade (of the 17th) marched down from Sakawng hill to milestone 109. The most dangerous Japanese roadblock on the Imphal-Tiddim road was thereby broken through.

Official Japanese records say that the evacuation was ordered by Lt. Gen. Motozo Yanagida, commanding general of the 33rd after he received a message from the 215th Regiment, which was blocking the retreat of the British 17th Division. The message said that the 215th Regiment encountered powerful enemy reinforcements (two brigades of the 23rd British Indian Division) coming from the other side of the road and was prepared to fight to the last man. Yanagida told the 215th to withdraw two kilometres to the west. And that removed the roadblock to the retreating 17th British Division.

On 27th March, Yanagida cabled Mutaguchi, recommending the "re-examination of the whole operation formula." Mutaguchi cabled back a message, asking Yanagida to give hot pursuit to the fleeing enemy immediately. Yanagida refused to obey. After one week had been wasted in the cable exchanges, Yanagida resumed the movement- but not as swiftly as before. During this week, the 17th British Division completed its withdrawal to Imphal.

As soon as Yanagida resumed the march, he elected to be very cautious and made it a rule that strong patrols preceded and beat the bush before the main force of the 33rd Division marched. Yanagida's unit reached Toibung, some 50 kilometres south of Imphal, on 10th April, four days after the 31st Division swarmed to Kohima, a vital junction mid-way between Imphal and Dimapur in Assam and one week after the 15th Division occupied hills overlooking the Imphal Kohima road. Nevertheless, the whole picture definitely looked favourable to the Japanese and INA forces, even better than expected and ahead of schedule.

When Imperial Headquarters issued a communique on 8th April saying that "Japanese troops, fighting side by side with the Indian National Army, captured Kohima early on 6th April", many Japanese began to expect Imphal to fall before the Emperor's birthday on 29th April.

Tojo, who was a scowling and sulking man for many months, was smiling again and felt happy. He issued a statement and made it clear that "whatever area the Indian National Army liberated should be placed under the administrative control of the Provisional Government of Free India. It is the aim of Japan to crush the enemy and help to place India under the complete control of the Indian people." Rash Behari Bose, who was critically ill with tuberculosis, rose from his sick-bed against medical advice and went to Radio Tokyo to record his speech expressing jubilation to be broadcast "when Imphal fell". He was carried back after he had recorded his speech at the studio. That speech, of course, failed to go on the air.

Netaji issued a statement announcing that the INA, fighting under the command of the Provisional Government of Free India, had embarked on its sacred mission with the cooperation of the Japanese Imperial Army. At that historical moment, when the Indo-Japanese troops had crossed the border and started marching deep into India, the Provisional government drew the attention of the world to the epochal event. He declared that the Provisional Government of Free India would continue to fight side by side with the Japanese Army until India was wholly liberated. On behalf of the Provisional Government of Free India, he further urged the Indian people to give their full support, block the US-British war efforts by resorting to sabotage and cooperate in bringing about the success of the struggle for freedom as early as possible. Netaji urged Indian soldiers serving with the British Army to refuse to fight for the rulers and come over to the INA and upon Indian officials working for the British Government to cooperate with the Provisional Government in fighting the holy war. He assured the Indian people that there was nothing to fear as long as they did not work as agents of the British and that the seat of the Provisional Government would, in due course, be shifted to Indian soil, liberated from British rule. He advised Indians to stay away from the US-British airfields, ammunition factories and other military installations to avoid being hurt as a result of Indo-Japanese attacks. He concluded by saying that at this crucial moment in history, India expected all Indians to do their duty. On 4th April, Netaji appointed Lt. Col. A C. Chatterjee as the governor of the newly liberated territories of India.

Paradoxically, the Battle of Imphal saw very little fighting in Imphal city proper during 1944, although clashes raged all around Manipur's capital and even occurred as close as Nungshigum, some 5 miles (8 km) to the north and Red Hill (or Maibam Loopaching), some 10 miles (16 km) to the south. However, barring some aerial attacks targeting the Imphal airfields by the Japanese Army Air Force, the city emerged relatively unscathed for the over four-month-long battle, the period when the city was under the siege of the Japanese-INA troops. For over two months, Imphal city was completely cut off from the rest of the world by land and kept supplied by air. However, militarily, it remained the nerve centre of the Allied forces. The actual hostilities pertaining to the Battle of Imphal were spread across the valley and hills of Manipur in different directions simultaneously to many clusters that also spilled over to certain parts of the adjacent Naga Hills, including Kohima (the present-day capital of the state of Nagaland). [11] [12]

INA forces that accompanied the Japanese in the liberation war of India did not have wireless transmitters/operators or any other means to regularly share with the INA Headquarters the details of their clashes against the Allied forces on Indian soil. Therefore, their side of the stories of the Battle of Imphal and, for that matter, the Battle of Kohima could not be adequately disseminated, even among their fellow soldiers and higher-ups. Also, it has not been possible to lay hands on the Japanese accounts, if there are any, of the battles. It is understood that because of the censorship of the Japanese History Textbooks during the Allied Occupation of Japan (1945–1952) just after World War 2, the chronicled records of the campaign have been rendered non-existent. Whatever reports on these crucial battles have so far been recounted, these are primarily based either on the local sources (in Manipur and Nagaland) or the Anglo-American versions of the conflicts, which clearly and wittingly ignored and played down the triumphant roles of the joint INA-Japanese soldiers in general, the INA fighters, in particular.

Thus, many books on the subject are replete with the success stories of the Allied forces narrating, for instance, how they broke the Imphal siege or how they won back Kohima from the control of the joint INA-Japanese forces. But the stories of how the British, in the first place, had lost their territories in India to the INA-Japanese joint forces are thin on the ground. Hence, barring some scattered records, here and there, of their early successes in Manipur and Naga Hills, proper accounts of the initial achievements of the joint INA-Japanese liberation forces in their clashes against the Allied forces through which a vast area of Manipur and substantial territories of Naga Hills came under their control and had remained so for a few months are few and far between.

The fact that the Azad Hind Fauj, backed by the Japanese, successfully penetrated the British Indian frontier in North-East India, occupied a large territory in Manipur and Naga Hills, and kept the occupied areas under their administration for four months bears the testimony that the defending British forces had suffered a significant setback in the confrontations and got a nice beating in their home ground from the Indian Liberation Forces. But books recounting such stories are scarce.

Earlier, it was highlighted that the Nagas, by and large, depended on oral tradition (passing stories from one generation to the other) and did not give importance to recording them in written forms. They considered the oral stories to be the most legitimate proof of any events or disputes that might have arisen between different parties, villages, or individuals. Things have changed in the recent past whereby the educated Nagas are in pursuit of documenting all those oral stories in writings and recordings (both audio and videos). One such story under the caption "Our Netaji Subhas Chandra Bose" thus appeared on 26th January 2022 in the Nagaland Post, Nagaland State's first and highest circulated newspaper. It provides a lot of significant insights into this historical battle. The following paragraphs are based on the same article:

> In 1944, the INA and the Japanese Army began Operation 'U GO', moving its troops across the Chindwin River towards its objectives: Imphal, Kohima and march to Delhi. On 15th March, they crossed the Chindwin River with their plan of crossing the Naga Hills to Dimapur railway and going to Delhi via Assam through their slogan, "Delhi Chalo".
>
> It is important to remember that the British started surveying Naga Hills in 1922 and came up with the Maps in 1943. As per Vikenyu Naga (a Naga British Labour Commander) account, one man stole the map and gave it to the Japanese, which helped them to write all the important villages, mountains, rivers and different routes in their own language. With the map in their hand, they were earnestly looking forward to meeting some Nagas from the Naga Hills for guidance from Myanmar to Kohima. During this time, the Japanese Imperial Army and the Indian National Army led by Netaji Subhas Chandra Bose already had a working relationship.

[15]A.Z. Phizo mentioned that he had no idea how the Japanese came to know that he and his brother were Nagas. But they came in search of them and asked them for help. The Japanese officers invited them to talk, and in their first meeting, they brought the map of Nagaland, showing all the minute details of villages, mountains, rivers and different routes. During this meeting, they were also introduced to the INA leader Subhas Chandra Bose. It is evident that with the maps and cooperation from the people, they became even more confident to enter the Naga Hills, probably taking British Inspection Bungalows as their reference point en route to Kohima.

There were three Japanese columns advancing on Kohima via different routes. General Sato sent Miyazaki with the main infantry group in the direction of the village of Ukhrul, where he would capture stores and then move to block the road at Kohima. Another battalion of the 58th regiment was sent through the wilds of the Somra tract to the North, while Sato's own column would travel the central route via Kharasom. The routes of advance were dictated by what passable tracks existed and took the advancing Japanese in the direction of three British garrisons. There was little room for improvising on the move, given the size of the Army and the wildness of the terrain. Lieutenant Nishidas's map-making foray would gain Sato vital time in his advance, but for the marching soldiers, the journey into India was a test.

Mention may be made that the Japanese vehemently opposed Subhas Chandra Bose's coming to the front, citing security reasons. Even then, Bose was making occasional forays into Imphal and Nagaland to cheer his man and study the battle on the ground, ignoring Japanese advice. When the Imphal offensive started, there was an information blackout for him for 15 days. Subhas Chandra Bose, with many INAs and Japanese troops, along with captured 1st Assam Regiment at Jesami,

---

[15] A. Z. Phizo, or Zapu Phizo (16 May 1904 – 30 April 1990), was a Naga nationalist leader with British nationality. Under his influence, the Naga National Council asserted the right to self-determination, which took the shape of armed resistance after the Indian state imposed the Armed Forces Special Powers Act in 1958. Naga secessionist groups regard him as the "Father of the Naga Nation".

went through the eastern route towards Kohima via Lozaphuhu, Phek BIB, Khuza, Mutsale, Ruzazho and later moved to Suthozu, Yoruba, Chozuba, Chesezu, Thenyizu, Chakhabama to Kohima which is the shortest route among all from Homalin, Chindwin to reach Kohima (Approx. 447km Arial distance via Google map). Some had gone towards K.Basa, K.Bawe, Thiphuzu, Phesachodu, Kikruma. Some troops went to Phugi, Thurutsuswu village camp, Khetsami and Dzulha. At the same time, some marched towards northeast of Kohima via Chepoketa British IB (Inspection Bungalow) and Satakha IB in the rear. Some soldiers pass through the Chindwin River towards the Zunheboto, Tuensang and Mon areas as the rear front of northeast patrol and security. [13].

In the same article, the author, who wrote it as the Convenor of India Freedom Fighter (INA) Children's Welfare in Nagaland, Mr Vevotso Sapu, correctly added, in his own words, that:

Historic moments and times cannot be hidden for long; it may be a little late to unearth the historical fact, but there is no definite time frame for such research. With this in mind, as there are hundreds of eyewitnesses saying the same thing from various villages and stories passing down even to their children and grandchildren about their association with INA and Bose, it gives much room for researchers to be excited to piece together the missing links of history. The Nagas have been taking the Oral tradition as the most authentic source of history for centuries, and hence, along with many other sources that speak of Netaji and INA's presence on the battlefront during the 1944 war, this particular event and the missing link has been collected and documented, as a window to further research. After all, Oral history is still a history and can't be ignored.

Thus, the imperative need for thorough and meticulous research on the Second World War's Imphal campaign by the joint INA-Japanese forces with a particular reference to the Battle of Imphal and the Battle of Kohima cannot be overemphasised to bring out the true history of the confrontation. While there is no doubt that the British war machine had kept the world body in general and the Indian public especially in the dark on the subject, it is unfortunate that more than seven and a half decades of the country's independence, authentic history of India's Liberation War that was fought by the INA in 1944 under the leadership of Netaji Subhas Chandra Bose with the Japanese support in this front of Northeast India has not yet been duly brought to light and chronicled.

Be that as it may, it is a historical fact that the advance of the joint INA-Japanese liberation force in the Imphal-Kohima region had been very swift at the outset. They overwhelmed a vast territory of Manipur and a large area of Naga Hills soon. However, before long, their early success was met with stiff defensive resistance from the British Army, primarily manned by the Indian soldiers on their payroll. The INA and Japanese forces wanted to stop a British offensive before it could reorganise or gather adequate strength. Accordingly, they continued their combative operations simultaneously in both the Imphal and Kohima sectors. However, the INA halted within three miles of Imphal due primarily to the absence of the necessary air support.

At the same time, the enemy Allied forces poured reinforcements into Imphal by air in a desperate last-minute stand. Lord Mountbatten, the British Commander, was to defend Imphal at all costs. The delivery of ninety-nine transport aircraft from Britain and the Mediterranean in April proved to be a serendipity for the British and a bolt from the blue for the Indian Liberation forces engaged in the Imphal campaign. Thus, in the defensive battle of Imphal, the Allied forces were able to adequately replenish their regular supply of consumables by air to meet the challenging situation in the war that was fought on their own ground near their own base, in the only areas where their existing lines of communication could adequately support them in a large-scale campaign. Besides, their air bases were also located quite close to the battlefront. It was totally in contrast to the prevailing position of the combined INA-Japanese troops. They greatly needed more air support to keep up their offensive campaign and maintain their dwindling supply of food, arms, and ammunition. The delay in vanquishing Imphal in three weeks, as initially calculated by Mutaguchi, put the entire Japanese plan of the Imphal campaign in jeopardy. Then, the rain came ahead of schedule, aggravating the difficult straits further. With their own supply line chocked, it became tough for the combined

INA-Japanese soldiers to manage the minimum ration for their survival and even to beat a defensive retreat properly.

It is pertinent to highlight here that the Imphal-Kohima region is a very inhospitable terrain. During the rainy season, which usually lasts from mid-May to early September, the jungle paths become very muddy, and small streams can quickly turn into big rivers. This place is very distressful because of the harsh living conditions. There are many types of insects here, like sandflies, ticks, mosquitoes, and leeches, which are particularly troublesome as they crawl up your legs at night and suck your blood until they are full. The mosquitoes here are some of the biggest and most annoying in the world. Some types of mosquitoes, especially those found around Mao in the present-day Senapati district of Manipur, can cause severe skin sores that look like smallpox.

Where there are lots of insects, there are usually lots of diseases. So, in this region, people are susceptible to different diseases like dengue fever, scrub typhus, malaria, cholera, scabies, yaws, sprue, and all types of dysentery. There's also a condition called Naga sore, which is caused by pulling off leeches and leaving their heads under the skin. After a few days, a small blister appears and grows until it's about five or six inches across. This blister can destroy not just the skin but also the flesh and muscles underneath. It smells awful and can be deadly if not treated properly. The best way to deal with a leech is to let it finish sucking blood and fall off on its own or to burn it with the end of a cigarette. In that case, no harm is done. [14]

That the joint INA-Japanese Imphal campaign during World War II in 1944 to liberate India from British colonial rule ended in tragic failure in the midst of all the above-mentioned challenges is now well-known. Different experts have attributed various causes to the fiasco from diverse perspectives. Some experts ascribe the INA-Japanese reverses to the lack of preparedness in the extension and consolidation of the supply lines to the battlefront and to the underestimation of the enemy's strengths. Some attribute the failure to the Japanese overconfidence, given their past experience with the British forces. Some Pundits also criticised the fact that the Japanese planners had failed to take into account that the Allied forces, in the meanwhile, considerably augmented their capabilities and duly factored in the same in their strategy during the planning stage of the operation.

However, the British propounded the idea that the Japanese had made a fatal mistake in supposing that as soon as India was invaded, there would be a nationalist revolution which would completely neutralise British and American military strength in India, thereby leaving the field open for Bose's so-called 'puppet forces' to fight for India'. Of course, it had nothing more than its vicious propaganda value, as is evident from the subsequent revelations.

When discussing military operations, it's easy to find faults in hindsight. However, when recounting history, it's crucial to consider the limitations and the compulsions of the time, and the events should be evaluated from a long-term perspective and their ultimate outcome. From the Indian point of view, the INA's aim of liberating the subcontinent from British rule eventually succeeded, and the sacrifices of the Azad Hind Fauj personnel in the Imphal campaign were not in vain, as evidenced by the events narrated in the next chapter.

From the Japanese perspective, the Imphal campaign was a decisive operation. Success, as noted by the Director of Military Intelligence, would have threatened the use of India as a British base. Conversely, failure implied that the Japanese would 'probably never launch another offensive'.

Simultaneously, the Army Headquarters in India acknowledged in a confidential dispatch that the results of the Japanese offensive could have been catastrophic for the British had they managed to establish a solid foothold in the area. The conquest of even a single Indian State by the Japanese would have had far-reaching effects on morale and politics, as the plain of Imphal was a prize whose capture might have significantly altered the course of the war in Eastern and Southern Asia and profoundly influenced the history of India and China.

Even a post-war British military historian has noted that if Imphal had fallen, one of the consequences could have been a revolt in Bengal and

Bihar against British rule, potentially on a much larger scale than the riots of 1942. It highlights the strategic importance of the Imphal campaign in the broader context of World War II. [15]

In the middle of the tumultuous backdrop of World War II, there is no denying that the INA-Japanese combined team had embarked upon a daring and high-risk venture. However, considering all relevant aspects, their calculated risks can be deemed justifiable given the circumstances prevailing during those wartime days. With a touch of luck in their favour, there was every chance for their endeavour to succeed, yielding substantial dividends for both India and Japan.

As ill luck would have it, the early rains turned the Kabaw valley through which the INA-Japanese supply route lay into raging torrents. It made it impossible for any wheeled traffic to move. This caused a complete stoppage of all supplies from the start of June 1944 onwards. The INA and Japanese troops had now to survive only on the dwindling stocks of supplies they were left with. These were fast petering out, and the troops on India's liberation mission were almost on starvation rations. There was no replenishment of arms and ammunitions to fight with or food items to survive on. It took time for the Japanese think tanks to recognise the enormity of the desperate straits. They gambled heavily on the capture of Imphal and its vast store of supplies, but they lost. That they had almost pulled off the impossible was a small consolation. The belated attack they had launched gave the enemy a chance to reorganise, and the premature arrival of monsoon simply washed off their early successes. The soldiers had been severely degraded by sickness due to malaria, typhus and dysentery. They had suffered heavily due to enemy air attacks, especially in the open plains of the Imphal valley, where the jungle canopy cover was far less dense. Now, they were reduced to abject starvation. It was a human tragedy of the most monumental proportions. A general withdrawal was ordered from the Imphal front on 18th July 1944, and the Japanese and INA Armies fell back in the line of the Chindwin River.

As the spring of 1945 unfurled, the Axis powers found themselves on the brink of defeat. The relentless march of the Soviet forces from the

East and the Western Allies from the West had Berlin in a vice-like grip. In a desperate bid to evade capture, Adolf Hitler and his companion Eva Braun chose death over dishonour, ending their lives in suicide.

On 7th May 1945, General Alfred Jodl of the German High Command signed an unconditional surrender of all German forces at Reims, France. Despite initial hopes to limit the surrender to forces fighting the Western Allies, General Dwight Eisenhower demanded a complete surrender, including forces fighting in the East. If not complied with, Eisenhower planned to seal off the Western front, leaving Germans in the hands of the Soviet forces. Following orders from Hitler's successor, Grand Admiral Karl Donitz, Jodl signed the surrender. With signatures from Russian General Ivan Susloparov, French General Francois Sevez, and General Walter Bedell Smith for the Allied Expeditionary Force, Germany was officially defeated.

Nevertheless, in the Asian theatre, Japan vowed to fight to the end despite clear indications that they had little chance of winning. By this time, the Axis powers, including the U. S., had already suffered significant casualties, but Japan showed no signs of accepting unconditional surrender. It created complications for the U.S. So, to force the Japanese to surrender without stretching the war further, President Truman authorised the use of atomic bombs. Accordingly, on 6th August 1945, the United States of America dropped one atomic bomb on the Japanese city of Hiroshima, which was followed by another atomic bomb on the Japanese city of Nagasaki on 9th August 1945. The back-to-back bombings of the two Japanese cities marked the first use of nuclear weapons in war. The immediate death toll was estimated to be 140 thousand. Besides, the long-term effects of radiation exposure caused a range of health problems, including cancer, leukaemia, and other potentially fatal illnesses, resulting in many more deaths and illnesses in the years that followed, including a profound impact on the environment and the economy of Japan. The unprecedented heartless acts of bombings by the U.S. on innocent civilian populations using 'weapons of mass destruction' left behind a legacy of destruction and suffering that is still felt today.

It is widely held that the USA resorted to the use of weapons of mass destruction against an enormous number of harmless people primarily due to the following reasons:

- The U.S. wanted to end the war hurriedly to minimise further casualties.
- However, despite being on the verge of defeat, Japan showed no signs of accepting an unconditional surrender. Accordingly, the U.S. forced the issue by using the weapon of mass destruction on innocent citizens.
- The only other alternative was to have a full-fledged invasion of Japan, which would have led to heavy casualties among Allied forces. The U. S. administration wanted to avoid this at all costs.
- By bombing Japan with two atomic bombs, the U.S. demonstrated the power of its new weapon to the world, particularly to the Soviet Union.

The unparalleled massive civilian casualties as a result of the use of nuclear weapons by the United States of America on unsuspecting Japanese civilians remains a subject of unending ethical debate.

After the bombing of Hiroshima and Nagasaki, everything changed abruptly. It became clear that Japan's surrender was imminent in a matter of days. From 12th August onward, Netaji had almost nonstop discussions at his Singapore residence with his top civilian and military colleagues on the next course of action of the Provisional Government of Azad Hind that was proclaimed on 21st October in Singapore. How the INA and the Indian Independence League (IIL) should respond to the end of the war and the British re-occupation of Singapore and Malaya was extensively debated, among other things. During the deliberations on the next course of action, Mohammad Zaman Kiani felt that Netaji should perhaps lead the INA surrender in Singapore, where the Indian National Army had been born three years earlier. But Netaji felt differently; his surrendering to the enemy was out of the question. The deliberations covered many other pressing matters and concluded at sunrise on 16th August 1945.

On the same day, 16th August 1945, Netaji issued a brief order on the letterhead of the Arzi Hukumat-e Azad Hind, the Provisional Government of Free India. It read: 'During my absence from Syonan (Singapore), Major General M. Z. Kiani will represent the Provisional Government of Azad Hind.'

Early on in these confabulations, [16]Colonel Cyril J Stracey walked in carrying a number of paper designs and miniature models of the INA martyrs' monument. Netaji had already laid its foundation stone in the previous month, on 8th July 1945, on the seafront of Singapore, where INA was born in 1942. While laying the foundation stone, Netaji had said: 'The future generation of Indians who will be born not as slaves, but as free men, because of your colossal sacrifice, will bless your names and proudly proclaim to the world that you, their forebearers, fought and suffered reverses in the battle of Manipur, Assam and Burma, but, through temporary failure, you paved the way to ultimate success.' That was indeed a prophetic statement from Netaji Subhas Chandra Bose more than two years before India could unshackle itself from the bondage of British colonial rule!

The Unknown Warrior, whose identity remains a mystery, symbolised the countless soldiers who had fought bravely and made the ultimate sacrifice in the INA's campaign against the British in an attempt to liberate India. The memorial was meant to be a symbol of the INA's dedication and determination to free India from colonial rule.

When Colonel Stracey brought paper designs and miniature models of the INA martyrs' monument, Netaji looked through them and selected

---

[16] Colonel Cyril John Stracey was a notable Anglo-Indian officer in the INA. Born in 1915 in Kurnool, India, he pursued his education at St. Joseph's in Bangalore before joining the Indian Military Academy in 1935. Stracey's journey with the INA began after the Japanese captured him during World War II. He played a significant role in the INA, leading a large contingent of new volunteers and contributing to the construction of the INA Monument in Singapore. Despite the challenges he faced, Stracey's dedication to the cause of Indian independence remained unwavering. His story is a testament to the diverse backgrounds of those who fought for India's freedom and highlights the contributions of the Anglo-Indian community to the nationalist movement.

one. He told Stracey that time was now very short and enquired if he would be able to complete the construction of the memorial.

'Certainly, sir', Stracey replied. Others present in the room looked sceptical, and they were not to blame for doubting that he would be able to find the materials and the workers to complete the task, given the fluid situation prevailing in Singapore at that time. However, with that confident reply, Stracey saluted smartly and went off.

About a week later, a marble monument of simple but elegant design, twenty-five feet tall, came up on Singapore's seafront. It consisted of three thick pillars, the middle pillar slightly higher than the other two. The INA motto was inscribed near the top ends of the pillars: Itmad (Faith) on the middle pillar, Ittefaq (Unity) on the left pillar, and Quarbani (Sacrifice) on the right pillar.

Every effort was made to complete the installation of the INA monument before Netaji left, but alas, it could not be done. However, when the monument was finally ready, Major General Mohammad Zaman Kiani, whom Netaji had entrusted with the responsibility of Singapore, performed the inaugural ceremony that coincided with the mourning ceremony of the most tragic death of the supreme leader-Netaji the Great! He lost his life in a plane crash at Taipei in Formosa (Taiwan) on 18th August 1945. Kiani recalled it in his memoir and added that it was a moment of profound poignancy. He admitted without being ashamed that almost all those who attended the ceremony broke down when eulogies to Netaji Subhas Chandra Bose were offered. The solemnity of the occasion was palpable, and the air was thick with grief as if the entire environs were weeping for the loss of such a great leader.

Less than 20 days after its inaugural ceremony that coincided with the most tragic death of Netaji, the INA martyrs' monument was dynamited to rubble at 6 p.m. on 6th September 1945 on the order of Lord Mountbatten (who, incidentally, was appointed by our leaders as the first Governor-General of India immediately our country became free from the British rule). A group of Indian soldiers of the 17th Dogra Regiment placed the charges at the base of the monument, and a British major checked the fuses before they were lit. A brigadier wearing a Scottish kilt – probably Patrick Mckerron, who would be Singapore's colonial administrator from 1946 to 1950 – then inspected the guard of honour by Dogra detachment and made a speech.

Since the British viewed the INA as traitors and collaborators, they wanted to erase any trace of the Azad Hind Fauj's presence in Singapore. They also wanted to suppress the nationalist sentiments that the INA had aroused among the Indian population in Singapore and Malaya. They feared that the INA might inspire a revolt against the British rule in India and other colonies. Accordingly, Lord Louis Mountbatten ordered the demolition of the INA Memorials as part of his policy of "denazification\" of Singapore. He wanted to remove any symbols or monuments that were associated with the Japanese occupation or their allies.

On the evening of 6th September 1945, when the INA martyrs' monument was being dynamited to rubble, a group of surrendered rank-and-file INA soldiers were squatting nearby in a huddle. They became agitated when they realised what was happening, and one of them loudly cursed Mountbatten by name, saying that one day he would meet the same fate as the memorial.

The curse that was once dismissed as a mere superstition turned out to be true! Although it's beyond the scope of this story, it might as well be mentioned that on 27th August 1979, Lord Mountbatten was blown to bits by a bomb planted on his boat by members of the Provisional Irish Republican Army (P-IRA) while he was holidaying in his summer retreat, a castle on the north-western coast of the Republic of Ireland. The reason adduced by the IRA for his execution was clear. According to them, what they did to him was what Mountbatten had been doing all his life to others!

Ruefully, in the late evening of the same day, 6th September 1945 on which the INA martyrs' monument was dynamited, many Singaporean Indians who either witnessed or came to know of the tragic incident of detonating the INA martyrs' monument by dynamites came to the site quietly under the cover of darkness and collected the fragments as if these were some precious objects. Today, one such fragment is reportedly in possession of the Netaji Research Bureau in Kolkata.

The fact that even today, many people cherish these pieces of the demolished INA martyrs' monument with utmost reverence and respect is a testament to their unwavering loyalty and admiration towards their beloved leader. After India gained independence, Prime Minister Jawaharlal Nehru personally gifted a fragment that had 'SUBHAS CH' on it to Cyril John Stracey, who had designed the monument at Netaji's instance. It's a touching reminder of Netaji's legacy and his unwavering commitment towards India's freedom struggle.

In 1995, the site where the INA Memorial once stood was marked by the National Heritage Board as a historical site. Subsequently, with financial donations from the Indian Community in Singapore, the Singapore Government rebuilt the Memorial to honour the INA soldiers who gave up their lives to liberate India from the clutches of British imperialism.

Earlier, the Japanese Prime Minister Gen. [17]Tojo resigned on 18th July 1944 in the wake of the disaster in Imphal theatre (though for different reasons). Despite the failure of the Japanese Higher Command in this critical operation, the sheer heroism of the troops and their willingness to obey orders, which caused them such harrowing levels of suffering, serves to highlight the Samurai spirit of not just the Army of Japan but also of the Azad Hind Fauj which it had helped raise and train and which seemed to have imbibed its military culture and ethos of militant nationalism as its prime motivational principle. Subhash Bose had been able to infuse the Samurai spirit of militant nationalism into this hastily formed force. That he succeeded in such a short time only highlights

---

[17] After resigning on 18th July 1944, Japanese Prime Minister Hideki Tojo was eventually tried and convicted for war crimes following Japan's surrender to the Allied powers. He was executed on 23rd December 1948 in Tokyo's Sugamo Prison for the so-called 'crimes against humanity'. The war crimes were tried by the International Military Tribunal for the Far East, established by a charter issued by U.S. Army Gen. Douglas MacArthur.

his unbounded charisma and sterling qualities as an inspirational military leader.

The combined Japanese-INA force had suffered staggering casualties of about 40,000 dead in their challenging endeavour to liberate India from colonial rule. The British had expected the INA to disintegrate completely in such terrible circumstances and surrender in droves. The miracle was, in the face of the intense human suffering involved, the INA morale held. Regardless of the fearsome toll taken by disease and starvation, the retreating INA units maintained their organic cohesion, good order and military discipline, unlike the British and their allies, who in 1942 had wholly disintegrated when routed by the Japanese having command of the air at that time. [16] [17] [18]

Despite being battered and bloodied, the Indian National Army emerged like a phoenix from the smouldering ashes of tactical defeat in the Imphal-Kohima theatre. Their banners may have fluttered in retreat, but the indomitable spirit of freedom blazed forth. Soon, an eternal flame danced across the synapses of every Indian soul. The colonial rulers failed to extinguish the fire of liberty ignited by the Azad Hind Fauj in the hearts and minds of Indians. Within a couple of years, this spark ultimately burst into flames of an uprising among fellow citizens and led to revolts within the Indian armed forces. Ultimately, this relentless struggle compelled the British to relinquish their hold on the Indian subcontinent. Thus, India's Liberation War, waged by the INA under the visionary leadership of Netaji Subhas Chandra Bose, was eventually crowned with success. This crucial moment echoes the history and awaits further exploration in the next chapter.

****

Chapter 7

Finally, the Victory!

Perhaps neither Subhas Chandra Bose nor the Japanese knew how the British war machine had kept the Indian public in the dark about the INA. Throughout the war, they had been depicting the Japanese as a brutal and inhuman race whose advance had to be resisted at any cost; the INA was characterised as a puppet army and Bose as a stooge of the Japanese. British counter-measures against Bose and the Japanese proved highly effective.

It was common for the British to ridicule and belittle Subhas Chandra Bose and the INA he led. The British depicted the Azad Hind Fauj, or the INA, as full of spies who would not hesitate to desert the Japanese and start helping the British at the first opportunity. At the same time, to create mistrust of the Japanese within the INA, it was propagated that the Japanese considered the INA unreliable and, hence, were using them merely as spies and stretcher-bearers. Anti-Japanese and anti-Bose propaganda were launched in Bengali, Punjabi, Hindustani, Tamil, Gujarati and English. The British narratives portrayed Bose as a dreamer who degraded Indian self-respect by calling on Japan to secure the freedom of India.

The main thrust of the propaganda was to drive a wedge and create discord between civilians and military elements of the INA, between the Japanese and Subhas Bose, and vice versa. One report commented in a radio broadcast: "We suggested that S.C. Bose was merely a tool in the hands of Rash Behari Bose and the move of the Headquarters of the Provisional Government of India to Burma was caused by its unpopularity in Malaya".

British psychological warfare contributed a lot towards the waning of the morale of the INA personnel. It was widely propagated that on account of this propaganda, many INA soldiers deserted. Inside the country, British propaganda heavily influenced the perception of the political leaders about Japan: they began to view her as a hustling aggressor to be resisted at all costs. The success of British propaganda nearly sandbagged the possible drive of the Azad Hind movement into India. It prevented the Indian people from appropriately appreciating the nature of the movement, which Bose had started to oust the British from India.

Despite the defeat, Bose was not willing to give up the fight for the liberation of India. At a public meeting in Bangkok, he said that the march to Delhi would continue to liberate India. The INA may not march to Delhi via Imphal, but it must be borne in mind that, like Rome, there are many roads leading to India. Maybe his reading of the international situation convinced him that after the war, there was bound to be a clash between the Soviet Union and the Western powers, which could be utilised for the achievement of India's freedom. He outlined a twofold task: first, to continue the armed struggle, and second, to agitate for Indian independence in the international field, making use of every conflict within the camp of the so-called United Nations and, in particular, the conflict between the Soviets and the Anglo-Americans. Towards the close of the war, Bose's stand was that to destroy the common enemy, Britain, both Japan and the Provisional Government should try every possible means and help each other. Therefore, he requested that Tokyo act as a go-between and approach the Soviet Union on his behalf.

After the Japanese surrender on 15th August 1945, Bose was asked to come to Tokyo for further consultation. General Terauchi gave him a special plane. The plane crashed on the way, and his tragic death and the surrender of the INA were considered the end of a vibrant chapter in India's struggle for freedom. After the war was doomed to failure, the subsequent events proved that the British attempted to denigrate INA officers by putting them on trial for treason. Wavell, the British viceroy, was undecided over this, as it was not known whether Bose was alive or dead. He wrote to the Secretary of State for India about the difficulties involved in handling the INA, as this was the first occasion in which an anti-British politician had acquired a hold over a substantial number of men in the Indian army, and the consequences were likely to be incalculable. Wavell wrote that many of the INA men had a great regard for Bose, and he might yet become a national hero. The viceroy wanted the British Cabinet to consider Bose's case carefully and observed that it would be good if he were disposed of without being sent back to India. [1]

During the Imphal campaign, about fifteen hundred INA soldiers were captured by the British Indian Army. Many more fell into the British hands in Burma, Thailand, Malaya and Singapore. The repatriation to India of the Indian soldiers who joined the INA started in May 1945 and continued till the first quarter of 1946. Although [18]some of the INA prisoners who were captured during the Imphal campaign were at once court-martialled and punished, the need for the Government of India to formulate a definite policy towards the INA personnel arose after the war came to an end. The Government of India did not take any steps against the civilian recruits of the INA from Southeast and East Asia. However, their decision to prosecute the former members of the Indian army who joined the INA had profound repercussions in Indian politics, which forms a significant aspect of the INA story.

Within a few days of the end of the Pacific War, it was known that the India Office in London would leave it entirely to the Government of India to formulate a policy towards the Indian soldiers who had joined the INA. The Government of India, more specifically the authorities of the Indian army, lost no time in taking the task. Within a week of the end of the Pacific War, a press communique issued by the Government of India stated that they were "Considering very carefully the treatment to be given to the Indian soldiers who joined the enemy."

The British were generally hostile to the INA and, more particularly, to its officers, who were considered responsible for having weaned over the ordinary ranks from their loyalty to the British Crown. Strictly

---

[18] According to the Secretary of the War Department of the Government of India, 27 were court-martialled and punished, and nine were hanged during the war.

speaking, there was no one view in the Indian army about the INA. In fact, on the INA question, one can trace at least two different opinions among the British officers in the Indian army. The senior British officers, such as the GOC Eastern Command, the GOC Southern Command, the Commanders of the Central Command and the North West Army, and the Adjutant-General of the Army Headquarters were very hostile to the INA. As professionals, these officers held stability in the army and loyalty to the higher authorities above everything else. These officers felt that discipline in the army should be maintained at all costs and that no other consideration should be allowed to stand in the way of administering discipline. They vehemently charged the INA officers with breaking the trust placed in them and characterised the INA officers as "rabble". The bitterness of this group of senior British officers against the INA as a whole can be partially explained by the fact that many of these officers had encountered the INA in the front.

Moreover, the opinion of some of them was coloured by their intense dislike for the INA's Supreme Commander. One senior British officer described Bose as "a plump Bengali Brahman of over-weening personal ambition" who "permeated the core of the INA body with a rigid, utterly intolerant, tightly closed and diseased mentality." These British officers were disposed to see the INA question by itself in isolation from any political consideration. They failed to foresee the political consequences that any vindictive measure against the INA might create in the country. In general, they viewed the INA question purely as a case of administration of military discipline. They suggested "routine treatment" for INA personnel for the crime of throwing off their loyalty and waging war against the British Crown. The logical corollary of this view would be the punishment of all the Indian soldiers who had joined the INA.

The higher military and civil authorities of New Delhi adopted a more cautious and considerate view on the INA question. In any case, the possibility of the release of the INA prisoners without any trial was ruled out, given the known opinion of the senior British officers - on whom the efficiency and, to a great extent, the existence of the Indian army ultimately depended. It would have been too great a blow to their faith in the higher authorities in New Delhi. On the other hand, the views of the senior British officers were not entirely shared by the highest military authorities, as the latter believed that the treatment to be meted out to the INA was not merely a military question. It was partly political, and the official policy's consequences were bound to impact Indian public opinion. It could affect the prospects of a satisfactory post-war political settlement between the two countries. The Government authorities in New Delhi supported the line of thinking of the Headquarters of the Indian army. [2]

In the book [19]"THE TRANSFER OF POWER 1942-7 (Volume VI)" edited by Nicholas Mansergh and Penderel Moon, some vital details of the INA personnel held in the custody of the British at the end of World War II are available under the caption "The treatment of Indian and Burman Renegades and Collaborators with the Enemy (INDIAN MILITARY OFFENDERS). These are furnished in Annexure I to India and Burma Committee Paper LB. (45) 16 L/WS/i/i577 No. 154 (ff 142-7). It's enlightening and gives an overview of how the British had planned to punish the INA personnel for their omissions and commissions in World War II.

The following details are an excerpt from THE TRANSFER OF POWER 1942-7 (Volume VI):

Item 154

(Annexure I to No. 154)

1. The main organizations composed of Indian personnel which collaborated with the Japanese or German forces, are,

---

[19] "The Transfer of Power 1942-7" is a comprehensive collection of documents that detail the constitutional relations between Britain and India during the final years of British rule. This 12-volume series was published by Her Majesty's Stationery Office (HMSO). The series includes unpublished documents from the India Office's official archives and private collections of Viceregal papers. This publication is invaluable for historians and researchers as it provides a detailed and nuanced understanding of the political and administrative processes that shaped the end of British colonial rule in India.

(a) Indian National Army (I.N.A. or J.I.F.S.). These are estimated to amount to —

20,000 men of the Indian Army, as well as

23,000 civilians (of whom 20,000 were resident ex-India)

(b) 950 Regt. (H.I.F.S.) (Hitler's Indian Foreign Legion). Of these men, some 3,000 are now in India.

The former compose the forces who, under the leadership of Subhas Chandra Bose, formed part of the Japanese Army. The latter correspondingly formed part of the German Army.

2. The individuals in each section when they have been recovered and questioned are divided into the following categories.

> (a) **Whites**: Those whose loyalty is beyond question. They are treated as any other recovered P.O.W. and will continue to serve in the Army.
>
> (b) **Greys**: Those whose loyalty was weak and who, subject to propaganda etc., broke down but who are not fundamentally and incurably disloyal. These are discharged as "services no longer required". They will forfeit pay for period spent as P.O.W. including time spent as a H.I.F./J.I.F., but not any amount issued as family allotment. They will not be given a war gratuity but, as an act of Grace, will be given leave with 42 days pay prior to discharge. They will be entitled to draw any pension earned by service excluding the period spent as a prisoner of war.
>
> (c) **Blacks**: Those whose conduct merits trial for a criminal offence or those whose release would be dangerous.

3. (a) Investigations into the INA activities show that of those who formerly belonged to the INA, 16,000 have been recovered, of whom

11,300 have been interrogated. The division into categories provisionally is as follows:

Black 2,565; Grey 5,091; White 3,644.

The above figures are provisional and may vary as the result of Courts "of enquiry which are yet to be held, and when statements by loyal P.O.W.s not yet recovered have been considered.

(b) In the case of 950 Regt. the 3,000 held in India have all been provisionally classified as Black. Further details of classification are not yet available.

4. As a result of interrogation, the following categories will be tried by court martial:

(a) Officers Indian Army 59

(b) V.C.O.s who became officers INA 29

(c) V.C.O.s who joined 950 Regt. 14

(d) Those who deserted from our lines, as opposed to being taken prisoner 40

(e) I.O.Rs who became officers 950 Regt. 12

(f) Those instrumental in causing death of any British or Allied subject in or out of battle 60

(g) Those guilty of brutal conduct, either to fellow JIFS/HIFS or to members of the Allied Forces 92

(h) Those who took part in capture or handing over to enemy [of] any British or Allied subject 53

(i) I.O.Rs who became officers INA and took a leading part in battle against us 240

(j) Fujiwara Volunteers (Men captured in Singapore and joining a force raised by the Japanese) 205

The C. in C. has directed that, in the first instance, the trials of those in trial categories other than (a), (b), (c), and (e) should proceed and that trials under these four categories should be postponed for the present.

5. As a result of the investigation, court-martial sentences are likely to be confirmed in the following cases:

(a) Persons causing death of any British or Allied subject whether in or out of battle **60**

(b) Brutal treatment to any British or Allied subject **92**

(c) Handing over to the enemy any British or Allied subject **53**

(d) The senior V.C.O. or I.O.R. of a party over ten in number which deserted and joined INA **40**

Numbers under other categories are not immediately available.

These offences in the "Black" category are serious offences for a soldier to commit, and the punishment is either Death or Transportation for life. To deal leniently with such cases would cause great offence to the Indian Army and, in particular, to those P.O.W.s who remained steadfastly loyal in spite of all the blandishments, propaganda, hardship and brutality to which they were subject. On the other hand, it should be remembered that Pandit Nehru and others are glorifying these men as true and long-sighted patriots.

It is estimated that death sentences may be imposed and continued [confirmed] and executed in approximately 50 cases mentioned above. The others would be commuted to varying periods of imprisonment. [3]

As mentioned earlier, some senior British Army officers were generally antagonistic to the INA personnel, particularly its leader, Netaji Subhas

Chandra Bose. This intense dislike prompted these British Officers to teach the captured Indian renegades and enemy collaborators certain exemplary lessons in a befitting manner for daring to go against mighty British Colonial rulers. They intended to punish them in such a way that no Indians would ever think of venturing into such audacious acts in the future. These British officers were determined to crush the spirit of independence Netaji Bose spawned in the INA personnel.

Accordingly, deviating from their standard procedure of military trial, the British government decided to keep an open trial and planned to arrange for the court martial of the detainees at Delhi's world-renowned Red Fort, Lal Qila, which historically served as the primary residence of the Mughal emperors. The idea behind holding the court martial at this iconic site was to give the widest possible publicity to the trial and make a mockery of Netaji's clarion call against the British Colonial rule in India, 'Chalo Dilli' that means 'Let's go to Delhi', from where Bose had intended to announce his victory.

Significantly, like never before, Subhas Bose's leadership in the INA had united people of all faiths for the cause of India, setting an example of communal harmony and reconciliation among the Indians. In the words of Sumit K Majumdar (EPW, 19 November 2016),

> *'Netaji had infected the once-mercenary Indian Army – which, in a policy of divide and rule had been organised along caste and religious lines by the British – with the viruses of secularism and nationalism. The united Indian soldiers now believed that they owed greater loyalty to Mother India's cause than to the characteristics of their own personal situations.'*
> [4]

That was an eyesore to the British rulers in India as it was dead set against their infamous practice of 'divide and rule' policy through which a handful of British so far managed to rule zillions of Indians for nearly 200 years. Therefore, in their retaliating plan of twisting the knife in the wound, they put one Hindu (Lt-Col. Prem Kumar Sahgal), one Muslim (Maj-Gen. Shah Nawaz Khan) and one Sikh (Lt-Col. Gurbaksh Singh Dhillon) in the first batch of accused to face the court-martial. Nevertheless, their sadistic design boomeranged on them in the final analysis.

The first and most significant of the highly publicised military trials began on 5th November 1945 inside Delhi's Red Fort. On the stand were three defendants — Shahnawaz Khan, Prem Sahgal and Gurbaksh Dhillon. All three were charged with treason as set out in Section 121 of the Indian Penal Code. Also, Dhillon was charged with murder under Section 302 of the IPC, while Khan and Sahgal were charged with abetment to murder. Arguing on behalf of the defendants were veteran Congressman Bhulabhai Desai, who was Chief Defence Counsel (CDC), Tej Bahadur Sapru, Jawaharlal Nehru, and Dr KN Katju. They had to present their case in front of a military tribunal comprising of senior British army officers.

The essence of the prosecution's arguments can be summed up by what Advocate General Sir Naushirwan Engineer said in court:

> The prosecution will submit that any plea that they [the accused] were bound or justified by law in doing what they did cannot avail them. Joining with rebels in an act of rebellion or with enemies in acts of hostility makes a man a traitor. An act of treason cannot give any sort of rights, nor can it exempt a person from criminal responsibility for the subsequent acts. Even if an act is done under a command where the command is traitorous, obedience to that command is also traitorous.

Once the prosecution was done making its case, CDC Desai took the floor. Over the course of 10 hours spread across two days, Desai presented a stirring defence without any interruption or notes. His argument was that:

> The issues at hand were matters for public international law, not British Indian municipal law. The Indian National Army was a properly constituted and self-governing army, run by Indian officers, with its own disciplinary code, ranks, uniforms and regalia, just like the British-run Indian Army on which it was closely modelled. It had two aims: the liberation of India

from British rule and the protection of Indian populations in Burma and Malaya, especially during the war. So, contrary to the prosecution's claims, it was not just a Japanese-run fifth column.

The INA fought on behalf of the Provisional Government of Free India, which complied with all the requirements of a proper state—control over resources, territories including the Andaman and Nicobar Islands albeit for 18 months, finances and the fact that they even enacted their own laws.

The Free India government was recognised as a sovereign government by Japan and a number of its allies, and following that, it declared war on Britain, which meant it could assume the rights of a belligerent state.

What Desai essentially did was turn the treason argument on its head on the point that under international law, an enslaved nation has a right to engage in battle for the overthrow of a foreign ruler. Shri Desai submitted that:

> It was a settled position in International Law that when two governments are at war with each other, the combatants acquire the status of belligerents, and the soldiers cannot be punished for murder and other offences under the municipal laws. The matter passes from the domain of municipal law to that of international law. Amidst the clash of arms, the ordinary criminal law becomes silent. Consequently, the charged INA officers were entitled to be treated as POWs.

Desai then asserted and explained, along the successive lines, the stage to which the international law has now reached if liberty and democracy are to have any meaning all over the world, and not merely just for a part of it, subjugated peoples' rights to fight for their liberation must be recognised and upheld:

> Any war made for the purpose of liberating oneself from foreign yoke is entirely justified by modern international law.

And it will be a travesty of justice if we were to be told as a result of any decision arrived at here or otherwise, that the Indian may go as a soldier and fight for the freedom of England against Germany, for England against Italy, for England against Japan. Yet, a stage may not be reached when a free Indian State may not wish to free itself from any country, including England itself. In other words, the erstwhile notion that only an independent sovereign state can validly declare war is outdated and allows for the furtherance of a vicious circle that people under subjugation would remain a subject race in perpetuity. Therefore, modern international law does recognise the conquered peoples' right to organise themselves and fight for freedom.

This is not politics; it is law, emphasised Desai.

Throughout the course of his arguments, Desai also kept returning to the question of allegiance of erstwhile soldiers of the British Indian Army joining the rebel Indian National Army. Were the three soldiers really required to maintain their allegiance to a government that had deserted them? On 16th February 1942, the British had surrendered Singapore to Japanese forces. British and Australian prisoners were sent to prisons and internment camps, but the 40,000 Indians surrendered troops from the British Indian Army **were given a choice** – either become POWs or switch allegiance to the Indian National Army.

Both the accused and witnesses had stated that the fall of Singapore had convinced them that Britain was incapable of protecting Indian interests and had therefore forfeited its claim to their allegiance . . . Shah Nawaz Khan testified that when forced to choose between King and Country, 'I decided to be loyal to my country'.

Despite the stirring defence put forward by Desai and his team, the court, on 31st December 1945, found all three men guilty of treason and one guilty of abetment to murder. The sentence delivered on 3rd January 1946 did not mandate the execution of the three officers, but they were summarily dismissed from service, ordered to forfeit all their pay and allowances, and sentenced to transportation (relocation of convicted criminals to a distant place). [5] (Emphasis by Subir)

During the war, there had been a complete blackout in India of any news about the INA. While young Indians had been listening in to Bose's radio broadcasts, their newspapers contained almost no reports about the INA's actual role as a freedom army that fought a war for India's liberation. So, when the newspapers began to carry detailed reports about the INA trials, the vast majority of Indians (and, especially, British residents of India) began hearing for the first time about the heroic fighting by an ill-equipped and poorly supplied but valiant freedom army of soldiers and civilian recruits, men and women, who had been prepared to lay down their lives so that India could be free. It had an electrifying impact on the nation, spurred further by the upright and attractive personalities of the three officers facing trial.

Demonstrations in sympathy with the accused INA soldiers occurred in Dhaka, Patna, Benares, Allahabad, Karachi, Bombay and many other places (with several killed in police firing), and the IB was especially concerned about a growing undercurrent of anti-European feelings evident in these demonstrations. Posters had appeared in Delhi and Calcutta threatening to kill twenty Englishmen for the hanging of every INA hero. British bosses were startled to hear their employees refer to Subhas Chandra Bose as 'the George Washington of India', with photos of him and the three INA officers taking on iconic status throughout the country. (In contrast, until then, Subhas Bose had been demonised in the English-language press.) Shops refused to serve British clients, and increasing evidence of racial hostility towards the British was manifested in mounting stories of insubordination across the country.

The Congress party - moribund in the wake of the crushing of Gandhi's Quit India movement - had been revived partly by this rush of patriotic fervour. The Muslim League, too, came out strongly in support of the INA, somewhat ironically so, given Bose's hostility to Jinnah in his broadcasts. The very fact that Muslims had such a prominent role in the Azad Hind army and government, made it impossible for the Muslim League to ignore the INA. Thus, in a rare moment of unity, joint Congress-League demonstrations were held in Delhi, Calcutta and Lahore backing the INA. **That was the last time the Hindus and the Muslims in undivided India fought for a common cause. Its result was there for everybody to see.**

Such was the patriotic fervour that Jawaharlal Nehru and Md Ali Jinnah, for the first time in their long careers, accepted the same brief - Nehru donning a barrister's gown after twenty-five years. Having effectively retired from the bar some two and half decades earlier, Nehru had decided to join the INA officers' defence team alongside the veteran Congressman Bhulabhai Desai and the seventy-three-year-old ailing barrister Tej Bahadur Sapru. This was an ironic twist for Nehru: when the INA was fighting in the trenches and forests of Manipur and Nagaland, Jawaharlal had provocatively travelled to Bengal and Assam and said that he would personally oppose Subhas Bose even at the head of his army. In the end, Jinnah and Nehru's membership of the defence team was little more than symbolic, as Bhulabhai Desai's eloquent advocacy needed no substitutes. [6]

Every word of this trial was reported by the press with befitting commentaries every day, and the three accused gained the sympathies of the whole nation.

The trial ended on 31st December. The British could read the writings on the wall to see the signs of time and acted wisely; whatever the original sentence of the court-martial, the Commander-in-Chief, Field-Marshal Sir Claude Auchinleck, reduced it to mere cashiering from service. They were finally released in the first week of January 1946. The reception that these three heroes of the Red Fort got was unprecedented in the annals of our history.

The release of General Shah Nawaz, Colonels Sehgal and Dhillon, under the compulsion of events, irretrievably damaged the prestige of the British Raj in India. It inspired all the patriotic forces in the country, including elements in our armed forces as well.

After their failure in the first trial, the British dropped the charge of waging war against the King. They still continued to tinker with the problem by holding a few more court-martial on the charge of committing atrocities. Indian people were not in a mood to tolerate anything of that sort.

Anger at racial discrimination and wretched service condition among the ratings – common sailors of the Royal Indian Navy (RIN) – had been simmering for quite some time. The passion to free motherland from tyrannical foreign rule had also taken hold as the INA trials progressed. The fuse was lit. The explosion came on the morning of 18th February 1946 when the ratings of the HMIS Talwar, a signal school located in Colaba, Bombay, started a mutiny. By the evening of the next day, the mutiny became widespread, involving 78 ships, 21 shore establishments, and over 20,000 ratings. In less than 48 hours, it completely crippled one of the most formidable navies of the Second World War. Naval ships were taken over, armouries broken open, and officers, British and Indian, ordered to leave their posts. Even the flagship of the Flag Officer Commanding RIN, Admiral John Henry Godfrey's, was taken over and converted into a control centre. The Union Jack and the White Ensign of the Royal Navy were pulled down and replaced with the tricolour of the Congress, the green flag of the Muslim League, and the red of the Communist Party.

The outbreak threatened to engulf all three arms of the defence forces, and the world was also watching this colossal revolt. It had all the elements necessary to administer a final push towards toppling the Raj. Three days later, Sir Claude Auchinleck, C-in-C of Indian armed forces, sent a desperate secret warning to PM Atlee: "We may be faced with complete rebellion, supported by the whole of the Indian armed Forces."

Barely 24 hours into the mutiny, on 19th February 1946, the British hustled to announce a Cabinet Mission, which was to travel to India and discuss the transfer of power with Indian stakeholders. Prime Minister Attlee announced this in the British Parliament on the very day he received news of the naval mutiny.

Naturally, the British were greatly alarmed. But more than the British, it was the great leaders of the Congress who were really upset and were now **ready to cooperate with the British to suppress this patriotic**

upsurge in the armed forces. A real business-like bargain based upon the spirit of give and take of all sorts was about to begin between our great leaders and the British. Gandhi came out most vocally against the ratings. Prominent Congress leader Sardar Vallabhbhai Patel condemned the ratings' revolt, terming it 'nothing but hooliganism', adding 'the ship of freedom was coming close to the shore of India; people should not go out and sink it'. On behalf of the Muslim League, Jinnah advised the ratings to surrender. Patel and Jinnah managed to persuade the ratings to surrender on 23rd February, giving an assurance that national parties would prevent any victimisation – a promise Patel had no authority to give nor the power to deliver upon. Nor was it kept. [7] [8]

How strongly the INA episode had rattled the British think-tank can be gauged from the notes of following deliberations of a British MP at a meeting at the official residence cum office of the Prime Minister of the United Kingdom, No. 10 Downing Street, on 13th February 1946. It is revealed from the records of the last days of British rule in India published in the Volume VI of the "THE TRANSFER OF POWER 1942-7", the relevant portion of which is quoted below:

426

Rough notes of points made by various Members of the Parliamentary Delegation at the meeting at No. 10 Downing Street on 13th February 1946

L/P&J/io/59:ff33~5.

Mr. Richards: The most definite impression on his mind was the urgency of reaching a solution, due to the increasing bitterness, almost hatred, towards the British; both the Muslim League and Congress are united on one point that they wish "the British to get out of India".

There are **two alternative ways of meeting this common desire (a) that we should arrange to get out, (b) that we should wait to be driven out.**

(In regard to (b), the loyalty of the Indian Army is open to question; the INA have become national heroes under the boosting of Congress; the possibility cannot be excluded that Congress could form an "Independent Indian Army").

If course (a) is to be adopted, it is suggested that a very early declaration should be made of the grant to India of full self-government forthwith. This might be made as soon as possible after the completion of the Provincial Elections. The suggestion is made that the declaration should take the form of a Royal Proclamation, complementary to Queen Victoria's Proclamation of 1858.

But a declaration by itself gets nowhere; it must be followed by action. Action recommended is (1) a commission to be formed to draw up the lines of the national treaty between H.M.G. and India working in London. (In reply to a question by the Prime Minister as to who would be the Indian representatives of such a commission and how they would be selected, Mr. Richards had no suggestion to offer). [9] (Emphasis by Subir)

The fact that the British finally chose to 'get out' in the next year, 1947, rather than wait to be 'driven out' is a well-known fact. The freedom struggle for which the INA was conceived finally came to fruition on 15th August 1947. As Bose had predicted, "when the British government is thus attacked... from inside India and from outside — it will collapse, and the Indian people will then regain their freedom". [10]

In the post-INA trial period, two touchy questions about the INA and Subhas Chandra Bose assumed substantial significance in certain academic circles: Was the INA a puppet or a genuine revolutionary army? Was it an independent army? Several Japanese witnesses called at the INA trial testified unanimously that the INA was an independent military arm of an independent government in exile. Besides, the detailed narrative embodied in this story corroborated this truth beyond an iota of doubt.

Was the INA then a genuine revolutionary army? No one can dispute the character of Bose as a revolutionary in every sense of the word. From early school days, he harboured a hatred of British rule, which became accentuated rather than softened during his years in British universities. His refusal to accept a post in the ICS, which he won through examination, was a significant step in the metamorphosis of Bose, the revolutionary. For Subhas Chandra Bose, there could be no cooperation with the imperialist powers. His conviction that the only way to rid India of British rule was to expel it by force was the decisive step in the formulation of Bose's revolutionary faith. But Indian revolutionary strength had to be supplemented by foreign power, and Bose turned to Italy, Germany, Japan, and finally Soviet Russia in search of outside help. Even Gandhi and Nehru, who broke with Subhas Bose earlier over the issue of the use of violence against the British, conceded during the INA trial that Bose was a true patriot. [11]

Be that as it may, consequent upon the backfiring of the INA Trial in Delhi, the British colonial rulers, in their haste to get out of the mess they had created in the sub-continent, resorted to the partition of the country along Hindu-Muslim communal lines. As a result, the unity between the various religious communities forged by Subhas Chandra Bose painstakingly in the midst of the colonial rulers 'divide-and-rule' policy was shattered. Brokered by the British, the frontline Indian leaders negotiated the terms of freedom, agreeing to the division of India, carving out from it Pakistan - a separate country for the Muslims. On the 14th/15th of August 1947, **these leaders celebrated the Independence Day** after the vivisection of motherland India was performed that involved profuse bleeding.

On the evening of 14th August 1947, in the Viceroy's House in New Delhi, Mountbatten and his wife settled down to watch a Bob Hope movie, "My Favorite Brunette." A short distance away, at the bottom of Raisina Hill, in India's Constituent Assembly, Nehru rose to his feet to make his most famous speech. "Long years ago, we made a [20]tryst

---

[20] According to Cambridge Dictionary, the word ¹tryst means, "a meeting between two people who are having a romantic relationship, especially a secret one".

with destiny," he declaimed. "At the stroke of the midnight hour, when the world sleeps, India will awake to life and freedom. **But outside the well-guarded enclaves of New Delhi, the horror of partition was well underway.** [12] (Emphasis by Subir)

Surprisingly, the INA saga's most profound revelation was brought to light by none other than Clement Richard Attlee, who served as the Prime Minister of the United Kingdom from 1945 to 1951 and led the British Labour Party from 1935 to 1955. During his critica tenure, the comprehensive spectrum of India's independence was up for resolution. Consequently, Attlee had to shoulder the pivotal responsibility of addressing this crucial matter. His perspective on the INA's role in India's independence, as narrated below, provides an illuminating insight.

> In 1956, Attlee came to India and stayed in Calcutta (now Kolkata) as a guest of the then-governor. At that time, P B Chakraborty was the Chief Justice of Calcutta High Court and the acting governor of West Bengal. He asked Attlee why, since Gandhi's Quit India movement had tapered off quite some time ago and in 1947, no such new compelling situation had arisen that would necessitate a hasty British departure, the British had to leave India.
>
> In his reply, Attlee reportedly cited several reasons, the main among them being the erosion of loyalty to the British crown among the Indian Army and Navy personnel **as a result of the military activities of Netaji Subhas Chandra Bose.**
>
> Toward the end of their discussion, Chakraborty reportedly asked Attlee what extent Gandhi's influence was upon the British decision to quit India. To this, Attlee's lips became twisted in a sarcastic smile as he slowly chewed out the word **m-i-n-i-m-a-l.**

It's an emphatic assertion from a key and critical decision-maker that highlights the vital role played by the INA and Subhas Chandra Bose in liberating India from British rule. (Emphasis by Subir) [13] [14]

References/Sources

Chapter 1

Busting the Myth

[1] "How Netaji Bose Set Up INA Camp at Ruzazho in Nagaland in April-May 1944" My India My Glory https://www.myindiamyglory.com/2018/09/25/how-netaji-set-up-ina-camp-at-ruzazho-in-nagaland-in-april-may-1944/

[2] *"Ruzazho village remembers Netaji Subhas Chandra Bose".* THE MORUNG EXPRESS dated 18th January 2023. https://mail.morungexpress.com/ruzazho-village-remembers-netaji-subhas-chandra-bose

[3] *"News channel adopts Ruzazho Village under CSR"* THE TIMES OF INDIA dated 24th January 2019.

https://timesofindia.indiatimes.com/city/kohima/news-channel-adopts-ruzazho-village-under-csr/articleshow/67665881.cms

[4] *Bose, Sumantra (Ed.) p.274-276. "NETAJI SUBHAS CHANDRA BOSE'S Life, Politics, & Struggle"by Krishna Bose. Paperback Edition 2023. PICADOR INDIA Pan Macmillan India.*

[5] *Werth, Alexander. p. 204-206. "A Beacon Across Asia: A Biography of Subhas Chandra Bose"* https://archive.org/details/in.ernet.dli.2015.201331/mode/1up

[6] *Bhattacharjee, J. B. "Presidential Address: WORLD WAR II AND INDIA: A FIFTY YEARS PERSPECTIVE." Proceedings of the Indian History Congress, vol. 50, 1989, pp. 365–98.* JSTOR, http://www.jstor.org/stable/44146070

[7] *Kipgen, Seikhohao. p. 296-297 & p.298. "The Anglo-Kuki War, 1917-1919" by Jongkhomang Guite and Thongkholal Haokip. (Edit) Routledge First South Asia edition 2019]*

[8] Bhattacharjee, J. B. "Presidential Address: p. 374. WORLD WAR II AND INDIA: A FIFTY YEARS PERSPECTIVE." Proceedings of the Indian History Congress, vol. 50, 1989, pp. 365–98. JSTOR, http://www.jstor.org/stable/44146070

[9] Khan, Shahnawaz p. iii. INA And Its Netaji 1946" Internet Archive. https://archive.org/details/in.ernet.dli.2015.49593

[10] Mohapatra, Dr. Biswajit. "SUBHASH BOSE AND THE BATTLE OF KOHIMA: MAINSTREAMING THE NORTH EAST INTO INDIA'S FREEDOM STRUGGLE" Jamshedpur Research Review, YEAR -VII VOLUME- IV, ISSUE XXXV, July-August 2019 https://www.academia.edu/39294429/Subhash_Bose_and_The_Battle_of_Kohima_Mainstreaming_the_North_East_into_Indias_Freedom_Struggle#:~:text=Subhas%20Bose%20and%20The%20Battle,Japanese%20and%20the%20British%20soldiers%2C

[11] Ethirajan, Anbarasan. "Kohima: Britain's 'forgotten' battle that changed the course of WWII" BBC News dated 14th February 2021. https://www.bbc.com/news/world-asia-india-55625447

[12] SAREEN, T. R. "SUBHAS CHANDRA BOSE, JAPAN AND BRITISH IMPERIALISM." European Journal of East Asian Studies, vol. 3, no. 1, 2004, pp. 69–97. JSTOR, http://www.jstor.org/stable/23615169

[13] THE NOBEL PRIZE: Winston Churchill Facts https://www.nobelprize.org/prizes/literature/1953/churchill/facts/

[14] "Winston Churchill has as much blood on his hands as Adolf Hitler: Shashi Tharoor" The Indian Express updated 22nd March 2017. https://indianexpress.com/article/india/winston-churchill-has-as-much-blood-on-his-hands-as-adolf-hitler-shashi-tharoor-4579549/

[15] Churchill, Winston. p. 181-182. "THE SECOND WORLD WAR VOLUME IV THE HINGE OF FATE" https://archive.org/details/dli.ernet.523562/mode/1up?view=theater

[16] Bhattacharjee, J. B. "Presidential Address: WORLD WAR II AND INDIA: A FIFTY YEARS PERSPECTIVE." Proceedings of the Indian History Congress, vol. 50, 1989, pp. 365–98. JSTOR, http://www.jstor.org/stable/44146070

[17] Churchill, Winston. p. 182-183. *"THE SECOND WORLD WAR VOLUME IV THE HINGE OF FATE"* https://archive.org/details/dli.ernet.523562/mode/1up?view=theater

[18] Kolakowski, Christopher L. *"'Is That the End or Do We Go On?': The Battle of Kohima, 1944."* Army History, no. 111, 2019, pp. 6–19. JSTOR, https://www.jstor.org/stable/26616950

[19] MacSwan, Angus. Reuters. "Victory over Japanese at Kohima named Britain's greatest battle. 21st April 2013. https://www.reuters.com/article/idUSBRE93K033/

[20] Chand, Dr. Somarani "Re-Reading Netaji Subhas in the Context of Imphal Expedition". Odisha Review, (ISSN 0970-8669) https://magazines.odisha.gov.in/Orissareview/2016/August/engpdf/23-26.pdf

[21] Unnithan, Sandeep. *"From the archives: When Nehru spied on Netaji."* India Today Insight UPDATED: 21st January 2021 https://www.indiatoday.in/india-today-insight/story/from-the-archives-when-nehru-spied-on-netaji-1761485-2021-01-21

[22] Dutta, Srishti B. *"The 'Forgotten Battle' Of Imphal-Kohima In 1944, When The Japanese Almost Invaded India"* Indiatimes NE Section dated 22nd August 2023. https://www.indiatimes.com/news/india/the-forgotten-battle-of-imphal-kohima-in-1944-when-the-japanese-almost-invaded-india-605536.html

[23] Dighe, Sandip. "Veterans commemorate the battle that stall Japanese invasion in northeast". Times of India dated 28th March 2022 https://timesofindia.indiatimes.com/city/pune/veterans-commemorate-the-battle-that-stalled-japanese-invasion-in-northeast/articleshow/90489413.cms

Chapter 2

Oatenization

[1] Bose, Krishna. Edited & Translated by Sumantra Bose. p. 367-369. "NETAJI SUBHAS CHANDRA BOSE'S Life, Politcs & Struggle." PICADOR INDIA Pan Macmillan India. Paperback 2023 Edition.

[2] Netaji Subhas Chandra Bose - The hero of India's freedom movement: Early Life https://www.netajisubhasbose.org/early-life

[3] Bose, Sugata. p.27-29. "HIS MAJASTY'S OPPONENT: Subhas Chandra Bose and India's Struggle against Empire." Penguin Random House India 2019 Edition.

[4] Bose, Krishna. Edited & Translated by Sumantra Bose. p. 367-369. xxxiv. "NETAJI SUBHAS CHANDRA BOSE'S Life, Politcs & Struggle." PICADOR INDIA Pan Macmillan India. Paperback 2023 Edition

[5] Werth, Alexander. p. 7-8. "A Beacon Across Asia: A Biography of Subhas Chandra Bose" https://archive.org/details/in.ernet.dli.2015.201331/mode/1up

[6] Express News Service Kolkata. "Nearly a century after he was expelled, Netaji finds pride of place at Presidency" The Indian Express dated 10th April 2010. https://indianexpress.com/article/cities/kolkata/nearly-a-century-after-he-was-expelled-netaji-finds-pride-of-place-at-presidency/

[7] Bose, Sisir K. (Edit) p.35. "NETAJI AND INDIA'S FREEDOM Proceedings of the International Netaji Seminar 1973" https://archive.org/details/dli.bengal.10689.12292/mode/1up?view=theater

[8] Bose, Sisir Kumar & Bose, Bose, Sugata (Edit) **An Indian Pilgrim:** An Unfinished Autobiography - Subhas Chandra Bose: https://ia800907.us.archive.org/33/items/ANINDIANPILIGRIMSUBHASCHANDRABOSE/AN%20INDIAN%20PILIGRIM%20-%20SUBHAS%20CHANDRA%20BOSE.pdf

[9] Bose, Nirmal. p. 438-439. "SUBHAS CHANDRA BOSE AND THE INDIAN NATIONAL CONGRESS." *The Indian Journal of Political Science*, vol. 46, no. 4, 1985, pp. 438–50. *JSTOR*, http://www.jstor.org/stable/41855198

[10] Khan, Akbar Ali. p. 148. Chapter V. "Netaji Subash Chandra Bose and the provisional government of Azad Hind an analytical construction" http://hdl.handle.net/10603/148350

[11] Bose, Krishna. (Sumantra Bose Ed.) p.362. "NETAJI SUBHAS CHANDRA BOSE'S Life, Politics & Struggle".

[12] Express News Service "Nearly a]century after he was expelled, Netaji finds pride of place at Presidency" The Indian Express dated 10th April 2010. https://indianexpress.com/article/cities/kolkata/nearly-a-century-after-he-was-expelled-netaji-finds-pride-of-place-at-presidency/

[13] Kearney, Robert N. "Identity, Life Mission, and the Political Career: Notes on the Early Life of Subhas Chandra Bose." *Political Psychology*, vol. 4, no. 4, 1983, pp. 617–36. *JSTOR*, https://doi.org/10.2307/3791058

[14] Toye, Hugh. p.22 "SUBHASH CHANDRA BOSE (THE SPRINGING TIGER) A Study of a Revolution."

[15] "'Netaji' Subhas Chandra Bose: 9 things you didn't know about the inspirational figure" India Today Web Desk dated 29th January 2018. https://www.indiatoday.in/education-today/gk-current-affairs/story/netaji-subhas-chandra-bose-952529-2016-08-18

[16] Subir. p. 101-108. "Story of Bengal and Bengalis: Ancient to Contemporary Era of Bangladesh & West Bengal: Genesis of Hindu-Muslim Discord". Notion Press 2020

[17] Unnitha, Sandeep. India Today Insight. "From the archives: "When Nehru spied on Netaji:. INDIA TODAY updated 21st January 2021. https://www.indiatoday.in/india-today-insight/story/from-the-archives-when-nehru-spied-on-netaji-1761485-2021-01-21

[18] Bose, Sisir Kumar. p. 53. "SUBHAS AND SARAT: An Intimate Memoir of the Bose Brothers". ALEPH BOOK COMPANY (2016)

[19] Bose, Sisir Kumar. p. 185. SUBHAS AND SARAT: An Intimate Memoir of the Bose Brothers. ALPEH (2016)

[20] Khan, Shahnawaz. p. iv "INA And Its Netaji 1946". https://archive.org/details/in.ernet.dli.2015.49593

[21] Khan, Shahnawaz. p. ix-x "INA And Its Netaji 1946". https://archive.org/details/in.ernet.dli.2015.49593

[22] Bose, Sugata in an interview with Thapar, Karan. 'If Netaji Had Been Alive No One Would Have Dared to Issue Calls for Genocide'". The Wire dated 28th January 2022 https://thewire.in/history/netaji-subhas-chandra-bose-sugata-karan-thapar-interview-full-transcript

[23] Raghavan, T.C.A. "How Singapore remembers Netaji Subhas Chandra Bose's legacy". NATIONAL HERALD dated 23rd January 2022. https://www.nationalheraldindia.com/india/how-singapore-remembers-netaji-subhas-chandra-boses-legacy

[24] "Hollwell Monument Removal Movement conducted by Netaji in 1940 at Calcutta": Freedom Movement detail. Azadi Ka Amrit Mahotsav. Report dated 5th August 2021 https://amritmahotsav.nic.in/freedom-movement-detail.htm?15

[25] Cartwrigh, Mark. "Black Hole of Calcutta" World History Encylopedia published on 11 October 2022 https://www.worldhistory.org/Black_Hole_of_Calcutta/#:~:text=The%20Black%20Hole%20of%20Calcutta%20refers%20to%20a%20prison%20cell,died%20of%20dehydration%20and%20suffocation

[26] Bose, Sisir Kumar. p. 102-105 "SUBHAS AND SARAT: An Intimate Memoir of the Bose Brothers". ALEPH BOOK COMPANY (2016)

[27] Khan, Shahnawaz. p. 1-2. "INA And Its Netaji 1946". https://archive.org/details/in.ernet.dli.2015.49593

Chapter 3

The Vanishing Act!

[1] Bose, Sisir Kumar. p. 109-111. "SUBHAS AND SARAT: An Intimate Memoir of the Bose Brothers" ALEPH (2016)

[2] Bose, Sisir Kumar. p. 108-143. SUBHAS AND SARAT: An Intimate Memoir of the Bose Brothers. ALPEH (2016)

[3] Bose, Sisir K., Werth, Alexander and, Ayer S A (Edit). p. 106-107 "A Beacon Across Asia A Biography of Subhas Chandra Bose" https://archive.org/details/in.ernet.dli.2015.201331/mode/1up?view=theater

[4] Bose, Sugata. p. 191-195 "HIS MAJESTY'S OPPONENT: Subhas Chandra Bose and India's Struggle against Empire" (Penguin Random House India 2019)]

[5] Bhaumik, Subir. "British 'attempted to kill Bose'". BBC News dated 15th August 2005. http://news.bbc.co.uk/2/hi/south_asia/4152320.stm#:~:text=The%20British%20told%20their%20agents,powers%20in%20World%20War%20II.

[6] Bose, Sugata. p. 208 "HIS MAJESTY'S OPPONENT: Subhas Chandra Bose and India's Struggle against Empire" (Penguin Random House India 2019)]

[7] Bose, Sisir K., Werth, Alexander and, Ayer S A (Edit). p. 108-115. "A Beacon Across Asia: A Biography of Subhas Chandra Bose". https://archive.org/details/in.ernet.dli.2015.201331/mode/1up?view=theater

Chapter 4

Across the Globe by Submarine

[1] Bose, Sugata. p. 83-91 "HIS MAJESTY'S OPPONENT: Subhas Chandra Bose and India's Struggle against Empire" (Penguin Random House India 2019).

[2] Bose, Sisir K., Werth, Alexander and, Ayer S A (Edit). p. 119. "A Beacon Across Asia: A Biography of Subhas Chandra Bose". https://archive.org/details/in.ernet.dli.2015.201331/mode/1up?view=theater

[3] Bose, Sugata. p. 203-205 "HIS MAJESTY'S OPPONENT: Subhas Chandra Bose and India's Struggle against Empire" (Penguin Random House India 2019)

[4] Bose, Krishna. Edited and translated by Sumantra Bose. p. 85-88. "NETAJI SUBHAS CHANDRA BOSE'S Life, Politcs & Struggle." PICADOR INDIA Pan Macmillan India. Paperback 2023 Edition.

[5] Werth, Alexander, p. 143, 158 - 164 "A Beacon Across Asia A Biography of Subhas Chandra Bose". https://archive.org/details/in.ernet.dli.2015.201331/mode/1up?view=theater

[6] Bose, Krishna. p. 111-159. NETAJI SUBHAS CHANDRA BOSE'S Life, Politics & Struggle. Edited and Translated by Sumantra Bose. Picador India (2023)

[7] Werth, Alexander, p. 164-165 "A Beacon Across Asia A Biography of Subhas Chandra Bose". https://archive.org/details/in.ernet.dli.2015.201331/mode/1up?view=theater

Chapter 5

The Born Revolutionary: Rash Behari

[1] Roy, Prasun. p.42-46. 52-64. A Samurai Dream of Azad Hind: RASH BEHARI BOSE. Vitasta 2022

[2] McQuade, Joseph. p. 644-645. "The New Asia of Rash Behari Bose: India, Japan, and the Limits of the International, 1912–1945. Journal of World History, Volume 27, Number 4, December 2016, pp. 641-667 (Article) Cambridge University.

[3] Elizabeth Eston. p. 40. "RASH BEHARI BOSE THE FATHER OF THE INDIAN NATIONAL ARMY Vol. 1" https://archive.org/details/rash-behari-bose-1-final/mode/1up?view=theater

[4] "Lahore Conspiracy Case trial", Wikipedia https://en.wikipedia.org/wiki/Lahore_Conspiracy_Case_trial

[5] Roy, Prasun. p. 121-127, p. 134-140. A Samurai Dream of Azad Hind: RASH BEHARI BOSE.Vitasta 2022

[6] McQuade, Joseph. p. 71-75. "Fugitive of Empire' Penguin Random House India 2023.

[7] Roy, Prasun. p. 184-188. A Samurai Dream of Azad Hind: RASH BEHARI BOSE.Vitasta 2022.

[8] McQuade, Joseph. p. 76. "Fugitive of Empire' Penguin Random House India 2023.

[9] Mukherjee, Uma. p. 143-150 "Two Great Indian Revolutionaries: Rash Behari Bose & Jyotindra Nath Mukhderjee. First Dey's Edition. August 2004.

[10] McQuade, Joseph. p. 647. "The New Asia of Rash Behari Bose: India, Japan, and the Limits of the International, 1912–1945. Journal of World History, Volume 27, Number 4, December 2016, pp. 641-667 (Article) Cambridge University.

[11] Eston, Elizabeth & Kawabe, Lexi. p. 45. "RASH BEHARI BOSE THE FATHER OF THE INDIAN NATIONAL ARMY Vol. 1" https://archive.org/details/rash-behari-bose-1-final/mode/1up?view=theater

[12] Nakajima, Takeshi. Motwani, Prem (Translator) p.51-72. "Bose of Nakamuraya: An Indian Revolutionary in Japan." Promila & Co. (2009.) [13] McQuade, Joseph. p.113-114. "Fugitive of Empire' Penguin Random House India 2023.

[14] Dutta, Nirmalya "India @75: Freedom On A Plate – Rash Behari Bose's Nakamuraya's India Curry". Slurrp dated 12th August 2022. https://www.slurrp.com/article/india-75-rash-behari-boses-nakamurayas-india-curry-1660307880310

[15] Pal, Sanchari. "The Other Bose: How an Indian Freedom Fighter's Curry Became a Sensation in Japan". The Better India https://www.thebetterindia.com/109063/rash-behari-bose-ina-nakamuraya-curry-japan/

[16] McQuade, Joseph. p.123, 125. "Fugitive of Empire' Penguin Random House India 2023.

[17] [Basu, Shyamal Krishna. "Unsung Warrior-I" The Statesman dated 13th June 2019. https://www.thestatesman.com/opinion/unsung-warriori-1502764724.html

[18] Guha, Ramachandra "THE BOSE WHOM JAPAN STILL REMEMBERS. The Telegraph, 13th June 2015. https://ramachandraguha.in/archives/the-bose-whom-japan-still-remembers-the-telegraph.html

[19] Nakajima, Takeshi. (Translation from Japanese by Motwani, Prem) p.178-179. "Bose of Nakamuraya: An Indian Revolutionary in Japan" Promila & Co. (2009.) [20] Rath, Radhanath (Edit) p. xxxvi xxxvii "RASH BEHARI BASU HIS: STRUGGLE FOR INDIA'S INDEPENDENCE" https://archive.org/details/in.ernet.dli.2015.99217/page/n42/mode/1up?view=theater

[20] Rath, Radhanath (Edit) p. xxxvi xxxvii "RASH BEHARI BASU HIS: STRUGGLE FOR INDIA'S INDEPENDENCE" https://archive.org/details/in.ernet.dli.2015.99217/page/n42/mode/1up?view=theater

[21] Kulim, Gurcharan Singh. The REAL founder of the Indian National Army (INA) - Giani Pritam Singh Ji Dhillon. Sikh Net dated 30th July 2015. https://www.sikhnet.com/news/real-founder-indian-national-army-ina-giani-pritam-singh-ji-dhillon

[22] Singh, General Mohan. LEAVES FROM MY DIARY- Memories and reflection of my INA Days.

[23] Ghosh, K. K. p. 28-63 "The Indian National Army: SECOND FRONT OF THE INDIAN INDEPENDENCE MOVEMENT. Meenakshi Prakashan, Third Edition 2022.

[24] SAREEN, T. R. p. 79. "SUBHAS CHANDRA BOSE, JAPAN AND BRITISH IMPERIALISM." *European Journal of East Asian Studies*, vol. 3, no. 1, 2004, pp. 69–97. *JSTOR*, http://www.jstor.org/stable/23615169

[25] Elizabeth Eston. p. 9-10. "RASH BEHARI BOSE THE FATHER OF THE INDIAN NATIONAL ARMY Vol. 1" https://archive.org/details/rash-behari-bose-1-final/mode/1up?view=theater

[26] McQuade, Joseph. p. 201-212. "Fugitive of Empire' Penguin Random House India 2023.

[27] Ghosh, K. K. p. 147-149 "The Indian National Army: SECOND FRONT OF THE INDIAN INDEPENDENCE MOVEMENT. Meenakshi Prakashan, Third Edition 2022.

[28] Eston, Elizabeth & Kawabe, Lexi. p. 9-10. 17 & 47. "RASH BEHARI BOSE THE FATHER OF THE INDIAN NATIONAL ARMY Vol. 1" https://archive.org/details/rash-behari-bose-1-final/mode/1up?view=theater

Chapter 6.

Serious Setback

[1] Ghosh, K. K. p. 157-158 "The Indian National Army: SECOND FRONT OF THE INDIAN INDEPENDENCE MOVEMENT. Meenakshi Prakashan, Third Edition 2022]

[2] Nakajima, Takeshi. (Translation from Japanese by Motwani, Prem) p.288-289. "Bose of Nakamuraya: An Indian Revolutionary in Japan" Promila & Co. (2009.)

[3] McQuade, Joseph. p. 213. "Fugitive of Empire' Penguin Random House India 2023.

[4] Werth, Alexander, p. 165-169 "A Beacon Across Asia A Biography of Subhas Chandra Bose". https://archive.org/details/in.ernet.dli.2015.201331/mode/1up?view=theater

[5] Ghosh, K. K. p. 162-163 "The Indian National Army: SECOND FRONT OF THE INDIAN INDEPENDENCE MOVEMENT. Meenakshi Prakashan, Third Edition 2022.

[6] Werth, Alexander, p. 188-190 "A Beacon Across Asia A Biography of Subhas Chandra Bose". https://archive.org/details/in.ernet.dli.2015.201331/mode/1up?view=theater

[7] SAREEN, T. R. 85-86 "SUBHAS CHANDRA BOSE, JAPAN AND BRITISH IMPERIALISM." *European Journal of East Asian Studies*, vol. 3, no. 1, 2004, pp. 69–97. *JSTOR*, http://www.jstor.org/stable/23615169

[8] Katoch, Hemant Singh. p. 48-50. THE BATTLE FIELDS OF IMPHAL. The Second World War and North East India. Routledge Reprint 2018.

[9] Katoch, Hemant Singh. p. 62, 83-84. THE BATTLE FIELDS OF IMPHAL. The Second World War and North East India. Routledge Reprint 2018.

[10] [Mairembam, Manindra Singh "'OPERATION U' - The Imphal Campaign" E-Pao Books https://books.e-pao.net/Heritage_Manipur/epShowChapter.asp?src=INA/operationu

[11] Katoch, Hemant Singh. p. 57 -62. THE BATTLE FIELDS OF IMPHAL. The Second World War and North East India. Routledge Reprint 2018.

[12] Werth, Alexander, p. 188-206 "A Beacon Across Asia A Biography of Subhas Chandra Bose". https://archive.org/details/in.ernet.dli.2015.201331/mode/1up?view=theater

[13] Sapu, Vevotso. "Our Netaji Subhas Chandra Bose". Nagaland Post dated 26th January 2022. https://nagalandpost.com/index.php/2022/01/26/our-netaji-subhas-chandra-bose/#:~:text=In%20September%201943%2C%20Netaji%20selected,to%20the%20Vicinity%20of%20Kohima

[14] Swinson, Arthur. p. 12-13. "KOHIMA The Story of the Greatest Battles Ever Fought". Paperback by Speaking Tiger 2016.

[15] SAREEN, T. R. "SUBHAS CHANDRA BOSE, JAPAN AND BRITISH IMPERIALISM." European Journal of East Asian Studies, vol. 3, no. 1, 2004, pp. 69–97. JSTOR, http://www.jstor.org/stable/23615169

[16] Bose, Sumantra (Ed.) p.210. 223-226, 228.232 286. "NETAJI SUBHAS CHANDRA BOSE'S Life, Politics, & Struggle" by Krishna Bose. Paperback Edition 2023. PICADOR INDIA Pan Macmillan India.

[17] Bose, Chandra Kumar. "What I learnt about the adoration for Subhas Chandra Bose in Singapore" DailyO dated 16th October 2017. https://www.dailyo.in/variety/subhas-chandra-bose-bose-memorial-singapore-ina-20100

[18] G. D. Major General. p. 167-179 "Bose: The Military Dimension. A Military History of INA and Netaji Bakshi" KW Publishers Pvt Ltd New Delhi. (2022).

Chapter 7.

Finally, the Victory!

[1] SAREEN, T. R. "SUBHAS CHANDRA BOSE, JAPAN AND BRITISH IMPERIALISM." *European Journal of East Asian Studies*, vol. 3, no. 1, 2004, pp. (90-94) 69–97. *JSTOR*, http://www.jstor.org/stable/23615169

[2] Ghosh, K. K. p. 222-225 "The Indian National Army: SECOND FRONT OF THE INDIAN INDEPENDENCE MOVEMENT. Meenakshi Prakashan, Third Edition 2022.

[3] MANSERGH, NICHOLAS (Editor-in-Chief). MOON, PENDEREL (Assistant Editor) p. 368-371 "THE TRANSFER OF POWER 1942-7: CONSTITUTIONAL RELATIONS BETWEEN BRITAIN AND INDIA." Volume VI .The post-war phase: new moves by the Labour Government 1 August 1945—22 March 1946." https://archive.org/details/transferofpower10006unse/mode/1up?view=theater

[4] Majumdar, Sumit K "The Rediscovery of Netaji: A Review Essay on the Life of Subhas Chandra Bose". Economic & Political Weekly Vol. 51, Issue No. 47, 19th November 2016 https://www.jstor.org/stable/44165877?seq=1

[5] Wangchuk, Rinchen Norbu. "Greatest Legal Argument Delivered in India': How a Gujarat Lawyer Defended INA" The Better India dated 10th January 2020. https://www.thebetterindia.com/212113/forgotten-army-sc-bose-ina-trial-delhi-bhulabhai-desai-history-india-nor41/#google_vignette

[6] Subir. p. 118-120. "Story of Bengal and Bengalis: Ancient to Contemporary Era of Bangladesh & West Bengal: Genesis of Hindu-Muslim Discord". Notion Press 2020.

[7] Singh. General Mohan INA. 422-423. The History of the Indian National Army: Soldiers' Contribution to Indian Independence. UNISTAR 2023.

[8] Kapoor, Pramod. P.11- 18"1946 LAST WAR OF INDEPENDENCE: ROYAL INDIAN NAVY MUTINY. Lotus Collection. 2022.

[9] MANSERGH, NICHOLAS (Editor-in-Chief). MOON, PENDEREL (Assistant Editor) p. 947 "THE TRANSFER OF POWER 1942-7: CONSTITUTIONAL RELATIONS BETWEEN BRITAIN AND INDIA." Volume VI .The post-war phase: new moves by the Labour Government 1 August 1945—22 March 1946."

https://archive.org/details/transferofpower10006unse/mode/1up?view=theater

[10] Grover, Priyamvada. "Remembering the Red Fort trials that tipped India towards complete freedom" in The Print dated 5th November 2018. https://theprint.in/india/governance/remembering-the-red-fort-trials-that-tipped-india-towards-complete-freedom/145260/

[11] Lebra, Joyce. "Japanese Policy and the Indian National Army". Asian Studies: Journal of Critical Perspectives on Asia https://www.asj.upd.edu.ph/mediabox/archive/ASJ-07-01-1969/lebra-japanese%20policy%20indian%20national%20army.pdf

[12] Dalrymple, William. "The Great Divide". THE NEW YORKER dated 22nd June 2015. https://www.newyorker.com/magazine/2015/06/29/the-great-divide-books-dalrymple

[13] Chatterjee, Shankar. "Bose Revisited." *Economic and Political Weekly*, vol. 51, no. 49, 2016, pp. 4–4. *JSTOR*, http://www.jstor.org/stable/44165914.

[14] G. D. Major General. p. liv-lv "Bose: The Military Dimension. A Military History of INA and Netaji Bakshi" KW Publishers Pvt Ltd New Delhi. (2022).

About the Author

Subir

Born in 1950 in Shillong Hill station, Subir is a science graduate who enjoyed a distinguished 35-year career in banking before making his debut in the literary field at 70+. His passion for uncovering hidden histories led him to write his third book. Subir's extensive travels across the seven northeastern states during his banking career gave him a deep understanding of the region's diverse cultures, communities and over 200 tribes. These experiences, combined with his fascination for India's liberation movements, particularly the pivotal Battle of Kohima in Nagaland and the Battle of Imphal in Manipur, inspired him to explore the overlooked aspects of these events. His year-long research ultimately reveals the hidden truths behind the so-called Japanese invasion of India, busting the Big British Bluff. The findings helped the septuagenarian to understand how these endeavours of the INA led by Netaji Subhas forced the British to get out of India.

www.ingramcontent.com/pod-product-compliance
Lightning Source LLC
LaVergne TN
LVHW091635070526
838199LV00044B/1081